The Last Weapon

Matthew McCluskey

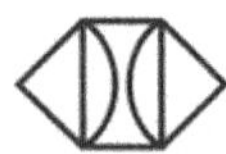

Confocal Media Edition, January 2014

ISBN: 061582322X
ISBN-13: 978-0615823225
Print version 140101

Published by Confocal Media
Confocalmedia.com

Send questions and comments for the author to:
mattmcc@alum.mit.edu

Cover artwork credits: Vladimir Kramer and NASA/Caltech
Author photograph by Jill McCluskey

To Lauren and Ryan

THE LAST WEAPON

PROLOGUE

The physicist skied against a backdrop of chiseled peaks and dark clouds. A lean man in his sixties, he wore a hat, gloves, and a full backpack. His pale blue eyes stared straight ahead. He moved smoothly, gliding, planting his poles precisely with each forward push of the alpine skis.

His name was Axel.

The plan was to rendezvous with members of the Committee. Axel knew the risks of such an unorthodox meeting, but he needed to deliver his message and it couldn't go through the usual channels. Time was running out. This was the last chance to save the project.

A few snowflakes fell from the gray sky. He saw a lone figure in the distance. As Axel skied toward him, he stayed close to the edge of a sheer mountain face. Below was an azure lake dotted with chunks of ice and snow.

"Axel," the man called.

He did not recognize the man.

"Come to me," Axel said. "And tell your two colleagues to join us."

The man walked toward him. He wore snowshoes. He was square-jawed and had dark, pitiless eyes. Two men, dressed in black snowsuits, came out of hiding. They carried weapons.

He knew this might happen. Still, it was disappointing. It

meant the Committee was compromised.

Axel shuffled back a few feet and put up his hands. "I'm unarmed," he said. "I would like you to deliver a message to the Committee."

The square-jawed man smirked. He made a gesture and the two men raised their weapons, aiming smooth black cylinders at Axel's chest.

"I see," Axel said calmly, and spread his arms wide. "Just one question, if you don't mind: who sent you?"

"Come with us," the man said, ignoring the question. "Slowly. Keep your hands up."

Axel did not move. After several tense seconds, the men stepped closer.

Axel turned his eyes toward the sky. He slid back, skis scraping on the rock. The men watched uncertainly. Axel fell backward and, with surprising abruptness, disappeared from view. Just like that, he was gone.

The men approached the cliff edge in shocked silence. It had happened so fast. They peered down and saw a billowing cloud of snow. No one spoke.

"He's dead," the leader said at last. "We'll hike down and dispose of the body."

FRIDAY, MAY 30

1

Professor Mike Harris felt a familiar mixture of frustration and apathy in his aching forehead as he listened to the Chair of the physics department.

"As you all know, we replaced the old printer in the department office. The new printer, regrettably, has had some problems." A balding, beleaguered string theorist, the Chair glanced around the room with the tired eyes of one who had abandoned research for administration. "As you know, the new drivers do not work. More accurately, they are not properly configured to the specifications of our new printer. While we think we have resolved that problem, a new one has since appeared."

Harris let his eyes wander to the tall windows of the conference room, which framed a view of rocky mountain peaks capped with snow. The view inside the conference room was less inspiring. Along one side of the table sat the "old guard," cranky holdovers who were professors back when Colton University was a two-year college. Bud Johnson, a hefty lumberjack of a man, stroked his bushy mustache as he stared absently into space. Dwight Jenkins sat next to Bud, grading papers. The eyes of Paul Quinlan, beady and paranoid, darted around the room as if trying to unravel the latest conspiracy against him. Several other members of the old guard, who showed up only to teach their mandatory sections, had not bothered to attend the meeting.

As the Chair's voice droned in the background, Harris considered the other faculty in his small department. Rachel Feld was a condensed-matter experimentalist who studied superconductivity. Wu Chen performed calculations that simulated nanocrystals. Next to Harris sat Seth Brenner, a gravitational theorist in his fifties. He wore, as always, a Hawaiian shirt and blue jeans. Today, Seth's curly hair had shades of purple.

On the other side sat some of the younger faculty–the future of the department, assuming they stayed around. David Schwartz recently received an award from the National Science Foundation to study biophysical phenomena. Jeff Lewis was a theorist who specialized in quantum computing. Matt Carter used lasers and scanning-probe techniques to investigate the interactions of atoms with solid surfaces, with an eye toward applications such as single-atom memory units.

The rising star was Stefan Schroeder, their newest faculty member. Stefan was a German scientist who made his name performing groundbreaking experiments with high-intensity lasers. Although Stefan had received offers from more prestigious universities, he came to Colton for the environment. Here he could work, hike in the mountains, and avoid the hassles of a city.

"I've asked the Dean for some support for the copier room," the Chair said, "but things are tight with the downturn in the stock market affecting the university endowment. I think we'll be in a limp-along mode for a few weeks."

Paul Quinlan pointed a finger at the Chair. "Does this mean we won't be able to make an offer?"

"No, Paul."

Over the past few weeks, the physics department had interviewed several candidates for a tenure-track theory position. Last night, Mike hosted a reception for one of them.

"But what I'm hearing is, cut *here*, cut *there*, cut *here*, cut *there*. When will it end?"

"We'll be able to fill the position, Paul," the Chair said. "We were talking about the copier situation."

Paul squinted his eyes and stammered. "I *know* what we were talking about. But this is the administration's pattern: first cut *here*, then cut *there*…"

Mike's phone rang. Embarrassed, he pulled the phone from his belt and looked at the identity of the caller. The picture on the display was a grotesque she-beast from a horror film. He felt a rush of anger and turned the phone off.

Next to him, Seth was smiling. "The ex?"

"Yep." Mike put the phone back. "Sorry," he mumbled to the Chair.

"No problem." If anything, he appeared to be grateful for the interruption. "Let's move on to the next item on the agenda: teaching assistant allocations for next fall."

Mike Harris, associate professor of physics, was dressed casually in Chinos and a long-sleeved shirt, with brown hair lightly touched by gray. As he approached forty, he had an increasingly distracted air about him. It was getting harder to focus.

He thought of his ex. His face burned with the raw emotion that had been awakened by her phone call. Along with his anger, though, he was curious about why she had called.

They had both arrived at Colton University ten years ago, and got engaged the following year. His fiancée, Jennifer Lawson, had a Ph.D. in finance, and finding positions for the two of them–solving the two-body problem–had been difficult. Colton was a compromise. While the university was no MIT or Stanford, it had potential and seemed to be on an upward trajectory. Over time, he grew to appreciate the area and its rugged beauty, and life with Jennifer was content.

Then everything fell apart.

She kicked him out of their house. He bought a new one in the outskirts, as far away as he could get in such a small town without moving to the country. He avoided her but couldn't stop thinking of her. Jealousy and other dark emotions simmered.

Weeks had passed with no contact. Now she had called him, out of the blue.

* * *

"Are you alright?"

Seth was looking at him, concerned. The meeting had ended.

"Yeah, I'm fine." Mike stood up to leave and Seth followed him out the door.

"Don't let your exes get you down." He looked around the hallway and lowered his voice. "Remember that girl in my 101 lecture?"

"You've mentioned a couple of them. Be specific."

"Okay, this is the one who sits in the fifth row. Tight mini-skirt whenever it's above freezing. You know how the seats are, right?"

Mike knew. The seats were arranged on a steep incline.

"She pulled a Sharon Stone."

"Who?"

"You know, the actress. *Basic Instinct*."

Seth raised his eyebrows, a satisfied grin on his face.

"Am I interrupting?" Stefan Schroeder walked up to them, eyes intense behind wire-rim glasses. His normally close-cropped hair was tousled, evidence of long nights in the lab.

"Hey, Stefan," Mike said. "Are we ready for the run?"

"*Ja*. The power generators are back online and the chilled-water loop is functioning. We'll begin in one hour."

"Okay," said Mike, looking at his watch. "I'll be there after my lecture."

"See you then."

Mike walked down the stairs to the lobby of the physics building, past displays of a chaotic pendulum and a towering Tesla coil. He brushed past some students and stepped outside. It was a sunny day, late in the spring quarter. Students and faculty found no shortage of excuses to go outside.

He walked past the library, with its glass dome ceiling and abstract sculptures, and reached the center of campus, a grassy ellipse ringed with evergreen trees. Behind the trees, the mountain range stood in full splendor. Students hung out, ate lunch, and passed out leaflets. Mike headed to the Cyber Café, a small coffee shop.

He ordered his usual, a tall latte with 2% milk, and sat at his favorite spot in a back corner. He unpacked his notebook computer, glad to be away from his office and its interminable interruptions. He logged on and checked his e-mail. After deleting several dozen messages, he found what he was looking for. Sipping his latte, he read:

Hello Mike,

As we discussed, isotope ratio in last crystal growth was not right. It was silicon-28 / silicon-30 mixture. Sorry about mistake. Furnace has been down too but we can fix it. I am optimistic we get things 'squared away' ;-)

Regards,
Oleg

An optimistic Russian, Mike thought wryly. *Now my day is complete.* He began to type a reply:

Oleg,

Don't bother. Seth's calculations indicate that it won't work.

-Mike

He thought for a moment, then deleted the message. There was no sense in dashing Oleg's newfound enthusiasm. Mike read a few more e-mails, logged out, and glanced at his course notes as he finished his latte. He had taught the course several times before and could deliver the lecture on autopilot.

He walked back to the physics building, the brick and glass structure that housed modern laboratories and classrooms. As he stepped inside the lecture hall, an image from the past hit him again.

The memory was etched permanently in his mind.

Mike stood in front of a projected display of a graph. He aimed his laser pointer at several data points.

"As you can see, the average occupation number for the excited-state energy increases with laser pulse intensity," he said. He looked out at the audience, thirty or so physicists in a small room at the convention center. His talk was one of dozens of parallel sessions at the American Physical Society March Meeting, a gathering of over eight thousand physicists in a range of sub-disciplines. He was allotted ten minutes for his presentation plus two minutes at the end to answer questions.

"However, after a critical intensity, the system appears to transition into a Bose-Einstein condensate."

A sudden motion in a dark corner of the room caught his eye. A tall man stood up and scowled.

Mike's voice faltered. "Now, of course, there are various interpretations for these data. However, it appears clear that our results are consistent with…"

"Laser heating!" the man said, his eyes glaring with rage. It was Hassan Zare, Harvard professor. Mike knew Hassan's reputation well. To Hassan, physics was a contact sport where collegiality was a sign of weakness.

"Well, we considered that…"

The Chair of the session stood up. "According to APS rules, questions are at the end of the presen…"

"This is not a presentation," Hassan spat. "This is a charade. Dr. Harris is presenting data on laser heating–nothing more, nothing less. Trying to portray these results as some kind of many-body quantum effect is a waste of our time."

The Chair, out-gunned by Hassan, a fellow of the American Physical Society and member of the National Academy, relented.

"As we *clearly* showed in our Physical Review Letter, the temperature of the sample increases with laser intensity, producing the very effect you are showing today. I noticed you have not cited our work."

"Well," Mike stammered. "I was going to mention it next."

"How do you know your sample temperature did not increase during exposure to the laser?"

The right side of Mike's face began to twitch. *Keep it together*, he admonished himself. Why couldn't he be stronger? "We measured it with a type-K thermocouple."

"Oh, a thermocouple. I see." Hassan savored the nervous

tension in the room. "Are you aware that thermocouples are susceptible to artifacts, due to the poor thermal conductivity of your sample?"

"No, I hadn't considered… I mean, we didn't look carefully at…"

"Apparently not." Hassan sat down, a malevolent expression on his face. "Please proceed."

After the talk, Mike went to his hotel room and locked the door. Feeling ill, he curled up in a fetal position on the bed. He thought of responses he should have given to Hassan's assault. Why wasn't he quick on his toes, like so many of these glib bastards? He had been humiliated, thoroughly, in front of his scientific peers. Mike entertained violent fantasies of what he could do to Hassan if he caught him alone in a dark alley or mountain pass. His anger was only intensified by the recurring thought that, on the technical merits, Hassan may have been correct.

The incident with Hassan occurred when Mike was a post-doc. When Mike joined Colton University as an assistant professor, Hassan's enmity only increased. Many of Mike's papers, reviewed by an "anonymous" referee, were torn to shreds. Proposals sent to the National Science Foundation would come back with three "excellent" reviews and one "poor." "We regret to inform you that your proposal cannot be funded at this time…" It felt like being stalked by a psychopath who hid, shamelessly, behind the shield of anonymity. Even worse, Mike suspected that, after shooting down his proposals, Hassan ran with the ideas and passed them off as his own.

He shook his head, trying to clear the negative thoughts that clouded it. He saw students sitting in the lecture hall, talking and texting. It was time for class to begin.

2

Professor Mike Harris stood with his back to the audience as he wrote an equation on the board.

"$E = mc^2$," he said with reverence.

Mike scribbled another equation next to Einstein's famous law. "As we saw last time, the complete relation is $E^2 = m^2c^4 + p^2c^2$, where p is the momentum of the particle. If we have a particle at rest, its momentum is zero. Then we get back $E = mc^2$, the equation of special relativity that has found its way into popular culture."

He turned to the class, a group of about thirty. Modern Physics, the course he taught, was popular among students in the physical sciences. He looked at their young, unlined faces. Part of him wished he could go back in time, back to when he was a student and life was simple.

"What does this equation mean? *E* stands for energy. With energy, I can make things move or heat things up. *m* stands for mass, the amount of matter in an object. And *c* is the speed of light, which is an extremely large number. *c* squared is even larger. So a tiny bit of mass can be made to produce an incredible amount of energy.

"This is what happens during nuclear fission. A big nucleus

like uranium or plutonium splits in two. But the sum of the masses of the two halves is less than that of the original nucleus. Where does the missing mass go? Into *energy*. Fission reactors use that fact to supply energy to homes, factories, and people. The fission bomb in Hiroshima used that fact to destroy homes, factories, and people.

"It is to Einstein's credit that he realized the importance of $E = mc^2$. Some scientists dismissed it as a mere algebraic artifact. But Einstein saw that this equation *demanded* that matter and energy be interchangeable. In his words, 'Classical physics introduced two substances: matter and energy. The first had weight, but the second was weightless. In classical physics we had two conservation laws: one for matter, the other for energy. We have already asked whether modern physics still holds this view of two substances and the two conservation laws. The answer is: "No." According to the theory of relativity, there is no essential distinction between mass and energy. Energy has mass and mass represents energy. Instead of two conservation laws we have only one, that of mass-energy.'

"We know from nuclear fission that mass can turn into energy. We also know that energy can transform into mass. In a particle accelerator, particles like protons or electrons are hurled at each other at terrific speeds. When they collide, their kinetic energy–their energy of motion–goes into producing a shower of new particles. The new particles did not come from nothing. They came from energy.

"This view of mass-energy is only one of many startling conclusions of Einstein's theory of special relativity. An even more counter-intuitive idea is the notion of time in different reference frames. The idea that different people perceive time differently can be explained as follows: If you're sitting on a hot stove, a minute can seem like an hour. But if you're sitting with your sweetheart, an hour can seem like a minute."

The students groaned.

"Seriously, different systems mark time differently. In our everyday experience, the effect is so small that we cannot discern it. But suppose a rocket ship flew past us at 80% the speed of light. Suppose further that this rocket had a big clock affixed to its side." Mike drew a laughably crude picture of a rocket ship. "The people on the rocket ship would see the clock hands moving at a normal speed. But people stuck on Earth would think the clock was running slow. They would see the second hand tick *every 1.7 seconds*.

"This discrepancy doesn't depend on what kind of clock we're using. If the earth people could look inside the rocket cabin, they would see the pilots moving and talking in slow motion. Everything on the rocket would appear 1.7 times slower than it should be.

"Think of the implications of this time dilation. Suppose Hans and Franz are twins, age 20, and Franz decides to leave Earth on a rocket ship that travels at 99% the speed of light. Hans watches his brother fly away from the earth for 10 years, turn around, and fly toward the earth for 10 years. Total Earth time: 20 years. Hans is now 40 years old, is married, and has kids in middle school. Franz, however, has only aged three years. *He's only 23 years old!* If Franz had traveled at 99.9% the speed of light, he would have aged only *one* year! The faster the ship, the greater the time discrepancy.

"Next lecture, we will examine Einstein's special theory of relativity more closely. Until then, I remind you that homework is due Monday at 5 o'clock sharp, and I do not accept relativistic excuses."

A glass of thirty year old BenRiach whiskey in his hand, Henry Colton watched the helicopter land. He stood in his spacious living room, admiring the view of the Whitefish mountain range while soft jazz played in the background. The helicopter touched down on the helipad, the engine turned off, and the rotors began to spin down.

Years ago, Colton and his sprawling compound engendered the usual resentment that California billionaires could expect from the local population. These rich snowbirds, people griped, drove up property values and imported political views from Hollywood. Henry initially confirmed the stereotype when he prohibited hunting on his hundred thousand acres of wilderness.

Over time, he methodically gained their trust, employing local labor and establishing nonprofit foundations that sprinkled his largess across the state. His most famous gift was a two billion dollar endowment to Northern Montana State College, an unprecedented act of generosity that converted the small institution into a research university. In turn, a grateful state legislature changed the name to Colton University. Colton U embarked on an ambitious growth program, hiring internationally respected faculty. It attracted students mostly from the northwestern United States and California, as well as a fair number of international students from Canada and Asia. New professors were willing to tolerate the university's second-tier status in exchange for the environment and potential for growth.

Henry Colton mused over the profound impact that could be delivered by the combination of money and will. Outside, he saw the helicopter doors open. His eyes were drawn to a beautiful Asian woman who stepped out. Henry's employee, an athletic man named James, greeted her.

"Watch your step," said James, escorting her down steps that led from the helipad to a stone pathway. He wore a Brooks Brothers suit and had an earphone in his left ear.

"Thank you for bringing me here."

They walked into a green courtyard in front of the mansion. The house had a stone base and wood siding that gave the impression it had risen from the earth. She surveyed the surroundings with watchful eyes. Several other buildings, built in a similar style, occupied the hilly area.

"That's the recreation center, complete with a swimming pool and indoor track," said James. "And that building contains a portion of Mr. Colton's extensive automobile collection."

"What about that building there?"

"Storage," he said, with a hint of hostility. "Follow me." She noticed a scar on the back of his neck.

They walked up a path toward the mansion.

When they reached the door, James turned to her stiffly. "If it were up to me, you wouldn't be here. Mr. Colton is a busy man.

He doesn't need this kind of interruption."

"Nice to see you, too."

James brought a small electronic device out of his coat pocket and waved it in front of her. It beeped once. "I'm going to have to ask you for your camera."

"Of course." She handed him a tiny camera from her hip pocket. "May I keep my pen and paper?"

"Yes. Mr. Colton is waiting." He opened the door.

Henry smiled warmly at the sight of her: lithe legs, long, satin hair, and a silky blouse that revealed just enough to draw attention. Her heels clicked on the hardwood floor and she opened her arms.

"I've missed you, Henry."

They embraced. Henry waved off James, who stood near the door with a disapproving scowl. James did an about-face and left.

Henry stared into her brown eyes. "I'm no fool, you know," he said playfully. "The editor of the *Times* knows I have a thing for beautiful, intelligent Asian women, so they sent their secret weapon."

"Who told you?" she asked, feigning surprise.

"I have my sources. You know, I read a story once about female interrogators at Guantanamo Bay who gave their victims lap dances as a method of torture."

"Oh? Maybe I'll have to try that technique."

"I'll never talk. *Never.*"

She brushed him off with a smile. Although of average height, Henry Colton possessed a calm self-assurance that gave him stature. In his late fifties, his gray hair was slightly unkempt but attractive in a professorial way. His sharp eyes, softened by wrinkles, regarded his guest. He had met Jing Shen, reporter from the *London Financial Times*, while speaking at an international conference on energy production. Her combination of intellect and beauty was devastating. The canny side of his brain told him that she used these assets to manipulate him. The rest of him didn't care.

They had talked about *everything* in the conference hotel lobby, from nuclear fusion to nonlinear dynamics and cultural trends. Henry learned that Jing's position at the *Times* gave her freedom to travel the world and pursue unusual stories. In return for such latitude, she repaid the *Times* with important leads, and let the editors take full credit. Henry found that kind of selfless curiosity charming.

Henry and Jing stayed in contact, exchanging flirtatious e-mails and occasionally speaking on the phone. Then, just a few days ago, she called to ask if she could interview him at his summer home in Montana. It took him a few microseconds to agree.

The screen displayed an array of color photographs. A technician named Troy sat at a computer in a windowless room. The computer was connected to Jing's digital camera.

"That's all of them," he said.

James walked up to the screen and scrutinized the pictures one by one. The first group of pictures showed a press conference with a government official.

"Find out who that is," he said, pointing.

"Already done. That guy is Thomas Harding, United States Undersecretary for Trade. The press conference was held last week. Items on the agenda included green energy, alternative fuels, pollution trading, carbon sequestration…"

"Fascinating," James growled. He moved to the next series of pictures, which were all scenic landscapes of Wyoming and Montana.

"She's quite an impressive amateur photographer, in my opinion," blurted Troy. "I especially like her use of high contrast."

James pierced him with stern eyes. "That woman has no business being two hundred miles from Mr. Colton. Give me the camera."

Troy handed it to him.

"Analyze the photographs for encrypted data."

"You think she's into industrial espionage?"

James frowned, turning toward a wall of screens that displayed different areas of the compound. He looked at a screen that showed an outside view of the mansion. Through a window, he could see the outlines of Henry and Jing, talking animatedly. "I don't know what she is. Just keep an eye on her."

"Yes, sir."

Jing sat on a leather sofa, legs crossed, and opened her pad of paper. "You're on the record now, Henry."

He sipped the last of his drink and set the glass aside. "Fire away."

"How does it feel being the richest person in the world?"

He winced. "Is that how I'm known?"

"To Forbes magazine, yes."

"I see."

When he was younger, he told her, such a title would have been the fulfillment of a dream. In fact, for most of his life, he had one goal.

He wanted to be the world's first trillionaire.

Through setbacks and crises, that single-minded goal kept him going. He had no family. He had no hobbies. The focus on money–not merely getting rich but breaking into uncharted fiscal territory–propelled him through work, eighteen to twenty hours a day, seven days a week.

In addition to his legendary capacity for hard work, Henry possessed a first-rate intellect. Understanding complex issues came naturally to him. His mind cut across disciplines, allowing him to forge revolutionary business ventures in biocomputing, telecommunications, and energy production. He had a unique ability to take cutting-edge research from the laboratories and develop it into profitable technology.

He would have achieved his goal, but something happened. Henry Colton, ruthless tycoon, transformed into the greatest philanthropist in history. In addition to his famous gift to Colton University, he set up major foundations to fund basic research in science and engineering. He also expanded the research laboratories of his corporate empire. Naturally, pundits questioned his motives. Everyone agreed, though, that he had become truly captivated by the power of science and how it could transform society.

"So, you ask, how does it feel to be the richest person in the world?" He shrugged. "Let me put it this way. I hope I'll be remembered not for how I made my money, but how I gave it away."

"Good one," she said, writing.

He gazed out the windows. "Don't get me wrong. I appreciate wealth. People who say 'money ruins the soul' have never been poor."

"Another good one."

"But a few years back, I realized I was getting sucked into a kind of black hole."

"So," she said, looking at him thoughtfully, "you decided to give your money away."

He laughed. "Some of it, yes."

Jing flipped through her notes. "The last I read, you gave ten *billion* dollars to your Pacific Research Center."

Henry stood up. "Eleven point two. My dear, I insist we continue this interview in the hot tub."

"I didn't bring a swimsuit," she said coquettishly.

And the problem with that is…? But Henry, the perfect gentleman, called a house servant. She showed Jing to the dressing room, which contained a selection of bathing suits.

3

Mike slumped in his chair, exhausted from the lecture. Jeff Lewis, the department's junior theorist, sat across from him.

"I'm concerned about this search," Jeff said, rubbing his bristly black hair. "I think the old guard are going to push for Harding. His research is a joke."

"Great teacher, though."

"Big whoop. Last thing we need is a wonderful teacher who's a mediocre researcher."

"How about Zheng?"

Jeff's eyes lit up. "He's perfect. How did he do at your house last night?"

"Fine, I guess." In truth, people at the reception were more interested in university gossip than candidate evaluation. "He's a smart guy."

"Seven Phys Rev Letters–you bet he's smart. Old Bud thinks his accent is too thick, of course."

After a few minutes of discussion, Jeff sensed Mike's disinterest and excused himself. Mike turned around in his chair and tried to focus.

He stared at the piles of books, papers, and journals on his desk and felt paralyzed. A stack of homework needed grading. Printouts of several proposals from the National Science Foundation were scattered on top. The NSF requested that he read through them and give a detailed review–ironic, since they had shot down his last two proposals. Buried underneath were folders pertaining to the faculty search, a *Physical Review* manuscript to referee, and a dissertation draft from one of his graduate students.

Several more stacks of paper sat on the dusty floor. One stack contained files from graduate student applicants, mostly unimpressive. Another stack–more accurately, a pile–contained a random collection of journal articles and printouts from the web. His shelves housed a jumble of books, spare electronic parts, product manuals and catalogs. To his right sat the computer, which listed hundreds of e-mails.

The prospect of cutting into this mess was daunting. One event required his immediate attention: the upcoming program review, to be held in Glacier Park the following week. At this point, his group had nothing to report. If they didn't produce something substantial, soon, their funding would vanish.

Mike remembered the genesis of the project like a distant, happy dream. He sat in Buck's Tavern along with Stefan Schroeder, Seth Brenner, and the program director, a veteran government official named Dr. Hansen.

"You know," Dr. Hansen said casually, "there's too much specialization in physics these days. Seth, you're a gravitational theorist. Stefan, you study lasers. Mike, you're a semiconductor guy. What do you three talk about?"

"Women," said Seth.

They laughed, but Dr. Hansen had a point. In the old days, things were different. Albert Einstein published three papers in 1905, each in a different field. In one paper, he explained Brownian motion in terms of molecules, silencing skeptics who didn't believe that atoms and molecules existed. In the second paper, he explained the photoelectric effect by introducing *photons*, particles of light, ushering in quantum mechanics. Finally, and most famously, he re-wrote the rules of space and time in what became known as the special theory of relativity.

Einstein's genius was extraordinary, but others managed to span a variety of sub-disciplines. Physicists were generalists, not specialists. After World War II, however, the explosion of knowledge made it impossible to keep abreast of the field as a whole. The *Physical Review*, once the journal that bound physicists into a single community, splintered into *Physical Review A*, *B*, *C*, *D*, and *E*, plus *Physical Review Letters*. Open access journals proliferated like weeds. The number of articles published each year grew exponentially. At the beginning of the twenty-first century, one hundred years after Einstein's famous papers, a gravitational theorist had almost nothing in common with a semiconductor physicist. Like an expanding universe, the community had drifted apart. Dr. Hansen considered it his mission to bring it together again.

Over pints of beer, their idea took shape, a revolutionary experiment that would fuse gravitation, high-energy lasers, and solid-state physics. It was crazy, but as the night wore on, fueled by creative energy and alcohol, it began to make sense. The more he thought about it, the more Mike believed that this was the Big One, the breakthrough that every physicist dreams of.

He recalled a story about Einstein, after he had completed the special theory of relativity. Einstein held an unshakable belief that nothing could travel faster than the speed of light, a deep faith that formed the foundation of his theory. He then pondered Newton's law of gravitation. According to Newton, an object exerted an instantaneous force on another object. "Action at a distance," it was called. If the moon suddenly disappeared, its tidal force on the earth would suddenly disappear too. But this was impossible–according to relativity, *nothing* could traverse the distance between the moon and earth instantly. Einstein realized he had to formulate an entirely new theory of gravitation.

It was, he said, the happiest, luckiest day of his life.

Mike now knew what Einstein meant. He felt a jolt of energy as he manically wrote equations and designed the proposed experiment. Stefan and Mike decided to knock out the wall between their labs and dedicate the combined space to their new project. Seth expanded his computing facilities, while Dr. Hansen laid the groundwork for long-term funding.

Mike's euphoria felt limitless. He fantasized about traveling to Sweden, with his wife Jennifer, to accept the Nobel Prize. But, in reality, who would receive the honor? There were four members of the team: himself, Seth, Stefan, and Dr. Hansen. The Nobel Prize could only be given to, at most, three recipients. Perhaps Hansen would miss out on the honor (ironic, since he initiated the project). Paranoia crept in. Maybe the Swedish Academy would decide Mike was essentially a technician, and award the prize to the other three. Perhaps someone–Hassan?–had already built the experiment, rendering his concerns moot.

After Einstein's euphoric insight, it took him ten years to complete the general theory of relativity, as he struggled through the tough world of tensor analysis. Mike's initial inspiration also gave way to the long, hard slog of research. Little problems cropped up everywhere. A graduate student assigned to the project suddenly decided to abandon physics for fine arts. The laser company delayed shipments and screwed up the specifications. A water leak ruined several computers and optical components. The electricians could not deliver the power they had promised. A computer virus wiped out priceless data. The headaches seemed endless.

The funding situation proved similarly rocky. At first, the Department of Energy showed great enthusiasm for the project, which fit into their mission of understanding matter under extreme conditions. After a series of scandals at the national labs, however, Congress slashed the DOE budget, and Mike's project ended up as one of the casualties. His NSF proposals went nowhere, thanks to Hassan Zare. Such setbacks would not have been so bad if he knew their idea would work. In reality, the entire enterprise could very well be a waste of time.

When it looked as though the project was doomed, he received an e-mail:

Mike,

I like your work. Keep it up.

Regards, –H.M. Colton

Like everyone else, he knew the legend of Henry Colton, the billionaire who owned a summer home not far from the university. He wondered whether Henry's interest in his research would translate into cash. The next day, the university Vice President for Research answered that question. He informed Mike that his project would receive a one million dollar, two-year grant from the Colton Foundation.

The project, a terminally ill patient, had just been given a new lease on life. Mike felt another rush of euphoria. He and Stefan rapidly completed the major components of the experiment: the high voltage system, laser array, and low-temperature cryostat. Oleg provided a high-purity semiconductor crystal. After a year, they managed to produce world record energy densities. Things were finally moving his way. He even began making wedding plans with his fiancée, Jennifer Lawson.

Then, recently, like a roller coaster, things turned downhill again. Seth's calculations showed that the project would almost certainly not work. The Colton Foundation grant expired. Most depressing was his phone conversation with Dr. Hansen.

"What do you mean, you're withdrawing support?"

"I'm sorry," said Hansen. "I've spoken with key people. They say no."

"What do you mean, *key people*?" Mike spluttered. Pale and trembling, he thought he might burst into tears.

"Key people."

"Then what's the point of this damned conference?"

"Give a solid presentation, Mike. Show some preliminary results. I might be able to turn this around."

Mike now turned to his computer and brought up a PowerPoint presentation, mostly blank slides. They had nothing. Perhaps after today's experiment, they would have some face-saving data to show. In the end, though, they were just going through the motions. Mike recalled the old adage that many beautiful ideas have been killed by a single ugly fact. The project had been a beautiful idea, all right. But it too was about to die.

* * *

"This is bull *scheiss*!"

Stefan burst into Mike's office, red faced.

"What's up?"

Stefan removed his glasses and rubbed his eyes. "We've spent *all week* aligning the *verdamten* optics, fixing the broken YAG laser, waiting for the chilled water supply to come back online…"

"I thought everything was ready to go."

"*Ja*, that's the damned point! I spent last night troubleshooting that piece of *scheiss* data acquisition program."

Mike took a breath. Stefan must be seriously pissed, he thought. He was mixing German and English curses.

"We *were* ready, dammit. Ready to go. Now we have a *verdamten* visitor in the lab!"

Mike's heart sank. "Oh, crap. I'm sorry Stefan, I completely forgot. I'll take care of it."

Stefan noticed Mike's pained expression and softened somewhat. "What is this person doing here?"

The visitor, Mike explained, was a nonfiction author who wanted to interview them and see the lab. The Colton Foundation, in addition to providing funds, also gave its grantees free publicity. They had referred the writer to Mike. A favor, to be sure, but the timing couldn't be worse.

They walked down the hallway toward the laboratory. They reached a door with a sign that read DO NOT ENTER WHEN RED LIGHT IS ON. The light was off. Several signs listed hazards due to intense lasers, chemicals, and high-voltage power.

Mike opened the door. He could hear one of his graduate students, Sarah Jacobson, explaining the details of the upcoming experiment.

"The silicon is placed in the liquid-helium cryostat," she said. "During our experiment, the sample is maintained at a temperature of two Kelvin."

Sarah emerged from behind the cryostat, a hefty stainless steel cylinder with small round windows. It was mounted on a several-ton table supported by vibration-isolating legs. Hundreds of optical components–prisms, lenses, mirrors, beamsplitters–covered the table. She saw Mike and Stefan, and smiled. "Hi guys," she said.

Mike felt his hair stand on end, as though he had walked in to find a venomous spider. The visitor turned to look at him. It was not the author.

It was Hassan Zare.

4

"Turn on the terahertz scanner," said James.

"With pleasure." Troy grinned like a nerd who had just been handed a pair of x-ray glasses at a sorority dance. He turned a knob and a fuzzy, black-and-white image appeared on a screen. The adjacent screen showed a color video of Jing Shen, sitting in a room. The black-and-white image came into focus. It was a low-quality version of the color video.

Troy turned two other knobs and zoomed in on Jing. The terahertz scanner virtually stripped away her clothes, revealing her underwear. Troy hummed a burlesque tune.

"Knock it off," James growled.

Troy refined the image further. They now watched a grainy image of Jing's naked body.

"Scan from the other angle."

A second image appeared and Troy repeated the procedure. "She just doesn't have a bad side."

"She looks clean," said James without irony. "Return the camera."

"Aye-aye."

* * *

As she waited in the windowless room, Jing recalled her conversations with Henry Colton. They had talked for nearly an hour in the luxurious outdoor hot tub with its splendid view of the mountains. Henry waxed philosophic about business, science, and religion, clearly overjoyed by the presence of an intelligent woman in a bikini.

"You seem to find *everything* interesting," she said, setting aside her empty glass.

"I suppose you're right." He thought for a moment. "Well, there are exceptions. Tax law, for instance."

"Let's pin it down. What will be the single biggest breakthrough of this century?"

"Now *there's* a question"

"I'm serious. You're all over the map. Biology, physics, computers, medicine… What's going to be the thing that historians, a hundred years from now, will write about?"

Henry watched her adoringly, captivated by her earnestness. So few people thought in terms of centuries, or even decades, anymore. In his world of business, Henry saw the insidious effect of short-term thinking. Public corporations served stock analysts who demanded quarterly profits. Under the crushing pressure of bean-counting scrutiny, the once-great industrial research labs had all but collapsed. Projects that lasted more than two years had no place in such a risk-averse environment.

When Henry abandoned his goal of becoming a trillionaire, he bought back stock and transformed his core company, Colton Enterprises, into a privately held entity. Freed from the tyranny of the financial markets, he embarked on long-term projects that nurtured creative concepts from basic research to product development. Most of the ideas generated during the basic research phase never panned out. But some, like the recently patented Biochip, proved lucrative successes that more than paid for the many small failures.

"Energy," he said at last.

"Specifically?"

"The world is becoming industrialized. The industrial revolution benefitted Europeans and Americans but left the rest of the world, literally, in the dust. Now, countries like China and India are rapidly catching up. They'll demand a lifestyle similar to ours, and rightly so. Whoever figures out how to supply energy to the entire world–not just parts of the world, but the whole planet, without ruining the environment–will go down as the greatest person of this century."

Henry's expression made it clear that he intended to be that person.

"Okay, smart guy," Jing said. "What about solar, or wind?"

"Marginal at best. You need to cover several square miles with solar panels just to put out as much power as an ordinary coal plant. Never mind the environmental impact of covering that much land with artificial structures, or the huge cost of producing so much silicon for photovoltaic cells. Wind? Nice idea, but it's intermittent. It'll always be a niche player."

"Nuclear?" she suggested, egging him on.

"Not bad, except for the radioactive waste that no one wants in their backyard."

"Hydrogen fuel cells?"

"Give me a break. Even if you could figure out how to store hydrogen safely and efficiently, you still need to produce the stuff, which requires a huge amount of energy. That just moves the problem from one place to another. No, we need something radically different. A technology that no one else has thought of."

"Like what, exactly?"

Henry smiled. "I have a few ideas."

Jing watched the slightly overweight man in a Motley Crue T-shirt as he tentatively approached her. He avoided her eyes. "Ma'am, here's your camera."

"Did you enjoy the pictures?"

Troy laughed nervously. "Visitors aren't allowed to bring cameras here. Sorry."

"Well, that's understandable," she said. "You can't tolerate Peeping Toms."

Troy laughed again, pathetically. Blushing, he scurried away.

A few minutes later, James entered the room. "I'll escort you to the helicopter. Follow me."

Jing walked silently behind James on the path to the helipad, where the helicopter and pilot were waiting.

At the helicopter, she extended her hand. "James, it's been a real pleasure. I hope we can do this again sometime."

James squinted at the afternoon sun. "Not if I can help it. Have a safe trip." He turned and headed back to the mansion.

Jing stepped into the helicopter. She carefully removed her contact lenses and placed them in her silk blouse pocket. After Jing buckled herself, the pilot started the engine and the rotor blades began to spin. A few minutes later, the helicopter ascended. She saw Henry through a window in the mansion, waving goodbye.

5

One side of the lab housed a grid of bulky capacitors behind a metal cage with signs that read HIGH VOLTAGE. Thick cords ran from the capacitors to twenty high-power lasers. The lasers, suspended from the ceiling by metal wires, pointed in the direction of the optical table.

Hassan, a tall man with a mane of gray hair, inspected the setup.

"I'm surprised you let graduate students in here," Hassan said. "These are petawatt lasers. Very dangerous."

"I don't believe we've met," said Stefan.

"Hassan Zare," he said, extending his hand. "You must be Stefan Schroeder."

Stefan shook Hassan's hand hesitantly. "*Ja*, but I should tell you, we do not have time for a tour right now."

"And *I* should tell you that our interlock procedures are fine. The students are perfectly safe."

Hassan regarded Mike with a supercilious smile. "Mike, good to see you."

"I didn't know you were coming by. What's the occasion?"

"The DARPA program review, of course," he said.

"That's not until next week."

"Indeed. I thought I would take the opportunity to see the sights."

Mike felt his blood pressure rise. Hassan obviously had an ulterior motive, but he was not about to divulge it.

Stefan's face turned redder. "Professor Zare, we should really continue this discussion in the hallway. We are getting ready for an experiment."

Hassan ignored Stefan and peered into the cryostat. "I know your trick. This idea about isotopically pure silicon–it's no longer a secret."

"Nothing we do is secret. This is basic research, remember?"

Hassan walked up to Mike and bored into him with angry brown eyes. "Cut the crap, Mike. You don't think I know what you three are working on? Let's see: a laser jock, a semiconductor guy, and a gravitational theorist. Hmmm. Maybe they're researching crystal healing! How stupid do you think I am?"

Mike felt the onset of panic–blood pumping, pulse pounding, dry mouth, headache… Why couldn't he stand up to this bully?

"I don't think you're stupid."

"Humor me," Hassan hissed, sensing fear. "Tell me the goal of your little science project."

"To study interactions between lasers and matter," he replied, his voice unsteady.

"Of course. Of course. Silly me. Well, I'll be leaving now." Hassan headed for the door, then stopped in mid-stride. "Oh, there's just one thing. What is Seth's role in this project?"

"What do you mean?"

"He's a gravitational theorist. Numerical general relativity. What the hell does that have to do with 'interactions between lasers and matter'?"

Mike looked at Stefan. They remained silent.

"We three know damn well that gravity plays no role whatsoever in solid-state phenomena." Hassan's eyes were wild behind strands of long gray hair. "Electromagnetic interactions are stronger by forty orders of magnitude! To hell with gravity–it just doesn't matter!"

Stefan began to speak, but Mike put a finger to his lips.

"No secrets," Hassan scoffed. "Basic research. You're a hypocrite, Mike. I play games, sure. But at least I'm honest about it."

With that, he turned dramatically and left the room. Stefan and Mike exhaled.

"Well *he* seemed nice," Sarah said.

Still shaking from his encounter with Hassan, Mike closed his office door and massaged his temples. Fingers of pain reached into his frontal lobes as he slumped into his chair. He opened a desk drawer and retrieved a plastic bottle. Hands trembling, he opened the bottle and popped two pills into his mouth.

What was Hassan up to? Somehow, he had discovered the real purpose behind their experiment. Mike could see that clearly in Hassan's predatory eyes. Someone had spilled the beans. Not the graduate students, though–they were kept blissfully in the dark. Who, then? Mike's old paranoia, about Hassan stealing their idea and taking the credit, resurfaced.

He felt his pulse race as he thought about the timing of Hassan's unwelcome visit. Perhaps he had beaten them to the punch and was taunting them. The esteemed Professor Zare was going to reveal the results of his groundbreaking experiment at the program review. The Nobel Prize would not be far behind. But before collecting his laurels, Hassan had to stick it to his old nemesis, just for old time's sake.

Calm down, Mike told himself. *Seth's calculations showed that the experiment wouldn't work*. The point was moot. Still, Hassan had figured it out. That much was certain.

"Let's see: a laser jock, a semiconductor guy, and a gravitational theorist. Hmmm. Maybe they're researching crystal healing! How stupid do you think I am?"

It was possible that Hassan had deduced their experiment's true aim from the available data. He may be a monster, but he's no fool.

A knock interrupted Mike's agitated thoughts. Shaking them off, he opened the door. A skinny graduate student named Charles stood, eyes wide with enthusiasm. He was wearing his typical uniform of jeans and a plaid shirt.

"We're ready to transfer the liquid helium," he said with a

toothy grin. His eyes were crimson from a long night of trouble-shooting.

"Great," Mike replied, trying to sound upbeat. "I'll come by the lab in a few minutes."

"Excellent," said Charles. Whistling, he walked down the hallway toward the laboratory.

Mike picked up the phone and dialed Seth's number. When he got voice mail, he hung up. He went to the hallway and took the elevator to the second floor.

"People used to think space and time were separate," Seth said smoothly, leaning closer. "Take us, for example. We occupy the same *time* but different *places*."

He spoke to a woman of about thirty with thick glasses, shoulder-length black hair with a hint of red, and a pale complexion. Bookish in appearance, she wore a plaid skirt and Mary Jane shoes. She seemed fascinated by Seth's private lecture.

"Let's trade places." He touched the small of her back and guided her to where he had stood. "Now, at a later time, you occupy the space that I did at an earlier time. To describe your position in space-time, we need four variables: x, y, z, for position and t, for time."

"I see."

"If, however, we occupied the *same* space-time coordinate…"

Mike walked in. The woman turned to him and extended her hand. "Professor Harris! I'm Valerie Norton."

"Thanks for coming," he said, managing a wan smile. "I see you found Seth's computer lab."

"Darned impressive," she said, gesturing to the rows of computers, over a thousand of them, chugging through massively parallel calculations. "This rivals the national labs."

"Unlike the national labs, I don't have to share my toy," said Seth with pride. "This entire facility is dedicated to one project."

Mike gave him a look that said *enough, Seth.*

"But tonight," he continued, "*I* have only one project: making dinner for you."

"Well, sorry, but I…"

"Seth understands," Mike said hastily. "Let's go down to my lab."

"Nice to meet you," said Seth as Mike escorted her out of the room. "Text me."

"This is *so cool*," Valerie enthused, snapping pictures with her camera.

Mike led her to one end of the laboratory. "These are the high-voltage capacitors, which store and deliver pulses of electricity to the lasers." The twenty lasers, each the size of a .50-caliber machine gun, pointed menacingly at a series of optics and a single planar mirror on the optical table. The mirror was mounted on a motorized stage.

"This is *so* Death Star," she said.

"What kind of book are you writing, exactly?"

She whipped out a notepad covered with scribbles. "It's a work in progress, really. Something tying together the greatest discoveries of the twentieth century with what will be the greatest discoveries of the twenty-first. This stuff here fits right in." She set the notepad down and snapped more pictures.

"Who's your publisher?"

"I'm shopping around. Hey, what does this do?"

"Madam, please don't touch that." Stefan, at the end of his rope, had walked into the lab.

"Valerie, this is Stefan," Mike said awkwardly.

Her eyes brightened. "Stefan Schroeder, the laser jock. Can I ask you some questions?"

"*Nein*, madam, we have work to do."

"That's fine, I'll just watch."

Stefan groaned and joined Sarah and Charles, who stood by the cryostat. Charles wheeled over a large steel Dewar of liquid helium. Sarah took a transfer line and stuck the tube into the opening of the Dewar.

"They're preparing to transfer liquid helium into the cryostat," Mike said.

"What's a cryostat?"

"It's that big metal cylinder there. Essentially a glorified

Thermos, with windows for optical access. The outer insulating region has been evacuated to less than a billionth of an atmosphere. When liquid helium flows in, our silicon sample will be cooled to a couple degrees above absolute zero."

She scribbled excitedly in her notes. "That is *so* cool. Literally."

Stefan climbed a ladder and stuck the other end of the transfer line into the cryostat. Charles flipped a switch on a large vacuum pump that sat on a vibration-isolating platform. The vacuum began to chug loudly. The vacuum, Mike explained, would suck liquid helium into the sample chamber. He showed her a digital readout of the temperature. Gradually, the temperature decreased from 298 Kelvin to 290, 280, 270, at a rate of a degree every few seconds.

"The samples are prepared in this part of the lab," Mike said, leading her to the wall furthest from the capacitors. There she saw a chemical hood, a locked cabinet labeled FLAMMABLE, and a polishing apparatus. "We need to polish the surfaces of the silicon sample to a high degree of perfection. Any scratch will get extremely hot during the laser irradiation, causing the sample to melt."

"Do you make your own samples?"

"No," he said, thinking of his encounter with Hassan. "Our Russian collaborators grow special samples for us."

"How are they special?"

Good question. "High purity," he said.

She snapped several pictures of the sample preparation equipment. "Darned impressive."

"Ten Kelvin," Stefan called. "Nine. Eight."

The temperature decreased rapidly and the vacuum pump began chugging more loudly.

"Four-point-two Kelvin. We have liquid helium."

Valerie walked over to the cryostat and peered inside. She saw a shiny cube supported by a copper rod.

"That cube is the silicon sample," Mike said. "After fifteen minutes or so, we'll get it down to two Kelvin."

"There's something I don't get. Absolute zero. What is it, exactly?"

I'll have to start from Adam and Eve, Mike thought.

"Let's go back to my office," he said.

Mike erased part of the whiteboard. He cleared a stack of product manuals, papers, and books off a chair and invited Valerie to sit down.

"Temperature, roughly speaking, is a measure of how thermally excited something is."

Valerie's eyes squinted behind her thick glasses. "Excited?"

"Yes. You can excite a system in a number of ways. Through vibration, for example."

Valerie snorted. "Are *all* physicists perverts?"

Mike blushed, not amused by the double entendre. In a different context, he might have laughed. But now, with the program review a few days off and an experiment running, he didn't have the patience to deal with an amateur.

He continued: "Remember that piece of silicon? At room temperature, 298 Kelvin, the silicon atoms were vibrating like mad. The vibrations are called *phonons*–literally, particles of sound."

"So, at high temperatures, crystals like silicon have lots of phonons."

"Correct. When we cool the sample down to a few Kelvin, the phonons all but disappear."

"And at *absolute* zero, there would be *no* phonons. All the atoms would be frozen in place."

Mike picked up a dry erase marker. "You're right, there would be no phonons. But the atoms would not be still." He drew a circle to represent an atom. Superimposed on the circle, he drew a bell curve. "The laws of quantum mechanics cause something called *zero point motion*–that is, motion even at zero temperature."

"Is that the Heisenberg uncertainty relation?"

"Yes. There's no way an atom can be perfectly still, due to the random quantum motion that everything has."

"Then why bother to cool your sample down? Liquid helium must be expensive."

"Over a thousand bucks per experiment. The reason is that, while the atoms always have quantum mechanical jiggle, their energy states are very well defined."

It was all about what you chose to measure, he explained. If you want to measure the *position* of an atom, you'll get a random probability distribution, given by the bell curve. If you decide to measure *energy*, however, you can get an extremely precise value. Such special quantities were denoted *eigenvalues* of the system.

In a silicon crystal, light could kick an electron into a higher energy state, forming something called an *exciton.* At temperatures near absolute zero, this exciton had a very well-defined, sharp energy. Stefan Schroeder's lasers were tuned to that exact energy. When they all fired a laser pulse at the same time, the silicon crystal would be suddenly promoted to a highly excited state.

"That sounds totally cool," she said. "But, if you don't mind me asking, *why*?"

"Basic research," he replied, somewhat wearily. "No one's ever done it before."

Hassan's voice rose into his thoughts. *"Basic research. You're a hypocrite, Mike. I play games, sure. But at least I'm honest about it."*

"In some sense, we're creating an artificial state of matter. Under normal conditions, you would *never* find a crystal in such an excited state."

Valerie chewed a pencil eraser as she pondered his comments. "So you're storing energy. Like a hydrogen fuel cell, or a battery…"

"Sort of…" It was true–when the silicon absorbed the laser pulse, it would store a tremendous amount of energy. But only for a brief instant. "The exciton lasts for a nanosecond," he explained. "Not long enough for a practical storage device."

He noticed Charles standing at the door, an energized grin on his face.

"We're there," Charles announced excitedly. "Two-point-two Kelvin. Ready to commence firing."

6

The pilot handed Jing an envelope. "Mr. Colton wanted me to deliver this to you."

"Thanks." She took the envelope and walked away from the helicopter, toward a parking lot on the small airfield. She waited until the helicopter took off before getting into her car, a black luxury sedan. When she started the ignition, a small screen turned on.

Messages: 1
Priority: urgent.

"Play message," she said as she drove up to a gate, which opened slowly.

Jing saw a familiar face on the screen. "Jing," he said. "It looks like the baby is premature. Things are happening faster than we expected. Please report to the hospital. End message."

This was not good. Just an hour ago, she was enjoying the rarefied atmosphere of Henry Colton's estate. After sitting in the hot tub, they donned robes and Henry, like an eager schoolboy, showed her his collection of science toys in the solarium. She marveled at the eclectic array of computers, telescopes, microscopes, electronic gadgets, and piles upon piles of books. One toy, probably from his telecommunications subsidiary, transformed her voice so that it sounded like various celebrities. Another device, a headband with light-emitting diodes, monitored frontal brain activity and served as a primitive lie detector. They giggled as Henry attempted to lie about his age, prompting rude beeps from the computer.

Obviously, Henry had a sincere love of science, and Jing enjoyed being around him. But now, she had a job to do. She pressed on the accelerator and the car sped up the mountain road.

"Seth, we need to talk."

Mike closed the door behind him. The large computing laboratory housed 16 rows of sophisticated computers, equipped with cryogenically cooled quantum-dot arrays for rapid calculations. Each row contained two levels, 32 computers on each level. In all, 1,024 computers labored continuously, lights blinking, day and night. To dissipate the heat generated by the processors, massive fans blew air past the computers. The spaces between the rows were like wind tunnels. Every time he saw it, Mike was amazed by the sheer power of the operation.

Seth stared at a whiteboard, where he had written Maxwell's equations, the formulae that governed electricity, magnetism, and light. Next to them were Einstein's equations of general relativity. "What's up?" he asked absently.

Mike looked around the room, making sure they were alone. "Hassan was here."

Seth whirled around. "Hassan Zare?"

"Yep. Just popped in, unannounced. Fired a few barbs, then left."

"What is that nutcase up to?"

"Good question. Listen," he said, lowering his voice. "He knows."

"He's bluffing."

Mike shook his head. He had seen the knowing, malevolent eyes of Hassan Zare.

"I don't believe it. Who could have told him? The students

know nothing."

Mike pressed his fingers to the left side of his forehead and sat down. He felt the throbbing pain return. "I might have let it slip. Back when I was with Jennifer."

"Pillow talk?" said Seth disapprovingly. "Jesus, Mike. She probably blabbed to the Boy Dean, who then told the entire Western World."

He saw Mike's crestfallen expression at the mention of the Dean.

"Sorry," he said. "That was low."

"It hardly matters," Mike said morosely. "Your damned calculations showed the whole project is a joke."

"About those calculations…"

The phone rang. When Seth answered, his ear was assaulted by high-volume Germanic invective.

After a minute, he hung up the phone. "You'd better get down to the lab. Stefan is about to kill our visitor."

The temperature controller read 2.2 Kelvin. Inside the cryostat, the silicon sample was immersed in a clear fluid: liquid helium, the coldest liquid in the universe.

Stefan marched up to Mike, face taut with pent-up rage. "Get her out of here, *now*," he hissed.

"Sorry," Mike mumbled. He gently touched Valerie's shoulder. "They're about to begin. We should leave."

"Oh, sure," she said, setting her camera on a lab bench. "Thanks, Stefan!"

Stefan muttered something under his breath as he fine-tuned the alignment of the optics.

Mike pressed a button by the door. With a buzz, the door unlocked.

"That's our interlock system," he said as he opened the door for Valerie. He still felt defensive after Hassan questioned the safety of his lab. "The door won't unlock if the lasers are on. That prevents someone out in the hallway from getting blinded by infrared radiation."

They headed back to Mike's office. Valerie reviewed how the

experiment would go, to make sure she had her information right. First, the high-voltage capacitors would charge up. Then, the lasers would fire intense pulses of infrared light at the optical table. The optics would combine twenty beams into a single, extremely intense pulse of radiation. The motorized mirror would direct the beam toward the cryostat. The pulse would slam into the cold piece of silicon, instantaneously creating a blizzard of excitons. For one nanosecond, the silicon crystal would be in a state unlike anything in the known universe. Then, the process would be repeated as the lasers fired pulse after pulse.

"Darned impressive," she remarked.

Valerie may be annoying, he thought, but she obviously had a competence for synthesizing information. Perhaps her book would sell. Still, he didn't have time for an extended discussion. He glanced at the blank PowerPoint slide on his computer screen. The DARPA review was next week. He needed something, *anything*, to present. He was not concerned about Dr. Hansen, the program director. It was Hassan he feared. What did that man have up his sleeve?

"Would you like to take some pictures?" he suggested lamely, trying to get Valerie out his office.

"Oh, shoot," she said. "I left the camera in the lab. I'll go get it."

Mike yawned as she strode into the hallway. He knew Stefan could very well blow his top, but he was too tired to stop her.

The laser tests, performed at low pulse intensities, were going well. Stefan felt tension ebb from his body. A familiar calm that came with the taking of data displaced his wound-up nervousness. There was nothing like it–pumps humming, computers plotting, lasers firing… It didn't matter what the experiment was, really. He always savored the moment when, after days of effort, everything converged and real numbers streamed in.

"Okay, clear the area," he ordered. Sarah and Charles walked to the side of the lab near the capacitors. He joined them. Now, the experiment was automated. They put on their safety glasses and watched.

"Here we go," Stefan said with a satisfied grin.

The blank PowerPoint slide seemed to taunt him. Even if the experiment went perfectly, Mike was not sure what he would present at the program review. They had promised "deliverable milestones" that had not been delivered and probably never would be. If their goal had been too lofty, that would be one thing. But if Hassan had succeeded where they had failed, then Mike's scientific reputation would never recover. Again, he asked himself what surprise Hassan had in store.

He recalled the time, during the euphoric early days of the project, when he told Jennifer about the experiment. They talked late into the night, and he discovered that she was genuinely interested in his work.

Apparently, Jennifer leaked the information. She must have told someone who told Hassan. Although her research was not in physics, the academic world was small. He cursed his bad judgment. They had all agreed to keep it a secret…

A scream interrupted Mike's thoughts. He ran into the hallway. Valerie was crouched on the floor.

"What's wrong?" he asked, confused.

She pointed to a fist-sized hole in the wall, next to the laboratory door. The edges were black, ringed with glowing red embers. He saw a similar hole on the opposite wall. The hallway filled with acrid smoke.

"Come here, *now*!" he yelled. Valerie ran toward him quickly. "Get into my office and call 9-911."

As she ran into his office, Mike approached the lab door. The red light was on. He tried to open the door but it was locked.

Stefan could not believe what he was seeing. The mirror had suddenly swung out of alignment. *Another computer bug?* Then, the lasers fired. Twenty invisible beams of light combined and reflected off the mirror's silvery surface. He felt heat as the pulse shot past his face, puncturing the wall.

"Oh *scheiss*."

The mirror, seemingly possessed, turned slightly and the lasers blasted. Stefan screamed in horror as his shirt caught fire. Another pulse tore into his chest and he doubled over. Blood spurt out of a gaping hole in his burnt flesh. With a sickened gasp, he collapsed onto the floor.

Charles staggered backward, eyes wide. The mirror spun wildly, sending laser pulses firing in his direction. Sparks flew as a laser beam hit a high-voltage capacitor. Panicking, he backed away from the mirror. After a brief lull, he heard the lasers fire again. Feeling a scorching pain in his shoulder, he jerked backward and slammed into the capacitors. Bright blue jolts of electricity arced from the capacitors to his arms. He twitched spasmodically as current coursed through one arm, surged through his heart, and exited out the other arm.

The mirror swung around and laser pulses shot in the opposite direction. The cabinet of flammable chemicals exploded in a bright orange fireball, sending shards of glass flying. Organic liquids sprayed onto the optical table. Sarah screamed, face bloodied by the explosion, and scuttled toward the door. A pool of flaming fluids blocked her path.

Mike heard the explosion, the screams, and the unrelenting lasers. He slammed his body against the door but it did not yield. He ran down the hallway. He spent every workday here, yet he couldn't remember where the damned fire extinguisher was! He turned right. Paul Quinlan emerged from his office, confused about the commotion.

"I need an axe!" Mike yelled.

Paul took one look at Mike's unhinged face and ran away.

"Dammit!" Mike spun around and saw the emergency equipment. Breathing heavily, he grabbed the fire extinguisher. He sprinted down the hallway toward the laboratory door. A laser pulse blasted through the wall, narrowly missing him. He dropped the fire extinguisher and kicked the door madly. Sarah's voice yelled for help.

"Hang on, Sarah!" He kicked the door a few more times,

then slammed his body into it with all his remaining strength. The door burst open. Mike tumbled into a wall of fire. Flames seared his flesh. He retreated and rolled on the hallway floor. He choked on black smoke and picked up the fire extinguisher.

Mike pulled the pin and squeezed the trigger, shooting a white spray of carbon dioxide at the base of the fire. He moved the spray in a side-to-side motion. Gradually, the flames subsided. Sarah made her way toward the door, past the liquid helium Dewar.

They heard another pulse fire, followed by a deafening *boom*. Liquid helium sprayed out of the Dewar, sending up frigid, billowing clouds. Sarah shrieked as the freezing vapor enveloped her body. Desperately, Mike threw the fire extinguisher at the mirror. Dozens of optical components shattered. The mirror tumbled onto the floor.

He saw Charles, who was stuck to the high-voltage equipment, paralyzed with electric shock. Horrified, he walked through clouds of cold vapor. His eyes watered from the sting of smoke and chemicals in the air. He looked at Charles' pale face, which stared back with zombie-like vacancy. He removed his belt and used it to pull Charles loose from the capacitors. Limbs stiff, Charles fell forward and landed with a thud.

"Sarah, help me pull Charles out of here."

Sarah lay on the ground, bleeding and shivering. Mike cursed as he abandoned Charles. He dragged Sarah out of the laboratory and into the hallway.

"Are you okay?" he asked, knowing the question was stupid.

Shards of glass had cut into her face, but her eyes seemed intact. She tried to speak but could not.

"Don't worry. An ambulance is on the way."

The lasers fired again. Instead of converging on the mirror, twenty individual beams struck the pools of organic fluid that covered the optical table. The flammable liquid ignited, sending up an inferno of orange flame.

"We need another fire extinguisher!" he yelled desperately.

A piercing fire alarm sounded as the hallway became choked with thick black smoke. Overhead sprinklers sprayed water. He could hear faculty and students rushing for the exits.

Valerie emerged from his office, holding a scarf over her mouth.

"We need to get Sarah out of here," he said between coughs.

They lifted Sarah and carried her past the lab, where the fire raged, unabated by the sprinklers. Sarah moaned in pain. They made their way toward the lit EXIT sign. Amid the chaos, a pair of surprisingly calm students opened the door for them. Mike and Valerie lugged Sarah to the assembly area and lay her down on the grass.

"Stay with her," Mike said, turning to reenter the building.

"Mike, no!"

He ran back in, pushing his way past groups of students.

"I need a fire extinguisher!" he shouted.

"Over there," a tall student said, pointing down the hall.

Mike ran down the hallway and grabbed a fire extinguisher from a mount on the wall. Sweating profusely, he scrambled toward the lab, entering a thick cloud of smoke. He made his way toward the fire, feeling the searing intensity of its heat. Through stinging eyes, he saw Stefan's body on the ground, engulfed by flames. Mike cried out and emptied the contents of the carbon-dioxide canister. White vapor mixed with black smoke. Mike fell to his knees, eyes closed, holding his throat, unable to breathe. He threw the canister at the capacitors. Through the fog, he saw a surge of bluish sparks, and the lights in the room flickered out. In the darkness, he collapsed to the ground and saw stars before all went black.

7

So when are you going to ask me out?"

Mike blushed, embarrassed by his lack of nerve. Jennifer sat on the table next to his computer, her white summer dress revealing beautifully tanned skin, supple legs, and gorgeous curves. Long, light brown hair rested on her shoulders and spilled down her back.

He stammered a bit, then offered: "How about Giovanni's?"

"When?"

"Tonight? Say, seven?"

She smiled. "Now that wasn't so difficult, was it?"

"I guess not."

Jennifer's angelic image faded into a pale white glow. He tried to touch her but could not.

"Second-degree burns over twenty percent of the torso," someone was saying. "Respiratory blockage due to smoke inhalation. Mild concussion. Dehydration."

A blinding white light sent a sharp pain into his head. He felt his body convulse with hacking coughs. Hands propped him up as he coughed up sooty phlegm.

"Mike, do you know what day it is today?"

Blurry images stood around him. Was this the DARPA review?

"Mike, if you can hear me, blink twice."

With effort, he blinked. The pain in his head was almost unbearable.

"Bring Jennifer back," he slurred.

Someone wiped his mouth. A female voice said, "Mike, do you know where you are?"

The images slowly came into focus. He moved his hand to his aching forehead and felt an intravenous line attached to his arm. He recognized the doctor. What was her name?

"You've been in an accident, Mike."

His heart froze as hellish images resurfaced: the chemical inferno, choking smoke, Stefan's body afire…

"Stefan!" he shouted. He struggled against restraining hands. "I need a fire extinguisher *now*!"

"Stefan's dead," the doctor said calmly. "Sit down, Mike. You did everything you could." She held his hand, soothing him with her serene voice. "You're a hero. Not the brightest idea in the world, running into a burning room. But brave. Very brave."

Stefan's dead. Mike felt sick. "Charles?"

"I'm sorry."

"Sarah?"

She squeezed his hand gently. "Alive, thanks to you. Stable condition."

His relief immediately gave way to guilt. Human error, not bad luck, caused accidents. He and Stefan were ultimately responsible for the safety of the lab. With Stefan gone, scrutiny would focus on Mike alone. What had he done wrong? The past couple of years felt like wandering through a fog. As his enthusiasm for the project ebbed, he relinquished more authority to Stefan. In truth, Stefan had become the project leader. Maybe if Mike had been more involved, he could have somehow prevented the disaster.

His thoughts turned to Charles, a true innocent, a student who trusted his mentors to provide a safe working environment. They had failed him, horribly. He imagined the shock and grief of his parents as they received the news. Their sadness would soon turn to anger. Lawyers would circle like vultures. They would expose each mistake, every miscalculation. Armed with 20/20 hindsight, lawyers would build their case: the university allowed Mike Harris to run a lab that was out of control. Colton University would spend millions to make the problem go away.

He felt dizzy as dark thoughts spun in his head. He closed his eyes and tried to fall asleep.

A fireman removed his self-contained breathing apparatus and spoke to a tall, slender man in a police uniform.

"We need a Hazmat team in here. There're organic solvents all over the place. Gotta secure 'em. No chemical inventory, near as I can tell."

Jon Patterson, chief of campus police, nodded. He stood near the yellow tape that demarked the boundary of the disaster area. Black smoke and the smell of ozone still hung in the air.

"Ventilation?

"It's working now."

"How's Mike?"

"Not sure."

Jon stroked his mustache as he took in the scene. The massive optical table in the center of the lab was covered with a sticky, tar-like film, and the cryostat lay on its side, windows shattered. Hundreds of painstakingly aligned optical components lay in ruins. Most of the lasers still hung from the ceiling, although a couple of them dangled by a single metal wire. On the left, fume hoods and chemical cabinets were obliterated. On the right, the bank of capacitors sparked intermittently.

A few minutes ago, emergency workers somberly removed the charred remains of Stefan and Charles. Owing to his training and years of experience, the sight of corpses did not perturb him. Jon felt a pang, though, when he saw Mike on the gurney, an oxygen mask over his mouth. The guy couldn't seem to catch a break.

Now, the cleanup was underway. While the scene looked chaotic to the uninitiated, Jon was familiar with the ballet between academic and municipal agencies that followed an accident. The fire department arrived first. They evacuated the victims and extinguished the remnants of the fire. Then, the university's Office of Environmental Health and Safety, working with the fire department, assessed the hazards and contained the toxic brew. The campus police department established a perimeter and interviewed witnesses. Later, lawyers and administrators would descend, eager to assign blame. Despite the obvious tragic dimensions of the laboratory fire, he felt calm, in his element, as the process unfolded.

The Hazmat team arrived, clad in yellow suits, and began taking samples from various areas in the lab. Jon overheard them talking about "butthead cowboy scientists" and their cavalier attitude toward safety. He noticed the computer, badly burnt, with a film of sticky fluid covering the monitor. He walked over to it.

"Computer's toast," said the fireman. "So much for their firewall."

"Can you get any data from it?"

"Heck if I know."

"I'll call one of our IT guys."

The fireman shrugged, not particularly interested in the state of the computer. Jon noticed the shattered mirror and fire extinguisher on the floor. Someone had thrown the extinguisher at the mirror.

"How about the female grad student?"

"Frostbite and some cuts to the face and arms. She's in shock."

"I'd like to take statements as soon as possible."

The fireman took a step back. "I didn't know this was a crime scene."

"It's not. Still, we'll be filing a report."

"We didn't find any accelerants, if that's where you're headed. Looks to me like their lasers got out of hand, ignited the flammable liquids, and ka-boom. Honestly, I'm surprised this crap doesn't happen more often."

"They're at the campus clinic?"

"Two at the clinic, two at the morgue."

"I'll have Sergeant Garrett do the interviews." Jon spoke into his radio.

* * *

This time, Mike was half aware that he was dreaming. He walked with Jennifer, hand in hand, back to her apartment. Their evening of wine and food took the edge off Mike's awkwardness. First dates were not his forte–he usually wished that he could skip to the second date right away. Tonight was different, though. Just holding her hand sent tingles through his body.

They reached the door of her apartment. Jennifer took keys out of her purse and opened the door. She turned around, her hazel eyes teasing and inviting. Without a word, uncharacteristically bold, he slid his hands around her waist. She returned the embrace. His eyes closed as their lips met.

Mike heard beeping and subdued voices around him. He tried to block them out but could not halt the unwelcome return of consciousness.

He rubbed his bleary eyes and sat up. The image of Valerie came into focus.

"Hi, Mike."

"What are you doing here?" he asked, a terrible ache throbbing in his head.

"Just wanted to see how you're doing. You're quite a hero, you know."

The word *hero* grated. "I'm sure it'll make a fine chapter in your book."

They sat for a few minutes of strained silence. Finally, she showed him her business card. "Call me if you want to talk."

She placed the card on a table. After gazing at Mike sympathetically, she gave him a smile and quietly left.

Mike felt annoyed when he heard her talking to someone in the hallway. *Get out of here, already.* After a moment, he recognized Seth's voice. He and Valerie chatted for five or ten minutes. Then, Seth entered the room.

"You look like crap," Seth exclaimed. He set several bouquets of flowers on the table. "These are from the department. And me."

"Thanks."

"You've just been through hell. Anything you need, let me

know."

Mike thought for a moment. "The DARPA review. Do you think you could make some PowerPoint slides…?"

"Forget the DARPA review. It's finished. You need to focus on your health. Everything else is tertiary."

"You talked to Hansen?"

"I called his cell but couldn't reach him."

"Did you e-mail…"

"Forget it, Mike. End of story. By the way, I'll cover your classes for the rest of the quarter."

"Thanks."

"Yeah, well, I was getting tired of all those nubile 101 students. It's time to diversify."

Mike smiled weakly.

"Listen, Mike," he said, serious now. "I'm afraid the administration is going to come down on you like a ton of bricks. They'll need to blame someone."

"I *am* to blame."

"Bullshit. We both know that Stefan was in charge of that lab."

"I should've been more hands-on. Maybe…" Mike felt the rush of guilt, the fresh memory of lasers out of control, Charles twitching from electrical surges, Stefan lying motionless on the floor…

"The fact is, neither of us knows what went wrong today. But I do know two things. Stefan was in charge of that lab. And, Stefan is dead."

"Making him the perfect scapegoat," Mike whispered.

"Forget about honor, Mike. Think about yourself."

Mike wearily looked out the window at the setting sun. Seth sat in a corner of the room, silently keeping him company. He was still there when, a half hour later, Mike fell asleep.

SATURDAY, MAY 31

8

After a night of feverish dreams, he awoke to the sight of a policeman, sitting where Seth had been. Sunlight filtered in through the window blinds. He wondered what time it was.

"How are you feeling, Professor Harris?"

"Call me Mike," he mumbled, sitting up.

"Anything I can get you–Mike?" the young police sergeant asked.

Mike rubbed his aching forehead. His throat felt dry but he doubted water would help. "Are you here to arrest me?"

The policeman laughed. "Hardly," he said, extending his hand. "Sergeant Garrett, campus police."

Mike returned the handshake weakly. "You want to know the details?"

"If you don't mind. Let's start from the beginning."

Mike recounted the nightmare that had been replaying continuously in his mind. Stefan, Charles, and Sarah were in the lab. He was in the office. Valerie was in the hallway. The lasers went out of control. By the time Mike could break through the locked door, Charles and Stefan were dead.

Garrett then interrogated: What kind of lasers are they? How are they controlled? How did the optics direct the beams? What were three people doing in a room with twenty powerful lasers? Did the computer have any problems? What about software bugs? Mike felt increasingly defensive as he groped for answers. In retrospect, his research group looked like an amateurish, seat-of-the-pants operation.

"Hold on," he said, grasping his hair. "We always did tests at low pulse intensity."

"What do you mean?"

"Before we ramped up the laser power, we always did a test run at *low power*. I'm sure Stefan would have done that."

"So, when Stefan cranked up the power, something must've happened."

"I guess, but…" There was nothing fundamentally different about running at high power or low power. The beams should traverse exactly the same path.

"It was the mirror," Mike said. "It's controlled by the computer."

"How?" asked Garrett, writing in his notepad.

Mike had seen the mirror, out of control, directing the deadly laser pulses around the room. He explained that a computer program sent signals from the USB port to a motorized mirror mount. Commands from the computer told the mount to rotate horizontally or vertically. In theory, a computer glitch could cause the mirror to spin out of control.

"Who was using the computer prior to the experiment?"

He tried to remember the days before the disaster. They seemed so long ago. "Stefan was working on software bugs all week. But they were related to the data acquisition, not the optics."

"What was Stefan's state of mind?"

"Tired. Stressed. Ready to get on with the experiment."

"I see. So maybe he tried to fix the program but made a mistake."

Mike felt ill. He knew that Stefan was perfectly competent. "I guess it's possible."

A few minutes passed as the sergeant absently flipped through his notes. Then he broke the silence: "To your knowledge, did Stefan Schroeder have any enemies?"

Mike bolted upright. "You're not implying…"

"I'm just asking."

"I don't understand. This was an accident."

"Any ex-girlfriends? Irate students? Jealous colleagues?"

Mike tried to get his bearings. The interrogation over the technical aspects of his lab had left him exhausted. Now, this new tack pushed him into uncharted terrain. "Everyone liked Stefan. I mean, it's inconceivable."

"Professional rivalries?"

"I… I just don't…" He felt weak. A chronic thirst burned in his throat.

Garrett placed a hand sympathetically on Mike's shoulder. "You've been through a lot, Professor. Get some rest. I'll leave my card."

"Okay."

"If you think of anything, even if you think it's dumb, give me a call."

"I will."

The question hit him like a truck.

Hours after Sergeant Garrett left, Mike's mind buzzed with morbid scenarios. Realistically, he knew the disaster must have been caused by some kind of error–software, hardware, electrical–that, in retrospect, would seem obvious. Nonetheless, foul play dominated his thoughts.

Why would someone want to kill Stefan? Mike knew nothing of his personal life, if indeed one existed. Interactions with Stefan were entirely straightforward. He cared about physics, the outdoors, and the occasional pint of beer. Plus, he was too junior to have accumulated a collection of professional enemies.

Mike realized something. If someone wanted to commit murder–and that was a big "if"–then that person might have assumed that Mike would be in the lab. Perhaps *he* was the real target…

He shook his head, trying to purge paranoid thoughts from his brain. He needed to talk to someone.

"Nurse!" he shouted. "I need to leave. *Now.*"

* * *

The doctor regarded Mike disapprovingly. She handed him a form on a clipboard.

"I've already told you that I think you should stay for another twenty-four hours," she said. "But, I can't force you to stay."

Mike signed the medical waiver. He had to escape the confines of the hospital, with its diseased odors and lack of privacy. He needed space to think.

"I'd like to schedule an appointment in a couple of days. If you're experiencing respiratory problems, we'll need to perform a bronchoscopy."

"Fine." He handed the clipboard back to her.

"Do you have anyone who can wake you up at regular intervals?"

"I have an alarm clock."

"Okay," she said, looking sympathetic. "Set it so that you wake up a couple of times during the night. I'll have someone call you, too. We don't want you slipping into a coma."

"Of course," he said.

After the doctor wrote prescriptions for respiratory congestion and headaches, a nurse unhooked the intravenous line. Mike stood up shakily and shuffled over to a mirror. A gaunt, unshaven face looked back at him. A shower and some real food were definitely in order, he thought.

He collected his wallet from the table, as well as the business cards from Sergeant Garrett and Valerie Norton. The one from Valerie had a high-tech look to it–perhaps it had a magnetic stripe that contained useless information.

Valerie Norton, Ph.D.
Author, Philosopher, Lover of Science

Besides these few items, Mike realized that he had nothing else, including transportation. He remembered Seth's words: "*You've just been through hell. Anything you need, let me know.*" He hated asking for favors, even small ones. At the receptionist desk, he phoned Seth, who graciously apologized for not offering a ride sooner. He would be right over.

A few minutes later, Seth pulled up in his red Viper, its sleek curves shimmering in the afternoon sun. Where he got the money for such toys was a mystery, Mike thought. Seth escorted him out of the hospital and held the passenger door open.

"C'mon, Seth, I'm not your grandmother."

"Get in," he said gently. "Watch your head."

Mike settled into the leather seat and fastened his seatbelt. The Viper accelerated out of the pick-up area and onto the boulevard, Seth showing restraint out of deference to his queasy passenger. They passed the professional malls and superstores that dominated the southern section of town. After a few minutes, he turned onto a gravel road that wound through a pine forest.

"I'll be around, if you want to talk," he said as he drove. "Any time, day or night."

Mike looked at the clock on the dash–2:30 PM.

"Thanks. Right now, I need a shower."

They pulled up to Mike's house, a modest cottage with a ten-year-old car parked in front. Mike got out of the Viper.

"Thanks for everything, Seth," he said.

Seth removed his shades. "Get some rest. Forget about everything else."

"I'll try."

With a wave, Seth took off. Mike walked up to his door and opened it. As always, it was unlocked.

Mike felt refreshed after a shower and shave. Nonetheless, the travesty still haunted him. He feared the nightmares that would visit him tonight. Beyond the emotions of fear and guilt, he was profoundly confused. As he pondered the events, murder made less sense. If someone wanted to kill Stefan, why not buy a gun and catch him alone? The collateral damage seemed like overkill: an innocent graduate student dead, a multimillion dollar laboratory destroyed...

He realized how callous it was to place scientific equipment on par with human life. In truth, he did mourn the lab, much as a captain might mourn the loss of his ship. Their project had been full of promise, at least in the early years. Now it was over, not with the expected whimper but with a bang.

His mind turned to the DARPA review. He needed to talk to Dr. Hansen, and soon. What had Seth said? Hansen was out of touch, or something along those lines. Mike's gut told him, persistently, that he needed to find him.

Unknown to the general public, Hansen was a legend in the physics community. As a young Swede, he earned a bronze medal in the biathlon at the Winter Olympics. He would have been a contender for the gold four years later, but chose instead to focus on academics. After graduating with top honors from Linköping University, he headed to Berkeley, where he completed a doctoral dissertation in three and a half years. His research showed an intriguing theoretical link between the gravitational and electromagnetic forces. This connection could lead to the holy grail of fundamental physics, grand unification.

With that discovery, he could have had his pick of prestigious professorships. After a postdoctoral stint at Princeton, though, he grew restless with fundamental physics and turned his attention to applied science. He delved into a broad range of subjects in engineering, science, and mathematics. Rather than perform solitary research, he wanted to bring disparate elements of knowledge together to improve society and national security. He became a United States citizen and rose quickly through the ranks of government agencies. For the past ten years, he served as head of the Defense Sciences Office at DARPA.

DARPA, the Defense Advanced Research Projects Agency, developed radical military technologies. Housed deep within the Pentagon, DARPA directed technology programs that funded high-risk research at universities, companies, and government laboratories. Some of these programs yielded famous breakthroughs, such as ARPANET, a telecommunications network that evolved into the internet, as well as artificial intelligence and speech recognition. Other developments included sensors, lightweight surveillance satellites, and stealth technology. Still other discoveries remained shrouded in secrecy.

As chief of the Defense Sciences Office, Hansen consistently championed long-range, innovative, high-risk technology, often butting heads with more small-minded people. So far, his combination of intellect and toughness had kept the federal dollars coming. In particular, he went to great lengths to protect Mike's project from the axe. After the disaster, though, not even Hansen would be able to save their program.

But maybe he could figure out what the hell had happened. Mike picked up a telephone and dialed. He heard an automated response.

"This is Axel Hansen. Please leave a message and a number where you can be reached."

9

Jing sat in a dark chamber, lit only by the glow of computer screens. The screens showed maps, streams of alphanumeric data, and live feed from cable news channels. Across from her sat the man who had left the video message. His head, nearly bald, reflected the iridescent light.

"Here's the target," he said. "Male."

He handed her a tablet computer that displayed the target's face and vital statistics.

"I've never seen him before," she said. "Where is he?"

"Near Colton University."

She groaned. "I was just there."

"I know," he said, putting up a hand. "We only received this intelligence in the last hour. You'll need to go now. The helicopter is waiting."

Jing donned a black leather jacket. She loaded a high-power sniper rifle and slung it over her shoulder. She placed extra ammunition, a tripod, and a scope into a handbag.

"Next time, I'd like some advance notice."

"My apologies."

She took the computer brusquely and stalked out the door.

* * *

Chief Patterson sat back in his chair and rubbed his chin pensively.

"It doesn't make sense," he said.

Sergeant Garrett sat across from Jon Patterson's desk, reviewing his notes. "If I had to guess," he ventured, "I'd rule out Mike Harris as a suspect. He seemed genuinely shocked by the suggestion of murder. But, I've been wrong before."

Jon hoped his memories of Jennifer and Mike would not cloud his judgment. Back when they were a couple, they lived in a house in the same cul-de-sac as Jon. The neighbor between their houses was a history professor who maintained a continual supply of cold beer in his garage. Those were the days. When fertility treatments brought Jon and his wife an unexpected gift–triplets–Mike and Jennifer babysat often. What had happened with them? They had seemed like the perfect pair. After the breakup, Mike left the neighborhood, while Jennifer remained in the house. After a few months, she too moved out, and the cul-de-sac was never the same.

"So it looks like an accident."

"I suppose," Garrett said. "These professors are kinda cavalier, you know. There really aren't any safety rules for labs at the university. Just guidelines."

"I expect that will change." Jon yawned, feeling the effects of sleep deprivation. "The thing I don't understand," he said, rubbing his eyes, "are these frigging lasers. From my perspective, they seem like guns. Blam, blam. Someone had to be aiming them, right?"

"Not necessarily. The whole setup was computer controlled. Maybe the computer went haywire."

"Keep looking into the homicide angle. I don't expect to find anything, but…"

They understood implicitly that if Garrett uncovered incriminating evidence, Jon would bring in the detectives or even the feds. Until then, Garrett would continue collecting information.

"I'll keep on it," Garrett said. "I'm on my way now to see the tech guy."

"I'll come with you."

* * *

The loud ring jolted Mike out of a half slumber. He reached for the phone, disoriented.

"Mike?"

He glanced at the clock–4:20 PM. His heart pounded. Almost exactly twenty four hours ago, he heard Valerie's scream outside his office.

"Mike, are you there?"

"Yeah," he slurred, trying to focus. "Who's this?"

"It's Jeff. Jeff Lewis."

"Oh. Hi." People from the department must have been talking nonstop about the lab disaster. They would be curious to hear his eyewitness account. Mike stood up and walked to the kitchen, where piles of dishes left over from the reception two nights ago remained in the sink.

"I heard about the accident. Is it true about Stefan?"

"Yeah. It's true."

"How awful." Jeff cleared his throat. "This probably doesn't seem like the best time, but we should start thinking about the effect this might have on the search."

"Huh?"

"It doesn't look like Zheng is the faculty's number one choice. But if the Dean can be convinced to let us fill *two* positions, I think he would have a shot."

Mike held on to the kitchen counter for balance. "My God, Jeff."

"I know it seems distasteful, but we're late in the hiring cycle. If we wait, it could be two years before we get someone. The department can't survive that."

"I have to go," Mike said, pressing his free hand against the left side of his head. He felt severe pain return, a relentless, pulsating hammer that pounded on one side of the brain. Dropping the phone, he headed to the bathroom near the entryway and searched the medical cabinet. He found a bottle of pain medication and opened it, hands trembling. He swallowed three pills.

The horror of the disaster roared up in his mind. He couldn't stop the cascade of images. Tears welled up in his eyes as he staggered into the kitchen. He opened the liquor cabinet and hastily poured a shot of Scotch. Somehow he needed to calm his nerves. He needed to think, to answer the question, *what happened?* He downed the shot.

Was someone out to get him?

Mike's pulse raced as he locked the deadbolt on the front door. He went to the back door, which led out the kitchen to a small deck and expansive yard. He locked it. What if someone had snuck in? He opened the closet next to the front door. No one there. He turned on all the lights. Should he dial 911?

I should call a shrink. In fact, he should have gotten help years ago. He realized that now. The past decade had been a gradual descent into a mental fog. If he hadn't been in such a funk, would Stefan and Charles still be alive?

He had to solve the problem scientifically. Figure out what happened. This was something he could do, he must do, but first he had to shove aside guilt and fear.

He drew up a mental list of the reasons why murder made no sense. One: Stefan had no enemies. Two: Even if he had an enemy, that person wouldn't choose such a complex means of rubbing him out. Three: Even if his enemy had a perverse desire to orchestrate a baroque murder, laboratory lasers made poor weapons. They were far too random; indeed, one grad student survived. The entire scenario of foul play, brought up by Sergeant Garrett's leading questions, collapsed under the weight of logic.

Mike sat down and pressed his fingers to his head. He felt paranoia gradually fade away. What was the source of the disaster? It must have been the computer, which seemed to have a mind of its own. The cause of software crashes was a mystery to him. He suspected the IT guys didn't understand bugs either—they just made up a mythology to guide them along. No one person truly comprehended the complexity of computer systems.

Somehow, they would find the bug. Perhaps blame would rest on the company that sold them the data acquisition software. Whatever the outcome, Mike knew what he needed to do. He would pour a couple more shots of Scotch. His nerves calmed, he would sleep through the night. In the morning, first thing, he would call a therapist. Something good would come of this tragedy, he vowed. Starting tomorrow, he would put his life back on track.

"I take it you've met Harry before?" said Sergeant Garrett.

Chief Jon Patterson nodded. They stepped into a musty office. Electronic components and computer magazines were scattered on desktops and on the floor. A small trash can overflowed with paper, old banana peels, chicken bones, and a half-eaten sandwich. The putrid odor of perspiration and stale food hung thick in the air.

Harry, an immense man of average height and enormous girth, grunted and heaved himself out of his seat. His dirty blue and white plaid shirt failed to conceal a prominent, hairy belly, which spilled out of his jeans and sloshed as he shifted his weight. A strained leather belt barely suspended a pair of old, faded blue jeans. Bits of solder, paint, and oil adhered to his musty clothes, along with copious perspiration. Graying, disheveled hair sat atop a gigantic head, and tinted glasses obscured his eyes.

"Chief," Harry said with a distinct Chicago accent.

"What do you have for me?"

Harry pointed at the burnt computer that rested on one of his desks. "She's seen better days. Her hard drive's pretty much fried."

"Can you recover anything useful?"

"You mean data?" Harry shook his head. "It's gone. Unless you got yourself a SQUID."

Patterson and Garrett exchanged glances.

"Superconducting Quantum Interference Device. SQUID. There's an outfit in Mountain View that uses them to get magnetic info from hashed hard drives. It'd cost you a few thousand, though."

"Pass," Jon said.

"Right now," Harry said, stroking his stubbly jaw, "I'm looking into the network. Information that went to and from this computer."

"There's a record of that?" Jon asked.

"Sort of. The server logs will give me an idea about network activity. Which computers were talking, et cetera."

"Seems like a dead end," interjected Garrett. "If there was a bug in the software, then that evidence is on the hard drive."

"Which has been baked," Harry said. He leaned back in his chair, which squeaked in protest.

"What do we know about the software?" Garrett pressed.

"Ah," Harry groaned, "these labs are all the same. Obsolete computers with a hodgepodge of crap from scientific equipment companies, intermixed with even worse, homemade, crap. Kluge city. Totally FUBAR. It's no wonder they crash so often. Don't get me started."

Jon had heard enough. "Figure out, as best you can, what software was on that computer. Call the vendors and see if they know of any problems. We can follow up with Mike tomorrow."

"It's gonna be tough, without the hard drive."

"That's why they pay you the big bucks."

10

The dark helicopter hovered quietly in the night sky, its rotors making a dull *thud thud thud* sound. Barely visible in the twilight, it had an angular appearance, like a Stealth fighter.

"Good luck," the pilot said. "You won't be alone."

Jing heard the pilot through an earphone in her right ear. "Roger that," she said into her mouthpiece. Grasping a rope, she rappelled quickly to the ground. The helicopter flew away, staying low, just a few meters above the treetops.

Jing ran to the base of a large tree. Peering through wraparound night-vision glasses, she saw her surroundings brightly illuminated in false color. A small map was projected on the upper right corner of her field of view.

She set the Heckler & Koch PSG-1 on the ground and opened her handbag. She attached the tripod and night scope to the rifle. With a quick glance around the area, she double-checked the extra twenty-round magazines and zipped up the handbag. Jing wore the handbag over her shoulder and grasped the sniper rifle. She made her way, swiftly and catlike, through the forest.

The map showed her position relative to the target. The terrain was hilly but she encountered no serious obstacles. Her head continually scanned the surroundings. After a half hour, she could see from the map that she was close. The sky had darkened considerably, revealing the Milky Way. Unfortunately, the quarter moon deprived her of the ultimate cover of darkness. She would have to make do.

The town lights were visible now. Assuming she was not too late, Jing knew how events would unfold. Sighting the target, she would pull the trigger, causing a firing pin to strike the primer of the 7.62 mm round. A pressure wave would stimulate chemical reactions in the primer, igniting it and setting off the explosive powder in the cartridge. The explosion would propel the bullet down the barrel. Polygonal rifling in the barrel, smooth contours that spiraled down its length, would force the bullet to spin rapidly. At supersonic speeds, the bullet would travel six hundred meters in a fraction of a second. It would then impact the target's skull, producing a massive shock wave that would blow brain and bone out the opposite side. Within an instant, the life of a man she had never met would end.

She stopped. According to the map, she had arrived at her designated location. Through the trees, she could see the back of a modest house. She lay in a prone position and set up the rifle.

"I'm at the target site," she said into her mouthpiece. "Mike Harris' residence."

Woozy, Mike set down the shot glass. He belted out the lyrics to "Heartache Tonight" as the Eagles blasted through stereo speakers.

He grabbed the bottle of Scotch and clumsily poured the remaining contents into his glass, spilling a good fraction. He downed the shot, savoring the smooth taste of twelve year old whisky, a generous gift from a Japanese colleague. A welcome numbness coated his nerves. In this state, he recalled his conversation with Valerie in the hospital. She had called him a hero. Maybe she was right. He did save Sarah, after all.

In the back of his mind, he knew the morning would bring back his usual self-doubts and insecurities. But now, he saw the situation in a more favorable light. He had done everything he could! He even used the fire extinguisher properly. Information from some boring safety video had rushed to the forefront of his consciousness and told him what to do.

He heard a chime, but it took a moment to register.

It was the door. Someone was ringing the doorbell. He threw his shot glass aside and staggered to the door. He opened it.

He saw a beautiful woman.

"Hi, Mike."

It was Jennifer. At five-foot-eleven, she had long, light brown hair that ended in curls midway down her back. She wore a charcoal gray wool suit, which enhanced her already broad shoulders, giving her an authoritative and strikingly attractive presence. Her eyes looked puffy. Had she been crying?

"May I come in?"

"Sure," he slurred. He picked up a few plates and carried them back to the kitchen. "Excuse the mess. Major physics party the other night."

"I heard about the accident," she said. "I'm glad you're okay."

Mike tossed the dishes in the sink and stared at her with a deer-in-the-headlights look. "Jennifer…"

"I got your phone call and I came right over. I really am glad you're okay, Mike. I was worried."

His eyes focused on the object on her finger. Carbon atoms, packed into the hardest natural substance in the universe. Diamond. A diamond ring. Diamond could cut anything.

"Jennifer. What the hell?"

Self-consciously, she looked at the ring. "Oh. We haven't made the announcement yet."

So that was it. Jennifer and the Boy Dean were getting married. Her boyfriend, Carl Wilson, Dean of the business college, had earned his nickname thanks to his youthful appearance and juvenile bearing. While the higher administration approved of his ability to bring in corporate money, most professors resented his push to water down academic standards. What Jennifer saw in him was something Mike tried not to fathom.

He walked over to the stereo and turned the music off. Jennifer noticed the bottle of Scotch. "How have you been, Mike?"

"You mean, other than losing a colleague, a graduate student, my lab…"

"Sorry," she murmured.

"What're you doing here, Jennifer? Come to ask me to be the ring bearer?"

She averted her damp eyes. "I should have taken the ring off. I didn't mean to…"

"Oh, yeah," he blurted, "shoulda concealed it from me. Like everything else."

She met his eyes evenly. "I never hid anything from you."

"How long were you sleeping with the Boy Dean before I found out?" he retorted belligerently. "My whole department knew before I did. Your whole *College* knew before I did. What else don't I know?"

She gestured to the disheveled living room and kitchen. "You know what, Mike? I don't expect you to take responsibility for anything. It's your life now. If you want to blame me, fine. I came over here as a friend."

Abruptly, she burst into tears and covered her eyes. The suddenness of it took Mike by surprise. He felt the rage evaporate.

"I'm…" he stammered. He approached her, but she backed away. His hand touched her hair gently.

"I'm sorry," he said after a while. Maybe it was the booze, but he sensed his old feelings for her return. "For everything. I mean, if I had to do it over…"

"I know," she said between sobs.

His hand rested on her shoulder. He thought of the old times, of them laughing and making love. What had destroyed that contentedness? Answering that question was like trying to focus on a keyhole in the dark. When you looked straight at it, it vanished from view.

"So why did you call me?" he asked.

She rested her head against his chest. He felt the moistness from her eyes. "I don't remember. It seems so long ago."

"You got that right."

"It was that Iranian guy," she said after a moment of thought. "Hassan. He called me, out of the blue. He wanted to know if you'd be in town."

"Hassan?" he asked, bewildered. "Did you tell him anything?"

She stepped back from him. "I think I… confirmed something. He had a good idea of what you guys were working on, and…"

"You confirmed it."

"Yeah. I did. I guess I screwed up."

"Well… yes. You did."

"Sorry."

He shook his head. He felt dizzy. "It doesn't matter anymore. It really doesn't. A couple days ago, I would have been pretty pissed. But right now…"

She wrapped her arms around him. "I'm just glad you're safe."

They remained in an embrace for a minute. Then, she disengaged gently and headed for the door.

"Thanks," Mike said as she opened the door.

"For what?"

"For coming over. You didn't have to."

She wiped away the remaining tears. "Of course I did. You asked."

Jennifer turned and walked out. Mike shut the door. He felt tears welling in his eyes. What a mess, an utter *mess*, he had made of things. She still looked so beautiful. Why couldn't he let his feelings go? *She* was the one who kicked him out of their house. Why did he carry so much guilt?

He felt sick. His plan of having a couple of shots and calling it a night was not working out so well. Through his drunkenness, something nagged at him. Something about Jennifer. Her ring, of course. He couldn't imagine it–Mrs. Boy Dean. The thought of them in bed–*don't go there.* It was something she said.

"I got your phone call and I came right over."

What phone call?

Was she toying with him? He knew, even in his current state, that he had not called her. Through his alcoholic haze, he felt paranoia rush in. His pulse quickened. Something was wrong. He felt it. He ran for the door.

As he frantically turned the knob, he heard a *boom* outside. He swung open the door and saw Jennifer lying on the ground.

"No!" he screamed, and fell toward her. Blood soaked her blouse. Her pale face turned to him. She looked as though she was trying to speak, but no words came.

Mike looked up and saw a dark figure with a weapon. Panicking, he staggered backward into the house. He ran past the kitchen, to the door that led to the backyard. He unlocked the deadbolt and sprinted outside. He had the premonition that this might be a trap, but he couldn't think of what else to do but run. He heard heavy footsteps behind him.

Then, a shot. He closed his eyes, ready for the bullet that would end the nightmare. His legs kept moving. He glanced backward and saw the dark figure collapse, like a marionette with its strings suddenly cut, blood spraying out of his head. The figure's large weapon clattered onto the deck.

A second gunman rushed at him from behind and pressed a gun to his cheek. The cold steel filled him with dread.

"Don't do anything stupid," the man hissed. "Walk backward slowly."

They inched backward, toward the open door. Through his terror, Mike hoped the gunman was just taking him hostage. At least then he would have a chance. They stepped inside the house. The man pushed him behind the kitchen counter.

"Lie down," he commanded. "Put your hands behind you."

Mike complied. The man slapped on a pair of handcuffs.

"If you move, I'll kill you."

Mike stole a quick glance at the gunman. Night vision goggles concealed the man's face. He wore dark clothing. From a back harness, he retrieved a large weapon. Crouching low, he ran out to the backyard. He quickly brought the weapon to eye level and fired. A bright flash illuminated the area as a projectile streamed toward a large tree. The tree exploded with an intense blue burst as sparks shot outward.

A woman in a leather jacket and wraparound sunglasses ran from the explosion. She turned her rifle toward the gunman and fired, shattering the kitchen window. Mike winced fearfully as glass showered down. The gunman returned fire, sending another projectile toward the woman. It curved in midflight and struck her shoulder, sending bolts of electricity over her body. She froze and collapsed to the ground.

The man returned to the kitchen.

"What do you want?" Mike asked, still lying on the floor. "My wallet's in my back pocket."

"Shut up." The man placed the large weapon back in the harness. He unloaded the magazine from his 9mm Beretta and slid it into a pocket. He locked and loaded a second magazine.

"Stand up and walk outside."

Mike walked out to the backyard, his hands still in cuffs. The man put the gun in Mike's hand.

"Don't get any stupid ideas. The gun is loaded with blanks. Point it at the trees and shoot."

Awkwardly, Mike tried to aim the gun. "I can't squeeze the trigger," he said with an unsteady voice.

The man cursed. "Like I said, don't get any stupid ideas." He unlocked the handcuffs. With a quick motion, he stepped back from Mike and retrieved the projectile launcher. He aimed the weapon at Mike's head. "Now shoot."

Mike pulled the trigger. The gun fired with a *boom*.

As he fired the weapon, he realized that this man was not going to take him hostage.

"What do I do now?" Mike asked, slowly walking toward the man.

"Put these back on." The man reached for the handcuffs on his belt. At that moment, Mike smacked the pistol across the man's face. The man staggered back, surprised. Mike fired the gun, point blank. He turned and ran for his life, heading for the trees. He tripped over something but scrambled back to his feet. Mike had no plan, he just had to run. He reached the forest. In the dim glow of the moon, he saw trees whizzing past him, as if in a dream. His head struck a branch, drawing blood, but he kept going. He felt no pain. His legs and arms moved automatically, his entire body galvanized to do just one thing: put as much distance between himself and the gunman as humanly possible.

He heard the man behind him, boots crunching pine needles and branches on the ground. He had the sinking sense that the man was not expending much effort. Running through the forest, gasping for air, Mike lost track of time. The man pursued Mike up a steep hill until they reached a clearing. Finally, he dared to look back, only to see the man fire his weapon. The next image was a blinding flash. His limbs went numb and he fell to the ground.

Paralyzed, he saw pulsating images of white and purple but nothing else. A slimy substance covered his lower back. The sound of footsteps grew louder.

"Nice try, Professor."

Mike felt the man's boot kick his side. He groaned in pain.

"First, you killed your ex."

He heard the man eject the magazine of blanks from the Beretta.

"Then, you killed yourself."

He heard, with a sense of final dread, the click of the other magazine as it locked into place. The man pulled back the slide, loading the firing chamber.

Then, the sound of shots, rapid fire, followed by–*impossible*–a helicopter. He heard the man topple to the ground. The dull thudding sound of helicopter blades faded away.

SUNDAY, JUNE 1

11

A lamp illuminated a small desk in the basement of their house. On either side, sturdy shelves housed textbooks, novels, old class notes, and photo albums. Mike shuffled into the room, miserable to the core.

Envelopes and cards covered the desk. Jennifer stared at him, tears in her eyes. Her expression was one of disbelief.

Mike tried to say something but could not. Finally, Jennifer broke the silence.

"When did you–*decide*–this?"

"I've been thinking. Over the past few weeks."

"Oh. And I suppose it's my fault for failing to read your mind."

"No," he said, choking up. "It's not your fault."

He stood there, dumb, not knowing what else to say. Several times, Jennifer started to speak but stopped. The words just didn't exist. At last, she brushed past him and ran upstairs.

Mike looked at the wedding invitations scattered on the desk. He saw a picture of the two of them, blissfully happy, on vacation in Glacier Park.

* * *

He awoke with a start to the sight of the gunman's pale face, illuminated eerily by the moon. He stood up unsteadily. His body had a tingling sensation all over. The slimy stuff on his back had dried into a flaky residue that fell to the ground when he stood. The gunman lay on the ground, his body riddled with bullets. Ants were already beginning to make a meal of him.

Feeling nauseous, he staggered across the clearing and down the hill. As long as he went downhill, he figured, he would eventually reach the valley and could hitch a ride back home. His head throbbed painfully. His heart beat faster as panic set in. Were they still after him? He stopped suddenly and whirled around, expecting to see another gunman.

He wiped sweat off his brow and continued down the hill. He ran faster. He imagined dark assassins, ninjas, hiding behind every tree trunk. Where was he? He couldn't be too far from town… or could he? As he glanced behind him nervously, his foot struck a rock and he tumbled forward, landing on the ground with a thud.

I'm going to die here, he thought as he lay on the ground, but at this point he just didn't care. He listened to the nocturnal sounds of the forest. Soon, exhaustion overtook him and he fell into a deep slumber.

He felt a stick poke his nose. His eyes opened wide. He saw the face of a curious black-haired boy, maybe nine years old. The boy retreated.

"Leave him alone," an older boy said. "He's a drunk."

The trees on the slope cast long shadows in the morning sun. Mike shivered uncontrollably, teeth chattering in the crisp air. His throat burned with thirst and his lips were painfully chapped.

"Can we bring him home?" The boys spoke with an American Indian accent.

"No, we can't bring him home."

"Should we tell Mom?"

"Yeah," the older boy said. "Let's go."

They ran off.

* * *

A warm, damp cloth covered his forehead. Mike shivered with a feverish chill. He lay on a well-worn sofa in a small room. Photographs of relatives and Native American quilts hung on the walls.

A portly woman brought him a cup of water. "Joseph is curious, just like his grandfather. Always finding stuff. Bugs, squirrels, field mice... Today, white guy."

He took the cup with a shaking hand. Joseph stood with his older brother, who eyed Mike warily. Two younger siblings, a boy and a girl, watched from across the room. Mike sipped the water tentatively.

"Am I on the reservation?" he asked, his voice hoarse.

The woman chuckled. "No, the rez is twenty miles west. Drink."

He drank the water. His throat hurt when he swallowed.

"I need to get back," he said. "Can I use your phone?"

"Don't got one." The woman took the empty cup to the kitchen. "The boys can take you to town when you're rested."

"What happened to you?" Joseph asked boldly.

"Joseph, what did I tell you?" she scolded. "Get back to your room."

"But Mom…"

"*Now.*"

The boy walked out of the room, griping under his breath.

"I'm from Colton," Mike said. "I'm a professor. Last night, some people…"

"Joseph always is asking questions. Never mind him."

"Some people… They…"

She put a finger to her lips and placed a fresh cloth on his forehead. After a few minutes, he fell asleep to the sound of her humming a melodious song.

He slept fitfully, tossing and turning on the sofa. He woke up every ten minutes and muttered incoherent phrases. The Indian woman shushed him, as if he were a child, and he would fall back asleep.

"Can you tell me a story?" he asked once.

"What kind?" she replied, chuckling softly.

"A bedtime story."

She laughed again, looking at the morning sun.

"A bedtime story? Sure, why not. I'll tell the one about frog and antelope."

Mike's sweaty, delirious face appeared to calm as she began telling the tale. Antelope was the chief of a village on Tobacco Plains. Of all the animals, he was the fastest. Frog was the chief of another village. Although frog was not as swift as antelope, he was intelligent. One day, frog and antelope were smoking a pipe in antelope's lodge. Antelope, as usual, bragged about how fast he was. Frog smiled and suggested he could beat antelope in a race. They would race from one village to the other and back. Whoever won would receive all the clothes from the loser's village.

Antelope agreed. He spent the evening in his lodge, laughing over his good fortune. What a fool that frog chief was! Meanwhile, frog gathered together the members of his village.

In the morning, the race began. Antelope ran confidently. Somehow, frog always seemed to be ahead of him. Antelope began to worry and ran with all his might, hooves pounding against the trail. Still, frog managed to hop ahead of him. Finally, they approached the finish line. Miraculously, frog won.

Antelope never knew the secret behind frog's victory. The night before, all the frogs had lined up along the trail, hidden. During the race, they hopped down the trail in such a way that antelope always saw a frog ahead of him. Since he could not tell them apart, he assumed that it was the frog chief.

"You're a fast runner," antelope said after the race, nearly out of breath.

"Not really," frog replied. "But I *am* a fast thinker."

The woman removed the cloth from Mike's forehead.

"He cheated," Mike whispered.

"Course he did," the woman replied.

Two corpses lay on a wide table in the center of a dimly lit room.

One of them had a single bullet wound in the forehead, just left of center. The second corpse was soaked in blood from multiple wounds in the torso. The bald man sat in a corner, observing silently.

A man in a lab coat and latex gloves turned the first body's head to the side, revealing a large exit wound.

"Bulls-eye," he said admiringly.

"It's a pity they weren't both clean shots."

They heard footsteps approach. Jing entered the room.

"Last-minute notice, no planning, uncontrolled variables… You should give me a medal." She walked over to the second corpse. "He had a bio launcher."

"Like what they used at Glacier."

"Probably," she said. She remembered lying paralyzed on a gurney as men lifted it into the helicopter. "A little heads-up would have been nice."

"Intelligence is rarely perfect."

She turned and walked out.

"You could have taken both of them out," he said to her back. "They were well within range."

She kept walking.

Mike made his way along the hilly path, following the two Indian boys, remembering what the woman had said to him before he left.

"I read about you in yesterday's paper. Says you were a hero, saving that girl."

"Hardly," he said, looking at the pictures on the wall.

"Be careful. People shift with the wind."

As he walked through the tranquil woods, he thought about what he would do. Obviously, he needed to talk to the police right away. They would probably have information about the assailants. He tried to recall what had been real and what had been a dream. The entire experience seemed to have occurred in a previous life.

"Do you live at the college?" Joseph asked.

"Not exactly," Mike replied. "I work there, though."

Mike looked around the woods. In the daylight, the forest didn't menace him the way it had under the cover of darkness. The landscape seemed completely transformed. He couldn't recognize the terrain. From the distance they traveled–about three miles so far–he figured he must have blacked out the previous night.

"How much further?" he asked, feeling the pain of blisters on his feet.

"One mile," the older boy replied.

They continued walking. After about fifteen minutes, Mike recognized a couple of houses, big expensive ones perched on hilltops. Movie producers or investment bankers lived in them.

"I know my way from here," he told the boys. "Thanks for your help."

"Look at what I found," Joseph said, showing him a small snake.

"C'mon," his brother admonished. He led Joseph back up the trail.

Mike descended into town, ragged and dirty, looking like a transient who had recently hopped off the train. From the hills, he emerged into a familiar neighborhood of well-kept houses and yards. He saw children playing. It must be Sunday, he thought. He shuffled along the sidewalk, making his way slowly toward downtown. A quick movement caught his eye. A mother, eyeing him warily, pulled her child into the house and shut the door. *Can't blame her.* He needed to clean up.

The police could put things in perspective. Who the bad guys were, why they wanted to kill him–cops, not physicists, had minds for this sort of thing. It must have been law enforcement–FBI, perhaps–who stopped the assassins last night. It would all get cleared up soon.

The police station was on the south side of campus, a short distance away. He turned onto a sidewalk that led down a hill to the small downtown. He would turn right and walk along Main Street until he reached the station. Mike paused to admire the stately brick buildings of Colton University, snow-capped peaks in the background. Despite the trauma of the lab disaster, he still felt at home.

After the police clarified things, he would eventually grieve the loss of life. He knew that intellectually but did not feel it in his gut. He was wearily detached, the horrors of the last forty-eight hours very much in the background. Jennifer's image remained in his mind, though. He knew he'd been telling himself a lie about Jennifer, a convenient fiction about how she had dumped him for no reason. Now, inexplicably, she was gone.

Another image rose before his mind's eye: Hassan Zare. Towering, arrogant Hassan, with his condescending smirk and vulturine eyes. Hassan, the man who waged a guerrilla campaign against Mike's scientific career for over a decade. The same man who dropped in on the lab just before it was destroyed. The same man whom Jennifer had spoken to about the project. Now Jennifer and Stefan were dead, and Mike was lucky to be alive.

He felt the adrenalin return. Jennifer, Stefan, Mike… *Seth!* He needed to find Seth. They would get him, too; it was only a matter of time. Why didn't he consider this earlier? Maybe he was too late. Sweating, he ran down the hill. He needed a phone. There was a gas station downtown, he could use theirs. He needed to warn his friend.

He heard a loud sound behind him.

"Drop to your knees," a voice said over a loudspeaker. "Put your hands behind your back."

He turned around and saw a police car, lights flashing.

"On your knees, *now*."

Mike dropped to his knees. Behind him, he heard two more police cars stop. Footsteps approached.

"Hands behind your back," a voice said from behind.

He complied, and the officer put handcuffs on.

"Please," Mike said, sweat dripping into his eyes. "I need to call Seth Brenner."

"Who?"

"Professor Seth Brenner. I have to talk to him, right away. It's important!"

"You can call him from the station," the cop said. "Stand up. We're taking you into custody as a material witness to the murder of Jennifer Lawson."

12

The bald man sat back in his chair. Several people were around the table in the conference room, including Jing, who sat opposite him. Large computer screens lined the walls and displayed a steady stream of data from around the world.

"Mike Harris was detained fifteen minutes ago," he announced, his baritone voice filling the room.

"We need to bring him in," Jing said, "along with Seth Brenner."

"Impossible," he replied with a dismissive gesture. "We'll continue to monitor them from a distance."

Jing pounded the table with the palm of her hand. "That's crazy! There is an obvious threat to their safety."

"Revealing ourselves at this juncture would be too risky."

Jalen, a slender black man in his twenties, cleared his throat. "Our information's pretty good right now," he said, avoiding Jing's eyes. "We got a lot of chatter after the incident at Harris' house. My team cracked a bunch of the encryption codes."

"A bunch?"

"Intelligence is rarely perfect," the bald man said.

"Tell that to Jennifer Lawson."

The bald man met Jing's stare with hawkish eyes, ignoring

Jalen. "There is risk in everything we do. Collateral damage happens." He pointed to the back of the room. "If you're uncomfortable with risk, there's the door."

"Uncomfortable with risk? I'm not the one who is obsessed with secrecy, with the *risk* of being revealed."

The man stood up, leaning on a cane. "This debate is over. I've made my decision. We will observe the situation from a distance."

Jing shook her head silently.

The man looked around the table. "Dismissed."

"What happened next, Professor Harris?"

The detective ran a thumb along his five-o'clock shadow, looking at Mike incredulously. He wore a cheap brown suit and a long tie that went well below his large belt buckle. He set his notepad and pen on a cluttered desk in the small room. Posters with safety messages hung from the walls. A large mirror was mounted on one wall.

Mike took a sip of weak coffee from a Styrofoam cup. "I heard a bang–a boom–outside."

"A gunshot?"

"Yes. I ran outside and Jennifer was lying on the ground. She was bleeding."

He shivered. Just moments ago, he had identified the body. He remembered the shock and guilt that swept over him as he stared at her pale face. Then they escorted him to the campus police station and, taking advantage of his vulnerable state, began the interrogation.

"Dead?"

"Excuse me?"

"You said Jennifer was lying on the ground, bleeding. Was she dead at that point?"

Mike pressed his fingers to his head. "I think so," he whispered, his eyes closed.

"What did the shooter look like? Old, young?"

"I don't know. It was dark."

"Caucasian? Hispanic? Indian?"

Mike sighed. "White, I think. It all happened so fast. He–I think it was a he–he wore dark clothes."

"So you ran."

"Yes, I ran. Like I told you before. Can I call Seth now?"

The detective casually reached for his notepad, ignoring Mike's request. "Then what, Professor?"

"Someone shot him."

The detective flipped through his notepad. "Ah, yes. The female Ninja."

"You think I'd make this up?"

A smile flickered across the detective's face, which quickly returned to deadpan. "Then what?"

"Another guy appeared. He pressed a gun to my head and forced me back inside."

There was a knock at the door. A female technician entered with a camera and a small plastic case.

"You've already waived your right to an attorney," the detective said as the woman opened her case. "Would you mind if Jessica here took some pictures and swabs from your hands?"

"Sure," Mike said, standing up. "I have nothing to hide."

Jessica quickly ran cotton swabs across his palms and the tops of his hands. She sealed each swab in a Ziploc bag. She took photographs and fingerprints.

"Thanks," she said after she was done.

"Thanks, Jessica," the detective said, almost friendly.

Mike sat back down. "I really need to call Seth. Please. He's in danger."

"So how did this guy take out the Ninja?"

"I already told you," Mike said, exasperated and short of breath, "he had some–I don't know, a bazooka or something."

The detective stared at Mike with a bemused expression. "A bazooka."

"I don't know what it was. Jesus, we've been through this already."

"Keep going."

Mike felt like he was drowning. The old headache returned with a vengeance, sharp daggers of pain sticking into him.

"I ran away from the guy but he shot me. I was paralyzed.

This slimy stuff was all over me."

"So," the detective said with a smirk, "he *slimed* you."

Mike pressed his hands to his forehead. "I know it sounds unbelievable. If I were lying, don't you think I'd come up with something better?"

"Then what, Professor?"

"He was about to kill me. Then I heard a helicopter. It shot him, and I escaped."

"Helicopter? Did you see it?"

"No, at that point, I was blind. I heard it."

The detective grabbed a binder from the desk and flipped through it. "Funny thing," he said with exaggerated befuddlement, "is that no one reported seeing or hearing a helicopter that night."

"It was a different kind of helicopter, I guess," Mike said. "Quieter."

"Of course it was. Probably invisible, too. Makes sense. They *are* ninjas, after all."

"I'm sure you must have found the bodies."

The detective shook his head.

"Then at least check for footprints!"

"Calm down, Professor. We did check for footprints in and around the house. There are loads of 'em. At least twenty."

Mike felt the ache press inward, from his skull deep into his brain. The walls closed in and he struggled to breathe. "I had a reception," he said, his voice weak. "The night before."

"A party?"

"Yes, a department thing. For a job candidate. I can tell you who was there. You can match shoes…"

"Like Cinderella?"

Mike looked at the detective imploringly. "I don't care what you think. But please, warn Seth Brenner. They're after him too."

From behind the two-way mirror, Chief Jon Patterson watched the interrogation. Dr. Leslie Kellerman, a therapist from the university clinic, stood next to him.

"This is painful," Jon said. "Can you figure him out?"

Kellerman shook her head. "Without an interview, I couldn't give you a diagnosis."

"Best guess?"

"He has a well-developed fantasy, which he probably believes. He also suffers from migraine headaches."

"How can you tell?"

"Watch his eyes. When the interview becomes hostile, you can see that he experiences chronic physical pain."

As if on cue, Mike eyes closed. He rocked back and forth in his chair, massaging his temples, trying to suppress the searing inflammation of the nerves and blood vessels around the brain.

"This guy should have seen me a long time ago," she said with a trace of sympathy. "He probably held it together, all these years. Fairly common, I'm sorry to say."

"Common, except that he murdered his ex-girlfriend. This county hasn't seen a homicide in ten years. Detective Casey covers an area the size of Connecticut."

"I'm sure you can handle it," she said, patting him on the shoulder. "And if you can't, don't be a typical male. Ask for help."

"Yeah, yeah."

13

Henry Colton stood on a stage, illuminated by bright lights, holding a glass of champagne. He wore a stylishly casual shirt and coat, with no tie, in contrast to the black-tie crowd in attendance. As usual, his mop of gray hair was unkempt. Billionaires could get away with that, he knew.

"Only one month ago," he announced, "we launched the Biochip, a device that market analysts said would be the biggest flop since the Edsel."

He looked out at the crowd, his eyebrows raised in amusement. The invitees were a mixture of venture capitalists, reporters, and politicians. Several of them had advised against the Biochip project.

The skeptics had a point. Who would want to implant a computer chip into the back of their head? It seemed ludicrous–insane, really. But Colton could see where things were headed. Over time, people gradually but inexorably surrendered their bodies to technology. Cosmetic surgery, tattoos, and piercings breached the outer defenses. Later came more invasive procedures such as eye laser surgery, stomach stapling, gender reassignment, genetic therapy, and a host of prescription drugs to cure whatever needed fixing.

Henry's epiphany came years ago when he sat in the plaza of his corporate headquarters in San Francisco. He saw a man talking to himself, not an unusual occurrence given the hordes of nutjobs in the Bay Area. Then he noticed the man was talking into a headset. He was communicating via cell phone. Historically, a man talking to himself on a street corner would have been considered insane. Today, he is normal. Society continually redefined deviance downward to accommodate technology.

"The Biochip can be implanted with a simple outpatient procedure," he said, as images were projected onto a screen behind him, "giving the customer a powerful organizing tool to manage the multitasking demands of work and family. Our initial trials left a scar on the back of the neck. Since then, Colton Medical has refined the laser microsurgery protocol so that the scar is essentially invisible. In addition to a scheduling application, we have partnered with a search engine company and GPS service to provide a wealth of information to the user."

He thought of Jing's comment: *"You're all over the map. Biology, physics, computers, medicine…"* She was right. He loved it all. But he also had focus. It would all come together, and soon.

Henry went through the rest of his presentation, discussing his company's plans to get FDA approval and making conservative profit projections. He raised his glass. "And now, a toast," he said, gesturing to the audience. "To our Brave New World, with such people in it."

The audience returned the toast with hearty applause. As Henry wandered into the crowd, James moved to his side protectively. James spoke into a hidden microphone, his eyes scanning the room. Two other men, also dressed in tuxedos, kept close watch on the assembled guests.

"Senator!" Henry enthused, approaching a man with reddish gray hair and wire rim glasses.

"Great speech, Henry," the senator said, shaking his hand. "This Biochip is going to be a knockout. I wouldn't worry about FDA approval."

"I was hoping you'd say that."

As they talked and made their way toward the balcony, several photographers snapped pictures. Something caught James' eye.

He moved rapidly, speaking in hushed tones into his microphone. He approached a bespectacled, short-haired young man who held a small briefcase.

"I need you to come with me," James said quietly.

"What for?" the man asked.

From behind, the two bodyguards gently but firmly grasped one arm each.

"Let's talk," James said.

Henry and Senator Conrad Schmidt stood on a balcony that faced the bay, admiring the view of the Golden Gate Bridge and Alcatraz. Ocean spray glistened in the late afternoon sun.

"Some of my constituents are concerned about off-shoring," Conrad said, sipping his glass of champagne. "They're economic primitives, but I can't ignore them."

"Of course."

"A lot of high-tech activities have moved from the Bay Area to that island of yours."

"The Pacific Research Center," he said, looking out toward the water.

"Now Henry, I understand business a hell of a lot better than most of the people in my party. I explain it to them 'til I'm blue in the face. Fact is, though, a lot of people see this as shipping jobs overseas, plain and simple."

A flicker of contempt crossed Henry's face. "A lot of people are morons, Conrad."

The senator chuckled stiffly and set down his glass. "I wish I could disagree, my friend."

"I assume this talk I hear about an 'off-shoring penalty' is going to die. Am I right?"

Conrad took a breath. "I think I can kill it. Won't be easy."

"On an entirely unrelated subject," Henry said, eyeing the senator cannily, "I'm happy to report that several thousand of my employees will be donating to your reelection campaign."

They watched several windsurfers speeding along on the choppy water. One of them wiped out, sending the board and sail flying.

"And, if I may go on a tangent, Henry," Conrad said, "I don't think you'll have to worry about FDA approval *or* the off-shoring penalty."

They dragged the bespectacled young man to a waiting van. Three men stepped out of the vehicle.

"We'll take the van," James said. "You two go back to the Yacht Club."

They unlocked the back door of the van.

"Open your briefcase," James said to the young man.

Hands trembling, he opened it. Inside was a lemon meringue pie in a plastic container.

"Eat the pie," James said humorlessly.

The man looked at James quizzically but decided to comply, scooping a handful and stuffing it into his mouth. "It's not a bomb," he said.

"Don't talk with your mouth full. Get inside the van."

"Excuse me?" he said, summoning an indignant expression. "This was meant to be a prank. A *prank*. You caught me. Good job. Now call the cops and be done with it."

"Mr. Colton is a great man," James said, jaw muscles tight, "but he is naïve. He doesn't know half of what I do to maintain his security. I intend to keep it that way. This was a prank, you say. Pretty soon, another prankster comes along and squirts him with a hose. Then, someone throws a rock. Then, someone pulls out a gun. It stops here, Jarrod."

"How do you know my name?"

"Your sister Kayley, age nineteen, has Hodgkin's lymphoma. Today she is recuperating in room 235, Alta Bates hospital."

From behind his glasses, Jarrod's eyes bulged out in a panic. "What the hell do you want with me?"

"I want you to get into the van," said James. "Now."

After Henry spoke to several other dignitaries, he found a quiet corner and dialed his phone. His eyes lit up when Jing answered.

"Jing! I'm sorry you couldn't make it."

"I'm sorry too," she said. "I've been working nonstop."

"I know. I read your article."

"Did you like it?"

"I *loved* it. I mentioned it to some of the people here."

"How's the schmoozing?"

"Ah," he said, shaking his head, "it takes a lot out of me. By the way, did you get my invitation?"

"I did," she said.

"And?"

"Let me check my schedule. I'll get back to you."

Henry placed the phone in his pocket. He hadn't felt this way in years. Sure, there had been women, plenty of them. There was something about Jing, though–intelligent, beautiful, with just a dash of recklessness and danger–that made him feel giddy like a schoolboy.

He rejoined the crowd, glad-handing and jawboning, the indelible image of Jing Shen lingering pleasantly in his mind.

14

Mike felt like he was about to burst. “I need to call Seth. Please.”

Detective Casey stared at him blankly. “Fine,” he said at last. “Follow me.”

They walked down a hall and stepped into an unoccupied, bare room with a desk. A partially open window let in a cool breeze. Casey handed Mike a phone.

“Dial 9 to get an outside line.”

Mike hurriedly dialed Seth’s number. He wiped sweat off his brow as he listened to the phone ring. Finally, someone answered.

“Hello?” said a female voice in a singsong tone.

“Is Seth there?”

“Seth?” she said, giggling. “He’s crashed.”

“Wake him up. Please.”

“Sethie babe… Wakey wakey…”

“Listen!” Mike shouted into the phone. “You’re both in danger! Come to the police station *now*!”

After a moment of silence, the girl spoke. “Who is this?”

“It’s Mike Harris. This is about our physics experiment. Someone is out to…”

"Sethie's asleep."

She hung up the phone.

"Hello! Hello!" Mike looked at the detective, eyes wide with panic. "Please, send a car."

"Forget it. Sit down."

Mike sat, his heart beating rapidly.

"Send a car to his house," he pleaded. "He only lives a few blocks away."

"You're in no position to tell me to do anything, Professor."

Mike buried his head in his hands. His hair and skin felt grimy, his clothes were torn, and the burns on his torso itched. His head and knees were scarred from his terrifying run through the forest. Maybe he was losing his mind. At the very least, he could hardly trust his judgment right now.

He looked up and saw Jon Patterson walk into the room.

"Hey Mike," Jon said, his face betraying sympathy. "What happened?"

"Jon," he said, relieved to see a friend. He stood up.

"Sit down," Detective Casey barked, "or I'll slap the handcuffs back on."

"Relax, detective." Jon walked up to Mike and patted him on the side. "Mike and I go way back."

"I didn't kill Jennifer," Mike said breathlessly, avoiding Casey's scowl. "You know I loved her, Jon."

"I know you used to love her. People do crazy things, Mike. Happens all the time."

"If it were up to me," Casey said belligerently, "I'd lock up the professor and throw away the key. It's one thing to kill his ex. It's another to lie to my face." He stalked out of the room and slammed the door behind him.

"No!" Mike protested, his voice hoarse. "I didn't do it. There were these guys, and a helicopter… Someone must've seen the helicopter."

"Mike, I'm trying to be on your side here. Detective Casey wants to nail you. I can talk some sense into him, but you need to cooperate."

Someone knocked on the door. Jon opened it. It was Sergeant Garrett. He whispered into Jon's ear. Jon nodded silently and closed the door.

"What is it?" Mike asked.

"Your hands tested positive for gunshot residue. And, your fingerprints are on the gun found at the scene."

Mike's knees went wobbly. His stomach felt like it was in free-fall. "Jon, you have to believe me," he said desperately, "They *made* me shoot the gun."

He then recalled, as if uncovering a repressed memory, what prompted him to hit the gunman in the face. As he shot the blanks, his subconscious mind figured out the plan. They were going to kill him and frame him.

"At least warn Seth," he pleaded.

"Who?"

"Professor Seth Brenner. They're after him too."

Jon shook his head sadly. "Mike, I'm your friend. I want to help you, so listen. Right now, you need two things. A lawyer and a psychiatrist."

"You don't believe me."

"I don't know what to believe, Mike. Something happened between you and Jennifer, and you've never been the same."

"You're right. But you have to trust me. Yes, I was angry at Jennifer. Angry at myself, really. But I didn't kill her! For Christ's sake, Jon."

Jon looked down at the ground, avoiding Mike's beseeching eyes as he removed handcuffs from his belt.

"What's going on? Jon?"

"It's better I do this than some stranger. Sorry, Mike." He approached his friend.

Mike became aware of the darkness outside. The sun was setting. He saw a vision, almost as clearly as if it were in front of him, of a helicopter flying stealthily over the horizon. Men in dark clothing rappelled out, taking up positions, checking their weapons, using hand signals to coordinate their attack. They advanced toward Seth's house.

"Michael Harris, you're under arrest for the murder of Jennifer Lawson."

The men burst through the door.

"You have the right to remain silent. Anything you say can

and will be used against you in a court of law."

Laser spots converged on Seth as he awoke, bleary-eyed.

Mike, apparently unbalanced, leaned on Jon. "Please understand," he whispered. With a swift motion, he removed the pistol from the holster and aimed it at Jon's head.

"Put the gun down," Jon said, the paleness of his face belying his even tone.

"No," Mike said, eyeing the door. "Handcuff yourself to the desk."

"Fine, Mike. See, I'm doing it." Jon put one cuff on his wrist, never breaking eye contact. He kneeled down and locked the second cuff to the leg of the desk. "Do me a favor, though. Take your finger off the trigger. No accidents, okay?"

"Okay," Mike said, breathing rapidly. "Throw me your keys."

Jon complied. "You're digging yourself into a deep hole, my friend."

Mike wiped the sweat off his brow as he glanced around the room. He locked the door and ran to the window.

"After I do what I need to do, I'll turn myself in. You have my word."

"Fine."

Mike pushed open the window and jumped out onto the grass. He ran into the darkness.

Even with the numbing jolt of adrenalin, his joints ached painfully as he ran through the dark streets, 9mm Beretta in his right hand. He felt blood trickle down from the scar on his forehead. He saw a police car on Main Street, a hundred meters away. He quickly darted into a side street and sprinted up a hill. His legs felt like they would give out at any moment.

He willed himself forward. Seth's house was not far away, but each step was pure agony. Hallucinations emerged from the darkness–ninjas, helicopters, policemen–that looked real enough to make him gasp in fear.

He turned left onto a winding street with moderately expensive homes. The residents would surely alert the police to the presence of a crazed gunman running through their well-manicured neighborhood. The clock was ticking. As much as he needed to rest, he had to keep going.

The road looped around and went uphill. The final stretch. Every muscle in his body screamed at him to stop, but he pushed ahead. Stinging sweat dripped into his eyes and blurred his vision. He wiped it away and saw blue Christmas lights strung across bushes. He recognized the quirky decoration. It was Seth's house.

He staggered up to the front door and pounded on it. He pressed the doorbell button frantically. After a minute, he heard footsteps.

The door opened. Seth, in his boxer shorts, took a step back, shocked by the image before him: Mike Harris, wild eyed, sweaty, bloodied, and gasping for air, clutching a pistol.

"Jesus, Mike."

"I need to come in," he said.

"Sure," Seth said, eyeing his friend suspiciously. "Make yourself at home."

Mike stepped in and shut the door behind him. His eyes darted around nervously.

"I'd appreciate it if you put down your gun," he said. "House rule."

Mike set the gun on a table and surveyed the house. A vintage Atari video game stood near the entrance. The smoky haze of cannabis and incense filled the house. The open living room, decorated with peculiar lamps and bean bags, had been the setting for numerous house parties over the years.

"Are your doors locked?" he asked, peering out the front bay window.

"Yes."

"Don't stand in front of the window."

"What the heck is going on?"

"Someone–some *ones*–tried to kill me. They killed Jennifer. I'm sure they're the same ones who blew up the lab."

"Sethie?" A slender young woman emerged from the haze, her nude body illuminated by the soft glow of the lamps. She looked about twenty–a student, apparently–and was blithely immodest. A shiny silver ring pierced her navel and she had a small tattoo above the left breast.

"Go back to bed, dear."

"Okay," she said with a giggle. "Who's this guy?"

"He's my accountant," he said, winking at Mike. "I'll be there in a minute."

The woman smiled vacuously, her long, light brown hair reflecting golden light. She turned and walked slowly back to Seth's room, giving them a view of another tattoo, inscribed just above her petite ass, before she disappeared into the haze.

"The 101 student?" Mike asked.

"Her? No." He chuckled, his hairy chest and belly rippling with laughter. "I met her a few weeks ago." Seth went into his room. After a minute, he emerged wearing blue jeans, a Hawaiian shirt, and Birkenstocks.

"Seth," Mike said, deadly serious, "there are people after me. They'll come after you too. We need to call the cops."

"The cops?" he asked, bewildered. "I heard on the news that you'd been arrested."

"I know. I was. Look, we need to get you someplace safe."

"Did you post bail?"

"No. I escaped. I came here to warn you. They'll arrest me again, probably throw me in jail, but at least we'll be protected from these people."

"Wait," Seth said, trying to get his bearings. "You want the cops to come here *why*?"

"There are people trying to kill you! Dammit, Seth, these people killed Jennifer. They almost killed me. We need to get into protective custody. *Now.*"

"Hold on," he said, watching the sweaty, bloodied face of his agitated friend. "You haven't thought this through."

"I *have*! First, they killed Stefan. Then, they tried to kill me. The project, Seth! They want to kill everyone involved in the project."

"I know. I'm a step ahead of you. I'm a theorist, remember? Think. Who's the fourth person on this 'hit list'?"

Mike stepped back, mouth agape.

"Axel Hansen," he said, his voice trembling. "Have you been able to contact him?"

"No," Seth said. "That's the point. But I have an idea where he might be."

"He's in danger!"

"If what you're telling me is correct–*if*–then yes, they'll come after Dr. Hansen. We need to find him."

"Where is he?"

A blinding white light shone through the front window. Seth and Mike moved away, toward the bedroom. Mike grabbed the gun.

"Did they see us?" Mike asked fearfully.

"I don't think so."

The woman, clad in one of Seth's T-shirts, walked toward them. "Is that the cops?"

"Yeah," Seth replied. "I want you to answer the door."

"No *way*!" she protested.

"Don't worry, the weed's legal. Just tell them I went to the convenience store and I'll be right back."

"You want me to lie?" Her previously blissful visage was replaced by one of paranoia.

"I'll make it up to you, I promise."

They heard the loud chirp of a police siren. Blue and red lights flashed.

Seth touched the woman's face tenderly and gave her a kiss. He turned to Mike. "This way," he said. They ran through a door.

The woman jumped at the sound of loud knocks on the door. She approached the door, eyes wide and dilated.

"Police! Open the door!"

She fumbled with the lock and opened the door. Cops burst in, blinding her with their flashlights.

"Is Mike Harris here?" one of them demanded.

"Who?"

"Where is Seth Brenner?"

"Seth?" she asked innocently, her acting skills well below Emmy standards. "He went to the… store."

They heard the automatic garage door open. A cop ran toward the door that led to the garage, yelling into his walkie-talkie. He kicked open the door and took cover. He shone his flashlight into the dark garage as his partner held his pistol at the ready. The partner entered the garage. The car nearest him was a sport utility vehicle.

"C'mon out, Harris," he said.

The other cop flipped on the garage light and drew his pistol. They both took cover behind the SUV.

"It's over, Harris. Put your hands up."

Seth stood up from behind the Viper. "He's crazy!" he said, eyes melodramatically wide.

Mike held a gun to Seth's head. "Back off or I kill him," he said with a trembling voice.

The cops slowly retreated. "It's alright," one said. "We can talk."

Seth held his hands in the air and walked to the driver side of the car. Mike kept the gun aimed at him.

"Put your guns down!" Mike shouted.

"No problem. We're leaving, see?"

Outside, a pair of police watched the unfolding hostage situation. They drew their weapons.

With a throaty growl, the Viper slammed into reverse, tearing off a string of Christmas lights as it bolted up the driveway. Tires squealing, it accelerated onto the street. The cops aimed their weapons but didn't fire. They jumped into their patrol car. The cop on the passenger side yelled into the radio as they gave chase.

Seth pressed on the gas and shifted into third gear as they rounded the loop. The car's rear end fish-tailed wildly at the end of the curve. He turned left and shifted into fourth as they headed uphill. The patrol car followed them, siren blaring. Mike felt groggy as the Viper swerved left and right through the winding streets. They reached the highway and Seth shifted into fifth gear. The cops were still behind them.

They roared uphill, ninety miles an hour. After vertiginous twists and turns, there was finally a long stretch of straight road. Amber reflecting lights on either side of the highway zipped past.

"Here we go," Seth said, shifting into sixth gear. The car's speed climbed up. Mike winced in fear, his stomach in knots. He thought of Bob Schrieffer, a physicist who won the Nobel Prize for helping develop the theory of superconductivity. At age 74, Schrieffer drove his Mercedes-Benz a hundred miles an hour and plowed into a van, killing one and injuring seven.

Mike turned his head and looked out the side window. The flashing lights and siren of the pursuing vehicle faded into the distance.

"Seth, there's a turn ahead."

"I know."

He tapped on the brakes and rounded the turn. The car, riding low, hugged the concrete.

Mike glanced in the rearview mirror. No one was behind them.

"What are we going to do?"

Seth saw a sign for an exit to a road that headed west. He pressed on the brakes and abruptly turned right, into the exit lane. Mike held on to the door handle, white-knuckled, as they rounded the bend.

"We're going to Glacier Park," Seth said. "That's where Axel Hansen is."

15

Jalen dipped Teflon tweezers into a saline solution and guided a pair of contact lenses into the path of an ultraviolet laser beam. As the contact lenses intersected the beam, they fluoresced bright blue. A microscope objective focused the blue light into an optical fiber, causing it to glow brightly in the dark room. A computer monitor displayed a message:

Downloading encrypted data...

Pictures appeared on the screen, photographs of Henry Colton's summer estate.

"Looks like it worked," Jalen said, satisfied.

Jing watched the screen from behind him. The contact lenses were coated with a transparent layer of holographic memory, fabricated from an amorphous oxide alloy, which stored visual information. An invisible chip was powered by a combination of solar energy and normal body heat. After Jing's surveillance mission, she carefully removed the lenses and placed them in the pocket of her silk blouse, and later transferred them to a Teflon container. Now, Jalen used a laser to extract the stored information, much like a video player read data from an optical disc.

A picture of a stern-faced, square-jawed man appeared on the screen. "That's James," Jing said. "Not his real name, I'm sure."

"I'll run a search on his mug," Jalen said as his slender fingers rapidly tapped on the keyboard.

While Jalen typed, another image appeared. It was the building James claimed was used for storage. Jing sat down at a workstation and pulled up several pictures. They were high-resolution satellite photographs of the Colton estate. She zoomed in on the building in question.

"This is the one," Jing said confidently.

She stacked three satellite images, taken at two month intervals. The bottom image, the most recent one, showed three delivery trucks lined up near the building's loading dock. "There's a clear pattern of increased activity."

"Whoa," Jalen said as data scrolled down his screen. "This guy's been around. Central America, the Balkans, Iran, Afghanistan. Looks like he joined Colton about ten years ago. Did you get any intel from him?"

"James is not the chatty type. I'm better off pursuing Henry."

"Something's going on," Jalen said, his eyes rapidly scanning the data on the monitors. "There's been a spike in money transfers between Colton Enterprises and its subsidiaries."

"I'll call Henry today," Jing said. She looked at the letter that Henry's pilot had given her:

Henry M. Colton
Respectfully requests the pleasure of your company
at
The Pacific Research Center
for
a unique presentation,

"*Colton Enterprises: Enter the Future*"

The letter contained detailed information about dates, travel, lodging, and menu options. This was an invitation she could not turn down, obviously, but the event would not occur for a few days. She needed information sooner than that.

"Where are they headed?"

Chief Jon Patterson, face still flush with anger, stood at the front of the room. His old neighbor was making a fool of him. Jon had let his guard down, a mistake he was determined not to repeat.

Several campus police officers sat at a small table. "They were headed north on 93 when they eluded our guys," Sergeant Garrett said. "We've put out an APB, two men in a red Dodge Viper. License plate, PHYSX 1."

Hardly inconspicuous, Jon thought. Then again, he knew how few cops per mile of road there were.

"Is Seth Brenner a hostage?"

"It would seem so."

"North on 93," Jon mused. "Are they headed for Canada?"

"Maybe. We alerted CBP."

Jon sighed. "You know what that means."

Garrett nodded.

"I'll call her," Jon said, and left the room.

Mike's head bobbed up and down as he oscillated between consciousness and sleep, the bumps on the road intermittently jerking him back to reality. Axel Hansen dominated his thoughts. In a lucid moment, Mike recalled sitting in a subcommittee conference room in Washington, DC, in one of those situations where he felt awkwardly out of place. Axel had asked him to deliver a brief statement on the feasibility of nuclear "bunker-buster" weapons. The issue was really outside his area of expertise, but he agreed to give the testimony out of gratitude for Axel's support. Mike read the statement and returned to his seat at the back of the room. Two days of travel for two sentences. It would be remembered by no one.

Axel, a taciturn man, got to the point early in his testimony. He explained that the main problem in knocking out underground bunkers was the mechanical mismatch between the air and the ground. If an explosive detonated above the ground, most of the shock wave would reflect back into the air. If, on the other hand, it detonated a few feet underground, a large portion of the explosive energy would reach the bunker. The only way to knock out an underground facility was to design a warhead that penetrated the earth before exploding.

This led some to speculate that a nuclear explosion could be used to destroy deeply buried bunkers. Axel explained that, in fact, increasing the tonnage of explosives only led to a marginal increase in damage to an underground bunker. The environmental and political costs, in his view, outweighed the benefits.

The Chair of the subcommittee thanked Axel for his testimony. He called the final expert.

"Dr. Damien Voth, from Lawrence Livermore National Laboratory."

Mike turned his head to see the famous nuclear-weapons physicist walk down the aisle. He instantly recognized the stooped, compact man, with his bronze skin, thick eyebrows, and crooked grin. The same age as Axel, he eyed his colleague with a look of amused disdain, dark circles under his murky brown eyes. Voth sat down and addressed the committee.

"Honored representatives," he began, his gravelly voice bearing a residue of Eastern Europe, "Dr. Hansen described for you some of the physical principles behind the so-called 'bunker-buster' explosive devices. I have no disagreement with him on these technical points. However, there is no reason to suppose that much more powerful weapons cannot be designed, with the proper funding level, thereby achieving maximum destructive power. It is true that such weapons would produce prodigious radioactive by-products and other collateral damage. Unfortunately, I regard Dr. Hansen's cost-benefit analysis as subjective, and, if I may say, betraying a philosophy of weakness."

A senior congressman shook his head. "Weakness, Dr. Voth? Dr. Hansen has worked on defense issues for over two decades."

"And the frail condition of our nuclear establishment shows the wounds of his meddling," he said, baring his teeth. "The stability of our entire society depends on a willingness to inflict and suffer mass casualties. If we project ambivalence about our will to strike with the full arsenal of destructive power, civilization as we know it shall cease to exist."

The room fell silent. Axel, a playful glint in his eye, said, "You have a point there, Damien. One cannot tolerate unclean outcomes."

"Precisely right," he said, eyes narrowing. "The nuclear option is extraordinarily clean, optimally so. It is a total-death machine that efficiently and totally wipes away the full spectrum of organic existence, bacterial to mammalian. The power of the sun is harnessed. I'm not referring to the pathetic inefficiency of solar cells. I am talking about the awesome power of nuclear fusion, which yields energy in an eruption that, indiscriminately and without favor, *exterminates life*." He paused and stared distantly. "Dr. Hansen is correct, for once. One cannot tolerate unclean outcomes."

The Chair cleared his throat. "Dr. Voth, the committee recognizes your many years of service to this nation, but I must take exception…"

"Of course you must," Voth hissed, his face deep crimson. Mike could swear he saw spittle issue forth from his mouth. "You spend your days shaking the hands of unwashed masses, infected by their weakness, their nanosecond attention spans, filthy transients on the street who demand the right to vote…"

The Chair banged his gavel. "I've heard enough," he barked indignantly.

"…women who give up their cocaine-addicted babies to drug dealers, deviants who provide cultures for the spread of viruses through unnatural coupling, contagious filth who cry out for the civil right to spread their disease…"

A pair of Capitol police grabbed him and lifted him out of his chair. The gavel banged, over and over, as he continued his rant.

That was the last time Damien Voth was invited to give congressional testimony.

Mike glanced at the dash and was relieved to see that Seth had slowed to ninety miles an hour. The two-lane road stretched ahead of them, brilliant stars overhead. "We may be too late," he said quietly.

"Axel cannot be killed."

He looked at Seth. "That's absurd."

"There's a lot you don't know about Axel Hansen."

"I know the Axel legend," he groaned. "Biathlete, scholar, scientist, government big shot..."

"You forgot the bit between biathlete and scholar. There's a gap."

Mike shrugged. "So maybe he backpacked across Europe."

"He backpacked all right. NATO special forces."

"You're kidding."

"Trust me on this one, Mike. Axel will die when he's ready, and not a minute before. The man cannot be killed."

16

The van stopped at the top of a hill, somewhere in the East Bay. They opened the rear doors and removed Jarrod's blindfold.

"Please don't hurt me," he whimpered.

The men led him on a dusty trail. The lights of San Francisco glimmered in the distance. After a few minutes, they stopped. James walked up to him, gun in hand.

"Tell me the name of your handler."

"What?" Jarrod protested. "This was supposed to be a joke. A pie in the face, that's it. I'm not some kind of terrorist. I'm sorry, okay? I'm really, really, really sorry."

James reached for his pistol. "I don't have time for this. Who is your handler?"

"I don't have a…"

James pressed the gun against Jarrod's head.

"There's a guy named Kevin!" Jarrod screamed, eyes pressed closed. "Kevin Larson. He's in the Anti-Globalization Alliance, the AGA. Please, I thought this was just a prank."

James put his pistol back in his shoulder holster.

"Take us to him."

"I don't know where he lives. C'mon, man."

"Jarrod, you will set up a meeting with Kevin Larson, or the last thing you see will be your sister being strangled to death."

Jarrod stood for a while, complexion pale, and started to wobble. The two men propped him up and led him back to the van.

"Okay," he said, depleted. "I'll do whatever you want. Tell me what to do."

Special Agent Gabrielle Sanchez strode down the hall toward the conference room. Five foot six with heels, she had straight black hair, dark complexion, and hazel eyes that betrayed nothing. An FBI ID with her photograph was pinned to the left pocket of her black business suit.

She knocked once and entered the room. Jon Patterson stood.

"Agent Sanchez," he said, unable to conceal his gloominess. "Thank you for coming on such short notice."

Gabrielle had traveled from Helena on a chartered flight, a signal of how serious the Bureau regarded the situation. "I should have been notified earlier," she said to the officers assembled in the room. "This is now a federal investigation. I am the lead agent on this case."

"Ma'am," an officer said insolently, "with all due respect, everything up to this point has happened in state. I don't see how the feds need to get involved in a local homicide."

Jon shook his head, embarrassed, as Gabrielle stared icily at the man. "First, officer, Customs and Border Protection, a *federal* agency, was alerted to the fact that Professor Mike Harris was headed north toward Canada. Second, you are operating under the assumption that Professor Brenner has been taken hostage, which I'm sure you realize is a *federal* crime."

"Of course."

She turned to Jon. "I'll need a briefing on the details of the lab incident and any information you obtained from Professor Harris."

"Certainly," he said.

Gabrielle turned and left.

Jon glared at the officer. "Get me that information," he said, "and stop making an ass of this department."

"Yes, sir."

Besides a couple of trucks and a near miss with a deer, they encountered little traffic on the two-lane road. Mike looked at the clock on the dash: 10:13 PM. They would keep driving until they reached West Glacier, the site of the DARPA review.

He thought about Seth's statement: *"Axel cannot be killed."* It was wishful thinking. He knew what these people, whoever they were, could do. He and Seth needed to find Axel before they got to him. Axel would have the answers.

"Do you believe me?" he asked.

Seth kept his eyes on the road. "What do you mean?"

"Do you think I killed Jennifer?"

"Would I be driving you to Glacier if I thought you were a murderer?"

"I don't know," Mike said. "I'm the one with the gun."

Seth laughed. "Do you even know how to shoot that thing?"

"Oh, I can shoot it. Hitting the target is my weak area."

The gun was locked in the glove compartment. Mike was not sure whether he would ever have the nerve to use it. Certainly, he never would have shot Jon Patterson. He wondered why Jon didn't call his bluff. Then he remembered that Jon, like the rest of them, figured him for a murderer.

Einstein never had to deal with this madness, he thought, but immediately realized that it was not so. Einstein, an intellectual pacifist with internationalist leanings, made a natural target for the Nazis, viscous thugs who labeled relativity a "Jewish theory." During the rise of Nazism in the early 1930s, Jewish scientists saw the writing on the wall and got out. With their exodus, the scientific center of gravity shifted from Europe to the United States. As he left the port of Bremerhaven, Germany, Einstein told his wife, "Turn around. You will never see it again." They never did.

The Nazis were so evil, so threatening to the ideals he cherished, they prompted Einstein to renounce pacifism and support the Allied military offensive. Later, he learned that the Nazis may be close to developing an atomic bomb. He knew that such a fearsome weapon was physically possible. He signed a letter that urged President Roosevelt to begin developing a bomb based on the principles of nuclear fission. The letter set in motion events that led to the Manhattan Project.

Along with the whirlwind of international crises, Einstein experienced turbulence in his personal life. At the Swiss Federal Institute of Technology, he had a stormy love affair with another physics graduate student, Mileva Marić. They had a daughter, Lieserl, out of wedlock in 1902 and gave her up for adoption or to an orphanage. What exactly happened to the baby girl was never made public, but it tormented Mileva for the rest of her life. They later got married and had two sons. Einstein's relentless pursuit of scientific truth–and other women–ultimately doomed their relationship and led to a painful divorce. Shortly after the ink on the divorce papers was dry, Einstein married his cousin Elsa, a matronly *Hausfrau.* His dalliances continued through his new marriage, as his passion for beautiful women nearly exceeded his love of physics.

Mike could empathize with Einstein's troubles, but at least the Nazis, monstrous as they were, were out in the open. The enemies pursuing Mike lurked in the shadows. Who were they? Who could engineer a laboratory "accident" and surgical assault on his home, with weapons he could scarcely describe? And who were his protectors, the woman in shades and the stealthy helicopter?

"You didn't," Seth said, startling Mike out of his thoughts.

"Didn't what?"

"You didn't kill Jennifer."

Mike felt empty inside. Sometime in the future, when he was out of danger, perhaps then he could grieve. "That's great," he said. "The only guy who believes me is stoned."

"The question before us, Mike, is: who did?"

"Hell if I know," he said, turning to look at the amber reflectors whizzing by.

"Hassan?"

"He doesn't own an army of mercenaries."

"The timing is awfully suspicious if you ask me."

Mike groaned. He had gone over this a hundred times in his mind. "Of course it's suspicious," he said. "The bastard comes by and, the same day, my lab explodes. Why the hell aren't the cops looking into *that* angle? Dammit, Seth, don't you think I *know* Hassan should be a suspect?"

"Then again, you're right." Seth continued, oblivious to Mike's agitation. "Hassan doesn't own an army of mercenaries. He must be operating within a larger conspiracy."

"And here I thought *I* was paranoid."

"We need to look at the interrelationships. Connect the dots. Find the patterns."

"For example?"

"Hassan and Axel travel in certain circles. DOD science clubs."

"How would you know?" Mike scoffed.

"I orbit close enough to know what goes on."

"Like what?"

"Secret stuff. Holiest of holies. This goes way beyond Q clearance. I only have the faint outlines."

Seth saw a sign for Highway 2 West toward Glacier Park. He decelerated and took the exit.

"Bottom line, Mike: we need to find Axel Hansen. He'll tell us everything we need to know."

They continued driving, at a moderate speed, on Highway 2. As they ascended in elevation, they could see patches of snow. Tall poles marked the edges of the road.

"What day is it?" Mike asked.

"Sunday, first day of June," Seth replied. "Why?"

"Has the DARPA review started?"

"It starts Tuesday."

Mike paused, calculating in his mind. "Maybe Axel hasn't arrived yet. If he flies in from DC, it takes…"

"No, Mike, you don't get it. Axel's a serious skier, remember?"

"Yeah. So?"

"Why do you think he chose Glacier for the review?"

"To be close to us," Mike said sardonically.

"Sure. Knowing Axel, I'd bet he's taking a cross-county ski tour before the meeting."

"I don't suppose he brought his cell phone."

"Not a chance. Finding Axel is going to be a serious pain, but we need to do it."

"I don't get it," Mike said, pressing his fingers to his forehead. "The project is a bust. Our experimental results are lame, our silicon samples aren't right, and your calculations showed that the goal of the project is impossible. If anything, someone out there wants to eliminate us for being inept."

Seth continued staring at the road ahead, accelerating slightly. "About those calculations…"

17

Einstein held a deep faith that the speed of light was constant in all reference frames. It didn't matter whether you were traveling on a bus, sitting on a park bench, or piloting a spacecraft. Mike recalled how he conveyed the strangeness of this rule to his students. Imagine you were watching a rocket cruise by at 99% the speed of light. The rocket fired a laser pulse. You would see the pulse travel forward only slightly faster than the rocket. You might conclude that the pilot in the rocket would observe the pulse shoot forward fairly slowly. From the pilot's frame of reference, the pulse should move away from him at 1% the speed of light.

"Wrong!" Mike would exclaim, mimicking a political pundit. Einstein's rule trumped everything. The speed of light was woven so tightly into the fabric of the universe, God insisted that it stay constant, in any reference frame. To enforce this ironclad law, time itself had to warp. "Moving clocks run slowly. Remember the clock, affixed to the side of the rocket? You would see it move in slow motion. It would move just slowly enough so that the pilot would see the pulse moving away from him at *exactly* the speed of light."

Along with this universal law came the universal speed limit.

Nothing could travel faster than the speed of light, 300,000 kilometers a second. If something happens 300,000 kilometers away, there's no way you will know about it in less than one second. Information cannot exceed the speed of light.

Einstein then had his great epiphany. The old gravitational theory postulated "action at a distance." If the moon wiggled, the earth would feel the tidal force wiggle, instantly. The information about the moon wiggling would travel to the earth with infinite speed. *Impossible!* Newton's law of gravitation had to be thrown out! In its place, Einstein proposed something truly radical. Massive objects did *not* exert a gravitational force on other objects. Instead, massive objects *warped space.* Other objects then felt the effect of this warped space.

Although these developments rocked the scientific establishment, they also hinted at the possibility of an all-encompassing, unifying Theory of Everything. Einstein felt frustrated that physics had separate theories for light, gravitation, and nuclear interactions. He spent the rest of his life trying, unsuccessfully, to develop a grand unified theory that would tie them all together.

The real problem lay in the huge difference between the gravitational and electromagnetic forces. Electrical forces kept atoms together. The electrical attraction between a nucleus and an orbiting electron was vastly larger than the gravitational attraction. In his mind, Mike heard Hassan's angry voice:

"Electromagnetic interactions are stronger by forty orders of magnitude! To hell with gravity–it just doesn't matter!"

Hassan was right, in principle. The gravitational force was very, very weak. The only reason we notice it at all is that the earth has a huge mass.

The point of the project was to get around this problem. They would create a state of energy inside a silicon crystal in which the normally meek gravitational force could compete with electromagnetism. Lasers would blast the crystal with such intensity that, for a brief instant of time, the energy density of the crystal would exceed anything in the known universe. This mass-energy, concentrated in a tiny spot inside the crystal, would produce a powerful gravitational field. Such an unusual state of matter had never been observed before. The results of their measurements could finally unearth the treasure of grand unification. Except…

"Your calculations showed that it wouldn't work," Mike said.

"We all make mistakes. Even I."

"What are you talking about?"

Seth exhaled, trying to think of how to explain his calculations to an experimentalist. "As you know, or at least you *should* know, my model involves three parts: the laser light, the crystal, and the gravitational warping caused by mass-energy."

Mike rolled his eyes. Of course he knew. Normally, theorists only included the first two parts, the electromagnetic field produced by the laser light and the quantum mechanics of the atoms in the crystal. Maxwell's equations of electromagnetism, combined with quantum theory, described the system perfectly, so long as gravity was negligible. Their project, however, aimed to create a high energy density such that gravity became important. Seth therefore had to take the extra step and include Einstein's equations of general relativity. This additional complication made the numerical simulations extremely difficult and time consuming.

To tackle the problem, Seth built a massively parallel cluster of high-performance computers. Each computer contained quantum-dot arrays that were specially designed to simulate quantum-mechanical phenomena. Light and gravitation were simulated by more conventional computer chips, with resources assigned adaptively according to the needs of the calculations. Even with this ingenious computing monster, it took an entire week to simulate a single nanosecond in the experiment.

"The problem," Seth said, "always boils down to accuracy versus time. If I had infinite time, I could give you a perfect answer. But, life is short."

"As are grant cycles."

"So I had to cut some corners. And, I cut them in the wrong places. My big mistake was in thinking the system would reach equilibrium after a few nanoseconds."

"But it *does*," Mike protested. "You showed graph after graph proving that everything reaches a steady state after one nanosecond. There's no point in running the simulation after that."

"That's what I thought. A month ago, I was about to terminate a high-precision simulation run and analyze the data. Then, I got distracted."

"Distracted?"

"Cherie is her name. I went to Europe with her for a couple weeks and accidentally left the simulation running. When I came back, I noticed that the system had veered wildly off equilibrium, four nanoseconds after the laser pulse hit the crystal. As of a few days ago, seven nanoseconds into the simulation, the deviation from equilibrium had grown exponentially."

"Numerical artifact," Mike said skeptically.

"I checked for that," Seth replied with a smile. "The only numerical artifact is the system reaching a phony state of equilibrium. When I increase the precision of the calculation, then this strange effect happens. The gravitational field increases over time, substantially. You should be able to measure it, Mike!"

"Except for two things. Oleg gave us a crappy silicon crystal. And, the lab blew up."

"The project would have worked," Seth said confidently. "I told Axel about my calculations last week."

"And he's God Knows Where."

Seth's smile faded. "Mike, there are people in the corridors of power who have wanted to terminate our project since day one. I don't know who they are or what their motivations might be. For a while, it looked like Axel could keep them at bay."

"You're not suggesting…"

"Look at the evidence. My calculations showed that the project would actually work. Oleg was about to grow a high-quality crystal. Stefan had the lasers running. The pieces were in place. Once we achieved a successful demonstration, *pow*, there would be no turning back. They *had* to stop us."

"But murder, Seth?" Mike said, his head spinning. "I can't imagine that some government bureaucrats would get together and say, 'Should we yank their funding? Nah, let's send in the hit squad.'"

"Why not?" Seth asked, his tone implying that Mike was hopelessly naive.

"Because," Mike spluttered, "our project isn't important in

that way."

"In what way?"

"In… You know, national security. It just doesn't matter."

Seth shook his head slowly. "That's where you're wrong."

MONDAY, JUNE 2

18

Agent Gabrielle Sanchez listened to the last part of the briefing silently. Sergeant Garrett recounted his discussion with Mike Harris at the hospital. At the time, Garrett explained, he didn't consider Harris a suspect, although he had kept an open mind.

After Garrett returned to his seat, Sanchez stood up. "Obviously, the first priority is locating Mike Harris," she said. "The APB went out and the media have been notified. Beyond that, we need information. What are his potential destinations? Does he have relatives nearby? Where are his usual haunts?"

Jon Patterson cleared his throat. "His relatives are out east. I think his parents live in Connecticut. As far as haunts, well, we've already checked Buck's Tavern. Buck's, his house, and campus pretty much cover his known whereabouts."

"He's an internationally known scientist," Sanchez said sharply. "He must go to meetings. Who are his colleagues?"

Jon started to answer, "I don't know," before his training stopped him. "I'll find out, ma'am."

"Interview the department, starting with the Chair."

"Sure," he said, looking at his watch. "First thing tomorrow…"

"Now."

It's past midnight, he thought, annoyed. He didn't relish the prospect of interviewing physicists in their pajamas. He pointed to Garrett, his gesture saying *it's your job.*

"The next priority is collecting forensic evidence," she said.

The door swung open and Harry stumbled in, breathing heavily, gray stubble covering his face. He pushed his tinted glasses up his nose and nodded deferentially to Sanchez, who stared at him without amusement.

"Ma'am," he said between breaths, "officers. Sorry I'm late."

"Have a seat," Jon said wearily. "Agent Sanchez, Harry is with the university's IT department."

"Have you scanned the hard drive?" Sanchez asked, ignoring Harry's beefy hand, which was attempting a shake.

"No, it's pretty much toast," he said as he sat down, rebuffed. "You guys want a crack at it?"

"We'll fly the computer and accessories to the Computer Analysis and Response Team in San Diego. I'll need someone to help identify and package the materials."

"I'm your man."

She looked at Jon. "My team will take pictures and collect evidence in the lab. I'll need the campus police to keep the scene absolutely secure."

"Okay."

"What about the residence?"

"We've secured that scene," Jon said, feeling a bit defensive, "with assistance from County."

"Fine," she said, "so long as the Sheriff has sufficient resources to search for Mike Harris."

"Understood."

"Gentlemen," Sanchez said, standing up abruptly, "you have your action items. We'll have another meeting in thirty minutes."

From the penthouse suite, Henry gazed at the lights of San Francisco. He sipped the last of his wine and set the glass on a table. He glanced back at the leggy redhead who relaxed on the sofa, city lights illuminating the gentle curves of her sheer black dress.

"Do you believe in Fate?" he asked.

"Sure," she said sleepily.

He walked over to another window and stared at the fog that was rolling into the bay. He reminisced, as he often did, about an encounter that occurred almost exactly thirteen years ago. Henry was in an upscale bar, with a young lady whose name he could not recall. They slammed shot after shot. He kept remembering, and ignoring, an old college adage: *liquor then beer, in the clear; beer then liquor, never sicker.* The lights of the bar seemed to spin. He nuzzled up to the woman, licking her neck, drunk in the moment. They started dancing, bumping into people, grabbing each other obscenely.

"Watch it," a man said.

Henry staggered toward the guy and swung wildly. The man and his friends laughed. Enraged, Henry charged, clutching the man by the throat. The friends started pounding on Henry, and everything went fuzzy after that. Rough hands threw him out onto his butt. He shuffled along a dark alley behind the bar. A minute later, he heard his date screaming at him.

"How could you leave me in there, asshole? Look at me when I'm talking to you. I said, *look!*"

He turned around and she stared at his bloodied face.

"God you're ugly," she said, squinting at him with intoxicated malice. "Rich, but ugly. Get a cab, loser." She staggered away, bellowing "loser!" every few seconds.

He pressed his hands to his forehead and then looked at his bloody palms. A wave of nausea overcame him and he dropped to his knees. He dreaded what was coming next. He convulsed painfully and vomited onto the asphalt, feeling like his insides would propel themselves through his throat. After several wrenching convulsions, his gut was empty and he got to his feet, his head pounding ferociously. He walked a few steps but had to sit down. The pain in his head was unbearable. He lay down, groaning pathetically. After a minute, he blacked out.

He awoke to the sight of a pair of polished black wingtip shoes. He slowly turned his head up to see their owner. The person wore latex gloves and handed him a box of tissue.

"Look at what they've done to you," said an oddly familiar voice.

Henry wiped his nose and face and looked up at the man. He stood maybe five foot six and wore a formal suit and tie, very old school compared to the San Francisco crowd. In the darkness, he could make out the slick black hair and large eyebrows. He recognized the gravelly Eastern European voice. There was no mistaking him. It was Dr. Damien Voth.

Dr. Voth crouched down and frowned, deep lines etched into his bronze skin. He pressed a cotton ball to the opening of a bottle of hydrogen peroxide. "This will hurt a bit," he said, and dabbed Henry's bloody face gently. Henry recoiled. "You need it. The streets teem with bacteria."

"Dr. Voth…"

"Call me Damien."

"Why are you here?"

"Call it Fate," he said, carefully wiping Henry's face. "I would be obliged if you could dispose of the cotton and tissues."

Henry stood up, still feeling woozy, and dropped the items into a Dumpster. Damien removed his gloves, taking care not to touch the outer surfaces, and threw them in too. He placed the bottle of hydrogen peroxide in his inside coat pocket.

"Are you in the mood for a coffee? There is a respectable café down the street a couple blocks."

"I suppose. You didn't answer my question, though."

They started walking slowly. They reached the street and headed down the sidewalk.

"We're two of a kind," Damien said. "I know you, Henry, but you don't know yourself."

"That doesn't make a damn bit of sense."

Damien's face grimaced into something resembling a smile. "It will, in the fullness of time. After you."

They stepped into a small café that hummed with a lively midnight clientele. They sat at a small table in a corner. Damien bought them espressos.

"This hits the spot," Henry said, his bloodshot eyes showing signs of life as he sipped the drink.

"You need hydration. Excuse me," he said to a passing barista. "My friend would like bottled water and a clean glass."

After a minute of silence, Damien said, "Why do you do this?"

"Do what?"

"Commit suicide," he said, a flash of gold behind his crooked grin. "That's what you're doing, you know. I assure you, there are much easier ways."

"Who are you, my mother?"

"For all you know, I am."

Henry got to his feet, ready to swing.

"Calm yourself, Henry. Do I look like a boxer?"

Henry sighed and sat down.

"I know you were adopted by a somewhat elderly couple who died when you were in college. You dropped out and started your first business…"

"Spare me," Henry said, angry but too tired to fight. "Spare me the psychoanalysis. I pay a guy good money for that. Abandonment stress disorder, he calls it."

"Must have been terrible, knowing your own mother gave you up."

"Not at all," he said, slamming down his palm. "You know that 'somewhat elderly couple' you mentioned? *They* were my parents. End of story."

Henry avoided Damien's probing brown eyes. "Of course," Damien said. "End of story."

"And what's *your* story, Mister Nuke? Hanging around pubs, waiting for drunken billionaires to stumble into the alley?"

"Still only a billionaire?" Damien said.

"Screw you."

"All your life's work, dedicated to piling up wealth, and to what end? For a one with twelve zeros. One trillion dollars US. After you have reached that summit, what then?"

Henry looked at him angrily, wanting to speak but not finding the words.

"I'll tell you what. You'll see those twelve zeros and realize they add up to *zero*. A life wasted, full of sound and fury, signifying nothing."

"Who are you to come in here…"

"*No!*" Damien hissed. "Who are *you*? Look around you. You're better than these people. This is a historic moment and you're heaving your innards in a germ-infested alley."

Henry saw a faint bloody print of his palm on the tablecloth.

"What do you mean, historic moment?"

"We live in decadent times," he said, setting down his empty cup. "The world's democracies are infected with sloth, waste, and weakness. Their impending extinction is inevitable. Consider yourself, Henry: a brilliant, self-made billionaire, the ideal person to lead a nation. Yet you would not stand a chance in a popular election."

Henry shook his head, trying to follow the threads of Damien's thought. "I'm not running for office."

"And why bother?" Damien said, his eyes alight. "The public wants to be spoon-fed platitudes about prosperity, peace, and a utopian society where no one gets hurt. A man who knows the truth, such as yourself, would stand no chance in such a charade. The democratic revolution of the Western hemisphere, led by visionary intellects, has given way to a fraudulent system of spineless, pandering politicians."

Henry pointed a finger at Damien. "I do pretty well working the system. I like my politicians weak, thank you very much."

A barista set a glass of water on the table. Henry held it unsteadily and took a sip.

"The definition of decadence," Damien said. "You know the system is wrong but feel you cannot change it."

"Why should I?" he asked defiantly. "It's been good to me."

Damien smiled sagely. After a few minutes, he paid the bill and they headed out to the street.

"We shall meet again," Damien said. "Think about who you are and what you can achieve."

He turned and walked down the sidewalk. Soon he vanished from view.

"Whatever," Henry grumbled, looking for a cab. "Freak."

Gradually, over the years, he came to appreciate the incisive intellect of Dr. Damien Voth, even as the public turned on the renowned scientist. After Damien gave his infamous congressional testimony, Henry was one of only a few who still supported him openly. Things went downhill when Damien focused his attention on the search for extraterrestrial intelligence, ranting against SETI and advocating a technique called "quantum gravity teleportation" to communicate with aliens. His reputation as an eccentric nutcase, a once-brilliant scientist who fell off the deep end, was assured.

If only that had been the worst of it, Henry thought.

He walked over to the redhead and stroked her silky hair. She hummed languidly and touched his hand.

"I need to get up early tomorrow," he said. "Make yourself at home. I'll leave a pot of coffee for you."

"Going to the island?" she asked, her eyes still closed.

"No, back to Montana. I need to finish some business there."

"'Kay."

"Good night," he whispered, kissing her on the forehead.

"'Night."

He walked toward the master bedroom and glanced back at the woman. For an instant, he imagined that she was Jing. With a yawn, he shuffled into the bedroom and got ready for a few hours of sleep.

19

Seth and Mike drove through the town of West Glacier and into the park. They drove along the Going-to-the-Sun road, with Lake McDonald on their left, glassy and still in the moonlight.

"We should change cars," Mike said nervously. "This thing stands out like a sore thumb."

"This 'thing' got us here," Seth responded, patting the leather upholstery affectionately, "and I won't abandon her."

As they proceeded northeast, Mike tried to piece together the bewildering events of the past few days. Everything started with a phone call. Jennifer had called him during the faculty meeting. He remembered his angry reaction–how petty he had been! Then, after the disaster, Jennifer appeared at his house. She told him why she had called.

"It was that Iranian guy," she said after a moment of thought. "Hassan. He called me, out of the blue. He wanted to know if you'd be in town."

"Hassan?" he asked, bewildered. "Did you tell him anything?"

She stepped back from him. "I think I… confirmed something. He had a good idea of what you guys were working on, and…"

"You confirmed it."

"Yeah. I did…"

She called to warn him about Hassan. At the time, the idea that Jennifer would call for an unselfish reason seemed impossible.

Then, a second call.

"I got your phone call and I came right over…"

Except that there *was* no phone call, at least not from him. Someone had lured Jennifer to his house. He recalled the cold, murderous voice of the man who calmly prepared to execute him:

"First, you killed your ex… Then, you killed yourself."

Murder-suicide. An open and shut case.

"What are we going to do, Seth?"

"We're going to get some rest," he said.

He turned left into the driveway of a rustic lodge and parked in a dark spot away from the lights.

"You should probably stay in the car," Seth said, putting on his shades, leather coat, and a baseball cap.

"You look ridiculous."

"I'll be right back."

Seth walked toward the entrance to the lodge. Mike glanced around nervously. He expected a park ranger to leap out from behind the trees, shine a flashlight at him, and tell him to give himself up. On some level, he wished they would catch him. At least then he could stop looking over his shoulder.

He opened the glove compartment. The Beretta was still inside. He closed the compartment and looked at the lodge. *What's taking so long?* Their pictures must have been shown on the evening news. Hopefully the lodge employee hadn't turned on the television.

Seth finally emerged from the lodge and walked back to the car, looking casual, hands in his coat pockets.

"What the hell were you doing in there?" Mike said, a nervous wreck.

"Calm down," Seth replied, removing his shades. "I got us a cabin."

He started the engine and drove slowly down a road that was lined with small log cabins. They stopped at cabin number 12.

"Did the employee recognize you?" Mike asked.

"No," Seth said as he opened the car door, "but check this out." He unzipped his coat and retrieved a newspaper, *The Kalispell Daily Inter Lake.* Mike read the front page as he walked to the cabin.

PROFESSOR FOCUS OF INVESTIGATION

The standing of Michael Harris, a physics professor at Colton University, has turned from hero to suspect. Just two days ago, he was hailed for reportedly saving the life of graduate student Sarah Jacobson from a fire in his laboratory. Campus police now say that he may be responsible for the murder of his ex-fiancée, finance professor Jennifer Lawson, at his home the night of May 31. His whereabouts are currently unknown. Police consider him armed and extremely dangerous.

"Nothing I didn't already know."

Seth unlocked the cabin door. They walked in and inspected the Spartan room: two twin beds with a nightstand between them, a dresser, and a closet-sized bathroom.

"What do we do now?" Mike asked as he sat on a bed.

"We rest," Seth said, yawning. "Tonight I was expecting to crash with Amy, not go on a road trip with you."

"At least hide your car."

Seth rubbed his eyes and stood. "Fine," he said groggily. "A little appreciation wouldn't hurt."

He left the cabin. Mike heard the low rumble of the Viper as Seth drove to a more concealed parking spot. He shuffled to the bathroom and looked in the mirror. His face, caked with blood and sweat, looked older than its 39 years. He ran cold water over his hands and splashed it on his face. He grabbed a white towel and pressed it to his forehead, where a scar was beginning to heal.

His thoughts turned to Hassan Zare. What had Mike done to earn his enmity? Apparently, he had trespassed on Hassan's scientific domain. Mike's talk at the American Physical Society was the first time he had presented his research on the interactions between high-power lasers and solids. Up until then, he researched basic properties of semiconductor crystals such as silicon. His work on excitons was generally well received but did not make top-tier publications like *Science* and *Nature*. Hassan, in contrast, continually sought the limelight, tirelessly promoting himself and the research of his well-funded Harvard laboratory. He must have regarded Mike as a nettlesome pest to be squashed as soon as possible.

For whatever reason, Hassan detested him. But why did he call Jennifer? He remembered that they had met briefly at a conference in Maui. Jennifer came as an "accompanying person," what in the old days would have been a "wife." It was the only time she had accompanied him on a business trip. He remembered how beautiful she looked, wading in the clear, warm sea, and felt a sharp pang of regret. He could see her now, water dripping down her tanned skin as she beckoned him to come in. No, he said, he had to attend a talk.

On the last evening of the conference, they went to a Luau with the other conference attendees. Hassan approached them. Mike felt his pulse race. Hassan smiled, bowed slightly, and extended his hand to Jennifer.

"Thank you so much for coming," he said charmingly. "Unfortunately, my wife could not make it."

"That's too bad," Jennifer said with a smile. "The snorkeling is great."

"Oh no no, she never goes in the water," he said, laughing.

Who is this guy? As they left for the airport the next morning, Hassan gave him a warm handshake and complimented him on his talk. On the plane ride back, Mike wondered whether he and Hassan had reached some kind of understanding. Alas, it was not to be. At the next conference, Hassan tore into him, just as he always had. Peer-reviewed proposals and papers came back with rejections that bore Hassan's unmistakably snide signature.

Mike envied Hassan's ability to turn himself from an ogre to a prince with the flip of a mental switch. His own face betrayed his emotions and insecurities. He would be the worst politician, spy, or actor imaginable. Mike shrank from awkward situations. Hassan thrived in them. Was that what drew Hassan to Mike's lab? Did he have a thirst for nervous adrenalin, like a Vampire seeking fresh blood?

Or was he just evil? The academic world that Mike inhabited

rejected the notion. There had to be forces, the theory went, that compelled people to behave in certain ways. A human could not possess innate badness any more than a brick could spontaneously float in the air. If you observe a brick in the air, an unseen force must be counteracting gravity. If a person acts outside social norms, deterministic forces must be pushing the person to behave that way.

Mike knew little about Hassan's background, except that he came from a relatively wealthy Iranian family and traveled to the United States to attend graduate school. Like many immigrants before him, he worked hard and became a US citizen. He labored tenaciously to build up a network of government sponsors. Like a fish in water, Hassan prospered in the cutthroat environment of science funding. Now, at the zenith of his career, his many contacts in the Pentagon and on Capitol Hill provided a steady stream of money. By any measure, he should be content with his success.

Seth said that Axel and Hassan traveled in the same Department of Defense circles. That comment reminded Mike of the depressing phone call with Axel.

"What do you mean, you're withdrawing support?"

"I'm sorry," said Hansen. "I've spoken with key people. They say no."

Was Hassan one of those key people? If so, why couldn't he be satisfied with choking off his source of funding? Why did he resort to murder?

The door opened and Seth walked in. He pulled the Beretta from his coat pocket and set it on the nightstand.

"The car's hidden," he said, "and I'm zonked." He threw his coat on the floor and unzipped his pants. "I call this bed."

Mike peered nervously out a small window.

"Give it a rest," Seth yawned, crawling under the covers. "If the cops find us, they find us."

It's not the cops I'm worried about. "I'll just keep watch for a while."

"Get some sleep," he murmured. "Big day tomorrow."

After a few minutes, Seth began to snore. Mike continued to look out the window. Then he went over to the nightstand and held the gun. He flipped the safety to the up position, revealing the red-you're-dead dot. He sat on his bed, holding the gun. As time passed, he felt exhaustion take hold, so he set the gun on the floor under the bed. He lay down, too tired to move but kept awake by adrenalin and fear.

20

Sergeant Garrett knocked on the door of the small home.

"Professor Quinlan?" he shouted. "Colton police. I have some questions."

He waited for a moment, listening to the sounds of crickets in the field behind the house. Then, he heard the unmistakable sound of a pump-action shotgun. He backed away from the house and drew his gun.

"Who sent you?" said a voice from the darkness.

"Campus police," Garrett said, moving toward his car. "Just here to ask questions."

"Put your gun down, mister."

"Sir, you need to come out. Show me your hands."

An old man in a pale blue bathrobe emerged from behind the house and walked cautiously toward Garrett, hands in the air.

"Are you Paul Quinlan?"

"Who's asking?" Paul asked, eyes wide. "Federal or local?"

"Campus police," Garrett said, holstering his gun and showing him a badge. "Professor, you're smart enough to know it's a bad idea to pull a gun on a cop. I could arrest you right now."

"Are you here about Mike Harris?"

"Yes."

Paul exhaled and relaxed. He put his hands down.

"May I come in?" Garrett asked.

"I'd rather you didn't."

"Fine," Garrett said, annoyed. He considered whether to haul the coot downtown, but thought better of it and pulled out a small notepad. "This won't take long. Think back to the lab fire. Did you witness anything out of the ordinary?"

"Other than a lab exploding?" he said. "I'll tell you what I saw. I saw Mike Harris running at me with murder in his eyes."

"What do you mean?"

Paul glanced side to side, as if checking to see whether someone was eavesdropping. "He had that crazed look, like he was on a rampage. I never trusted the man, I'll have you know. He kept taking things from my office."

"Do you have a lab?"

"Oh, no," he said with a dismissive wave. "My research days are long gone. The federal agencies discriminate against my kind."

"Why didn't you trust him?"

"Mike? He's one of these young hotshots who thinks he's too good for Colton. I've been here thirty-three years. I've put in my time. He hasn't."

They felt a chilly breeze. "Are you sure you don't want to go inside?"

"He always sent others to do his dirty work," he said, ignoring Garrett's question. "My black pens kept disappearing. I had evidence that it was his student. You see," he said, his voice dropping to a whisper, "that's why he killed him."

"To cover for the theft of black pens?"

"Not just pens," he retorted. "Other supplies as well. Binders, paper, dry-erase markers... My departmental allowance is only one thousand a year. One thousand. It's been flat for the last eight years. Mike has federal grants, he should get his own damn supplies."

"Does Mike have any other enemies?"

"Oh, I don't know that I'd call myself an enemy. Live and let live, I say. Speak softly and all that."

"Does he have any enemies, period? People who might want

to hurt him or sabotage his research?"

"We're a friendly bunch," he said, his eyes two narrow slits in the moonlight. Goose bumps from the chilly night caused the gray hair on his arms and legs to stand on end. "I don't think you can pin this on anyone other than Mike Harris. The man is not to be trusted."

"Thanks for your time," Garrett said, putting his notepad away. "We might come by again. I'd appreciate a better greeting."

"You've got nothing to fear from me."

Paul watched Sergeant Garrett get into his car and speed off into the night. When he was out of sight, Paul pulled a small audio recorder from the pocket of his robe. He turned it off and shuffled back into his house.

Jalen felt the thick tension in the room. The confined space added to his discomfort. He didn't know what he could say to smooth things over. They had lost track of Mike Harris. Jing's face burned with anger when the bald man delivered the news.

"We should have brought him in," she said through clenched teeth. "This is exactly what I said would happen."

"Our mission," the bald man said, his baritone voice calm, "is *not* to protect Professor Harris."

"Our mission will fail without Harris!"

"No, the mission would be set back. Your single-minded focus on preserving his life ignores the larger strategic landscape."

"I think you both make valid points," Jalen said tentatively.

"Oh stop," Jing said, getting up to leave.

"Just hear me out. On one hand, we should make an effort to find Harris and bring him in."

"Impossible," the bald man barked.

"On the other hand," Jalen said, raising his voice, "if we cannot find him, we should cut our losses and revert to the contingency plan."

Jing wrinkled her forehead and pressed her fist to her lips.

"We cannot bring in Mike Harris," the bald man said emphatically.

"We may have to," Jing said.

A minute passed while Jing and Jalen stared silently at the bald man.

"If Harris is lost," he said at last, "we proceed with the contingency plan. If we find him…" He paused. "If we find him, we bring him in."

"Fair enough," Jing said, exhaling.

"Now," Jalen said, eager to change the subject, "check this out. I've compiled recent financial activity by Colton Enterprises and its subsidiaries." He walked over to a computer screen. Several dozen boxes appeared on the screen, representing different companies, color coded according to their relationship to Colton. "In addition to shifting assets around the globe, they've gone on a stock buying spree. It looks like they've targeted about forty corporations."

Jalen tapped a button on a keyboard. A list of medium-sized corporations–pharmaceuticals, heavy equipment, telecom, retail chains, government contractors, internet companies–appeared on the screen. There appeared to be no common link, except that none was a giant like Microsoft or General Motors.

"How much money are we talking?" Jing asked.

"Nearly a hundred billion dollars."

"Good Lord," the bald man exclaimed.

"They're not great investments," Jalen said, "unless there's some inside information I don't know about. Colton bumped up their prices substantially just by purchasing so much stock."

"What about physical assets?" the man asked.

Jalen pressed a key and the screen showed overhead satellite imagery of Colton's summer home in Montana. "They're offloading huge amounts of equipment. Jing pointed us to this building after her reconnaissance mission. You can see trucks here, here, and here."

"What kind of equipment?"

"We're not sure," Jing said, "but from the size of the trucks and number of shipments, it's thousands of tons."

"Where is it all going?"

Jalen smiled. "For a long time, we didn't know. Then I got us a drone so we could follow one of the convoys. As you can see, they changed vehicles along the way." He pointed to an infrared movie of men loading equipment from one semi to another, in the middle of the Nevada desert. "The trucks then split up and went to different ports on the west coast: San Diego, Los Angeles, Oakland, and Puget Sound."

"Then where?"

"The cargoes were loaded onto shipping containers that went on merchant vessels, which we tracked." The screen showed cranes loading containers onto ships at the four ports. The view expanded to show a map of the Pacific Ocean. Yellow lines traced paths from the ports. The lines converged on one point in the Pacific Ocean.

"The Pacific Research Center," Jalen said. "Everything went to Henry Colton's island."

21

In his dreams, Mike saw the Indian woman. He couldn't understand what she was saying. She led him by the hand through a forest populated with antelopes and frogs.

"Look out," she said.

He looked down and saw an enormous spider. The blurry face of Hassan appeared. He tried to run but his feet became stuck in the muddy trail.

Mike heard scratching, soft at first and then louder. His heart leapt.

He awoke with a start. His head turned toward the small window. Eyes stared back at him. Mike screamed and dove under his bed. He grabbed the gun.

"What?" Seth exclaimed, bolting upright.

Mike aimed the gun at the window, hands trembling.

A claw scratched the window. Mike could hear his heart beating like a bass drum.

"It's a bear," Seth said.

Mike continued to point the gun.

"A *black* bear. He can't get inside. Put the gun down."

Mike breathed and flipped on the safety. He set the gun on the floor.

"Get a grip," Seth said grumpily, his eyes half shut. "We need to rest."

Mike watched the curious bear wander away from their cabin. "They can't find us, right?" he whispered.

"Not for a while. They're looking for my car, I'm sure, but…"

"Not the cops. The bad guys."

"Oh," Seth said, sitting on the edge of his bed. "No. Impossible. How could they know where we are? Don't sweat it."

Mike thought back to the night when they attacked his house. He remembered Jennifer's eyes as she lay dying. She had a look of acceptance, it seemed, but she had every right to hate him. She had a tenured professorship and was engaged to a man who could actually commit. Perhaps she would start a family. A full life lay ahead of her…

He collapsed onto the bed, tears in his eyes, and buried his head in a pillow.

"Don't blame yourself," Seth said, as if reading his mind. "Just try to stay focused. This'll all get sorted out." He placed his hand on Mike's shoulder.

"I can't take much more of this," said his muffled voice.

"After we find Axel, we can turn ourselves in. It'll all be over soon."

After a few minutes of silence, he said, "Hey, Seth."

"Yes?"

Mike looked up at him. "Want to hear a story?"

"A what?"

"There was this Indian woman. She told a story about a… some animal."

"Get some rest."

"A deer, I think. Antelope. That's it. It was an antelope…" Mike voice drifted off.

"Good night, Mike."

"And these frogs. There was a contest."

Seth climbed back into bed. "Good night," he said, more firmly.

"Night, Seth."

* * *

After a deep, dreamless sleep, Mike awoke to sunlight shining through the small window. Seth was already dressed in his blue jeans, sandals, and Hawaiian shirt. His purple hair dye had faded, revealing brown and gray.

"We need a change of clothes," he said, "not to mention hiking boots."

"Boots?" Mike asked groggily, rubbing his bleary eyes.

"Stay here. I'll buy some stuff at the gift shop."

He donned his coat, shades, and baseball cap, and went out.

Mike walked into the bathroom and turned on the shower. He took off his clothes and examined the cuts and bruises that covered his body. He gingerly stepped into the shower and winced as water hit his flesh. As steam filled the air and hot water ran over his body, his mind slowly began to clear. He thought of Seth's words: *"After we find Axel, we can turn ourselves in. It'll all be over soon."* The thought of jail time did not bother him. He just needed answers. Axel could supply them.

They *had* to find Axel. He needed to focus on that goal. Axel would gaze at them wisely and reveal the secrets of the conspiracy. He would tell the authorities, too. Mike would be exonerated.

The problem was that the clock was ticking. The story of Mike Harris taking a hostage would be in the morning papers. They had only a few hours, at best, before someone reported a red Viper cruising in Glacier Park. The park ranger police, a force trained to deal with armed fugitives and terrorists, would close in fast. Mike and Seth needed to locate Axel before that happened.

After a long shower, Mike stepped out and dried off. Fortunately, there was no television in the cabin–otherwise, he would not have been able to resist watching news accounts of his criminal activities. He peered out the window, looking for Seth. He realized that this was the site for the DARPA review. Two dozen attendees would start arriving today. If one of them recognized him, they were finished.

After a few minutes, he saw Seth sauntering back to the cabin with two large shopping bags filled with merchandise. Seth opened the door and stepped inside.

"I got ripped off," he said, dumping the contents of the bags onto the bed.

They changed into the clothes. They wore matching blue Glacier Park T-shirts, jeans, and hiking boots.

"Goodness," Seth remarked, looking in the mirror, "we look like a couple of guys on a honeymoon." He put on his leather coat and placed a small pair of binoculars in the inside pocket.

"Did you see anyone we know?"

"No. It's possible someone recognized me, though. We need to get moving."

Seth opened the door, letting in the cool morning breeze. Mike followed but Seth abruptly slammed the door shut, banging his nose painfully.

"Hey!" Mike said, staggering back. He held his nose, which started to bleed. "What the…"

He felt a chill as he heard Hassan's voice outside. Heart pounding, he pressed his ear to the door.

"…morning, Seth," Hassan said in a haughty tone. "I assume you heard the news last night."

"Yeah," Seth said. "That's something."

"Have they caught the bastard?"

"No," he said awkwardly. "I guess he's still on the lam."

"Terrible. I never thought much of him, to be perfectly blunt, but *murder*. Well, even *I'm* surprised."

Mike felt blood rush to his face. He wanted to strangle the man.

"So," Seth said uneasily, "have you seen Axel?"

Mike peeked through a gap between the drape and window frame. He saw Hassan standing with his arms crossed, a snake-like grin on his face, staring at Seth malevolently.

"Aren't you the least bit curious about your colleague?"

"I don't know what to think, Hassan. I thought maybe Axel would have some insight."

Hassan stepped closer to Seth and jabbed a finger into his chest.

"If you think Axel can revive your little project, think again."

"What are you talking about?"

Hassan leaned in close and hissed something that Mike could

not hear. Seth stepped back slowly and Hassan stalked off. When Hassan was out of sight, Seth opened the cabin door and quickly slipped inside.

"Shit," he said.

"What did he say?"

"He obviously didn't see the news this morning–yet. We need to move. My car is that way." He pointed in a direction opposite to where Hassan had headed.

Seth opened the door and looked both ways.

"Run!" he said.

They ran across the road, toward a small parking lot sheltered by trees. They passed several parked cars before Mike saw the Viper, partially camouflaged by a group of pines. They jumped in and Seth turned the ignition. He backed out of the parking lot, sped down the road, and accelerated onto the Going-to-the-Sun Road. The glacial lake, glassy and blue, was on their left, situated before chiseled, snow-covered peaks.

Mike fumbled with the seatbelt and put it on. He opened the glove compartment and got a tissue, which he held to his bloody nose. "What did he say?"

"I asked him about Axel," Seth replied, his face paler than usual. His hands gripped the steering wheel tightly.

"And?"

"He said he had 'neutralized' him. That was his exact word. Neutralized."

22

Mike felt ill as they turned around a bend. He was not worried about Seth's driving. To the contrary, he almost wished they would plummet down the steep mountain edge. At least that would provide a definitive conclusion to his nightmare. The thing that gnawed at him was the prospect that Axel might be dead. To a large extent, he had bought into Seth's confidence: *"Axel cannot be killed."* He knew such a statement was ludicrous. Still, he wanted to believe. Without Axel, he didn't know where to turn.

"Where are we going?" he asked, his voice weak with worry.

"Logan Pass," Seth answered, accelerating.

"Why?"

"I talked to a hiker in the lobby. He saw Axel–someone who matched his description, anyway–and said that Axel planned to ski up Highline Trail."

"So we're going to hike up the trail?"

"That's right."

Mike looked out his window, at the steep, rocky face of the glacier-carved mountain. He imagined how the car would appear from above, a tiny red speck winding its way along a thin strip of pavement. Next to these colossal features of geology, they must look insignificant.

"What if he's not there?" Mike asked.

"Well, we know he's not at the lodge," Seth replied testily. "At least we have a lead."

"It seems a bit early in the morning…"

"He was NATO special forces, for crying out loud." Seth kept his eyes fixed on the road ahead. "I've had it with your negative energy. Think positive."

"Jennifer was thinking positive, I'm sure," Mike replied glumly. "She had a lot to look forward to. What's the point, Seth? Any minute could be our last."

"*That's* a good attitude," Seth grumbled. He put on his shades.

They continued in silence for a while, the ten-cylinder engine purring contentedly as they cruised up the winding road. Seth moved into the left lane and swiftly overtook an old-fashioned bus full of tourists.

The closer they got to their destination, the more Mike felt, in the pit of his stomach, that they wouldn't find Axel. He wished he could be optimistic, like Seth. Did Seth know something? He always gave the impression that he was a step ahead of everyone else. More often than not, the impression turned out to be correct. Seth had last talked to Axel about his most recent calculations, the ones that proved their idea would actually work. Perhaps that conversation gave him insight that Mike lacked.

"You mentioned something yesterday," Mike said. "About our project."

"Yes?..."

"That there were people who wanted to kill it, for reasons of national security."

"Something like that."

"Why?"

Seth sighed. "Think about it, Mike."

"Just tell me," Mike said. "I'm not in any mood for games."

Seth smiled, his amused eyes concealed by shades. "If the project had succeeded, what would we have produced?"

"We both know the answer to that."

"*Energy!*" he said in a dramatic B-movie voice. "Energy can be used for good–or *evil.*"

Mike shook his head and looked out the window again. He couldn't stand Seth sometimes. "Give me a break."

"Seriously, Mike, remember when we had DOE funding? The Department of Energy studies high energy densities *why*? So they can model nuclear explosives! If we had managed to pull off this project, can you imagine what new weapons might be possible?"

"You can make a weapon out of anything," Mike said. "We already have enough nukes to flatten every city on the planet. Nothing we do will change that."

"Do you know who Alfred Nobel was?"

"Don't patronize me, Seth."

"Before he established his prizes, Alfred Nobel invented dynamite. He thought it would make the ultimate weapon, a weapon so powerful that it would render war obsolete. That was in 1867, before the worst wars in human history."

"Yes, Seth, I know."

"And here you are, telling me that nukes are the worst possible weapons, that nothing could possibly exceed their destructive power. Nobel said that about dynamite, now you're saying it about nuclear bombs."

"But it's been more than sixty years, and no one's invented anything to take their place," Mike said, frustrated by Seth's circumspection. "Certainly not *us*. The reason DOE funded us was that our data would help them model nuclear explosions, not invent some new super-weapon."

Seth swerved to avoid a bighorn sheep that had started to wander into the road. Unfazed, he said, "Sure, Mike. The Stockpile Stewardship Program. Preparing the nation for the Comprehensive Test Ban Treaty. And what about DARPA? Why are they interested?"

"You tell me," he said. "You're the one who talks to Axel."

"Yes, I do. And if we find him, he'll make everything clear."

As they approached the Continental Divide, the increase in altitude prompted a new round of bleeding. Mike opened the glove compartment and retrieved more tissues for his nose. They continued cruising up the vertiginous road. On their left, the mountainside plunged into a valley with a roaring river. After a few minutes, the road veered away from the river and steepened. They saw a sign for the trailhead and Seth hit the brakes.

"That's it," he said.

Seth darted into a small parking area. He parked as far from the road as possible; unfortunately, his red car would still be easy to spot. They got out and Seth popped the trunk. He took the Beretta and slipped it into an inside pocket of his leather jacket. They walked to the trailhead, where they found a kiosk that contained maps, grizzly bear warnings, and a visitor log. Seth opened the visitor log and ran his finger down the page. He pointed to a signature on the list:

Axel Hansen May 30

"May 30?" Mike said, feeling panic rise inside him. "That was…"

"Three days ago."

"Shit!" he exclaimed, pressing his hands to his head. "He's long gone!"

"Calm down," Seth said. "Breathe in. Make a whisper sound deep in your throat. Then exhale…"

Mike pounded the kiosk with his fists. "I need to find Axel!"

"I know. Focus, Mike. Your negative energy waves are out of control."

Mike paced frantically around the wooded area, cursing and pulling at his hair. After a minute, Seth said, "We should at least re-trace his steps. Let's take a quick hike and then come straight back. Maybe we'll meet someone who saw him."

"Maybe, maybe…"

"Fate runs both ways. I was lucky running into that hiker who had seen Axel. I was unlucky running into Hassan. We're due some luck now. Yin and Yang." Seth walked up the trail. "Are you coming?"

Mike grumbled incoherently and followed Seth up the trail. They walked along a narrow path on a steep, rocky mountain face. As they gained in elevation, the damp snow gradually became more prevalent until it covered the ground completely.

Snowy peaks stood in the distance. Overhead, wispy clouds blew by.

Mike recalled that he had proposed to Jennifer at Glacier Park. Where was the spot, exactly? Somewhere off the Going-to-the-Sun road, down by the river. She cried when he showed her the ring. She embraced him tightly, her tears falling onto his chest. It was mid-July, much warmer than it was today. They ran up the trail to the car and drove to the lodge, where they wasted no time in checking into their room. They made passionate love all afternoon.

"Keep up the pace, Mike."

Mike jogged, slipping once, to catch up with Seth. They continued the uphill hike until his feet felt numb. He stuffed a wad of tissue in his nose, which kept bleeding as they ascended. Finally, the trail leveled off. They turned right onto the trail and hiked up the gradual incline. Mike's boots and socks were soaked. He wondered, miserably, why they had gone on this chase. Axel must be long gone by now. By the time they made it back to the trailhead, the park rangers will have spotted Seth's car.

"Not far now," said Seth, leading the way.

As he walked, Mike examined the ground for signs of ski tracks. Nothing. What were they hoping to find, anyway? A thought hit Mike suddenly. The Nobel Prize could only be awarded to, at most, three people. They were down to Axel, Mike, Seth, and Oleg. Now, Seth had led him to a remote spot in Glacier Park. And he had the gun. *My God*, the thought, trembling, *was that why he seemed so nonchalant when I came to his house? Is that why he has such confidence now?* Seth had computer skills, especially when it came to networked systems. He could have hacked into the lab computer and programmed it to fire the lasers…

"What's wrong, Mike?"

Mike snapped out of it. "Nothing," he mumbled. "How much further?"

"We're there."

They jogged up to the summit and surveyed the area. Below them, they saw a brilliant blue lake dotted with chunks of ice. Behind it stood rocky peaks, carved in sharp relief by millennia of geological forces.

Seth quickly retrieved his binoculars and looked down at the lake. He focused them and staggered backward.

Mike squinted and saw a group of men. He took the binoculars from Seth, who seemed woozy. He looked through them and saw that the men were park rangers. They were using ropes to hoist a lifeless body from the lake. The body had a blue jacket. As the men pulled it out, it flopped to one side limply. Mike zoomed in on the corpse's head and gasped.

He dropped the binoculars and walked shakily back down the trail. He bent over and convulsed, racked by painful dry heaves.

"How could they?" he said, falling to his knees.

"I can't believe it," Seth said, stunned, his usual self-confidence gone. "I was sure…"

"How could they?" Mike repeated. "Did you see what they did to him?"

"We need to get back to the car," Seth said weakly, his face pale.

Mike's stomach felt like a bottomless pit. Finding Axel was the one goal that had kept him from total despair. He felt betrayed by Seth, who had proclaimed so confidently that Axel Hansen could not be killed. What nonsense. The only realistic thing to do now was to surrender to the authorities. Tell them the whole story and plead for mercy.

He stood up. As he pondered Axel's fate, he felt an intense sensation sweep over him. Inexorably, a feeling of pure, simmering rage displaced fear and uncertainty. Mike looked at Seth, who was muttering to himself, still baffled by how this could have happened.

"Seth," he said in an icy voice, "we need to find Hassan."

23

He ran down the trail, pumped with anger. Seth followed some distance behind him. Through his rage, Mike realized they should have confronted Hassan back at the lodge.

Hassan said he had *neutralized* Axel Hansen.

The arrogant bastard! He couldn't resist sticking in the knife. Like when he paid his surprise visit to the lab. His propensity to brag would be his weakness, Mike decided. He would find Hassan and put a gun to his head. Hassan would spill the beans, half out of fear but half out of arrogance, a desire to show how damned smart he was.

"Wait up," Seth called, out of breath.

They stumbled wildly down a steep, snowy part of the trail. Their new clothes were dirty and torn. Eventually they reached the parking lot.

"Give me the gun," Mike said, his face sweaty and grim.

Seth reached into his coat and handed over the Beretta. "Be careful, Mike."

"Let's go."

They got into the car. The windows fogged up instantly, so Seth rolled down the windows.

"Mike," he said as he started the ignition, "we need to think this through. Hassan has probably seen the news about me being a 'hostage.' He's not an idiot. I'm sure he put two and two together and called the cops."

"Drive."

Seth drove out of the small parking lot and onto the Going-to-the-Sun Road. He headed west, back toward the lodge.

"Did he mention his plans?" Mike asked.

"No. I have no idea where he is right now." He rolled the windows back up.

"We have to assume he's still at the lodge."

"We have to assume *park rangers* are waiting for us there."

Mike felt blood rush to his face. "I know you think you're a genius, Seth, but you were dead wrong about Axel."

Seth stared silently at the road.

"We're going back to the lodge," Mike said angrily. "If he's not there, we'll ask where the hell he went."

"Fine," Seth sighed, putting on his shades. He shifted into sixth gear and let the car accelerate smoothly around the bend. On their right, stone markers stood between the road and a sheer precipice.

Mike found strength in his newfound reservoir of anger. For years, Hassan had toyed with him the way a cat plays with a wounded rodent. Mike always tried to slink away, passively and quietly, hoping Hassan would move on to another victim. Those days were over. The thought of Axel Hansen–scientific visionary, government servant, and, if Seth was to be believed, NATO special ops soldier–killed by ruthless thugs… Yes, Mike drew courage from the searing rage inside him. Hassan would see the look in his eyes and know that Mike was not afraid to pull the trigger.

He knew Hassan was not acting alone. But he also knew that Hassan's arrogance would not allow him to keep quiet. Hassan would lead to the truth.

Mike and Seth suddenly inhaled. They both saw it. An oncoming white rental car passed them on the left. There was no mistaking the driver's mane of gray hair, his erect, regal posture.

"It's him," Mike breathed.

Seth pressed on the brakes. Seeing no one approaching, he

cranked on the steering wheel and the car spun around, wheels squealing against the road. He shifted into low gear and jolted forward with a burst of speed.

"Did he see us?" Mike asked.

"I don't think so."

They followed Hassan at a safe distance. Mike held the pistol grip firmly.

"See, Mike," Seth said, trying to sound upbeat. "Luck works both ways."

"Not for Axel and Jennifer. Stefan, Charles…" He clenched his jaw and faced the road ahead. "I won't let Hassan slither out of this one. He's gone too far, Seth."

"I know. Just don't do anything rash."

Gabrielle Sanchez opened her eyes at the sound of her phone ringing. She awoke instantly.

"Agent Sanchez."

After a moment, she said, "I see. Glacier? I'll meet you at Saint Mary. Have Stebbins take care of the west entrance."

She stood up and turned on the light in the small room. She opened the door and strode down the hall. Jon Patterson saw her approaching.

"I thought you'd be getting some rest," he said, trying to sound collegial.

"Glacier Park rangers received a call from Professor Hassan Zare, a scientist who is attending a workshop there. He reported seeing Seth Brenner this morning."

"What about Mike?"

She ignored the question and dialed her phone. "Carsen? I'll need to take off right away. Airport in five." She walked briskly toward the exit. Jon followed uncertainly. "No sign of Harris," she said without looking back. "I expect you to continue the investigation here."

Jon watched as she went out the door. "Yes ma'am," he said.

The passenger in the sport utility vehicle, a hard, muscular man with a buzz cut, watched the red Viper as it followed a white car up the Going-to-the-Sun Road. He looked through binoculars at the two cars as they climbed the mountainside. The driver was a fair-skinned woman with medium length black hair. She wore a sheer, long-sleeved white top covered by a black vest.

"They're following Zare," he said.

The woman spoke into a headset. "Central, they're definitely following him. Awaiting instructions." After a pause, she said, "Roger that."

"So what do we do?" the man asked.

"Improvise," she said.

"Is Harris armed?"

"Yes. He stole a 9mm Beretta."

The rear seats of the SUV were folded down to accommodate two aluminum-plated cases. The man reached back, opened a case, and looked inside. "Improvise," he said, and started to whistle.

24

Where do you think he's going?" Seth asked, keeping his eyes on the white car.

Mike's thoughts were elsewhere. He tried to keep his mind off revenge. Rationally, the best chance he had of preventing further bloodshed was to get information out of Hassan. To do that, he needed to be cold and calculating, even cruel, but he also had to keep his rage from boiling over. The temptation to inflict pain, to wipe the smirk off Hassan's pompous face, would be immense.

"His turn signal's on," Seth said, tapping on the brakes.

The white car slowed and turned left, toward a picnic area off the road. Seth pulled off to the right, keeping a distance of a hundred yards between him and the turnoff. Next to them, rivulets of water dripped down a rock wall and splattered onto muddy puddles on the ground.

They waited a couple minutes. Then Seth moved the Viper forward slowly. He turned into the picnic area and saw Hassan's car parked in the lot.

"Where is he?" Mike said.

"I don't know," Seth said, looking around.

He parked the car next to Hassan's. They got out, Mike holding the gun in plain sight. They saw several picnic tables in a grassy area overlooking the river, but there were no people at this early hour.

Seth motioned for Mike to follow him. He gestured toward a sign that pointed the way to a one-mile loop trail. They followed the trail, which led into a thick forest. The air was still and quiet, save for the burbling sounds of rapids in the background.

"Amazing, isn't it?" called a voice.

Twenty meters away, Hassan stepped out from behind a huge, moss covered boulder. He wore hiking boots and carried a map. Sunlight, filtered through the trees, made patterns of dark and light on his tall frame and leonine hair. He regarded the boulder clinically. "It's much taller than I, probably three meters high. How much would that weigh?"

Mike hid the gun behind his right leg and approached slowly.

"A volume of roughly twenty cubic meters," he said, rubbing his chin. "Density, about five metric tons per cubic meter. That makes one hundred tons. Geophysical processes pushed this hundred-ton rock from up *there*"–he pointed to the mountain range in the east–"all the way down *here*. The forces of nature dwarf us all."

Mike felt sweat drip from his brow. His heart pumped furiously, throbbing in his eardrums.

"I already notified the authorities," Hassan said casually, turning toward the two. "I gather Seth is not a 'hostage' as the media have claimed."

"We know what you did to Axel," Seth said. "Tell us the rest."

Hassan grinned. "Or what?"

Mike pointed the gun, his hand shaking. "Or I'll blow your fucking brains out," he spat, his eyes full of wild rage.

"Calm yourself," Hassan said, taking a step back. "There's no need for theatrics."

"Tell us, *now*," he said, pressing the gun to Hassan's cheek.

"Please," Hassan whispered, "remove that thing. You don't need to take another life."

"I'm innocent and you know it," he said, his hand shaking.

Hassan stared nervously at Mike's trigger finger. "If you say so."

After a tense few seconds, Mike pulled back the gun but kept it aimed at Hassan. "Go ahead."

"I'm not the only one," he said between short breaths. "There is a civil war going on, Mike, a war fought not in the open but in secret, in the highest echelons of government agencies. You know nothing of this, of course, but allow me distill this battle into its essential components."

"I'm listening."

"There are two sides. Each side has allies in Congress, the White House, and the vast defense-science complex. I am on one side. Axel was on the other."

"So you *neutralized* him," Seth said.

They all turned to the sound of footsteps approaching from the picnic area. A young couple with day packs stopped and stared, open-mouthed, at the scene.

"We were just leaving," said the man, a long-haired guy with a loose flannel shirt. He and his girlfriend held hands and scurried back up the trail.

Mike cursed. They were running out of time. "What the hell did you mean by *neutralized?*"

"He took your side. I'm sorry, Mike, but we could not let your research continue. Axel's influence had to be neutralized. Life is not fair."

Mike felt another jolt of anger. "So he, and everyone else, are just–collateral damage?"

Hassan stood up haughtily. "As in your research, Mike, you analyze this situation with an overabundance of simplicity." He gestured to the surroundings. "You lack a broad picture of the world. You don't even possess the security clearance required to understand what dangers lurk in the world's dark shadows. I do. I can tell you with absolute certitude that there exist dire threats to civilization that justify actions we would never consider in peacetime. Against the backdrop of such evil, the fates of Axel and others fade into insignificance."

Mike's body trembled. He felt he could pull the trigger at any moment. "Why Jennifer? She was innocent."

"You tell me, Mike," he replied, the corner of his mouth curling into a sardonic grin. "You're the one who killed her in a jealous–"

Mike slammed the gun against Hassan's face. Hassan staggered back and shook his head. He held his hand to the side of his head, feeling for blood. There was none.

"Jennifer confirmed what I already suspected," Hassan said. "I needed confirmation before approaching the Committee."

"What committee?"

Hassan stared at him defiantly, saying nothing.

"What did you need confirmation for?"

"Your little project," he said, regaining his arrogant smirk. "As a final test, I paid a visit to your laboratory at Podunk U. There was no doubt after that."

"So after you got the information you needed, you *neutralized* Jennifer and destroyed the lab."

"No."

"Then you killed Axel."

Hassan stared back at Mike. "What the hell are you talking about?"

"We saw Axel's body," Seth said, "at Grinnell."

A look of surprise registered on Hassan's face. "You're not serious."

"You admitted it," Mike said. "You're in a 'civil war.' Axel was collateral damage."

Hassan furrowed his brow, acting genuinely perplexed. "Axel was a naïve idealist. To be frank, he had no business in the arena of national security. Yes, I helped push him aside, and of that I am proud. But murder? You misjudge me."

"Don't play stupid."

"When I said 'neutralized,' I didn't mean…"

Hassan jerked to the side and collapsed to the ground, clutching his throat. Blood spilled onto his hands. Mike rushed to him and crouched down.

"What happened?" he yelled, panic rushing over him.

"Jason," Hassan wheezed, his face contorted in pain. Air escaped through a bloody hole in his thorax. "Go to…" he gasped, and his eyes rolled back.

Mike stood up. Seth barreled into him and they both collapsed onto a patch of ground next to the boulder. They heard a muffled shot. Mike grabbed his gun off the ground.

"Over there!" Seth pointed.

He peeked around the edge of the boulder and saw a black outline in the foliage. He aimed and fired.

"Run back to the car," Mike said. "I'll cover you."

Seth looked at him uncertainly. He took a breath and scrambled up the trail, hopping over Hassan's body. Mike fired wildly into the trees. He caught a glimpse of the shooter, a man with a large rifle. The muzzle flashed and the round exploded into the boulder. Mike knew he couldn't hit the man at this distance. He sprinted after Seth. He heard the Viper's engine start. He ran up the gentle slope to the parking lot and saw the red car with the passenger door open. He tumbled inside and slammed the door. Seth pressed on the accelerator and the car vaulted forward, tires squealing. He jerked the steering wheel. Abruptly, the car spun around and drove onto the Going-to-the-Sun Road.

Mike could barely hear his own voice above the roar of the engine and his own heartbeat. "He let me escape!" he shouted.

"What?" Seth shouted back, shifting into high gear.

"They're setting me up," he said, looking nervously at the rearview mirror. "That guy could've taken me out."

"He *would* have if I didn't knock you out of the way. You're welcome, by the way."

They drove up the road, toward the pass. The road curved around a precipitous mountain.

"What did he say?" Seth asked.

"Before he–" Mike felt sick to his stomach. Was Hassan innocent? It seemed impossible. "Before Hassan died, he said something about 'Jason.'"

A look of understanding registered on Seth's face. "Of course."

"Who is Jason?"

They saw an oncoming SUV. Mike caught a brief glimpse of the driver, a woman with a long-sleeved shirt and black vest. She suddenly swerved into their lane. Seth yelled hoarsely and slammed on the brakes. The broad side of the SUV rushed toward them. The road seemed impossibly narrow. On their left, a sheer drop to the valley below. On their right, a rock wall. Seth chose the rock wall. The Viper's right tires rode up onto the rock, tilting the car like a nauseating roller coaster. The black SUV sped past. Its metal scraped the left side of the Viper with a piercing shriek. Seth turned left, back onto the road, but that made the car tilt even more. Mike felt sure they would flip over. Seth corrected and the right side of the car landed with a thud. He nearly hit the rock wall before finally straightening their trajectory.

Mike turned back and saw the SUV behind them. The Viper hugged the road as ten cylinders pushed it furiously around a bend.

"Seth, slow down."

"I don't think so."

Mike looked in the rearview mirror. "You're going to kill us if you go any faster."

Seth ignored the advice and accelerated as they emerged from the bend. The car shot up the mountain road. Mike's head spun from the combined effects of vertigo and the shock of Hassan's death.

Seth was intent on putting miles of road between them and the SUV. He turned sharply around another bend, which ended in a straight, level path with a sweeping view of the valley. An object caught his eye.

Mike felt a fresh jolt of fear. A helicopter hovered in the air, a speck in the distance, at roughly the same altitude as the road. Slowly, it turned to face them.

25

The man with the buzz cut looked both ways before running into the road. A second SUV was waiting for him. He threw his rifle in the back and got inside.

"How did it go?" asked the driver, a gray-haired man with steely eyes and a trim gray beard.

"We got lucky," Buzz Cut said. "We should be able to wrap this up in time for lunch."

"Just follow the plan," the driver said, frowning.

"Fine by me, chief." He retrieved his binoculars and peered ahead.

The driver spoke into a headset briefly. "All right," he said to Buzz Cut. "She's in position."

"Slow down, Seth," Mike said in a quavering voice.

The white helicopter approached the mountainside. It hovered about a quarter mile ahead of them.

"We need to keep going," Seth said. His knuckles were white and his face was pale.

A trail of smoke streaked from the helicopter, followed by an explosion on the rock wall. Rocks tumbled down and crashed onto the road, shattering into pieces and falling off the sheer face on the other side.

Seth swerved to miss a large boulder and slid into the rock wall, shattering the window on Mike's side. They continued moving forward. A rock lodged itself between the front of the car and the road, making a horrible grinding noise as they spun out of control. The car bumped against a barrier that stopped them from plummeting down the sheer face. Seth put the clutch in reverse and slammed on the pedal. The rear tires spun rapidly, burning rubber, sending rock and dust into the air. After an agonizing pause, the car broke free of the boulder and jerked backward.

They drove up the road. The helicopter shadowed them. Mike looked through Seth's window and saw lettering on the side of the helicopter: GLACIER ECO-TOURS. A man aimed a large black cylinder out the open side door.

"Look out!" Mike shouted, and they both ducked.

A projectile hit the front of the car. Intense blue arcs of electricity shot out from the point of impact, enveloping the engine. They heard a small explosion–perhaps the battery–and smoke escaped from the edges of the hood. The dashboard lights flickered brilliantly and died.

Seth pressed the accelerator in vain as the car slowed down. "The spark plugs are toast," he said. "I need to find a turn-off."

"Just stop here," Mike said.

"I don't have much choice."

He stopped the car. The road was narrow, with no breakdown lane. Mike reached for the door handle.

Before he could open the door, the SUV roared up from behind them and rammed them forward.

"Dammit!" Seth yelled, turning back to see the black SUV. "What's her problem?"

He pressed on the brakes. Mike fumbled with the gun and looked back in time to see the SUV rush forward. It bashed the right corner of the rear bumper, sending them skidding across the road.

Mike tried to open the door but it was damaged and refused to yield. He pointed the gun and shot through the small rear window. He heard the loud report, followed by ringing, and the rear window disintegrated. The bullet made a small divot in the SUV's windshield, far left of the driver. The SUV rammed them again. The impact sent the Viper crashing into the stone barrier. Mike slammed his upper arm and shoulder against the door, which started to budge. He pushed it again, furiously, and it swung open. He tumbled onto the ground.

He scrambled to his feet. He saw the SUV crash into the car, which lurched forward. Its front tires slid off the edge of the cliff and the car tilted downward. Seth pounded on his door. As the SUV backed up, Mike ran to the driver side. His ears still rang painfully. He saw the woman, a determined look in her face, as she prepared to accelerate forward again. He aimed the pistol and emptied it into the side of the door. The SUV stopped.

Mike tossed the spent gun onto the ground and ran to the crumpled Viper. The car balanced on a pivot point just behind the front tires. Seth sat motionless, his foot planted on the brake pedal. Like the rest of the car, the door was thoroughly bent out of shape.

"Is the door stuck?" Mike yelled.

Seth nodded.

Mike walked over to the passenger side, where the door was open. "Seth, you're going to have to crawl over to my side. Keep your weight toward the rear of the car."

Seth slowly engaged the emergency brake and took his foot off the pedal. Through the cracked windshield, he saw the valley, hundreds of feet below. As sweat dripped from his forehead, he unbuckled his seat belt and slowly pushed himself back. The car responded, sliding a few inches downward. Seth held his breath.

"All right," Mike said, trying to sound confident. "I'm going to push down on the trunk, to keep the car from tipping over."

Seth nodded silently.

Mike walked to the rear and put both hands on the trunk. The rear tires were suspended a few inches off the road. He pressed downward and felt the delicately balanced car respond.

"Okay, Seth…"

"Turn around," said a female voice behind him.

Mike looked over his shoulder, keeping his hands on the

trunk. He saw the woman in a black vest. She held a submachine gun.

"What do you want?" Mike asked.

"Put your hands in the air," she said coldly.

Mike gradually released the pressure on the trunk and put his hands in the air. The trunk tilted upward and the car slid down a few more inches. Inside, Seth crawled toward the passenger door.

"I don't understand," Mike said, unable to conceal the fear from his voice. "What do you people want? I can give you information, if that's what you're after."

"I'm not here to negotiate," she said. She had thin, colorless lips, fair complexion, dark hair, and athletic body. "Get inside the SUV."

He felt a glimmer of hope. If she had wanted to kill him, surely she would have done it already. He opened the front passenger door and got inside. The woman pressed on a remote control and he heard the doors lock. He fiddled with the door controls but couldn't unlock it. He saw the woman walk to the Viper. Swiftly, she put her boot to the rear and gave it a kick.

"No!" Mike shouted.

The rear of the Viper lifted into the air. The car slid rapidly across the rocky edge, the rear tires bumping off the lip and sending the car tumbling, end over end, down the sheer cliff face. The front of the car smashed into the ground, compressing like an accordion. Both doors blew open as the remaining windows shattered. The fuel tank ignited, erupting in a thunderous orange fireball. Birds scattered from the trees near the impact as the resinous pines caught fire.

Mike pounded desperately on the door. He watched in a panic as the woman walked toward him. She pressed a button on the remote with her left hand and the door popped open. She dropped the remote and held the submachine gun firmly. "It would have been more convenient, Professor Harris, if you had gone with your colleague. Now I'll have to dispose of your body."

"You didn't have to do it," he said, feeling a new wave of anger and fear. "Seth never hurt anyone."

"He knew too much."

"What do you want from me?" Mike implored. "Surely there must be something."

"Just your silence." She aimed the gun. He saw the look in her eyes and knew the discussion was over.

A rock slammed the back of her head. The gun fell out of her hands as she lurched into the vehicle. Seth wrestled her from behind and threw her onto the road. Mike grabbed the gun and stumbled out the door.

"Who are you?" he yelled, aiming the gun at her head. "Who sent you?"

The woman looked at him with unfocused eyes. She stood up abruptly and her hand slipped into her vest. With startling speed, she pulled out a pistol. Mike squeezed the trigger on the submachine gun. A bullet tore the vest fabric, revealing Kevlar beneath. Blood stained the upper left sleeve of her sheer white top. She fired the pistol with her right hand. The bullet missed Mike and ricocheted off the armored surface of the SUV.

Mike fired another round, blasting away the bottom of her face. Blood gushed through her shattered jaw, soaking her shirt, spilling onto the ground. She recoiled backward and fell off the cliff. Her body collided limply against rocks, tumbling down, down like a rag doll, before disappearing into the fiery blaze that raged around the remains of the Viper.

Seth scooped the remote off the ground. "Can you ride shotgun?"

Mike nodded, stunned.

"I need to figure out how this thing works," Seth said. He stared at the black device, the size of a handheld video game, with an array of nine buttons. He pushed one and the open door suddenly swung shut, followed by the sound of locking doors. "Oops."

"The shooter," Mike said, looking down the narrow road. "He'll come after us."

"Don't be negative. Let's see…" he pressed another button, then the one he pushed before. Nothing happened.

Mike tried to open a door, without success. "We need to get moving, Seth."

"Let's try that one." The engine shut off. He pushed the button that he had tried before and the engine restarted. "I think I'm getting it."

Mike looked up fearfully. "Seth, I hear the helicopter."

Seth stopped and listened. They both heard it now. The sound was getting louder.

Seth pressed two buttons at once and the driver door popped open. "Jackpot."

Mike didn't wait for him to figure out how to open the other door. Clutching the submachine gun, he climbed over to the passenger side. The helicopter appeared from behind the steep mountain face, curving in a tight arc. Seth rushed inside and slammed the door. He pressed on the pedal and they barreled forward. The helicopter overtook them and fired a volley at the mountain face, sending an avalanche of rocks spilling onto the road.

"There you go again," Seth said, weaving around the rocks. The front tires hit two simultaneously and the SUV lifted upward; the rear tires followed suit. They cleared the rocks and accelerated up the road. The helicopter rose higher, out of sight.

"It's above us," Mike said.

"Shoot it."

Mike flipped a switch on the door and the window opened. He poked his head outside and looked up. The helicopter was above them, maybe a hundred feet.

"Can you hit it?"

"I don't know," Mike replied. *I've never tried to shoot a helicopter.* He crawled out the open window and held on to the roof rack with one hand. With the other, he tried to aim the gun. *Should I lead the helicopter? We're both traveling at the same speed, but air resistance…* He fired randomly at the helicopter, hoping to hit something. After shooting a dozen rounds, he crawled back into the SUV.

"It's hopeless," he said, shaking his head. "I'm not trained for this."

"Think positive," Seth said.

He slowed down as they approached a bend. They turned to the right and went over Logan Pass. Mike thought of how he had seen Axel's body, through the binoculars, and how his death changed everything.

Mike looked in the back of the SUV. The seats were folded down to make room for two large, aluminum-plated cases. He set his gun down and crawled back.

"What are you doing?" asked Seth.

"There's some stuff here," he mumbled. He opened one case but it was empty. He opened the second case. Inside, there was a long black weapon that looked like a rifle with a harpoon protruding from the barrel.

Seth tried to look up at the helicopter. He could hear it but not see it. "Did you find anything?"

Mike crawled to the front seat. "I don't know what this thing does."

"My friend," Seth said as they turned a sharp corner, "now would be a good time to find out."

Mike held the large rifle and stuck his head out the open window. His hair whipping in the wind, he looked up.

"Stop!" he yelled.

Seth slammed on the brakes. The SUV shuddered as the antilock system engaged. As they decelerated, the helicopter moved into view. A projectile exploded in front of them, radiating fluorescent, whitish blue sparks. Mike lifted the heavy rifle and aimed at a point slightly above the helicopter.

He squeezed the trigger. The harpoon launched into the air, pushed forward by a fiery propellant. It remained connected to the rifle by a thin cable that uncoiled rapidly. The cable went taut and a net of thin black fibers shot forth from the harpoon's tip. The fibers rapidly became entangled in the tail rotor. Mike felt a sharp tug as the rifle leapt from his grip, throwing off his balance. He shouted as he swayed away from the SUV. Seth jerked the car to the right, the sudden acceleration setting Mike straight again. Mike scrambled back in through the open window.

Ahead of them, they saw the helicopter's tail rotor, caught in the web of fibers, grind to a halt. The helicopter began to rotate, slow at first and then faster, out of control. It descended and crashed onto the narrow road, bending the skids. Seth pressed on the brakes but it was too late. Mike caught a glimpse of a gunman struggling to open the door as the SUV bumped the helicopter, sending it sliding to the edge of the road. Slowly, it tipped over the edge, metal and glass striking the rocks as it tumbled down the steep slope, becoming more crumpled with each impact.

Seth drove down the road, his brow drenched with sweat. From the corner of his eye, he saw a brilliant flash as the helicopter ignited.

26

Minutes later, Mike still checked the rearview mirror, fearing that Hassan's killers might be pursuing them. He knew they could not afford to relax.

"Who are these people?" he asked in a hoarse voice.

"I don't know, exactly."

"What do you mean, *exactly*?"

Seth tapped on the brakes as they approached a curve. "Hassan told us something."

"You mean before he died. He mentioned someone named 'Jason.' Who's Jason?"

"Not who. *What.*"

"What do you mean, *what*?"

"You of all people should know."

Mike grimaced. Here they were, only moments after evading death, and Seth was back to telling riddles.

"C'mon, Mike. JASON. All caps. Do I need to spell it out for you?"

Mike's jaw dropped. "You're not serious," he said. But he knew it could be true.

* * *

The yellow and blue seaplane flew in from the west, framed by rocky snow-capped peaks that made it look like a small insect in the sky. It descended at a good clip, approaching a glassy lake. After a minute, it splashed down, sending a wake rippling across the smooth, cold water. The propeller whined as it pulled the seaplane toward a small dock. Several men ran onto the dock to meet the plane. They wore black windbreakers with yellow lettering: FBI.

The door opened and Agent Sanchez stepped out.

"What's the status?"

A man with sunglasses and brown hair spoke. "Hassan Zare was the Harvard prof who called the park rangers to report the location of Seth Brenner."

"And?"

"Professor Zare was just found dead, a single 9mm round to the neck."

"Was Harris involved?"

"Yes."

They stepped off the dock and walked to a waiting Jeep. Agent Sanchez and the man got into the back seats. Another agent and a driver sat in front. The driver started the engine and they drove rapidly along a dirt road.

"A couple of hikers called the rangers. They saw two men matching the descriptions of Brenner and Harris. Harris was pointing a gun at Zare. The hikers managed to flee the scene. By the time the rangers arrived, Zare was dead."

"Have there been any reports of…"

"Hold on, ma'am."

The man listened to his earphone. As he listened, his expression became grim.

"Automobile accident near the Going-to-the-Sun Road," he said. "Red Dodge Viper."

"Any survivors?"

"No. There's one body, burned. The crash site is still too hot for an ID."

The man listened for a few more seconds. "There are reports that a tourist helicopter crashed, same area. Witnesses heard shots before it went down."

"Was that before or after the car crash?"

"Not sure. After, I think."

"He's out of control," Sanchez said clinically. "His state of mind is degenerating. This rampage will continue until he's stopped, one way or another."

The dirt road merged with a paved, two-lane road. They drove along the road, the placid lake to their left. The FBI agents in front scanned the area.

"I want amended rules of engagement from headquarters. We need deadly-force authorization."

"I'll call it in."

As they drove along the Going-to-the-Sun road, Mike pondered what Seth had said about JASON.

Mike knew about the secret society, founded in 1959 to advise the government on scientific matters vital to national security. Every year, the members met in a secure location and produced classified reports for DARPA, DOE, CIA, and FBI. Who the members were, exactly, was not public knowledge. Even the origin of the name JASON was a mystery. Some claimed that it came from the biblical story of Jason and the Golden Fleece. Others speculated that the letters stood for the months when the secret meetings took place.

It made sense that Hassan was a member–he was a well-connected scientist who worked on high intensity lasers. The military applications resulting from that line of research were obvious. He recalled Hassan's explanation for why he called Jennifer and later paid a visit to Mike's lab. Hassan needed confirmation before approaching the "Committee."

The Committee, Mike surmised, must reside within JASON. According to Hassan, they were in the middle of a civil war: one side was trying to kill the project while another side was trying to keep it alive. Hassan wanted to verify the project's true goal before making his case to the Committee.

Mike told Seth what he was thinking. "Hassan must have met with the Committee right after he visited my lab. The Committee must be *here*."

"Perhaps," Seth replied skeptically. "But they could have just as easily met electronically."

"Regardless, it sounds like the Committee, whoever they are, made the final decision. They decided to kill the project."

"They killed more than the project."

Mike felt queasy as he thought of what they were up against. Just yesterday, he dismissed the idea of a government conspiracy as a paranoid delusion. Now he wasn't so sure.

"What do we do?" he asked weakly.

"Avoid the federal government."

"You sound like Paul Quinlan."

"Think about it," Seth said. "This conspiracy involves the feds. We know that now. We need to get out of this *national* park and turn ourselves over to the state authorities."

"State, federal, what's the difference?" Mike protested.

"I seriously doubt the Montana Highway Patrol is in on this. If we surrender to them, at least we'll have time to call lawyers and alert the media before the feds swoop in."

Mike felt the onset of a headache and tried to ignore it. "How long will it take?"

"We're almost at St. Mary Lake. After that, it should only take fifteen minutes to reach the east exit."

"Okay," he said, rubbing his temples. "I'm tired of running."

The van parked in front of a large house in the Oakland hills. James stepped out and opened the rear doors. Jarrod squinted into the sunlight, dark circles under his bloodshot eyes. He had spent the night locked in the back of the van, drifting off to sleep a few times only to wake in a panic. In the morning, they asked him for his handler's contact information. He gave it to them, of course. Given the state he was in, he would have told them anything.

He walked unsteadily up stone steps, past Eucalyptus trees and an electric car parked in the driveway. James and two men walked behind him. He reached the door and pressed the buzzer with a trembling finger. A moment later, he heard footsteps. A man in his late thirties with jet black hair, dressed in jeans and a

T-shirt, answered the door.

"I'm sorry," Jarrod blurted, "these guys made me come here."

The man looked at James uncertainly. "Are you FBI?"

"No. Are you Kevin Larson?"

"That's what my mailbox says."

"You're the head of the Anti-Globalization Alliance?"

"There is no 'head,' no 'leader,' 'el presidente,' et cetera, so obviously the answer to your question is *no*."

James stared at Kevin with steely eyes. "Jarrod, get lost."

Jarrod walked cautiously down the steps, eyes darting around. When he reached the street, he sprinted away from the van and down the hill.

"What do you guys want?"

"We want to do business."

Kevin regarded James skeptically. "Tell your friends to wait in the van."

James nodded and the two men walked back to the van.

"Okay, look," Kevin said, "you're obviously FBI or CIA, so let's cut the crap. The AGA is not a terrorist organization. We post stuff on the web, that's it. I thought it would be cool if the SUVs at Union City Ford got firebombed. So, I put my opinion–not an order, not even a suggestion–but just my opinion, on the AGA site. 'If someone firebombed those SUVs, oil dependency would be reduced and lives would be saved.' If you disagree with me, then fine, start a right-wing web site. No one was more surprised than I when some idealistic individual did the deed. So, I crossed Union City Ford right off the list."

"That's very convenient," James said.

"If you want to arrest me for standing up to the corporations, be my guest. I have a good lawyer." He held up his wrists.

"I told you, I'm not law enforcement. I represent a benefactor who wishes to donate to your cause."

Kevin put down his hands. "Donate? As in, cash?"

"Of course. Unless you're a terrorist organization..."

"I already told you we're not. We put stuff on the web. That's it."

"I want you to put something on your web site." James

reached into his coat pocket and pulled out a piece of paper. "The address of a warehouse for a sweatshop in East Asia that manufactures clothing for a global retail chain. Hours are long and unions are banned."

James handed the paper to Kevin, who looked at it thoughtfully.

"I don't get it," he said after a minute. "Most supporters don't come to my place dressed in Brooks Brothers."

"Post that address on your site. You will not be disappointed." He reached into his pocket again and this time retrieved an envelope, which he gave to Kevin.

"Well," Kevin said, looking at the hundred-dollar bills in the envelope, "in case you're wired, let me just say this for the record. First, I thank you for your cash donation. Second, I am not condoning any illegal acts."

"Of course," James said. "There's more where this came from."

Jon Patterson stepped into the disheveled office and was greeted by a humid wave of body odor. Harry sat, his jowls adorned with the beginnings of a gray beard, hunched over a program manual.

"I got the data from CART," he said without looking up.

"CART?"

"Computer Analysis and Response Team. FBI, down in San Diego. They were able to partially reconstruct about thirty percent of the sectors. Not bad for hard-drive flambeaux."

Harry gazed at his computer screen, which displayed columns of alphanumeric characters. "I was able to get some fragments of the data acquisition and control program."

"The one that controlled the experiment?"

"Yep. I compared the fragments to the original code. The fragments match, mostly, but there are some differences."

Jon looked around the office, at the stacks of manuals, electronic gadgets, and computers in various stages of repair. "Mutations?"

"Yeah, something like that." He held up the program manual. "The problem is, I only have the original code for version 2.0, and they were running 2.2. The differences in the code might just be the upgrades in the new version."

"What's the company?"

"They're a little outfit in Menlo Park called Silicon Research Systems."

"Get version 2.2," Jon said firmly. "If they give you any crap, I'll give them a call."

"Okay, Chief," Harry said, as he wheeled his squeaky chair over to the telephone.

27

As they approached the park exit, Seth squinted his eyes and cursed.

"What's wrong?" Mike asked, worried.

"Park rangers. It looks like they're searching cars."

He pulled off to the side of the road. The park exit was a hundred meters away. They saw two park ranger vehicles parked by the kiosk. A family waited while a ranger examined their SUV.

"This is not good."

Seth stepped out of the automobile and looked around.

"What are you doing?"

"Thinking," he said. He looked toward the exit, blocking the sun with one hand. He resembled a befuddled tourist.

"We'll have to turn ourselves in," Mike said, rubbing his forehead.

A sedan pulled up beside them and stopped. The driver cut the ignition. Mike slowly grasped the submachine gun.

The driver opened the door and stepped out of the sedan.

"Hey guys!"

It was Valerie Norton. She wore large khaki hiking shorts, a fanny pack, glasses with flip-up shades, and a Glacier Park T-shirt. White sunscreen covered her nose. The afternoon when she visited his lab seemed to be from another lifetime.

"This is so cool! I mean, what are the odds?"

Mike and Seth stared at her, dumbstruck.

"Isn't this beautiful? You're here for that meeting, right?" Suddenly, her face went from cheerful to somber. "Oh, and I really am sorry about that lab accident. Just this morning, I was thinking, I hope it wasn't my fault."

Mike thought, *she hasn't heard that I'm the prime suspect.*

"It wasn't, right?"

"Wasn't what?" Mike said.

"My fault. The lab… fire? I can't bring myself to watch TV. I came here to escape, actually."

"No," Seth said. "It wasn't your fault, dear. It was just one of those random space-time coincidences. Like our meeting, here and now."

"Wow," she said, walking around her car. She approached Seth. Mike awkwardly concealed the gun beneath his legs. "You guys look like you've been wrestling grizzly bears. What happened?"

"You could say we came here to escape, too," Seth said.

"Escape what?" she asked, her curious eyes magnified by thick lenses.

"The media," Mike blurted. "You're right not to watch television."

"They're animals," Seth said, "a real pack of wolves. No offense to wolves."

Mike saw the park rangers in the distance, one of whom was watching them through binoculars.

"Valerie," he said, "I think you'd better do something with your car."

"Right." She walked to the car and stopped. "Oh my word. I'm such an idiot."

"What's wrong?" Seth asked, touching her arm gently.

"Locked the keys in the car." She thumped her forehead with her hand, getting sunscreen from her nose onto her wrist. "This is really not my day. Do you guys know how to pick locks?"

"No," Mike said, his jaw clenched.

"Can I bum a ride, just to St. Mary? There's a locksmith

there, I'm sure…"

She tried to open the rear passenger door of the SUV but it was locked.

"That door doesn't work," Seth said. "Climb in through my door."

Mike gave Seth a look of sharp disapproval as she climbed in.

"Nice ride you got here," she said. "When did you get it?"

"Practically yesterday," Seth said, while Mike kept his legs pressed together to hide the gun.

Seth accelerated slowly. At the entrance gate, two park rangers were watching them. One of them spoke into his radio.

"It's over, Seth," Mike said.

"What's over?" Valerie asked distractedly, checking out the view.

"You really haven't watched TV or listened to the radio?"

"I didn't come to Glacier Park to…"

A van squealed to a stop behind them. Mike turned and saw men in black body armor pile out. They carried shotguns. Several more gunmen, camouflaged, emerged from the woods.

Seth put his foot on the brake and held his hands in the air. Mike put his hands up, too.

"What the heck is going on?" Valerie screamed.

"Calm down," Mike said, his voice tired and weak. "Just don't do anything sudden."

A black SUV roared past the kiosk and stopped fifty yards in front of them. Three men stepped out, followed by a woman in a business suit. One of the men handed the woman a bullhorn.

"Mike Harris, I'm Agent Sanchez, FBI. I'd like to have a conversation with you. First, let the hostages go."

"You heard her," Mike said. "Get out of the car."

Seth and Valerie sat in tense silence.

"Forget it," said Seth, his hands still in the air.

"We're surrounded. We don't have a choice. It's over. We'll have to take our chances..."

Valerie pounded on the window of her door. "What the heck is wrong? The door is locked!"

"Stop it," Mike said. "We told you that door doesn't work."

"*Unlock the door*!" she yelled, hysterical, pounding on the window.

Mike whirled around angrily. "Dammit, will you stop…"

A loud *crack, crack, crack* punctuated the air. Mike inhaled as he saw bullet holes appear in the windshield–except that they weren't holes, they were spots where the glass absorbed the shock of incoming rounds. Seth pressed on the accelerator. They lunged forward, a volley of bullets sounding like a hailstorm. They sped past the FBI's SUV and the kiosk, blowing through the gate. Sirens blared as the vehicles took up pursuit. In the back, Valerie maintained a continuous scream.

"See what I mean?" Seth said, eyes wide. "We need to get away from the feds!"

"Letting *her* in the car didn't help!"

Seth cranked the steering wheel as they rounded a bend. Mike looked out the open window of his passenger door and saw the van behind them. He grabbed the submachine gun and fired at the van's tires.

"What are you doing?" Valerie shouted.

Mike ducked back inside just as an FBI agent returned fire. Seth slowed down as they came up behind a large flatbed truck piled with lumber. The van stayed close behind. The road straightened; in the distance, they saw a semi in the opposite lane.

Mike saw the look in Seth's eyes. "Careful," he said.

"Almost there…"

"What–the *heck*–are you doing?" Valerie said.

"Almost there…"

Seth pressed on the accelerator and swerved into the left lane. The approaching semi honked and flashed its lights. They sped past the logging truck, leaving the van behind. The semi got closer. Mike felt his stomach drop as Valerie screamed. At the last moment, Seth veered into the right lane, cutting off the logging truck, which honked loudly in reply.

The semi driver had slammed on the brakes, and now the rig started to jackknife. The logging truck reacted, turning sharply to the right. The rigs' brakes screeched loudly. The semi's trailer collided with the flatbed of the logging truck, sending logs tumbling onto the road. The FBI van tried to turn but plowed into a rolling log, its driver ducking quickly as a second log smashed through the windshield.

Seth drove at a frightening speed, leaving the pileup behind them.

"We need to turn ourselves in," Mike said.

"I know," Seth said, scanning the horizon, "but not to the FBI."

He turned onto a dirt road that wound through wooded hills.

They drove for a few minutes of relative quiet, the tires kicking up thick clouds of dust.

"What the heck is going on?" Valerie asked, breaking the silence.

Seth turned on the radio.

"…visitors are warned that Michael Harris is armed and extremely dangerous. Harris is described as medium build, five foot ten, brown hair, wearing jeans and a T-shirt. Authorities believe he is driving a stolen black sport utility vehicle and has at least one hostage. They are asking anyone with information to call 911. To repeat our top story, Michael Harris is now a suspect in at least two murders, possibly more, and is currently at large, believed to be in Glacier Park…"

He turned it off. Valerie's pale complexion seemed to whiten further.

"Maybe I should get out now."

"I'm not who they say I am," Mike said. "It's a long story."

"We're going to surrender," Seth said, looking at her in the rearview mirror. "But first we need to get away from the FBI."

"Why?"

He pointed at the bullet-pocked windshield.

"Mike's got his problems," Seth said, "but he's not a murderer. The federal government is trying to frame him and suppress our research."

"The laser stuff?" she asked, curious. "I thought you said it was basic research."

"It is," Mike said, annoyed by Seth's comment.

"Explain it to me again," she said, apparently transforming

from a scared hostage to an eager student.

Seth summarized the ideas behind the experiment. High-power lasers blasted a piece of silicon, creating excitons within the solid. The density of excitons increased until something amazing happened: their energy created a gravitational field. The gravitational field would tug on the crystal, warping it in a way that they could measure with laser interferometry.

"At least," Mike interjected, "that's how it was supposed to work."

"You never told me that bit about the gravitational field," she noted.

"That was our secret," he said. "Had we succeeded, it would have been… well, huge. It would have unified quantum mechanics, light, and gravity."

"Until someone blew up your lab. Was it a competitor?"

"That's what I thought," Mike said, "at first." He told her about Hassan Zare and Axel Hansen, and how both were killed in Glacier Park. Hassan's last words pointed to JASON, a secretive group of scientists who advised the government on national security. Apparently, a smaller group within JASON, the *Committee*, had made a final decision: the project must be terminated.

"I don't get it," she said. "I mean, no offense, but why would they care? It's a cool experiment, sure. But murder? Cover up?"

"Good questions," Mike said, staring out the window at the thick evergreen forest. "I wish I had the answers."

After a minute, he looked at Seth, who had a smug look on his face.

"What?" Mike asked.

"You still don't get it," he said.

"Get what?"

"The true aim of the project. I've been trying to tell you, but you won't listen."

"The 'true aim'? I think I know the true aim of the project."

"Okay," Seth replied, and the smug look reappeared, amplified. "If you say so."

Mike stared out the window again, peeved at Seth's cryptic arrogance. The presence of a woman only encouraged his tendency to act like a know-it-all.

"So it wasn't just basic science?" Valerie ventured. "Grand unification of fundamental forces?"

"Of course not," he scoffed. "The 'D' in DARPA stands for Defense."

"Out with it," Mike grumbled.

"You really don't know?" Seth asked in a disappointed tone. "After all these years?"

Mike continued looking out the window.

Seth turned back to Valerie. "Do you know what a black hole is?"

"Yeah… sort of."

"We were about to make one."

28

Mike's head whirled like it had been slapped. "That's ludicrous!" he shouted.

Seth smiled broadly, enjoying Mike's response. "My calculations proved it. There's no doubt. A few nanoseconds after the laser pulse strikes the silicon, the high exciton density initiates a nonlinear process, causing a runaway mass accretion that inevitably culminates in a space-time singularity."

"Well *that* explains it," Valerie snorted.

"He's bullshitting," Mike said, annoyed but a little intrigued. "Don't listen to him."

"At least tell me what a black hole is."

"It's an astrophysical object," Mike said, "not something you create in a laboratory." He recalled how he explained it to his Modern Physics students. A star experienced two forces that balanced each other, gravity and nuclear fusion. Fusion occurred when atoms of hydrogen were squeezed into helium, liberating huge amounts of energy. That energy radiated outward and made the star shine. Just as important, the pressure generated by nuclear fusion pushed against gravity, keeping the star from imploding.

Eventually, though, the nuclear fuel would run out. When

that happened, gravity would squeeze the star's core into a cold, dense object the size of a city. This object, called a neutron star, was held together by the Pauli Exclusion Principle, a kind of force that made particles like neutrons repel each other. A neutron star was extraordinarily dense–a teaspoonful of a neutron star would be so heavy, it would tunnel straight through the earth.

If the mass of the neutron star was sufficiently large, then something else happened. The Pauli Exclusion Principle broke down. No force in nature could resist the gravitational collapse. The star contracted until it vanished utterly, into an infinitesimal point called a singularity. The gravitational field from the massive singularity warped space so profoundly, objects that ventured too close got sucked in, never to return. Even photons of light could not escape the bond; hence the name, *black hole.* If any particle wandered past the event horizon–the radius that defined the black hole–it was history. Nothing could recover it, ever.

"We can 'see' black holes because they bend light," Mike said. "Light from a star behind a black hole is tugged by the gravitational field. This gravitational lensing effect warps the image of background stars. But making a black hole in the lab? Well, let's just say that Seth has an active imagination."

Seth drove into a deserted campsite and screeched to a stop. "We need to ditch the car," he said. "It may have a GPS transponder."

They stepped out onto the dusty road. A thick pine forest surrounded them.

"Where are we?" Valerie asked.

"Middle of nowhere," Seth said, looking at a map. "There's a town a couple miles down this road."

They walked swiftly for a few minutes in silence. Valerie seemed unconcerned that she was traveling with fugitives.

"No signal," she said, looking at her cell phone.

"Like I said," Seth replied, patting her shoulder. "Middle of nowhere."

Mike groaned. They were in mortal danger and Seth couldn't keep his hands off Valerie.

"So Seth," Mike said, "humor me. How exactly were we going to create a black hole?"

"It's all about energy density," he said. He turned to Valerie. "Einstein showed us the way when he wrote $E=mc^2$. Energy and mass are interchangeable. If you create a point of high *energy* density, it'll have a gravitational field just like a point of high *mass* density."

The dirt road turned to gravel. They saw a sign that read CHESTER–½ MILE. The area was quiet, with the sounds of insects and birds but no automobiles or people.

"What Seth isn't telling you," Mike said, "is that *c squared* is a huge number. A tiny amount of mass is equivalent to a huge amount of energy. You would have to produce enormous energies to create any measurable gravity."

"True. But with isotopically pure silicon, the sharpness of the excitonic resonance is such that…"

"Hold on," Valerie protested. "What's iso–pure–?"

"Isotopically pure," Mike said. "Most silicon crystals, like those in computer chips, have different isotopes of silicon–atoms that are chemically identical but with slightly different masses. Natural silicon contains a mixture of silicon-28, silicon-29, and silicon-30."

In the old Soviet Union, Mike explained, nuclear laboratories separated the various isotopes for every element, from hydrogen to uranium and beyond. After the Cold War ended, they had shelves filled with the stuff. Scientists from the West collaborated with the Russians and produced new materials composed of pure isotopes. These materials had surprising properties. Pure silicon-28, a silicon crystal that was depleted of silicon-29 and silicon-30, exhibited spectral features that were much sharper than those of natural silicon. The sharp excitonic lines enabled Mike's lasers to produce high energy densities in the crystal.

"Oleg sent us the wrong crystal," Mike said, "a mixture of silicon-28 and silicon-30 instead of pure silicon-28. Just one in a series of blunders." The silicon mix-up seemed a disaster at the time, but events since then put things in perspective.

"It would have worked with the right crystal," Seth said. "According to my calculations, the exciton resonance requires a nanosecond incubation period, after which time the polaritons form a runaway Bose-Einstein condensate. The energy field would then be unstable to perturbations, and *wham*." He clapped his hands. "Singularity city."

"Okay," said Valerie, who had been watching their back-and-forth like a ping pong match, "suppose you did create a black hole. Wouldn't it just–suck everything up? Like, the whole town?"

"Fortunately not," Seth said, giving Valerie's back a reassuring rub. "The black hole would be as small as a pinhead. The amount of matter sucked in per second would be miniscule. It wouldn't devour the earth any more than a vacuum cleaner would."

They continued walking along the dirt road. It turned into a paved two-lane road and a sign read CHESTER, MT–POPULATION 205.

"Finally," Mike breathed.

They approached downtown Chester, which consisted of a post office, diner, gas station, and a few scattered houses. The population estimate seemed overblown.

"Are you sure you want to turn yourselves in?" Valerie asked. They looked at her. "I mean, how do you know you won't go to jail for years and years? You seem like nice guys. I'd hate for that to happen."

After an awkward silence, she looked at her phone. "Still no signal."

"This will all get sorted out, somehow," Mike said unconvincingly. "I have to believe that."

Seth led them into the diner, which was empty save for a solitary waitress. "Excuse me," he said, "could you tell me where the sheriff is?"

The waitress, a fifty-something-year-old brunette, looked him over. "The sheriff?" she asked skeptically. "Why do you want to know?"

"We'd like to report something," Seth said.

The waitress raised an eyebrow. "Sheriff's station's a ways down the road. You want to use the phone?"

"Yes," said Mike.

She pointed toward a hallway at the back of the diner, where there was a single restroom and a black phone on the wall. A handwritten "Exit" sign was posted on a door at the end of the hallway. Mike walked to the phone and dialed 911.

Seth sat down at a table near the window. Valerie sat across from him.

"I'll have a coffee, black," he called to the waitress. "You want anything, dear?"

"No thanks," Valerie said, checking her cell phone again.

The waitress handed them menus and returned to the area behind the bar. She grabbed a pot of black coffee, probably an hour old, and poured it into a cup.

Seth scanned the menu. "I'm starving. A buffalo burger would be nice right around now."

"I'm curious about what you said earlier," Valerie said, "about JASON wanting to kill your project. It seems like they would want to fund it–I mean, creating a black hole in the lab, how cool is that?"

"It has to do with the applications of this research. Imagine the space-time singularity is your hand." He brushed his fingers lightly against hers.

"Okay," she said.

"It sucks in matter. *Whoosh.* The black hole we were going to create was tiny. No big deal. But the same technology could produce a big black hole…"

"The phone doesn't work," Mike said from the back.

"You're not using it properly," the waitress said, annoyed.

The windows shattered. Mike turned to see a black SUV crash through the front of the diner with an eruption of drywall, wood, and glass. Seth tumbled forward from the impact and landed on the glass-covered floor. Valerie jumped out of the way and crouched by the door. Two men entered the room, dark figures in the dust. One aimed a laser-sighted rifle at the waitress and fired. A spot of blood appeared on her forehead and she fell instantly. Valerie screamed.

Mike bolted for the exit. He tried to open the door but it was locked. He looked back and saw two laser beams cut through the dusty air and land on him. The lasers then did a dance and the rifles dropped onto the ground. The two figures collapsed.

"Mike Harris," said a female voice.

An Asian woman with shades and a leather jacket stepped over the two bodies. She held a large weapon equipped with a silencer. He recognized her. She was the one from his house. It had been dark and confusing, but there was no doubt. She was the one who had saved him before.

"Come with me," she said firmly. "There isn't much time."

Valerie stood up. "Who are you?" she asked.

"Jing. Follow me."

"What about Seth?" Mike said.

Seth lay motionless on the ground, a trickle of blood flowing from his mouth. Mike kneeled by his side.

"Seth," he said. "Can you breathe?"

Seth nodded silently. His eyes were glazed and his face was pale. Two paramedics appeared and brushed Mike aside. They worked with silent efficiency. One checked Seth's pulse while the other shone a flashlight into his eyes.

"We need to go, *now*," Jing said firmly. "It's not safe here."

"What about Seth?"

"He'll be taken to a medical facility. Let's move."

They followed Jing out to the street, where a few townsfolk were beginning to gather. A Mercedes SUV was waiting. Mike and Valerie got into the back seat. Jing rode shotgun. The driver was a young man with wraparound glasses. They sped forward.

"What the hell is going on?" Mike said.

"We're taking you in," she said, and the windows darkened until they were opaque. The driver increased the speed. Mike felt nauseous.

"How can he see where he's driving?" Valerie asked.

"Phase-modulated glasses," Jing replied. "We're taking you to a heliport but we need to keep its location secret. From there we'll fly to headquarters."

"Headquarters?" Mike asked.

"We will explain everything there," she said, handing them pills. "For now, I suggest taking Dramamine. Sickness bags are in front of you."

* * *

Back at Colton University, in the musty confines of his office, Harry stared at two lists of code on his widescreen monitor. His eyes were bleary. He took a sip from a large cup of soda and stuffed chips into his mouth.

"Hold on," he said, bits of chips landing on the desk.

He moved the windows side by side and highlighted sections of code. The two lists were nearly identical, but the second list contained an inserted list of commands.

```
MOV AX, BX
XOR BX
JMP 0A872FFF
...
```

He scrolled down further and found a longer section of inserted code. He highlighted the section, turned the text red, and saved the file.

"Upgrade, my ass," he muttered and picked up the phone. "Chief. Harry. Someone messed with the code all right. Remotely."

Mike and Valerie got out of the car, hoods covering their heads. Jing guided them across a field and they stepped onto a concrete landing pad. They climbed into a helicopter. Mike and Valerie got into the back seats and someone fastened the seatbelts for them. The engine started and in a few minutes the helicopter ascended.

The helicopter ride was smooth. After an hour, they landed at another heliport. Jing guided them to a waiting vehicle and they got in. She removed the hoods. They were sitting in the back of an SUV with blackened windows, similar to the one before.

They could see the back of the driver's head, which was bald. "Please excuse the precautions," he said in a baritone voice. "Standard procedure."

"Who are you?" Mike said. "Where are you taking us?"

"All in good time, Professor Harris. And who is your friend?" he said, his voice turning colder.

"Valerie Norton," she said. "You can drop me off wherever

you like."

"We're taking a risk by bringing you in," he said, his head turning slightly toward Jing, revealing a firm jaw and prominent nose. Like the previous driver, he wore sunglasses. "I trust you appreciate that."

"Oh, we do," Valerie said. "Thanks a bunch."

Mike settled back into his seat. Asking this man questions would get him nowhere. He thought about the long road that had brought him here. Along that road, one thing had shocked him the most, even more than the sight of Jennifer dead. It was the sight of Axel Hansen's body dragged from a frigid lake in Glacier Park. They had done more than kill him. They had mutilated him. Through the binoculars, he had seen it clearly.

They had cut off his face.

29

After a half hour, the driver pressed a button and the windows became transparent. He removed his sunglasses. In the rearview mirror, Mike saw a pair of perceptive eyes.

"My name is Gunnar Stone. I run an organization charged with protecting the free world."

They sat in silence for a moment.

"Is that all?" Mike said with angry sarcasm. "And here I thought you were somebody important."

"You've been through a lot, Professor, and you need rest. We're taking you to headquarters."

"I don't need rest, Mr. Stone–if that's your name–I need to know what the *hell* is going on."

"As soon as we get to headquarters."

Headquarters. Mike imagined what that place must be like. A military base protected by razor wire and electrified fences. They would enter a front office and pass through metal detectors. Retinal and fingerprint scanners would verify their identity. A terahertz imager would check for weapons or surveillance devices. Guards would open a thick steel door and they would enter a room full of government agents.

They drove along dry, hilly terrain for fifteen minutes. It was a sunny, early evening. Mike sulked in the back seat, the events of the past two days replaying in his mind.

Gunnar turned onto a dirt road.

"We've all been through a lot. Do you like wine, Ms. Norton?"

"Sure," she said uncertainly.

"There's an excellent place up the road."

After a minute, he pulled into a parking lot in front of a warehouse. He parked next to a rusty white delivery truck. They stepped out of the vehicle and approached the door. Gunnar walked with a confident stride but had a distinct limp.

A wooden sign read

Golden Fleece Winery. Tasting daily, 2-6 pm

He glanced at his watch. "We're late, but I know the owner."

What's with this guy? Mike thought. He saw from Valerie's expression that she was thinking the same thing.

Gunnar knocked on the door. After a moment, a man in his fifties, with graying hair and beard, answered. In contrast to Gunnar's athletic build, the man had a paunch and the overall appearance of someone who had lived well.

"We're closed," he said curtly. His face broke into a grin and he patted Gunnar on the back. "Good to see you, my friend. I've got a cab that's been breathing all afternoon."

Mike and Valerie followed Gunnar into the winery, while Jing remained by the SUV. It was cool and damp inside. They walked past oak barrels and crates of wine bottles to the tasting room. The man set up several bottles of red wine and three glasses. "I'm Rob," he said. "The first selection is our cab-merlot-Syrah blend. Optimized for taste and affordability."

Mike put his hands to his head. "What the hell are we doing here?"

"Being civilized," Gunnar said. "Humans have been perfecting winemaking since Neolithic times. The wine that we drink today has been optimized to a degree unparalleled by any other innovation. Relax, Professor Mike Harris, and enjoy this pinnacle of human achievement."

Mike froze. Gunnar had said his name. What if Rob had seen the news reports? He might call the FBI.

But Rob seemed to take no notice. He poured wine into the three glasses and handed them to the guests. Gunnar swirled his glass and put in his prominent nose.

"Good bouquet," he said, and took a drink.

Mike gulped the wine from his glass and set it aside. "I want some answers," he said, "and I'm not waiting until we get to headquarters."

"No need to wait," Gunnar replied, returning Mike's stare. "We're here."

Agent Sanchez stepped out of the park ranger pickup truck and surveyed the scene. A black SUV was lodged in the entrance of a small diner. Glass, wood, and plaster littered the front sidewalk. The area around the diner, essentially the whole downtown, was cordoned off by police barricades.

She showed her badge and walked inside the diner. Two men lay dead on the floor. One was a muscular man with a buzz cut and the other was a gray haired man with a beard. Each had been killed by a single shot to the back of the head.

"It looks professional," said a brown-haired man with sunglasses and an FBI windbreaker. A field agent based in Kalispell, his name was Doug Ashcroft. "Same with the waitress."

"Does Professor Harris have weapons training?"

"Not that we know," Ashcroft said. "Campus police interviewed his colleagues at Colton University, and we pulled up a security clearance that he got for his DARPA project. He has no military or law enforcement background and apparently has never owned a firearm."

They walked to the counter and saw the body of the waitress behind it, one bullet hole in the forehead.

"There's something else," Ashcroft said, lowering his voice. "Some witnesses report that a Mercedes SUV pulled up, and–depending on who you talk to–between one and five people got out. Then, some number of people got into the SUV and it took off."

"That's odd," Sanchez said, biting a pen.

"It gets weirder. Some of the witnesses said that paramedics carried off an injured victim. But we know that by the time *our* paramedics arrived, everyone was dead."

"How reliable are those witnesses?"

"As good as any," he said. "They could have been confused. With all the panic, we have to take their testimony with a grain of salt. Still, I'm having trouble believing Mike Harris is acting alone."

Agent Sanchez' phone beeped and she looked at it.

"Message from Chief Patterson," she said. "He wants to meet."

"The Cold War was simple," Gunnar began, leading his guests down a narrow stone corridor. "The world was defined by two opposing superpowers, both rational. The product of that decades-long standoff was a measure of stability that we can only appreciate in retrospect."

He opened a wooden door and held it open for Valerie. She walked through and Mike followed. Gunnar closed the door behind them. They walked down a dimly lit staircase.

"Today, the primary threats to the democratic world are not nations but individuals," he said, his voice echoing off the cold walls. "These charismatic, wealthy, nationless leaders attract bands of fanatically devoted followers. Their aim is to destroy civilization. With recent advances in technology, they now have the capability to achieve that goal."

They walked into a cool space with small oak barrels and bottles of wine. Gunnar walked up to a door.

"We know you're innocent, Professor Harris. And, we can explain everything."

He opened the door. The glow of computer screens filled the space. They stepped into a chamber with dozens of screens that showed maps, streams of alphanumeric data, and live feed from cable news channels. A pair of technicians hovered over pieces of equipment covered with wires. One of them pointed a remote control at a large screen.

"I believe you have heard of Henry Colton," Gunnar said, as an image of the billionaire appeared on the screen.

"Of course."

"Our intelligence indicates he is preparing to move to the Pacific Research Center, the primary research and development division of Colton Enterprises."

A second screen zoomed in on a crescent-shaped tropical island in the Pacific Ocean, dotted with several buildings along a volcanic ridge.

"Satellite imagery detected container ships delivering cargo to the Pacific Research Center as well as increased construction activity. Computer analysis revealed irregular financial transactions consistent with a relocation to the island. Colton used his political connections to avoid paying tax penalties for moving his operation overseas."

"It's a free country," Mike said, trying not to be swayed by the computer graphics and Gunnar's confident assertions. "He can move wherever he wants."

"True, except for one thing. Follow me."

They walked down another corridor to a spacious, brightly lit office with an open door. Windows and a skylight showed a sunny, tropical scene outside.

Jalen turned from his computer and noticed the puzzled looks of Mike and Valerie. "The view is computer generated," he explained, and stood up. "Mike Harris and Valerie Norton. I'm glad you're safe."

He shook their hands and pointed to the computer screen with a long, delicate finger. Henry Colton's picture appeared, with statistics listed on either side.

"A recent recon mission to Colton's compound in Montana revealed a number of suspicious buildings," he said, as images appeared on the "window" behind the computer. They were the pictures Jing had taken. Next to those images, thermal satellite photos showed workers unloading objects from the warehouses and loading them onto trucks. "These buildings contained military-grade weaponry. Trucks delivered the weapons to cargo ships in Puget Sound, which then journeyed to the Pacific Research Center."

A picture of James, Henry Colton's square-jawed assistant, appeared.

"This man goes by the name of James Tyrell, although he has numerous aliases and passports to match. He's a mercenary with a long resume, having worked in Central America, the Balkans, Iran, and Afghanistan, to name a few. He joined Colton ten years ago to direct the company's security operations."

"He directs more than security," said a woman's voice. They turned around to see Jing, who had entered the room silently. "He directed the attack on your house."

"But why?" Mike said, trying not to linger on the horrors of the past few days. "What did I do? What did Jennifer do?"

"It's not what you did," Gunnar said. "It's what you know. Colton's strategy was to fund research and capitalize on the biggest discoveries. You discovered something that he wanted. In order to keep the discovery secret, he attempted to eliminate everyone who knew about it."

"Jennifer," Mike said, his heart sinking. "If I hadn't told her about the experiment, she…"

Valerie put a shaking hand to her mouth. "Will they come after me?"

"Yes," Gunnar said curtly. "You're both in danger. You'll need to stay here until we have neutralized Colton's operation. Jing will show you to your rooms."

"This way," said Jing, leading them out of the office and down a dark passageway. "Try to relax and get some rest. You're safe here."

Agents Sanchez and Ashcroft sat in the back of a van. A screen displayed an image of Chief Patterson sitting in his office.

"Someone tampered with the code that controls the lasers," he said. "Our technician is certain that it was done remotely."

"How can you be sure?" Sanchez asked skeptically.

"I won't pretend to understand the details, but I trust Harry's judgment. It was done by an automatic upgrade feature of the data acquisition program. Instead of upgrading the software, it inserted a block of code that allowed an outside user to control the lasers."

"An outside user?" Doug Ashcroft said. "Who?"

"No way to tell. They used a proxy server."

"And what about feedback?" Ashcroft persisted. "How could they see the target?"

"We don't know."

Sanchez gazed distantly, lost in thought. "I wonder…" she said.

"Ma'am?"

"I wonder about the breadth of the conspiracy. The coordination, secrecy, and professionalism."

A look of understanding registered on Ashcroft's face. "You think?"

She turned to Patterson's face on the screen. "What I am about to say must remain confidential."

"The link is secure," Patterson said. "Go ahead."

She hesitated for a moment, then said: "One month ago, we detected a spike in intelligence chatter within the region. We cross-correlated the data with the Bureau's central database. The analysis showed that a group known as the Praetorians was operating in the state."

"The who?"

"The Praetorians," Ashcroft said, "named after the Roman soldiers who guarded the empire. I always thought it was one of those spooky stories that federal agents told around the campfire."

"According to that story," Sanchez said, "the Praetorians are a group of highly trained personnel who banded together to target and eliminate terrorists. They operate worldwide and above the law."

"Why would they target Mike Harris?"

"That's not clear. They may be protecting him, for now. The danger is that, according to the information we have, the Praetorians will kill anyone who knows about them."

"They have Mike?" Patterson exclaimed.

"This is all speculation," Sanchez said, "but if they have Mike, then he is in extreme danger."

30

Kuwat moved through the dark streets confidently. The air was humid and warm. This was a rusted, industrial part of the city, not far from shore. The streets were lined with dilapidated buildings and the occasional bum. Trash littered the sidewalks, left over from the weekend when the area filled with prostitutes and their inebriated customers. He strode toward a vacant wooden building with broken glass windows. He carried a jug of kerosene.

Kuwat entered the building.

"Get out!" he yelled.

There was no response. He unscrewed the cap on the jug and poured the fluid onto the floor. He heard a sound, and walked over to a set of rickety stairs.

"Get out, I said!"

A grizzled man stumbled down the stairs, muttering incoherently. The man glanced briefly at Kuwat and left.

Kuwat continued his job. He spread kerosene around the floor methodically, applying a uniform layer. After a few minutes, the room smelled strongly of fuel. Throwing the jug carelessly onto the floor, he walked to the door. He lit a cigarette and took a drag. He tossed the match into the building and turned away. The fumes caught fire instantly, billowing outward. Kuwat had done this enough times to know that the initial flash would not hurt him. He imagined that he must look bad, walking away coolly from a fiery explosion, cigarette in his mouth. He picked up the pace as the fire spread, maintaining his tough-guy look and savoring the payment to come.

Mike sat on the edge of the bed, lost in thought. The underground room was simple and furnished with tasteful antiques. A screen, like that in Jalen's office, displayed a realistic outdoor nighttime scene. He read the card from the gift basket:

Golden Fleece Winery and Bed & Breakfast
Robert Kendrick, Proprietor
For in the hand of the Lord there is a cup, and the wine is red.
--Psalms 75:8

He tossed the note aside. The events of the past days had controlled him. He was a pawn, unable to affect the outcome of a game played by higher-level people. For the next couple of days, he would be safe, protected by–whoever they were. It was time to rest.

Mike walked over to a small oak table that had a bottle of Golden Fleece CMS, a corkscrew, and two glasses. He uncorked the bottle and poured. While the thought of a drink did not really appeal to him, he figured it might help calm the nerves.

He jumped slightly at the sound of knocking.

He looked out the peephole. It was Valerie. He unlocked the deadbolt and opened the door.

"Hey," she said. "How's your room?"

"Okay I guess," he said, looking around. "Care for a glass?"

"Sure, why not," she said, walking in. She wore a long Caltech T-shirt, sweat pants, and slippers. She didn't have her glasses on.

He poured wine into a glass and handed it to her.

"I can't think of a toast," he said.

"To being alive," she said, and they clinked glasses. "That's good stuff," she said after taking a sip.

"I'm sorry I got you into this mess," Mike said in a tired monotone. "A lot of people close to me…"

She held his hand gently. "*You* didn't do anything wrong. Keep reminding yourself of that. I'll remind you. You did *nothing wrong.*"

"Except…"

She put a finger to his lips. "Except nothing. You're a good guy, Mike. You never asked for any of this."

He looked down at his glass, which he swirled absently. "I guess we're safe for now."

"I don't know," Valerie said. "My phone gave me the GPS coordinates for this place. They did nothing to keep the location a secret. How do they know we won't just blab to the media when this is over?"

"Maybe they trust us."

She stared into his eyes. "Mike, they don't trust us. We can't trust them."

He sighed and set his glass down. "I don't see how I have a choice. I'm tired of running."

"I think we're in danger," she said. "I mean, who are these guys? Military? Vigilantes?"

"I don't know," he said, feeling his headache intensify.

"Sorry," she said, seeing his pain, "I didn't mean to make things worse. Sit down." She pressed her fingers to his temples and rubbed gently. "Is that better?"

"A little," he said.

She continued massaging. Gradually, Mike began to relax and his eyes closed. After a few minutes, she leaned toward him and gave his forehead a kiss. "Get some rest."

She walked to the door. "Thanks for the wine. My place next time?"

"Sure," he said, managing a smile. "Good night."

On the island, it was afternoon. Clouds rolled in and sprinkled the jungles along the eastern shore. A two-lane road led from the airport and harbor to the central part of the island, which was dominated by twin dormant volcanoes. In a high elevation region called the Saddle, named after the peculiar topography, there was a network of buildings. Graders and dump trucks worked on roads while two cranes assisted the construction of new buildings. Workers, mostly Indonesian, labored in color-coded uniforms and hardhats.

"You're behind schedule," said a man named Dr. Sauer. He wore khaki shorts and a tropical shirt, but his face was all business. "The experiment should have been conducted two days ago."

A man in a lab coat walked next to him. His badge identified him as Dr. Kevin Lipman. "The lasers kept burning out," he said, his voice weak from lack of sleep. "The laser crystals are only made in China. We just received good ones yesterday."

"I'm not interested in excuses. Neither is Henry Colton."

Lipman pressed his palm against a reader and steel doors slid open. They walked into Building G36.

"The lasers are online, but I'm still not sure about the isotope ratio," Lipman said, rubbing his fingers through a mop of black hair. "If we had another week…"

"You don't."

They walked into a locker room and put on cleanroom attire, the booties, coat, and cap known as the "bunny suit." Lipman swiped his badge through a reader and they entered a hangar-sized room with amber lighting. Suspended from the high ceiling by fine wire was a massive array of lasers, all pointing at a gleaming stainless-steel cryostat. Snakes of wires led from the lasers to a high-voltage power grid. Vacuum pumps and computers surrounded the cryostat. The floor was vibrationally isolated from the rest of the world and the cryostat stood on another vibration-isolating platform. A shiny black crystal sat in the cryostat, maintained at a temperature of two degrees above absolute zero.

Several technicians stood at a control panel and looked at Lipman expectantly. Lipman and Sauer donned safety goggles and Lipman nodded. A technician flipped a switch and red DANGER lights lit up.

"Clear the area," a female voice intoned over a loudspeaker. "Laser test in progress. Clear the area."

Power generators ramped up to their operating voltage. Lipman nodded again and the technician pressed a large green button. Dozens of intense laser beams converged on the cryostat, filling the room with light. A reddish glow flashed from inside the cryostat. The red turned to bright white.

"Cut!" Lipman called.

The technician pressed a red button and the lasers turned off. The glow inside the cryostat subsided. Smoke billowed out. A pressure relief valve popped, sending up a plume of helium vapor.

"Dammit," Lipman grumbled, walking toward the cryostat. He peered through the small windows. The crystalline silicon cube was a molten glob.

"What happened?" Sauer demanded.

"Dammit, dammit, dammit!" Lipman yelled, throwing his lab notebook across the room. "The isotope ratio was off."

"Why?"

"Because we have no clue! Growing these crystals is tricky. You can't just dial in the ingredients. It's an art."

Sauer stared at Lipman. "Who can grow a crystal with the correct isotope ratio?"

"There's a guy. Oleg Sinitsky, at the Ioffe Institute in Russia. He's a wild card, though, an eccentric, which is why we avoided approaching him. Plus, he works with Mike Harris."

"*Worked*," Sauer replied through clenched teeth. He took off his goggles and headed for the exit.

TUESDAY, JUNE 3

31

Sleep hit Mike hard the night before. He awoke groggily to a computer-generated sunrise. A pot of freshly brewed coffee was on the table. He shuffled toward it, savoring the aroma, and looked at the clock: 9:32 AM. After a luxuriant shower, he slowly got dressed and poured a cup.

There was no television or newspaper in the room. He wondered what the outside world was saying about the fugitive professor. So many people close to him had been caught up in the violent storm. Now, Valerie Norton, another innocent, was in danger.

Just a few days ago, he was thinking about a science experiment. His problems then had been trivial. He recalled the e-mail from Oleg:

> Hello Mike,
>
> As we discussed, isotope ratio in last crystal growth was not right. It was silicon-28 / silicon-30 mixture. Sorry about mistake. Furnace has been down too but we can fix it. I am optimistic we get things 'squared away' ;-)
>
> Regards,
> Oleg

Oleg was probably still thinking about the experiment. He had no idea what was happening.

Mike froze. His cup dropped to the floor. He ran to the door and opened it.

Gunnar was standing in the passageway.

"Oleg Sinitsky's in danger," Mike said.

"We know," he said. "Follow me. We need your help."

Gunnar led him down the passageway. Valerie ran to catch up with them.

"What's up?" she asked, her hair wet from a recent shower.

"Oleg," Mike said. "He's my Russian collaborator. He's the only one in the group who hasn't been attacked."

"Correction," Gunnar barked. "We intercepted an e-mail that he sent to you."

He handed Mike a printout:

Mike,

Some bad guys came by lab. I took sample and headed for another location. Give me call on cell number immediately.

-Oleg

"We need to help him," Mike said frantically. "Can't we–I don't know, call the embassy or something?"

"Negative," Gunnar said.

He led them to a stainless steel door and waved his palm in front of a reader. The door slid open. They walked into an underground warehouse. High-tech equipment sat alongside oak barrels and crates of wine. Like the rest of the headquarters, the room had a temporary feel. The machines were mounted on pallets that could be moved in or out quickly. In the center was a Mercedes SUV. A hefty Asian man in a lab coat stood next to it, inspecting the windows.

"Robert Chen," Gunnar said. "This is Valerie Norton and Mike Harris."

Robert faced away from them. "Nice to meet you, Professor," a voice said, right next to Mike's left ear. He turned. No one was there.

"Over here!" a voice said to his right.

He turned again. No one. Valerie looked at him, puzzled.

"Did you hear that?" he said.

"Hear what?"

Robert faced them, grinning. He held a small microphone, which he placed in his lab coat pocket. "Acoustic focusing," he said proudly. "Using sound-wave interference, we can localize an audio transmission to within a centimeter."

Robert walked toward them, extending his hand. Mike noticed the MIT class ring, the Brass Rat, on his finger. Robert turned to Valerie, enjoying what he saw. "Ma'am," he said, his eyes gleaming behind tinted safety glasses.

"Valerie Norton," Gunnar said. "She was with Mike when we took him in."

"I see," Robert said, captivated. "Echo five."

"Huh?"

Behind her, something beeped. Valerie turned around and saw a hand grenade on a small table. Blue LEDs on the grenade flashed on and off.

"Boom. You're dead. Voice activated grenade. Don't worry," he said, chuckling, "it's just a dummy."

"Show us your creation," Gunnar prompted.

"Oh, this," Robert said, resting his hand on the SUV. The vehicle had dull black paint, like primer, and the windows were shaded. "Soccer mom stealthmobile. Absorbs electromagnetic radiation from radar to UV. Nine hundred horsepower electric engine is all 'zoom' and no 'vroom.' Quiet as Leisure Village on Sunday but a lot faster. Take a look inside."

He tapped the side door, which slid open. They saw a rotating back seat with joysticks on the armrests. The inside of the windows lit up, displaying vectors and numbers like the heads-up display in the cockpit of a fighter jet.

"Directed-energy weaponry pops out the roof,"–a laser rose from the roof of the SUV and started pointing around–"and automated targeting does the rest."

The laser looked like a black telescope with power cords connected to the SUV. Grinning broadly, Robert climbed into the SUV and sat in the rotating chair.

"Glasses!" he yelled.

A technician handed safety glasses to Gunnar, Valerie, and Mike. As they donned the glasses, a human-shaped paper target descended from overhead. Robert pressed on the joysticks. The laser swiveled around and locked in on the target. Robert pressed a red button on the left joystick. An intense green beam shot forth from the laser, perfectly silent, and punctured the target, which caught fire. A fire extinguisher doused the flame.

"Cool!" said Valerie.

"Impressive," Mike said, facing Gunnar, "but what are we going to do about Oleg?"

"I told you, Professor Harris, we need your help. This way."

They walked across the underground warehouse and passed through another set of steel doors. Mike felt his blood pressure rising. Gunnar was stringing them along. He never seemed to give a straight answer.

"Where are you taking us?" Mike demanded.

"We need to visit an old friend," Gunnar said.

They entered a hangar that housed a helicopter, painted in the same type of dull primer as the SUV. It had angled sides reminiscent of a Stealth fighter.

Robert rushed to the helicopter.

"This is my baby," he said, stroking the side. "The Comanche helicopter was designed to be silent and stealthy, but the project was canceled back in 2004. Some of us rescued it and made modifications. Noise cancellation acoustics make it nearly silent from the ground."

Mike realized this helicopter, or one just like it, had saved him in the hills behind his house.

"Are we riding in this?" Mike asked.

"No," Gunnar said. "We're taking the jet. It's quicker. Follow me."

Mike and Valerie followed Gunnar across the dark hangar. "Who are we visiting?" Mike demanded.

"Like I said, an old friend. I'm sure you've heard of him. His name is Damien Voth."

32

The surgeon set aside his scalpel and pulled the black computer chip from the back of the man's neck. He set the chip on a stainless steel tray. Using a pair of Teflon tweezers, he retrieved a smaller chip, about the size of a postage stamp, from a container. He placed the chip into the man's neck.

"I'm attaching the nerve bundles now," he said.

The network of nerves, which led to the brain and spinal cord, had been fit with gold electric contacts. Using tweezers with fine points, he guided the contacts onto the chip. After about five minutes, he used a precision soldering gun to fasten the contacts permanently.

"Walk in the park."

Whistling, he sewed up the incision and placed a bandage over it.

"When will the upgrade take effect?" the man asked. It was James.

"Couple of hours."

James recalled the last time the Biochip came in handy. It was at the Yacht Club in San Francisco, where Henry Colton was giving a speech.

Something had caught his eye. James had moved rapidly and

approached the bespectacled, short-haired young man, Jarrod, who was holding a small briefcase.

It was a setup. He was expecting Jarrod, with his lemon meringue pie. The little twerp had thrown pies at politicians and dignitaries for years. It was easy to predict when he would strike. Still, the Biochip gave him an instant lock on Jarrod as soon as he entered the room. It was like having a door gunner in his head, looking out for insurgents while he concentrated on piloting. The upgrade would further enhance his situational awareness.

"How did it go?"

James turned around. It was Henry.

"No problems," the surgeon said, removing his mask. "You should be able to remove the bandage in twenty-four hours."

"Could you excuse us?" James said.

Henry nodded and the surgeon left the room.

"Sir, I have some news from the Pacific Research Center."

"I heard," Henry said, sitting on a stool. "They can't get the isotope ratio right."

"We should have a crystal from St. Petersburg soon."

Henry nodded distractedly.

"I'm leaving for Indonesia in three hours," James said. "I expect to find a suitable target within the day."

Henry shook his head slightly. "Terrible," he said softly. "It's a terrible thing we're about to do."

"Terrible, but necessary."

"True," Henry said with a faraway look in his eyes. "All great civilizations arise from blood. We must be strong."

James gazed at Henry with admiration. Henry Colton was the only true visionary James had ever met. Henry knew that governments beholden to democratic whim were weak and prone to superstition. Despite a century of scientific progress, common people refused to embrace technology wholeheartedly. Sure, they were content to have electronic gizmos, cosmetic surgery, and prescription drugs. But with the important things–energy production, genetic modification, defense–they had an irrational fear of progress. No nuclear power. No GMOs. No war. Rather than enlightening the masses, educational institutions indoctrinated students with gauzy platitudes about diversity. Politicians, who used to come from the highest echelons of society, now pandered to the lowest common denominator.

It was time to start over. A new civilization would arise, led by scientists and philosophers rather than slobs who sat on the couch and drank beer and complained about gasoline prices. Cast in the mold of Plato's republic and the government envisioned by H.G. Wells, enlightenment, science, and reason would be the guiding principles for a new golden age. Biotechnology and genetic modification would be utilized to their fullest potential. The new society would have an unlimited energy source, freeing them from dependence on corrupt governments and greedy corporations.

Like ancient Greece, this new civilization would arise on an island.

But first, they had a problem to solve. Their silicon crystal, key to everything, had the wrong isotope composition. Everything else was in place. They just needed a good crystal.

"You'll be able to manage the Russian angle?" Henry asked.

"We're on it," James said. "Just concentrate on moving to the island."

"Yes sir," Henry said, chuckling at the role inversion. He knew he needed his subordinate to push him, especially when it came to matters of physical conflict. "Will your neck hold out?"

"Never better," James said, standing up. "I'll see you at the island."

"At the island," Henry said, and they shook hands.

Mike squinted at the sunlight as they stepped outside. He, Gunnar, and Valerie walked out the back of the Golden Fleece Winery, toward a small jet on a short runway strip. The jet looked like a Lear.

"What does Damien Voth have to do with anything?" Mike asked, his frustration growing by the minute. "We need to help Oleg."

"There's something you need to understand," Gunnar said.

They reached the jet and the pilot opened the door. Gunnar

gestured for Valerie and then Mike to step in. They sat in the back seats.

Jing emerged from the winery, wearing shades.

Gunnar turned to her. "Prepare headquarters," he said. "Delta nine."

"Delta nine," she repeated, and stepped back into the building.

Gunnar got in and sat in a seat that faced Mike and Valerie. The engines started.

"What do we need to understand?" Mike said, putting on his seatbelt.

"Excuse me?"

"You said there was something we need to understand."

Gunnar took his time fastening his seatbelt. He turned to the pilot and told him to proceed. Then he looked at Mike.

"Oleg is expendable," he said.

"What about me?" Valerie protested. "Am I expendable?"

"Yes."

"Like the waitress at the diner?" Mike said, burning with anger.

"Yes."

"So you just let her die."

"Negative," Gunnar said calmly. "We could have saved her if circumstances had been different. But saving her was not the mission objective. We needed to hang back and wait for them to strike. Hold on."

The engines blasted flame and they shot forward. Valerie yelped and grabbed Mike's hand. The pilot pulled back on the joystick and the plane lifted upward. Mike felt his stomach drop.

"We don't have much time," Gunnar said over the scream of the engines.

"I don't understand," Mike yelled. "Why didn't you move sooner?"

"Chatter," Gunnar responded after the engines quieted. "We intercepted a spike in encrypted messages in the minutes leading up to the attack. We expected words like 'Harris,' 'Glacier,' and so on, to be in those messages. Using those clues, Jalen cracked the code. Had we rushed in earlier, we'd still be flying blind."

A few minutes later, the jet climbed through a layer of clouds and the engines fired up again. The roar of an afterburner shook them.

"Mach 1," the pilot announced.

"We intercepted communications that led to Damien Voth," Gunnar shouted. "Evidently, he found a way to communicate from prison."

33

Like everyone else, Mike was shocked by the news five years ago. Everyone knew Voth was odd. His rant at the congressional hearing and his subsequent obsession with extraterrestrial intelligence ensured his place in the pantheon of eccentric scientists. But genocide? It seemed unthinkable. And yet, if the media reports were true, mass death had been his plan.

The facts surrounding the case were murky. A messianic cult leader named Jacob Seitz apparently contacted Voth with the intention of building a nuclear bomb. Seitz and his band of twenty Revolutionaries lived in a house in the hills above Berkeley, California. Their guiding philosophy was an eclectic mix of leftist revolutionary theory, Eastern mysticism, and cyber-libertarianism. Many of the members were educated, with PhDs in engineering, chemistry, and physics. To become a full Revolutionary, a member had to endure excruciating initiation rites where they were tortured and branded. At the end of the initiation, the Revolutionary was thoroughly brainwashed, ready to die for the collective.

Somehow, the Revolutionaries acquired materials for a workable nuclear device. Their plan was to detonate it on Telegraph Avenue, next to the University of California campus. Before they could execute their plan, FBI agents descended on the Revolutionaries' house. It was never revealed who tipped them off. During the gunfight that followed, the house burned to the ground. The fire spread, destroying dozens of homes in the Berkeley Hills.

Over the next weeks, investigators pieced together evidence from the smoldering remains. They reached two conclusions. First, all the Revolutionaries perished in the fire. Second, the nuclear device was dangerously close to operational.

That led to the question: Who had supplied them with the bomb?

With surprising speed, the White House announced that agents had apprehended Dr. Damien Voth and moved him to an undisclosed location. After several days of interrogation, they said, Voth had confessed to supplying the terrorists with nuclear material and classified information needed to construct a bomb. No motive or evidence was made public.

After the initial shock subsided, Congress and the press questioned the secrecy surrounding Voth's internment. They raised constitutional objections. Human rights groups pressured the government to give Voth a fair and public trial. As months wore on without any new information, public sympathy for the famous nuclear scientist grew.

In January, a new administration took control of the White House. Eager to repair the country's international reputation, they struck a deal with Voth's lawyers. Voth would spend the rest of his days in a comfortable, minimum-security prison on the West Coast. He would have a big window that faced the beach, all the medical care he required, and a high-speed internet connection. In return, he signed a nondisclosure agreement with the government. He promised to never reveal any details about the case.

Less than an hour later, the afterburners shut off and the jet entered a steep descent. Valerie squeezed Mike's hand so hard that it turned white. They dove through the cloud layer. Mike looked out a window and saw an arid landscape dotted with farms. They approached the ground rapidly. He saw a landing strip in the distance.

The ground rushed up at them. Surely the pilot was going too fast. Mike held his breath as they landed with a thud on the landing strip, prompting another yelp from Valerie. The jet decelerated abruptly. Mike, pale, wiped his sweaty forehead. He felt sick.

They taxied to a small building. "Welcome to California," the pilot said. "Please remain seated until the plane comes to a complete stop."

After a minute the plane stopped and someone opened the door. Gunnar gestured for Valerie and Mike to exit. They walked unsteadily toward the building. Before they reached it, a black SUV drove onto the tarmac.

"Get in," Gunnar said.

Mike and Valerie got into the back seats. The driver was a woman with shades. Fortunately, the vehicle didn't have blackened windows like the last one. Mike was not sure he could endure more nausea.

"Damien Voth doesn't like me," Gunnar said from the front seat. "That makes me the bad cop. You're a physicist, Mike. You're a wanted man. He'll relate. That makes you the good cop."

"You're joking," Mike said, pressing his hands to his forehead. "That's why you dragged us here?"

"You don't know Voth like I do. Be empathetic. You're two misunderstood scientists, persecuted by the government."

"Fine," he said miserably. He was tired of arguing with this guy. For now, Mike would go along with the plan.

The SUV wound its way through the hills of northern California. The driver kept the speed between eighty and a hundred. After a half hour, they could see the ocean.

"Jalen hacked into the prison database," Gunnar said with some measure of pride. "Voth will be expecting two well-wishers. That's us."

"What about me?" Valerie asked.

"You'll wait in the lobby."

She looked out the window petulantly. "Then what am I doing here?" she muttered under her breath.

"Here we are," Gunnar said as they approached a concrete building. The grounds were well manicured, with basketball hoops and a putting green. A group of men in orange jumpsuits congregated behind a fence. A sign read:

Kenwood Coast Federal Correctional Facility and Wellness Unit

They pulled up to a guard post. The driver showed the guard her ID and they were waved inside. They parked in the visitor lot and walked toward the entrance. The driver remained in the SUV.

"Pretty mellow place," Valerie said. "Aren't you worried Dr. Voth might walk out?"

"That's not going to happen," Gunnar said with a wry grin.

Mike noticed that Gunnar's limp became more pronounced as they approached the building.

They entered the lobby, where Gunnar signed the visitor sheet. The room had a skylight and reasonable décor. Security was light. A woman behind the desk waved Mike and Gunnar in, while Valerie searched for magazines in the lobby. They followed signs to the Wellness Unit.

"Play the sympathetic role," Gunnar said as they walked down a brightly lit corridor, "but do not forget what he is."

"And what is that?"

"A brilliant sociopath."

They reached an empty waiting room and walked up to a window with a sign that read CHECK IN. Gunnar gave the clerk two phony names.

"Dr. Petersen will be right with you," she said.

"Thank you."

From a south-facing window, they could see arid land on the left and a rocky cliff on the right. The cliff gave way to a narrow strip of beach.

"This business about Voth being misunderstood," Gunnar said, his face reddening slightly, "is fiction."

"I'm sure people are saying that about me," Mike retorted.

Gunnar arched an eyebrow. "Good," he said. "You're getting into character."

"Mr. Warner?"

A young doctor in a white coat approached them. He had sandy blond hair, freckles, and long eyelashes. He extended his hand, a genuinely friendly smile on his face.

"That's me," Gunnar replied, shaking his hand. "We're here to see our friend Damien."

"Great," he said, and shook Mike's hand too. "There was a time, a couple years back, when practically no one visited him. It's better now, though. More people are coming by, scientists mostly, from the national labs or wherever. Follow me."

They passed several rooms where motionless patients lay, some groaning, others silent. That smell peculiar to hospitals–urine, blood, bleach–filled the stuffy air, reminding Mike of his hospital stay a few days ago.

"Most of the inmates aren't much for conversation," Dr. Petersen said, chuckling, "but Voth is great. He knows about everything, it seems. I've learned a lot from the guy. And here's a secret: he's all bark and no bite."

They walked into a dark, spacious room. The curtains were drawn. A computer monitor was suspended from the ceiling. It showed stock quotations.

They approached a large steel cylindrical drum that lay on a bed. A pump made a sound that was a slow, mechanical imitation of breathing. A pair of arms, covered by long light blue sleeves, stuck out of the drum and lay limply on the bed. The right hand rested on a keypad. Mike noticed that the hand was burnt crimson.

Voth's head was propped on a stainless steel support. He faced away from them, watching the computer monitor.

"Gunnar Stone," he said, his voice barely a whisper. He paused as the iron lung inhaled. "You need to fix that leg."

"This is Mr. *Warner*," Dr. Petersen said loudly, as if addressing a senile or deaf patient.

"Of course it is. You may leave, Dr. Petersen."

Petersen left, smiling, and gave them a conspiratorial wink. "All bark," he said on his way out.

Gunnar and Mike walked along the bed. Mike inhaled sharply when he saw Voth's face. The right half was horribly burned, the skin like red wax dripping from a candle. His right eye, pale blue and bloodshot, drifted to the side. The left half of his face had two deep scars that extended from the jawbone to the forehead. He had no eyebrows or hair. Lines from a fractured skull showed through the skin.

"We know you're communicating with Henry Colton," Gunnar said without preamble, pointing accusingly at the monitor.

Voth's good eye focused on Mike. "I've seen you in the news," he said. "They're looking for you."

"Yes they are," Mike said unsteadily. "I guess I know what you went through."

Voth bared yellow teeth as the iron lung inhaled. "Don't play games with me, child."

"I tried to tell Mike that you're psycho, but he wouldn't listen," Gunnar said, getting in Voth's face. "He thinks he can reason with you. I prefer more direct methods. Your choice."

Voth looked at the screen. "Ah," he said. "My DenTech stock is up again." *Inhale.* "When I get out, I may be a rich man."

Gunnar laughed spitefully. "What do you know about Colton?"

"Wealthy fellow. Needs direction"–*inhale*–"why do you ask?"

"I'll shut down your internet connection, Voth. Is that what you want?"

"You have no authority."

"I don't need it," Gunnar hissed. "The same hacker who got us in here can shut down your little chat room, so stop screwing with me. *What is Colton doing?*"

"Something terrible," Voth said, his mouth curling into a grin.

Gunnar stared at Voth silently, the mechanical pump the only sound in the room.

"I'm finished with riddles," Gunnar said, and stormed out.

"Subtlety–is not his strong suit."

"What…" Mike stammered. "Do you know what's happening? Because I'm just confused, to be honest."

"They're after you," Voth breathed. "They think you're a

murderer."

"Yes."

"You've been set up, boy." Voth's hand tapped on the keypad. "They won't stop until you're dead–or as good as."

Mike looked into Voth's eye. He tried not to let his revulsion show. "I'm not sure what to do."

Voth's face softened a bit. Gunnar leaving the room seemed to take a load off his mind. "You cannot trust that man," he said paternally. "He tortures. Be careful, boy."

"What about Colton?"

"I can stop him," Voth said. "That is why I–contacted him. He is misguided."

"What is he planning to do?"

"Kill many people."

Voth's hand pressed a button on the keypad. The image of a burning warehouse appeared on the screen. Text in a sidebar read:

> Surabaya, Indonesia–Authorities have ruled that a fire that destroyed an empty warehouse in an industrial part of the city, owned by the multinational corporation KJR, had "suspicious origins." Further tests, they said, will be performed to confirm that the fire was arson. Authorities in the United States are investigating the Anti-Globalization Alliance (AGA), whose web site listed the warehouse as a facility that should be "shut down immediately." After the fire, the web site showed the warehouse as crossed off a list of "global entities that oppress workers and destroy the environment." A member the AGA, who spoke on the condition of anonymity, said, "I'm glad that KJR's property was destroyed, but we do not condone illegal actions."

"Why would Colton do that?" Mike asked, genuinely befuddled.

"He is misguided–maybe insane. He wants to demonstrate his power."

Mike shook his head. How did torching an abandoned warehouse in Indonesia accomplish anything?

"He's setting them up," Voth said, as if reading his mind. "The AGA will take the fall."

"Take the fall? For what?"

"For the Big One," he said, his eye intense with what looked like fear. "The world will blame AGA–but the top echelons of government will know it was Colton. It will be a–warning."

A heart monitor began a continuous *beep* and Voth's eyes pressed shut, a look of pain on his face. A pair of attendants came and adjusted an intravenous line that led to Voth's left arm.

Dr. Petersen rushed over and looked at Mike suspiciously.

"I think you need to leave," he said.

The beep stopped and Voth's eyes opened wide.

"Stop Colton," Voth said, before his eyes shut again.

34

Mike staggered back to the lobby, bewildered, and found Gunnar and Valerie there waiting. As they left, he told them about what Voth had said.

"That confirms it," Gunnar said. "Colton is planning a terrorist attack."

They got into the SUV and took off.

"That doesn't make sense," Mike said.

"It makes perfect sense. He's sending a message."

Mike held on to his seat as the driver accelerated around a bend. "If he wants to send a message, why not do it openly? Why all the secrecy?"

Gunnar looked back at Mike from the front seat. "People might demand a response. Though weak most of the time, the populace will rise if provoked sufficiently. Colton knows this. He's covering his tracks. Only select people in the government will know the truth. They will know that they must acquiesce to Colton's demands, whatever they may be. If that happens, he wins."

Valerie listened skeptically. "I don't get it," she said. "What does Colton have that is such a major threat?"

"He doesn't have it yet. That's how we're going to lure him

out."

They reached the small airport a half hour later. During the ride, Mike felt his simmering rage grow steadily. They got into the jet and buckled up. After the jet reached cruising altitude, Mike's anger boiled over.

"You're jerking us around," he said, his voice quavering. "You said you would help Oleg. Now do it."

"What do you think we're doing?" Gunnar asked, with a *you don't get it* look of superiority on his face.

"I have no idea what you're doing or who you are."

"You owe him an explanation," Valerie interjected. "He helped you back there."

"Henry Colton wants isotopically pure silicon. He'll kill Oleg to get it."

"So what are we going to do?" Mike demanded.

"Get Colton," Gunnar replied. "And you're going to help."

Mike felt Valerie hold his hand. Maybe she was trying to calm him down. Maybe it was a sign of solidarity. Either way, it felt good.

"When you say, *get* Colton…"

"Termination," Gunnar said in his baritone voice, his eyes fierce. "We're going lure Henry Colton out into the open and kill him."

James walked into the opulent mansion, his face hard and unimpressed by the garish display of wealth.

"Good day, Mr. Tyrell," a servant said as he closed the double doors behind him. "Santoso will be with you in just a moment." He gestured for James to sit but James remained standing. The man turned to leave.

A few minutes later, Santoso, a jovial man with graying temples and a pot belly, walked into the room. He wore a silk *batik* shirt with intricate patterns.

"Mr. Tyrell," he said, smiling, "I'm honored that you have traveled so far to visit us. Please, let me get you something to drink."

"I'm not thirsty," said James. "And, I'm on a schedule."

"Of course," Santoso said, his smile fading. "Follow me."

They walked down a hallway lined with portraits and stepped into a plush office with a conference table. Santoso sat at the head of the table. James took a seat.

"We're getting hassled by your bureaucrats," James said. "I thought we had an agreement."

"Mr. Tyrell, any friend of Mr. Colton is a friend of mine. We welcome his generous investments. When you talk about 'my' bureaucrats, well, you must understand our political system. It's complicated. They are not 'my' bureaucrats. I have influence, to be sure, but they can be quite independent."

"Despite Colton's exemplary safety record, workplace accidents do occur. When that happens, Mr. Colton has been more than generous in settling the claims."

"Of course, I understand," Santoso said, spreading his hands magnanimously. "With any large-scale operation, there are risks."

"We hashed out the details in this very office," James said, his jaws tightening. "Imagine my surprise when I heard that you are *investigating* our operations. After the economic windfall to your little island here, not to mention to you personally, the idea of being investigated rankles."

"James," Santoso said affably. "I consider you a dear friend. You have brought opportunities to my people, and for that I am personally thankful. It's just… we have rabble rousers here, just like anywhere else. They dig around and make trouble. Some days I'd like to lock these guys up, but what can I do?" He spread his hands again. "I'm not a dictator. And, to be blunt, the questions they raise are hard for me to answer."

"Such as?"

"Well…" Santoso paused, as if trying to break bad news to a friend. "The missing workers are a sore point. Many of the families would be satisfied with a proper burial. But when workers just vanish, well…" He exhaled. "It's tough."

"And the investigation?"

"There's nothing I can do," Santoso said flatly. "It will proceed."

"I see," James said, standing. "Then I have wasted my time." He turned and walked out of the office.

As he left, he thought, *we have our target.*

35

The encounter with Voth sent Gunnar's thoughts to a desolate place, five years ago.

He felt the sting of Antarctic wind. His leg burned with pain. He should have been in a hospital.

Soldiers in cold-weather battle gear shouted as the helicopter landed. The door opened and they lifted a gurney out of the helicopter and onto the snow. The gurney had little skis instead of wheels.

Gunnar hobbled toward the gurney. The soldiers pushed it toward a small building. The site was an abandoned physics experiment, AMANDA, the Antarctic Muon and Neutrino Detector Array. Now it served a different purpose.

He followed them into the building. Government interrogators were already shouting questions.

Damien Voth lay on the gurney, blood still dripping from his head. Medical personnel applied gauze and set up IV lines while the interrogators did their work.

"Step away from him," Gunnar said.

The interrogators hesitated.

"Now. We don't have time."

The government agents moved away. They knew that, for the

time being, Gunnar had authority.

Gunnar leaned toward Voth's ear. "Let me tell you what I'm going to do if you don't talk," he whispered.

Voth listened.

"No," he croaked. "No, no, no," he repeated, each "no" getting louder, building in intensity until a terrified scream propagated across the frigid landscape of the Antarctic Detention Facility.

"That's barbaric," Valerie said, bringing Gunnar back to the present. "You can't just kill someone because you think he might do something bad."

Mike looked out the jet window. After the meeting with Voth, he felt a brief feeling of satisfaction. He thought he had *helped* for a change. Now, he felt sick. Once again, someone was going to die because of him.

"Valerie's right," Mike said wearily. "If you have evidence, then arrest Colton."

"With respect," Gunnar said icily, "you don't know what we're dealing with."

"Try me. Maybe I'll understand. I'm a professor, in case you forgot."

"I didn't forget. Professor Harris, the academic."

"And what's wrong with that?" Valerie demanded, indignant.

"Our civilization is under attack," he replied coolly. "Who do you trust to defend it? Universities?"

"Why not?"

"Let's envision this collegiate army. Professors who can't remember to tie their shoes. Pampered youth who throw rocks at police over the latest trendy cause. Multi-culturists who see nothing wrong with terrorist attacks but get whipped into a hormonal frenzy at the merest whiff of harassment or discrimination. This is your army. *This* is your defense against evil."

Valerie muttered under her breath and stared out the window.

"You said you needed my help," Mike said, sitting up straight. "I'll help you, on one condition: don't kill Henry Colton."

"Impossible," Gunnar said, shaking his head emphatically. "There is no other way."

"Find a way," Mike said firmly.

They sat quietly until the plane approached the landing strip at the Golden Fleece Winery.

The jet landed and taxied to the rear of the winery. It stopped and they got out. Valerie and Mike were scowling from their conversation with Gunnar. The Stealth SUV was parked next to the runway. Robert Chen, still in his lab coat, fussed over it.

"We attack tonight," Gunnar said. "The SUV will get us past the outer defensive perimeter of the Colton compound. After that, Mike will lure him into the open. Jing will take Colton out with a single shot to the head."

"You're nuts," Mike said.

"If we don't move now, Oleg will die."

"Then arrest Colton!"

"Easier said than done," Jing said from behind them, a Heckler & Koch PSG-1 rifle in her hands. "We don't have enough evidence to hold him. As soon as he's released, he'll get on a jet and escape to his island."

Mike felt a chronic frustration. Whatever he chose, it seemed, someone would get hurt. Maybe it did make sense to take out Colton. Perhaps that was the least of many evils.

"You say I can lure him out," Mike said, calming down. "How?"

Robert pulled a shiny cube from his lab coat pocket. "Silicon," he said.

"Colton needs silicon," Gunnar said, his eyes gleaming in triumph. "Jalen faked an e-mail transmission from you to Oleg, saying that you received the 'isotopically pure silicon.' Colton intercepted the message. He believes that you possess the key. Once we're inside the perimeter, you will call him. Tell him to meet you alone. If anyone else comes, threaten to crush the crystal."

Comprehension dawned on Mike's face.

"When Colton gets into the open, Jing will take him out."

Was there method to Gunnar's madness? Mike wondered. He looked into his eyes, then Jing's. They were ready. They had no doubts about what they needed to do, or so it seemed. Then he saw Valerie, who stood next to him. Her eyes beseeched him: *don't do it*, they said.

"I'll help you," Mike said after a long pause. "I'll help you capture Colton. When he gets into range, don't kill him. Grab him. My final offer."

Gunnar appraised Mike for a long while. "Very well," he said. "We'll apprehend him."

Mike felt Valerie's hand hold his gently.

"We'll meet in fifteen minutes," Gunnar said gruffly, turning to enter the winery. Robert and Jing followed.

Valerie turned to Mike. "I'm proud of you," she said.

He looked away. How could he be sure he had made the right decision? What if a dozen people died in the attempt to capture Colton? What then?

Valerie's fingers turned his head toward her. She pulled him close and pressed her lips against his. He stepped back unsteadily, surprised. He recovered and put his arms around her waist. They kissed slowly. Gradually, he felt a warm sensation coat his tense body.

"I guess we'd better get inside," Valerie said, breathless.

"Yeah," Mike said absently, as they walked into the winery.

For the first time in what seemed like ages, he smiled.

Monitors displayed overhead images of Colton's compound in northern Montana. Red dots showed the locations of guards. A blue line highlighted a security fence that encircled the area.

"We will enter here," Gunnar said, his resonant voice filling the dark room.

On the screen, a dotted line traced a path up a winding road and stopped at an entrance with a guard post. Valerie and Mike stood together, apart from Jalen and Jing. Two men in their thirties watched intently and chewed gum. They had an ex-military look about them.

"The guards will be neutralized." He looked at Mike. "Non-lethal force, Professor, don't worry. The SUV will proceed inside the compound. Mike will step out. These two gentlemen will cover you. You will speak into this," he said, showing him a phone. "You will recite a prepared text. Colton will come out."

"How do you know?" Mike asked skeptically.

"He will," Jalen said. "We've developed a detailed psychological profile on Colton. He wants the silicon, really bad. And, in fact, he wants to meet you. Wants to kill you, too. Kind of messed up."

A green square, representing Colton, approached the SUV. Two dots, presumably the military guys, moved to intercept.

"When he gets into range, we'll take him down," Gunnar said, "hogtie him, and throw him into the back of the SUV."

The team members discussed details about the operation: points of entry, contingency plans, rules of engagement, and expected resistance. The consensus was that, while Colton's people were armed, they were not suicidal. They would not fight to the death.

The meeting adjourned. Mike was ambivalent about the plan. He knew almost nothing about this group. Were they government? Not one of them had shown identification. Gunnar spoke in riddles, revealing little. Still, he felt like he owed them some trust. They had saved him. Twice.

"What's on your mind?" Valerie said, running her fingers along his furrowed brow.

"Confusion. I'm a physicist. I prefer well-posed problems."

She moved her hands to his tight shoulders and rubbed them soothingly. "You're doing pretty well if you ask me," she said. "You got info from Damien Voth and convinced Gunnar not to commit murder. Not bad for a day's work."

Valerie's fingers, tender but firm, massaged the knots in his muscles.

"That feels good," he said, closing his eyes.

"Saddle up!" one of the military guys shouted, startling them both. "The bird's about to fly."

In a small computer room, Gunnar's eyes bored into Jing.

"I need to know that you can do this," he said.

"Of course I can," she said, somewhat defensively. Her usual combative tone was gone. She looked away.

"You've spent time with Colton. I need to know with absolute certainty that you will not hesitate."

She met his eyes. "This is an apprehension, right?"

"Wrong. Proceed with the original plan."

She inhaled unsteadily, trying to get her bearings. They were going to terminate Colton after all. Even though she always knew she might be called upon to use lethal force, she felt relief when Harris forced Gunnar to back down. Except Gunnar didn't back down–he just lied.

"You know better than anyone that apprehending Colton is a fool's errand," he said. "When he gets into range, take him out."

She nodded, again turning her gaze away from him.

"Jing, can you do this?"

"Yes," she whispered. She forced herself to look at Gunnar directly and swallowed. "Yes," she said. "I'll kill him."

36

Valerie stood with Mike as he prepared to board the helicopter. The late afternoon sky was clear and there was a light breeze.

"Be careful," she said.

"I will." He gestured toward the winery. "Open a bottle and enjoy."

"Call me," she said, and put a scrap of paper into his hand.

Mike turned and climbed into the dark helicopter. He was followed by the two ex-military guys, who wore flak vests and helmets, and Jing. One of the guys sat in the co-pilot seat and manned the weapons. The other sat next to Mike and handed him a headset. The pilot started the chopper.

The guy next to Mike identified himself as Dave and they shook hands. The helicopter ascended and headed out over a golden yellow landscape of rolling hills, keeping low to the ground. Dave explained how the quiet helicopter came to be. The Army spent twenty years and seven billion dollars developing a stealthy, high-tech helicopter, culminating in the RAH-66 Comanche. The Comanche skin, made of a composite material, had angled surfaces that deflected radar. It was also acoustically engineered to be quiet–it had a "small noise signature," as Dave phrased it–making the Comanche the ultimate stealth helicopter. However, budget pressures forced the Army to cancel the project in 2004.

After the Army abandoned the Comanche, DARPA continued secret research within the network of military laboratories. Government scientists improved the stealth technology and increased the crew size. They scrapped the Hellfire missiles in favor of lighter laser weapons and additional fuel for long-range deployments. The mission changed from general combat to special operations.

The helicopter rose and descended smoothly as it followed the topographic contours of the hilly landscape. After a half hour, the sun began to set. The land became mountainous as they approached northern Montana. The pilot spoke into his headset. A few minutes later, they landed at a desolate heliport. The black SUV that Robert Chen had shown them was parked there.

They got out and climbed into the SUV. Dave drove and Mike sat in the front passenger seat. The other guy, who went by the obviously fake name of Hal, sat in the back and manned a computer console. They accelerated away from the heliport and sped down a two-lane road.

"Memorize your lines," Dave said, pointing at the windshield. A heads-up display showed text:

> This is Mike Harris. I have a sample of silicon with the isotope ratio you are looking for. I am alone and unarmed. I want to talk, man to man. If anything happens to me, the silicon crystal will be destroyed. Come out, alone, and we can deal with this like gentlemen.

The statement seemed designed to appeal to Colton's macho side–"man to man," "gentlemen,"–as well as the persona of a CEO who likes to close a deal. Colton probably respected Mike as a scientist, even as he tried to eliminate him. He would find the opportunity to talk face-to-face irresistible.

Mike felt little fear, only numbness and resignation to the fact that events were outside his control. Perhaps fear would come when he set foot on the Colton compound. It would not be difficult for Colton to call his bluff. On the face of it, the plan was reckless. Still, Mike didn't have a better idea.

After an hour, it was dark. Dave pressed a button on the dash and the windows lit up with artificial-color images of the outside. It resembled daylight, although the colors were off, a little psychedelic. Mike moved his head side to side and noticed that the images were three-dimensional.

"Holographic night vision," Dave explained as he turned off the headlights. "Transparent laser diodes on the windows create the illusion of 3D. You know more about that than I do, Professor."

The dark SUV wound through a mountain road. Inside, the heads-up display pointed in the direction of the Colton compound.

"Guard post in ten miles," a female computer voice intoned.

In the back, Hal tapped on his computer, checking the weapons systems. "Laser ready," he said. "Modulation frequency: eighty-two hertz." He pressed a button on a joystick and his seat wheeled around. The laser popped out of the roof.

"Set phasers to stun," Dave said.

The SUV approached the guard post quietly. Yellow lamps illuminated a thirty foot radius around the post. A man sat inside, reading a paper, bored. He didn't notice the vehicle. Before the SUV entered the illuminated area, Hal pressed a button on the joystick. Silently, the laser flashed bright blue, pulsating rhythmically. The guard dropped his paper and staggered out, clutching his gun.

"You're off resonance," Dave said.

"I know." Hal turned a knob. The laser pulsed more quickly. The guard stood upright, his eyes staring like a deer in the headlights. His mouth dropped. Hal turned the knob slightly and the man's body jerked spasmodically. He fell to the ground. His arms and legs flailed. He twitched violently like someone having an epileptic seizure.

Dave pressed on the pedal and they accelerated silently past the guard post.

* * *

Gunnar watched the operation on a bank of screens. He sat in the back of a van, well outside the Colton compound.

"We've neutralized the guard," said Dave's voice.

"Very well," Gunnar said. "Proceed to the drop site."

On another monitor, he watched Jing rappel from the helicopter. Dressed in dark leather, carrying a sniper rifle, she moved with feline grace through the forest.

The SUV approached a green courtyard in front of the stone and pinewood mansion. Mike's hands began to tremble as he repeated his lines to himself. His heart beat faster as fear set in.

Dave handed him a phone. "Wait two minutes to let your eyes adjust to the dark. Then, walk to the center of the courtyard and press 'send.'"

"What if he doesn't answer?" Mike asked, his voice cracking a bit.

"Then get into the SUV and we'll go to plan B."

Mike stepped out of the SUV. After the false illumination of the vehicle's interior, the outside appeared frighteningly dark. He watched the clock on the phone. Two minutes seemed to take forever. His breathing sounded loud in the still night.

Gradually, his eyes adapted to the dark. After two minutes, he walked toward the courtyard, his heart pounding like a drum. The courtyard was bathed in a soft yellow light. He felt vulnerable, dangerously exposed.

He pressed the SEND button on the cell phone. He heard a ring. Then another, and another.

"Henry," said a voice, smoothly. It must be his personal line, Mike thought, the number he gave to his lady friends.

Mike cleared his throat. "This is Mike Harris. I have the silicon sample."

"Professor Harris?"

"Yes. Uh, come out and we can talk. I'm alone."

Gunnar cursed. "He's flubbing his lines. Jing, are you in position?"

Jing spoke softly into her headset. "Ready," she said, peering through the night-vision scope. She lined the cross-hairs up with

Mike Harris, who stood alone.

Beads of sweat formed on Mike's forehead.

"Why should I believe you?" Henry asked, peering out the bedroom window.

"I've got the silicon," Mike said, improvising. "It has the right isotopic ratio. Ninety-seven percent silicon-30, one percent silicon-29, two percent silicon-28."

"Silicon-29?"

"The silicon-29 nucleus is the only one with nonzero spin. That's the secret."

Henry pondered this for a moment. "I'll send someone outside."

"No," Mike said firmly. "I want to talk to you, man to man. I want to make a deal. The silicon for my safety."

"Fine," Henry said. "Come to the front door."

"No way. I want you to come out here and give me your word, as a gentleman, that you won't harm me or my friends."

Inside the mansion, Henry walked out of his bedroom, wearing a robe. "Okay," he said, searching for a second phone. "Just let me get dressed…"

"No," Mike said, "this deal expires in thirty seconds. I'm not going to wait while you call security."

"Fine," Henry said, putting on a pair of slippers. He pressed a red button before he opened the main door.

"He's coming out," Gunnar said. Jing looked through the scope but Henry was not in view.

Henry stepped out of the mansion, his hair mussed. He closed the double doors behind him. "Hello Professor," he called, staying on the spacious porch. His eyes searched Mike for weapons. "You've been in the news. I hope you aren't here to 'do me in.'"

Mike reached into his shirt pocket and retrieved the shiny silicon cube. "It's right here, Henry. Isotopically purified silicon. But it's fragile. If I drop it, the collision with the ground will ruin it. It's pure. The slightest defect and it's worthless. So tell your goons to stay away."

Henry walked down the stone steps, mesmerized by the crystal. "That's it?" he said as he approached Mike.

"It's yours. I don't care what you do with it. Just leave me alone."

"Why would you do that," Henry mused, "come here, all alone? Doesn't make sense."

"Because you're a bastard, Colton, but you're a man of your word." Mike held the silicon cube between his thumb and index finger. The yellow light gleamed off its polished surfaces. "I just want your word. That you'll leave me alone."

Colton stared at the crystal, then at Mike's eyes, scrutinizing him. "Professor, you have yourself a deal." He walked toward him, extending his hand, a conciliatory smile on his face. "Let's shake on it."

A flash of white light blinded Mike. Henry turned toward the light, confused.

"Get down!" called an amplified voice.

Henry put his hands up and got to his knees. Mike turned back to where the SUV had been. It was gone. A second white light blinded him. He squinted and dropped to his knees. Rough hands pushed him to the ground. He felt handcuffs tighten on his wrists. He heard shouts of "FBI!"

Jing tried to aim at Colton, but a swarm of agents surrounded him, making a clean shot impossible. She felt relief when she heard Gunnar's voice in her ear.

"Abort," he said.

She held the rifle and backtracked quietly through the forest, toward the rendezvous point.

37

The SUV's electric motor propelled it down the winding mountain road. Dave drove with trained intensity. In the back, Hal manned the weapons.

"We've got company," Dave said, seeing several dots on the heads-up display, "ninety meters ahead."

"Increasing power to lethal," Hal replied as the humming sound of the laser power supply grew louder.

"Vehicle ahead," the female computer voice intoned, "thirty meters."

Hal jerked the joystick to the right and his chair swiveled around. He faced forward. He saw the scene outside, lit in false color. A van was parked in the middle of the road, thirty meters ahead. Roadblock.

Hal positioned the crosshairs on the center of the van and pressed the button. An intense green beam shot from the SUV and cut through the van. The flash of light illuminated FBI agents, who dove for cover. Sparks flew from metal as the laser scanned vertically, slicing the van in two. The halves of the van collapsed and the SUV blew through it. Bullets pelted the SUV, bouncing off the composite skin. Dave stared ahead as they continued down the road, the bifurcated van's fuel igniting in an orange ball of flame.

After fifteen minutes, they allowed Mike to stand. The silicon crystal lay on the ground, shattered into several shiny pieces. Henry Colton stared at it longingly.

"It was a fake," Mike spat. "Ordinary silicon. I'm surprised that a man of your stature was dumb enough to take the bait."

Henry regained his composure. He showed Mike his wrists, which were free. "You're the one with the handcuffs," he said with a tense grin.

The area crawled with agents. A few Colton employees stood around, apparently cooperating with the FBI. Agent Sanchez approached Mike and showed her badge.

"You've led us on a long chase, Professor Harris."

"Agent Sanchez," Colton said charmingly, "I cannot thank you enough. I've informed my staff to provide you with whatever you require."

"Thank you."

Colton looked at Mike coldly. He turned and walked back to his mansion.

"You're letting him go?" Mike exclaimed. "He's a murderer!"

"Come with me," she said as a pair of agents escorted him. "You have some explaining to do."

James paced in the five-star Indonesian hotel room as he waited for Henry Colton to pick up the phone.

"Are you okay?" James asked when Colton answered. Colton went through the story sheepishly, knowing his security man would be irate that he had acted so impulsively. It was worth a shot, he thought. He knew the crystal might have been phony, but if it had been real, their problems would have been solved. He hadn't earned success in business by playing it safe.

James cursed as Colton related the details. If only he had been there, he thought. Things are falling apart in Montana. The idiots out there could not be trusted with security. Colton needed to get out to the island right away.

"Don't do that again," James said, trembling. "You're too important. Stay put until transportation comes."

He hung up the phone and poured a glass of whiskey. He downed it and threw the glass against the wall. The glass shattered. "Dammit!" he shouted.

Mike told the story in a monotone, barely believing it himself. Sanchez and two other agents stood in the room. He knew how it all must sound. He and Seth tried to find Axel Hansen–but someone killed him. They confronted Hassan–but someone killed him. They went to a diner–and someone killed the waitress. Where was Seth? Well, I don't know. Not to mention the unidentified bodies in the burnt Viper and the crashed helicopter.

He told them about the winery; Gunnar, Jing, and Jalen; the stealth helicopter and SUV. One agent, perhaps playing the bad cop but probably just amused, kept chortling with each new, improbable detail.

When he mentioned Damien Voth, the room got quiet.

"You spoke to Voth?" Sanchez asked.

"Yes. You can check the visitor log. Gunnar and I gave them phony names." Suddenly he had a thought. "I have a witness. Valerie Norton."

"Who is that?"

He explained that Valerie was a freelance writer who visited his lab at Colton University. Later, when he and Seth were fleeing Glacier Park, they ran into her. Ladies' man to the end, Seth let her into the SUV–a decision that nearly cost them their lives. Sanchez, holding a bullhorn, told Mike to surrender. Valerie panicked and pounded on the glass. Sanchez interpreted that as a hostage in distress. She ordered the snipers to fire. The bulletproof SUV survived, and they escaped.

The SUV belonged to a woman who had tried to kill them. The charred body near the destroyed Viper was hers. The agents seemed to value the information, even as they maintained skeptical looks. They were also interested in his identification of Axel Hansen.

He returned to the subject of Valerie Norton. "She said that she got the GPS coordinates of the winery. That's why she was worried. These people, whoever they are, made no effort to keep the location secret."

Sanchez nodded, thinking of the Praetorians' reputation for eliminating people who knew of their existence. "Can you contact Valerie?"

"I don't know." Then he remembered. She had given him a piece of paper before he left. He fished it out of his pocket. Valerie's name and number were written on it.

An agent handed him a phone. He dialed hurriedly, realizing how badly he wanted to talk to her. She answered immediately.

"Are you okay?" he asked.

"I should ask you."

"I'm with the FBI," he said.

"That's good," she said, sounding relieved. "Is Colton okay?"

"Yes," he said, somewhat peeved. Why should she care about Colton? Then he remembered how pleased she had been when Mike refused to go along with the plan to assassinate Colton. Like him, she objected to it on principle.

"Mike," she said in a hushed voice, "I'm glad you're away from Gunnar's people. I don't trust them."

"Where are you?"

"At the winery. They won't let me leave. There's a lot of activity…"

"I need the coordinates."

"The GPS coordinates? I'll text them to you."

He waited for a moment and the cell phone beeped.

"Got 'em."

"Are you going to come here?"

"I think that's the plan," Mike said. "Just hold tight."

"I'm scared."

"We'll get you," Mike said. "I promise."

He hung up and handed the phone to the FBI agent, who read off the GPS coordinates.

"That's it," Sanchez said to Mike. "If your story is true, this is where we'll find the Praetorian headquarters."

WEDNESDAY, JUNE 4

38

The FBI helicopter that Mike Harris and Gabrielle Sanchez boarded was standard issue, nothing like the high-tech marvel that the Praetorians used. The helicopter transported them to Kalispell, where they boarded a small jet and flew to an airport in Lewiston, Idaho. FBI agents met them and drove to southeast Washington state, toward the site of the Golden Fleece winery. It was almost dawn.

Sanchez and Harris sat in the back seat of an SUV, which was in the center of a five-vehicle convoy. Sanchez probed him about the Praetorians. He felt intimidated by her interrogation. At times, her skepticism almost convinced *him* that he was lying.

Still, he welcomed the closure that the FBI raid might bring. The renegade death squad would be reined in. Valerie would be saved.

They drove along dry, hilly terrain for fifteen minutes. Dawn broke. The convoy turned onto a dirt road. The SUVs turned off their headlights.

After a minute, they pulled into a parking lot in front of a warehouse. A wooden sign read

Golden Fleece Winery. Tasting daily, 2-6 pm

Agents poured out of the SUVs, armed with rifles and bulletproof vests. One agent knocked on the door and shouted "FBI!" He waited a moment and then nodded to a team that carried a battering ram. They approached the door.

Before they reached it, the door opened. A man in his fifties, with graying hair and beard, answered. His bleary eyes stared at the law enforcement personnel. He had a paunch and the unshaven appearance of someone who had lived well.

"That's him!" Mike exclaimed. "His name's Rob. This is the place!"

"We're closed," Rob said curtly.

The agent showed Rob a search warrant. Rob squinted at the paper, argued a bit, and finally shrugged his shoulders.

"C'mon in," he said. "I've got nothing to hide."

Sanchez escorted Mike as they followed the team into the winery. It was cool and damp inside. They walked past oak barrels and crates of wine bottles to the tasting room. "Are you here for the cab?" Rob asked. He caught Mike's eye and winked.

A pair of agents remained in the tasting room and guarded the entrance. The rest of the team went past the tasting room, down a narrow stone corridor. They pushed open a wooden door and proceeded down a cold, dimly lit staircase.

They walked into a space with small oak barrels and bottles of wine. Mike walked up to a door.

"This is it," he said. "The Praetorians' nervous system lies behind this door."

"You can't go in there," Rob said, his eyes now focused, his hung-over act finished. "It's off limits."

"We have a warrant," Sanchez said. She nodded to an agent. "Proceed."

An agent pushed the door open. The room beyond was dark. They aimed flashlights into the cavernous space.

The room contained a dozen oak barrels, arranged horizontally on a wooden rack, and little else.

Mike's jaw dropped. Where were the computers? Where were the screens that showed maps, streams of alphanumeric data, and live feed from cable news channels?

"We keep this room secret," Rob explained. "We've been aging our cab select for the past five years. It'll debut at the Unified Wine and Grape Symposium." He looked at Mike, his eyes playfully mocking. "I'd appreciate it if you kept this to yourselves."

Sanchez walked into the large, cool room. She examined one of the barrels. "I'll need to inspect the contents."

"Of course," Rob replied. He removed the stopper from a barrel. "I ask that you use sterile instruments. By all means, feel free to taste."

The agents tested, but did not taste, the contents of the barrels. They concluded that the liquid was, in fact, wine.

"Where's Valerie?" Mike insisted. He exited through a corridor toward Jalen's office, the one that had shown a computer-generated tropical scene. Now, the office was empty, save for a desk and an unimpressive desktop computer.

"What the hell?" Mike said, exasperated. Rob's smug look enraged him. He remembered that "headquarters" had had a temporary feel to it. All the equipment was portable. They must have whisked everything away.

"Where is Valerie?" he said, feeling dizzy. He stumbled down a dark passageway, toward the bedrooms. He pushed Valerie's door open. The room was empty. His room was also empty.

"Where have you taken her?" he shouted. He pointed an accusing finger at Rob. "You're a liar! Tell them what this place is!"

Sanchez regarded Mike with disdain. He could read her thoughts clearly: *I never should have trusted you. My original assumption, that you're an out-of-control lunatic, was correct.* "I'm sorry to have disturbed you," she said to Rob. "We'll complete the search and be on our way."

The staff at the Colton compound worked frantically. They knew Colton had dodged a bullet, literally, and that James' wrath would descend on them. There was no excuse for letting Henry Colton come so close to being captured or killed. Colton had to be protected, from himself if necessary.

Colton left the mansion and walked toward the helipad, surrounded by a phalanx of security guards. They got him into the helicopter, which took off as soon as it could. Men armed with rifles surveyed the landscape. As the helicopter faded into the horizon, the tension at the compound slowly began to subside.

The FBI drove Mike to a small federal building in downtown Lewiston, not far from the Snake River, and dragged him, handcuffed, into a bare room. The tone was different this time. Before, they seemed interested in the value of his information. Now, they wanted to extract a confession. Agents shouted at him as Sanchez looked on. His mind was reeling. He couldn't get his bearings.

The agents' questions came at him from all angles, making it difficult to perceive a coherent timeline. The axioms that held the story together–that Colton was behind the conspiracy and the Praetorians were the good guys–crumbled under the FBI's interrogation.

The agents kept yelling, their voices melding into an angry chorus. After the emotional volatility of the past days, Mike felt himself shut down. He couldn't hear individual words. He closed his eyes and wished he would pass out.

After a time, he noticed it was quiet. Sanchez looked at him intensely. "Damien Voth," she said. "Will he remember you?"

"I think," he said. "Why?"

"That's the only part of your story we can hope to corroborate. After the winery, though, I'm not inclined to waste more time."

"He'll remember me," he said without conviction. Voth's health was shaky. Mike could only imagine what the FBI would do if it turned out that Voth had died right after meeting the fugitive professor.

"Will he talk to you?"

"Yes," he said. "I think he empathizes. I mean, we're both scientists…"

Sanchez scanned his face, looking for deception. Finding none, she turned to an agent. "Set up a visit with Damien Voth."

The agent nodded and walked out of the room, dialing on a phone.

She turned back to Mike and pressed her finger into his chest. “If this turns out to be another dead end, I’ll see to it that you spend the rest of your life behind bars.” She walked out of the room, leaving him with a half dozen guards.

39

Mike wished he could sleep as they traveled by Lear jet to California, back to the prison that held Damien Voth. Handcuffs rubbed painfully against his wrists. His heart beat faster as they approached the site. After the experience at the winery, he feared they would arrive to find the prison hospital wing evacuated. "Damien Voth?" they would exclaim. "We've never had a patient by that name…"

As bad as things were, he thought, the worst the FBI would do was throw him in a federal penitentiary. Valerie, Seth, and Oleg faced more uncertain fates. The Praetorians had a reputation for eliminating people who knew of their existence. Colton's henchmen, proven killers, pursued Oleg. With each passing moment, three innocent people faced increasing danger.

The jet encountered turbulence. Mike felt nauseous and his head pounded painfully. The agents watched him, unconcerned about his discomfort. After a time, the ride became smooth. His headache persisted but his stomach began to settle.

At noon, they descended onto the tarmac of a secluded airfield. Dark clouds obscured the sun. The agents escorted Mike out of the jet and into a white sedan with government plates.

He wasn't sure what they would do when they met Voth. He

hoped he would corroborate Mike's story, but Voth had no real incentive to do that. Maybe he would play games. Perhaps Gunnar was right, that he was a "brilliant sociopath." On the other hand, Voth may have been right about Gunnar. *"You cannot trust that man,"* he had said. *"He tortures."*

After driving through the hilly terrain of northern California, they pulled into the well-manicured grounds of the Kenwood Coast Federal Correctional Facility and Wellness Unit. The driver showed his FBI badge and the guard waved them through. They parked in a space reserved for law enforcement.

They got out of the car. Sanchez unlocked his handcuffs and removed them. She and Mike walked toward the prison while the other two agents waited by the car. They entered the lobby, where Sanchez showed her ID and signed them in. They walked to the Wellness Unit and checked in with the clerk there.

After a minute, Dr. Petersen appeared and greeted them.

"I'm not sure you should be here," he said to Mike, his camel's eyelashes fluttering nervously. "You had a bad effect on him last time."

At least that's confirmation I was here, Mike thought.

"Does Dr. Voth not want to speak with us?" Sanchez asked pointedly.

"No," said Dr. Petersen. "Just go easy on him, okay?"

"Sure," Sanchez said.

They walked down a corridor, past rooms that held decrepit criminals in their final days. They entered the spacious room that housed Damien Voth. The back of Voth's head was burnt red, cracks from his fractured skull showing through the thin skin. Four stainless steel arms supported the head. The iron lung inhaled, mechanically, at regular intervals. Everything was as Mike remembered it.

"You're safe," Voth said, his good eye locking on to Mike like a laser. "I'm glad."

The screen above Voth's bed showed stock quotations and news updates.

"We were going to capture Colton," Mike said, uncomfortably aware of Sanchez watching him. "Did you warn the FBI?"

"Of course," Voth said, his mouth curling into a grin. "Why

wouldn't I? I'm a–concerned citizen."

"He got away," Mike said, casting an angry look at Sanchez. "Colton will continue killing people."

"What about Gunnar?" Voth said, nearly spitting the name.

"What about him?"

"I said to stop Colton, not kill him." Voth paused to look at the stocks for a moment and then focused on Mike again. "I could not let Gunnar kill a man in cold blood."

"That wasn't the plan," Mike said. "I mean, originally it was, but I talked Gunnar out of it."

"They would have killed Henry Colton–had I not warned the FBI."

Mike saw a look of certainty on Voth's face. He looked at Sanchez, who nodded slightly.

"Gunnar told me they would arrest him!" he protested.

"You're a physicist," Voth said. "You are used to physical systems–that play fair. Gunnar Stone, by temperament and–training, deceives."

Mike took a step back. He felt, once again, like an amateur, in over his head. Voth and Sanchez seemed to regard him as a naïve child. As he thought about it, he knew they were right. Why would Gunnar honor his verbal agreement? He needed Mike to get close to Henry Colton. After he eliminated Colton, Mike's value as an asset would cease.

"Where is Colton?" Sanchez asked.

"Out of the country," Voth replied, "en route to his island."

"Isn't there some way to grab him?" Mike said plaintively. "Stop him at the border or something?"

"Too late," Voth said. "The FBI chose not to apprehend him."

"We have no evidence that he committed a crime," Sanchez said flatly.

"He murdered a half dozen innocent people!" Mike shouted, feeling pain surging in his temples. "Does that mean nothing to you?"

"Perhaps," Voth said calmly, "Professor Harris and I could speak in private."

"Of course," Sanchez said, giving Mike a look that said *watch yourself.* She left the room.

Mike sat down and pressed his hands to his temples. He didn't want to look at the disfigured scientist.

"My boy," Voth said, "let the professionals handle Colton."

"But Oleg, Seth … and Valerie."

"Ah. So there's a woman."

"She's being held by the Praetorians."

"Is that what they call themselves?" Voth said, grimacing. "Such hubris."

"Will they harm her?"

"I wish I could reassure you."

"Did they torture you?"

Voth's eye drifted up to the screen. The room was silent, save for the mechanical breathing of the iron lung, for a full minute.

"You cannot understand cruelty," he said at last, "until you have been interrogated by Gunnar Stone."

Mike sat for a moment as the iron lung continued its respiration. He found it impossible to get a fix on who was good and who was bad. His first instinct was to trust the Praetorians, at least partially, because they had saved him from Colton's henchmen. Gunnar convinced him that Voth was a brilliant sociopath who had helped terrorists acquire a nuclear bomb. If the Praetorians had truly cared about him, though, they would have taken him into protective custody early on. To them, he was just a pawn. From that angle, he had to treat everything Gunnar said with skepticism.

"I'm going to die in this room," Voth said clinically. "I know that. My only fear is that, being–physically immobile, I will succumb to infection."

Mike noticed Voth wince as he said the word *infection.* He wondered how Voth ended up in a helpless state that precluded suicide. Gunnar Stone, he knew, must have played a role.

"I still have friends," Voth said. "Scientists from Livermore developed a–portable respirator for me. I will try it soon."

"That's great," Mike said, trying to sound upbeat.

"Henry Colton," Voth said abruptly. "I met him in San Francisco." Voth told him about their first meeting. Over time, Voth convinced Colton that he could benefit society by supporting science and technology. Although Colton initially regarded Voth as an eccentric, he gradually warmed to the idea that he could change the world through scientific progress.

Colton's fervor for science increased. He established a foundation to support physical and biological research across the nation. He testified before Congress, urging them to support basic research. His company, Colton Enterprises, pioneered revolutionary discoveries. Voth took satisfaction in Colton's zeal. After years of working on nuclear weapons, he said, he finally did something he could be proud of.

"Tragically, Colton took it too far," Voth said. "He now believes he can–remake the world in his own, reborn, image. A man named–James Tyrell convinced him that violent force was–required to achieve this goal." He went silent as his eye drifted upward.

"So now you want to stop him?" Mike asked.

"Yes," Voth said, his eye turning back to Mike, "through legal means. Too many people–have died."

"But they let him go. Nothing will stop him now."

"The FBI lady was right," Voth said. "They had no evidence. If you want to save your friends–and yourself, cooperate with the authorities."

They heard a knock at the door. Sanchez entered.

"Mike has done nothing wrong," Voth said. "He wants to cooperate."

She arched an eyebrow skeptically. "Is that true?"

Mike stood up. His body, from sore feet to aching lower back and throbbing temples, felt battered and weary. "Of course," he said. "I want to help. That's what I wanted all along."

Sanchez scrutinized him, her expression one of distrust.

Voth's finger tapped his keypad. The screen switched from stock quotations to a map of the Pacific Ocean. The display zoomed in on Colton's island.

The success of Colton's new society, Voth explained, relied on radical developments in biological and physical sciences. On the biological side, his researchers developed implants that heightened sensory processing, enabling his bodyguards to have lightning reflexes. The implants, called Biochips, served a second purpose. Colton knew that all revolutions started with idealism but eventually gave way to apathy and corruption. To counter that natural trend, Biochips would subtly influence the thoughts of all the citizens of his new society. It wasn't total mind control; rather, a positive feedback mechanism to keep the populace on the right ideological track.

In parallel with Mike Harris' nightmare, a researcher at Johns Hopkins developed a crucial interface that allowed the Biochip to work reliably. Shortly after making the discovery, his wife found him in their garage, in his car with its engine running. He had died of asphyxiation. Police ruled it a suicide.

Colton's pattern was clear. He used his foundation to fund research in areas where he needed radical innovations. Then, when researchers hit upon solutions to his problems, he eliminated them and took the technology.

"We need to stop him," Mike said to Sanchez, desperately. "Send in the military or something."

"I'm sure I don't need to remind you that the FBI is a civilian agency," Sanchez said. "While Dr. Voth has provided interesting information, we have no evidence that would allow us to issue a warrant for Colton."

"To hell with warrants!" Mike exclaimed. "Just *get* them!"

"Now," said Voth, "you sound like Gunnar."

"What about the Praetorians?" Sanchez said. "How can we get to them?"

"They are protected," Voth said, "by well-placed individuals in–governments here and abroad. Professor Harris is your best hope."

Sanchez turned to Mike.

"Forget it," he said. "I'm tired of being used."

"This woman of whom you speak," Voth said. "Valerie…"

Mike felt his pulse quicken. For the past week, Mike felt pushed to do things, never choosing for himself. Events controlled him. He seemed to have no free will. And now, once again, he felt compelled–by an external force–to act.

"I don't know where the Praetorians are," he said. "If I did, I would tell you."

"They will contact you," Sanchez said confidently. "The

phone you have is theirs. They'll call it sooner or later. When they do, lead us to them."

Mike closed his eyes and shook his head.

"Even if you do not care about this–Valerie," she said, "consider that you are a wanted man. You are not in a position to negotiate."

"Fine," he said angrily. "I'll do it for Valerie, not myself. You can throw me in a dungeon for all I care. But if anything happens to her…" He choked up.

Sanchez led him out of the room. The sound of the iron lung's mechanical breathing faded as they walked down the corridor. They reached the waiting room, where one of the FBI agents stood. He slapped handcuffs on Mike's wrists. They walked back to the SUV and got in silently. The third agent drove them along the winding road, away from the prison.

40

Chief Jon Patterson knocked on the door, which was plastered with test scores from physics courses and NASA space photos. The door creaked open, revealing the beady eyes of Professor Paul Quinlan.

"What do you want?"

"I'd like to ask some questions," Jon said, "if you don't mind."

Paul looked him up and down, considering. After a moment, he opened the door and gestured him in. He led Jon past columns of papers and piles of dusty electronic equipment. Papers with numbers and Greek symbols scratched on them covered the walls. Paul sat down behind his desk. Jon sat on a creaky chair opposite him. They looked at each other through a narrow gap between stacks of books.

"You're not federal," Paul said, "so I'm going to give you the benefit of the doubt." He removed a folder from the middle of a stack of papers, sending the rest of the stack sliding into a larger pile. He thumbed through the papers and found the one he was looking for.

"Postage stamps," he said in a hushed voice. "Note the rate increases."

"The what?" Jon asked, his forehead wrinkled in befuddlement.

"The United States Postal Regulatory Commission increased the rate of a first-class stamp 13 times, a prime number, between 1975 and 2007. They never explained why. In particular," he said, his voice lowering to a whisper, "they never explained why the prime-numbered rates became more common over time."

"Prime-numbered rates?"

"Consider this," Paul said, his face drawing nearer. "As numbers get bigger, prime numbers get rarer."

"Huh?"

Paul sat back, disappointed. "Prime numbers!" he barked. "Numbers that can only be divided by themselves and one! Like the number 5. You can't divide it by 2, 3, or 4. You can only divide it by 1 and 5."

"Okay…"

Paul groaned and stood up. He walked over to a whiteboard and tried to write with a blue marker. It was dry. He threw it across the room and tried a red one, which worked. He wrote a series of numbers:

2, 3, 5, 7, 11, 13, 17, 19, 23, 29, 31, 37, 41

"Now look," he said. "There are 4 prime numbers between 1 and 10. There are 4 prime numbers between 11 and 20. But there are only 2 primes between 21 and 30, and only 2 between 31 and 40."

"Is that a coincidence?" Jon asked.

"Hell no!" Paul said, throwing the red marker in frustration. "Supercomputers have calculated primes up to–well, huge numbers–and they get rarer as the numbers get bigger. It's a mathematical fact!"

"Okay," Jon said, holding up his hands. "I believe you."

"So," Paul said, the redness in his face fading, "if the Postal Commission had chosen rates *randomly*, one would expect *fewer* prime-numbered rates as time went on."

"Yeah," Jon said, "I guess you're right."

Paul grinned and threw a paper onto the desk. The paper was

a printout from the Postal Regulatory Commission's web site. "And yet," he said triumphantly, "the exact opposite occurred. On New Year's Eve, 1975, they raised the rate from 10 to 13 cents. 13 is a prime number. Between 1968 and 1990, a period of 22 years, 13 cents was the *only* prime-numbered rate. The rest of them–6 cents, 8 cents, 10, 15, 18, 20, 22, 25–were not prime."

Jon nodded his head.

"Then, a change occurred. 1991: 29 cents. 2002: 37 cents. 2007: 41 cents. *Three prime numbers in only 16 years!* The exact *opposite* of what one would expect had the Postal Commission chosen rates irrespective of primeness."

"So you're saying that, after 1990, they deliberately chose prime numbers?"

"Of course," Paul whispered. "That is beyond dispute. The real question is: *why*?"

Jon sat back, enjoying his discussion even as it veered away from the matter at hand. Listening to eccentric professors beat handing out minor-in-possession citations on College Hill.

"The answer is simple," Paul said with a sly grin. "Manned space exploration."

"You know, Professor," Jon said with a laugh, "I was just about to say that."

"You think I'm joking, but look at the data. The 13 cent stamp began in 1976. What else happened that year?"

"The bicentennial," Jon said.

Paul's eyes formed narrow slits. "The space shuttle," he said. "NASA's first space shuttle rolled out on September 17, 1976."

"I see."

"Then, in 1991, the 29 cent stamp appeared. Two months later, astronauts performed an unprecedented *spacewalk* at the International Space Station. This was the next logical step in mankind's domination of space."

"Wow."

"In 2002, the Postal Rate Commission unveiled the 37 cent stamp. Do you know what else happened that year?"

"No."

"LIGO, the Laser Interferometer Gravitational Observatory, began its search for gravitational waves."

Jon shrugged his shoulders, uncomprehending.

"Gravity waves!" Paul squealed. "Warped space! Ever watch *Star Trek*?"

"You mean, warp drive?"

"How else will we perform interstellar travel?" Paul said slowly, as if explaining to a toddler that two plus two equaled four.

"So you're saying that the Postal Rate Commission deliberately chose prime numbered rates whenever we made advances in space exploration."

"Exactly."

"Why?"

"Good question," Paul said, pleased that the cop finally understood. "Good question indeed. They're signals."

"Signals? For who?"

Paul looked past Jon to make sure no one was eavesdropping. "Aliens," he whispered.

"Space aliens?" Jon asked, suppressing a chuckle.

"It's the only explanation."

They sat silently for a while. "Wow," Jon said. "You've given me something to think about. But, you know, as much as I appreciate that information, and I *do* appreciate it, Professor, it's really not why I came here today."

Paul sat back, a disappointed look on his wrinkled face. "I see."

"I'm here to talk about Professor Mike Harris."

Paul growled. "Harris," he said grumpily. "You still haven't caught that nutcase?"

"No. Maybe you can help us."

"Go on…"

"Sergeant Garrett talked with you a few days back."

Paul grinned, recalling the moment when he pulled a shotgun on the policeman who came to his house. It had been in the middle of the night. Paul told Sergeant Garrett that Mike Harris was behind the killings, to cover up the fact that he sent his graduate student to steal Paul's office supplies.

"I'm curious about this office-supply theory you have."

"A theory that has been proven," Paul said authoritatively.

"The continual disappearance of my black pens has ceased."

"And the name of the grad student was…"

"Charles. He was the thief, sent on the orders of Mike Harris."

"You know that for a fact?"

"Absolutely."

"How?" Jon asked, his relaxed demeanor stiffening a bit.

"I know." He folded his hands across his chest and smiled smugly.

Jon pointed to Paul's computer, half concealed by stacks of dusty papers. "Why are you recording this conversation?"

Paul's eyes widened. "Wha-at?"

"I asked you a question: why is your computer recording our conversation?" He walked over to the computer, brushing past piles of scientific journals. He grabbed an inconspicuous microphone that sat on the tower and yanked it loose. Paul jumped at a sharp sound that burst from the speakers.

"I must've left it on," Paul stammered. "It's not a crime."

"Then you won't mind if we scan your computer."

"Wha– Why, that's a violation of my civil liberties!" he cried, his hands shaking. "I'm a tenured professor!"

"The computer belongs to Colton University."

"I don't see what that has to do with anything," Paul spluttered, his face crimson.

"I'm sure you have useful information recorded on this puppy," Jon said, putting his hand on the mouse. "Lots of good stuff."

"Stop," Paul said, panicking. "I insist!"

Jon turned away from the screen and looked into Paul's fearful eyes. "I dunno, Paul, you haven't been too cooperative. I asked you a simple question and you didn't answer. I'm thinking that scanning your hard drive will be a lot easier."

"What do you want to know?"

Jon casually returned to his seat. "How did you know that Mike Harris' student was stealing your supplies?"

"I just know."

Jon got up.

"Wait!" Paul shouted. "Wait." He exhaled. "I'll show you."

41

Mike sat on a squeaky chair in a windowless room in the Lewiston federal building. Besides a door that led to a small bathroom, the room was spare. The agents who guarded him ignored his requests for reading material. One of them held a phone. Sanchez predicted that someone from the Praetorians would call. Mike hoped it would happen soon. Nothing in his training or background prepared him for long periods of idleness. The agents didn't seem to mind. It seemed, from their impassive expressions, that they could endure boredom indefinitely. He envied them.

Hours went by. His mind wandered. He thought of the women in his life: a high school sweetheart, college girlfriends, Jennifer, Valerie. The faces of those who had died in the past week haunted him.

Mike felt regret over the distance he maintained between himself and other people. Seth had acted with kindness, visiting him at the hospital and sticking by him as he was pursued by the law. He had always been a good friend, but Mike never returned the friendship fully. At one point, he even suspected that Seth was part of the conspiracy. Oleg, a close collaborator, was far away geographically. They saw each other annually, at conferences, but otherwise communicated via e-mail.

Now, he waited for a phone call that might never come. He wanted to do something, anything. He had lost Jennifer. There was nothing he could do about that now. But Valerie was different. She was, he hoped fervently, alive. He resolved to do whatever it took to save her.

He jumped at the sound of the phone ringing. An agent handed it to Mike. The other agent used his phone to listen in.

"Professor Harris?" said the voice on the other end. It was Gunnar Stone.

"Where's Valerie?"

"With us," he said. "Hold on, I'll get her for you." The line went quiet. Mike examined the phone, puzzled. A message read:

Downloading encryption key…

Complete.

"They can't hear me now," Gunnar said. "Act like the phone doesn't work. Listen, Mike: you're in danger. In one minute, ask to go to the restroom. Tell them you have an upset stomach."

The line went dead.

Mike shrugged. "Doesn't work," he croaked, his mouth suddenly dry. He handed the phone to an agent. His heart pounded. He didn't trust Gunnar, but what could he do? Gunnar had Valerie.

He put a hand to his stomach and groaned. "I need to use the restroom," he said weakly. He didn't need to fake the symptoms.

The agent inspected the phone suspiciously. His brow furrowed. "No signal," he said.

"You're kidding," the other agent said.

"Excuse me," Mike said, standing up.

"Go ahead," the first agent said, nodding toward the door to the bathroom.

Mike stepped into the bathroom. He hoped the agents would not notice his trembling hands and the nervous sweat on his back. He closed the door and turned on the light. His pallid face stared back at him from a mirror. He ran the tap and splashed water onto his eyes and cheeks.

"Don't talk," said a voice, right next to him.

He looked around. No one was there.

"They can't hear me." It was Gunnar's voice. It sounded like he was speaking into his left ear. "I'm using acoustic focusing. Respond by tapping on the sink three times." Mike tapped. "Okay. Listen carefully. In three minutes, I will call the cell phone again. You will demand that I meet with you. I will agree. The FBI will escort you to an SUV. When the door opens, go in as fast as you can. Tap once if you understand, twice if you want me to repeat."

Mike tapped once.

"Got it," Gunnar said.

Mike opened the door, walked back into the room, and sat down. He felt sweat drip from his forehead to his jaw and down his neck. The room became chilly and he started to shake. Three minutes felt like an eternity.

The phone rang. Like before, the agent handed it to Mike while the other agent listened in.

"This is Gunnar Stone. We have Valerie Norton."

"Where are you?" Mike demanded. "I want to see her."

"Are you alone?"

"Yes."

"Very well. I'll text you my GPS coordinates. Come alone. If you bring anyone else, you'll never see Valerie again."

Mike shuddered, unconvinced that Gunnar was just acting.

"Fine," he said.

A moment later, the phone beeped. The text message showed a pair of numbers. The agent nodded.

"Come with us," he said.

The two agents led him out of the room and down the stairs. They walked through a small foyer and out the rear exit, where Gabrielle Sanchez was waiting. The four of them stepped out onto the street. A black SUV roared up and screeched to a stop. The rear door opened and a man in shades beckoned him in.

Mike rushed into the SUV. Gabrielle stared at the man with shades.

"Wait. Show me your badge."

The door slammed closed and the SUV lurched forward.

"Wait!" Sanchez yelled, reaching for her sidearm. The agents drew their weapons, confused. Sanchez fired at the tires, but it was too late.

"Where is Ashcroft?"

"He was supposed to be in the SUV," the agent said.

She looked around, running down the street, gun at the ready. Two more agents joined them.

"I've got Ashcroft's coordinates," one of them said.

Sanchez nodded and followed him. They ran down the street and turned left. A black SUV was parked on a side street. Sanchez saw Ashcroft through the tinted windows. She opened the door. Ashcroft stared straight ahead, unblinking, his expression blank.

"Doug. It's me. What happened?"

The driver was in a similar catatonic state. An agent waved his hand in front of his eyes.

"Doug," Sanchez said, holstering her gun. "Snap out of it." She slapped him.

"Flashes," Ashcroft slurred. "Praetorians."

"Who were they?"

He blinked and his eyes gradually began to focus. "Blinded us," he said. "Some kind of strobe light. I think it was the Praetorians. Must've been."

Sanchez cursed. She had intended to use Mike Harris as a pawn, to get to the secret group. But they captured the pawn.

Mike sat in the left rear seat of the SUV, which sped out of Lewiston. They crossed a bridge over the Snake River and headed toward steep yellow hills. The SUV turned right onto highway 12 and the windows went black. The driver wore glasses that allowed him to see through the windows. Mike's stomach lurched as they rounded a sharp curve.

Gunnar sat in the front passenger seat. "We're going to a secure location," he said. "Oleg sent you another message. He has the silicon crystal."

"Is he okay?"

Gunnar turned back to look at Mike. "He'll be dead in twenty-four hours if we don't get to him first."

"What about Valerie?"

"Oleg trusts you," Gunnar said, ignoring the question. "You can lure him out of hiding. Then we can protect him–and the crystal."

"What about Valerie?"

"We'll leave for St. Petersburg, Russia, within the hour."

"I need to see her first," he said.

Gunnar faced straight ahead and put on a pair of glasses. "She's safe," he said.

Twenty minutes later, the driver parked the SUV and they got out. The sun was setting behind rolling hills covered with yellow grass. They walked along a dusty path toward a nondescript warehouse.

"We don't have much time," Gunnar said.

They approached the door and Gunnar pressed his hand against a smooth black panel. The door unlocked.

They walked into the dark building. Mike saw a woman rush at him. It was Valerie. They embraced. Mike felt a swell of emotion as her body pressed against his. They kissed, their passion tempered by the presence of the Praetorians.

"Mike," she said, "I'm so glad you're safe."

"I know. I was worried…"

She pressed a finger to his lips. "I think we need to trust these people."

Mike disengaged slowly, uncomprehending. "You were the one who didn't trust them."

"I know," she said, "but I do now. There's someone here you need to meet."

They walked down a dark hallway. The air inside the warehouse felt cool, like a cave. Along the right side were windows, through which they could see a large hanger with an aircraft inside. They reached the end of the hallway. Gunnar opened a door.

"I believe, under the circumstances," he said, "that introductions are not required."

Mike stared in disbelief at the man who stepped into the passageway.

It was Axel Hansen.

42

Axel knew that the meeting in Glacier Park was a risk. He would probably be searched. Bringing a gun was out of the question. He filled his backpack with hand warmers, a small knife, and an innocuous radio transmitter. His ski poles had sharpened tips.

He signed his name in the visitor's log, to give authorities a clue in case he didn't make it back.

When it turned out to be a trap, he knew what he had to do. Familiar with the landscape, he fell backward onto a patch of snow and tumbled down the cliff, triggering a minor avalanche. At the bottom, he activated the hand warmers and hid. One of the men, using an IR camera, approached the hand warmers. He thought the thermal signature was Axel's body. From behind, Axel sliced his throat.

He used a ski pole to dispatch the second man.

That left the leader, who chased him toward the glacial lake. Axel plunged in, feeling the shock of frigid water. He swam to the bottom and waited.

He surfaced for a breath and heard the sound of a helicopter. He knew the sound well. It was a quiet, muffled throb, unlike any other aircraft.

He saw the brilliant flash of a laser. The leader tumbled into the lake, blood gushing from a gaping wound in his chest.

The helicopter landed. Axel got out of the lake and dragged the corpse with him.

Gunnar Stone approached the corpse, knife in hand.

"Give me your coat," he told Axel.

Axel handed him his blue coat. Gunnar filled the pockets with weights and put it on the corpse. Clinically, he took the knife and carved a line around the pale face. Blood trickled out. He pinched the chin between his thumb and forefinger and slowly lifted it up. He peeled the skin off the face, revealing muscles and eyeballs. He threw the skin into a bag.

Axel turned away and headed for the helicopter. Gunnar took out a pair of wire cutters and chopped off the corpse's fingers, one by one, and placed them into the bag. When he finished, he dumped the body into the lake.

"Is that the last one?" Chief Patterson asked.

Paul Quinlan's beady eyes darted from side to side. They stood in the hallway outside his office, not far from Mike Harris' lab, which still had yellow police tape covering the door. Paul had revealed three cameras and microphones in his office, as well as a wireless microphone he had planted in the Chair's office. He also showed, reluctantly but with some pride, the camera in the hallway. It was a tiny webcam that sat innocuously in a glass display case, along with an educational holography and laser demonstration. The camera continuously transmitted a wide-field image to Paul's computer.

"Yes," Paul said, "that's the last one."

"Show me the videos."

"Fine," Paul said, leading Patterson back to the office. He brushed aside a layer of papers that covered a pile of hard disk drives. The disk drives had dates written on them. After a moment, he found the one he was looking for.

"This is it," he said, setting it by his computer. He plugged it in and browsed the contents.

He clicked on a thumbnail. A window opened, showing an

empty hallway. A time stamp read 1:16 PM. A skinny graduate student with a plaid shirt and jeans entered into view, walking along the hallway. He looked around for a moment.

"That's Charles," Paul said, "the student whom Mike used to steal supplies."

Charles opened Paul's door. A second window on the computer screen showed the scene in Paul's office. Charles walked in, grabbed a Sharpie pen off the cluttered desk, and walked out.

"There!" Paul squeaked, rewinding the video. They watched it a second time. "There's your evidence, Chief Patterson!"

"Where were you during that time?"

"Teaching," he said. "Years ago, I suspected that someone was stealing my supplies. I set up the cameras. Then, I deliberately left my door open the entire semester."

"A sting operation," Patterson said, amused.

"Exactly."

"Have your cameras been running continuously?"

"Yes," Paul said, gesturing toward the pile of hard drives. "I recorded everything."

Patterson nodded his head, thinking. "That's interesting," he said.

The sun set over the Pacific Ocean, its deep orange light reflected by calm water. Wispy pink clouds stretched across the horizon. The Kenwood Correctional Facility, perched on a rocky cliff, had an enviable view. Damien Voth admired it from his room. A pair of biomedical engineers checked the valves on his iron lung.

"I think we're set," one of them said.

Dr. Petersen watched, smiling. "This is exciting," he said. "It's so wonderful that Dr. Voth still has friends at the labs."

A scientist stood silently in a corner of the room. He was gaunt, with sallow skin and black hair, and wore dark glasses despite the hour. Like the engineers, he was from Lawrence Livermore National Laboratory.

"This is a real marvel," Petersen said.

He walked over to a vest that sat on a small table. The vest had several rubber tubes that were connected to a pump, which was attached to the back of a wheelchair. A cable led from the vest to a laptop computer, which monitored its performance.

"The hydrogen bomb was a marvel," Voth said. "This is simple engineering."

"Still, it'll get you out of this old thing," he said, patting the iron lung.

"Call the nurses," an engineer said.

"Right," Petersen said. He stepped out of the room.

"We'll just have a few seconds," the engineer explained to Voth. "When the iron lung is at atmospheric pressure, we'll open it. Two nurses will lift up your back. We will snap on the vest. If there are any problems, we'll take off the vest and put you back in the iron lung. Got it?"

Voth nodded.

The other engineer walked to the laptop and clicked on a button. The pump turned on and the vest inflated. Then, it deflated. It continued the rhythm, imitating the much larger iron lung.

Dr. Petersen returned with three nurses. Two of them took up positions behind Voth while the third held the intravenous line connected to his left arm.

"Are we ready?" Petersen asked.

The engineer went through a checklist and nodded. He waited for the iron lung to reach normal pressure.

"Open the iron lung."

The other engineer turned off the iron lung pump. Both engineers quickly unlatched the iron lung and opened it, revealing Voth's frail frame. The two nurses gently propped him up. Dr. Petersen brought over the vest and the engineers snapped it on.

"Can you talk?" Petersen asked.

Voth shook his head. His face, already scarred by burns, turned a shade redder. The vest inflated, then deflated. Voth moved his mouth but no sounds came out.

"Abort," the engineer said.

Voth shook his head vigorously.

"Wait," the scientist in the corner said.

"He isn't breathing," Petersen said. "Take the vest off."

"Keep it on," the scientist said.

The engineers paused. Petersen gave them an incredulous look. "I'm the doctor here. Take off the vest!"

"No," Voth said. "I can…" He paused as the vest filled his lungs with air. "I can breathe." His mouth curled into something resembling a smile. "Now get me out of this bed."

Petersen exhaled a whoop of relief, overcome by joy. The nurses, who had a fondness for the grandfatherly Voth, shared in the celebratory moment. They didn't notice as the scientist with dark glasses quietly exited the room. Over the next few minutes, aided by the engineers, they carefully lifted Voth off the bed and onto the wheelchair.

43

Mike stared, disbelieving, as Axel shook his hand.

"You're alive," he said dumbly.

Axel's blue eyes crinkled into a smile. "Observant as ever," he replied.

"He made a mistake," Gunnar said, his baritone voice interrupting the moment. "He thought he was dealing with reasonable people."

Gunnar led them down a passageway and opened a door to the hangar. "We cannot negotiate with Henry Colton and his army. The best we can do is annihilate them and move on to the next battle."

"That's barbaric," Valerie protested.

"So is the world."

They walked into the dark hangar. The aircraft had a smooth polymer black skin, like a B-2 without the sharp angles. It had two jet engines under the V-wings and an afterburner. A metal ladder led up to the cabin, which had room for eight to ten passengers. Two pilots sat in the cockpit.

"Where are we going?" asked Mike.

"Russia," Gunnar said. "We need to find Oleg Sinitsky. Climb the ladder."

"Ladies first," he replied, gesturing to Valerie.

"Negative. She's staying here."

Mike crossed his arms defiantly. "Then I'm staying too."

"Oleg trusts you. We need you to make contact with him. If you don't go, he could die."

"Then you should listen to my request."

"How much blood do you want on your hands, Professor?" Gunnar spat, his face inches from Mike's. "I'm giving you a chance to save your colleague. Don't push your luck."

Mike stood silently, his heart pumping. With effort, he met Gunnar's stare.

Gunnar turned to Valerie. "Get in," he growled.

"Thanks," Mike said weakly.

Valerie climbed up the ladder, followed by Mike and Axel. They stepped into the spacious cabin, bathed in soft light from polymer panels on the deck and overhead. Valerie looked out the window and saw Gunnar talking to Jing. After a minute, Jing turned and left.

Gunnar joined them and they buckled up. They sat in four seats around a small table. Mike and Valerie faced forward, Gunnar and Axel faced aft.

The hangar door opened slowly. Outside, it was dark. The engines turned on and the aircraft rolled out onto a runway.

"Do you know where Oleg is?" Mike asked.

"No," Gunnar said. "When we're in the air, you will e-mail him."

After a moment, the engines roared to life and the aircraft accelerated forward. It lifted into the night sky.

After they reached cruising altitude, Gunnar pointed a finger at Mike. "There is no reason why I should trust you," he said. He aimed his finger at Valerie. "Or you." Turning back to Mike, he said, "You betrayed our headquarters to the FBI."

"If you're the 'good guys,' why hide from the FBI?"

Gunnar's face reddened. "They're a bureaucracy, Mike, hindered by rules, regulation, and oversight. When it comes to arresting people after a crime, they are without peer. When it comes to preventing an attack, they're impotent."

Axel observed the exchange with an amused expression.

"This is a war, Professor," Gunnar continued. "The future of civilization is at stake. If you think you can fight this war with warrants and subpoenas, then you're every bit as naïve as I suspected."

"Who are you, exactly?" Mike asked. "Government agents? Mercenaries?"

"We're people dedicated to civilization, something professors don't give a damn about unless it affects them directly. You remember Jalen, our computer guy? He's claustrophobic. Can't stand enclosed spaces. Yet every day he came to work in the basement of a wine cellar. Why? Why would he do that?"

Mike sat in silence.

"Because he cares about the survival of *civilization*," Gunnar shouted. "Do you know how important this is? Academics expect civilization served on a platter. They'll squeal about the importance of free speech, *their free speech*, but don't expect them to give an ounce of sweat or blood to defend it."

"Now Gunnar," Axel said, patting him on the shoulder, "there are exceptions."

The aircraft encountered mild turbulence and rocked. The pilots took it to a higher altitude and the ride was smooth again.

"I disagree with Gunnar about many things," Axel said, his blue eyes calm and sharp, "but he's right about one thing. Henry Colton must be stopped."

"Was he responsible…" Mike fumbled for words. "For Jennifer? For the lab?"

"Yes. There was nothing you could do, Mike. Once Colton's machine was set into motion, Jennifer and the others were doomed. You're only alive, as am I, thanks to luck–and the Praetorians."

Mike's mind flashed back to Jing, who saved him twice, once at his house and again at the diner.

"Colton's plan is to take your discovery and eliminate everyone who knows about it. He needs the ability to create a black hole. It is central to his scheme to create a new society."

Mike shook his head. He didn't even know that creating a

black hole was the true aim of the project until Seth told him. Why would Colton care about such an esoteric discovery?

"Your research reached the stage where Colton could take over," Axel said. "First he orchestrated the lab disaster. Then he used proprietary technology to emulate your voice and lure Jennifer into a trap. He needed to tie up the loose ends. Hassan and Seth were on the list. Oleg is too."

"And me," Valerie said quietly.

"You're not the only ones. Alongside the black hole project, Colton pursued the development of the Biochip."

"What's that?" Mike asked.

"A computer chip that enhances the human mind. The chip itself is not remarkable, but the techniques for interfacing with the brain are cutting edge. A researcher at Johns Hopkins, sponsored by the Colton Foundation, had a breakthrough."

"Let me guess," Valerie said. "That person is dead."

"Correct. The police ruled it a suicide."

"Of course they did," Mike said.

The Biochip had two purposes, Axel explained, confirming what Voth had said before. The first was to give operatives like James Tyrell enhanced sensory capabilities. The second was to control the population of Colton's new society.

The researcher at Johns Hopkins demonstrated that he could attach wires from the computer chip to primates' nerve bundles, which led to the brain and spinal cord. Human trials were awaiting approval. Before they could begin, Colton's people killed the researcher and framed it as a suicide. They took the technology, most of it unpublished, and proceeded with secret human trials at the Pacific Research Center.

After a year of intensive effort, the Biochip was implanted in James Tyrell for field testing. The initial trials were judged a success. Other operatives had Biochips implanted. Tyrell got an upgrade.

"There was a second innovation," Axel said to Mike, "with which you are familiar. The bio launcher."

"Those bazooka things?"

"They are the culmination of decades of research into non-lethal arms technology."

The idea of non-lethal weapons, he explained, was pioneered by a former Army Special Forces soldier named John Alexander. In 1980, Alexander published an article in Military Review in which he described the "new mental battlefield." He envisioned new weapons that could interfere with the brain's electrical activity and impair the enemy's judgment. Although the mental weapons idea never got off the ground, the idea of non-lethal weapons caught the interest of a lot of people. Alexander went to Los Alamos in 1988 and teamed up with Janet Morris, a science fiction writer. They enlisted the help of Ray Cline, a former deputy director of the CIA.

DARPA got involved and funded research into stun guns, computer viruses, and laser rifles that could flash-blind people. One project was a drone aircraft that sprayed metal-eating microbes on enemy weapons. Another weapon used a cloud of tiny metal fibers to short electronic circuits in enemy tanks and personnel carriers. Mike recalled the rifle that he used against the helicopter in Glacier Park. It shot a harpoon that cast a net. Such a weapon could capture people alive.

The bio launcher shot spheres that immobilized the enemy by delivering a high-voltage shock. The spheres were made of a complex organic composite that mimicked the tissue of electric eels. A network of neurons and kinesin motor proteins permeated the sphere, giving it the ability to adjust its trajectory in midair to hit a moving target. When the slimy mass struck, it unleashed multiple pulses of direct-current electricity. Similar to a Taser gun, the electric shocks caused muscles in the body to contract involuntarily, effectively paralyzing the person. Its mission complete, the sphere "died." It underwent rapid decomposition, drying into biodegradable flakes that sublimated into the atmosphere. The sphere left virtually no trace.

"Colton used the bio launcher against you outside your house," Axel said. "The plan was to immobilize you, shoot you, and plant the gun on you."

"Murder-suicide," Mike said. His voice faltered. Valerie's hand rested in his. "Why Jennifer? How did Colton know…"

Axel and Gunnar glanced at each other briefly. "There are some uncertainties," Axel said, "but this much is clear. Hassan had some hints about the project, so he called Jennifer to press her for information. She confirmed that the project's aim was to create a gravitational field using high-intensity lasers. Hassan used that information to lobby against funding our project."

At the DARPA conference in Glacier Park, Axel and Hassan were scheduled to present their cases to the Committee. On the way to the conference, Hassan appeared at Mike's lab, unannounced. He wanted to see the experiment with his own eyes before making his arguments.

"What is the Committee?" Mike asked.

Axel and Gunnar exchanged glances again. "The Committee is a group within JASON. Gunnar and I are not members, in case you're wondering, nor was Hassan."

"Who *are* members?"

"We can't answer that," Gunnar said.

"The Committee formed after the incident in Berkeley, where a group of amateurs nearly detonated a nuclear device on American soil," Axel said. "It was decided that JASON needed to be more–proactive–about preventing such attacks in the future."

"Hassan talked about a 'civil war,'" Mike said. "What did that mean?"

Axel smiled wryly. "The Committee split into two factions. One wanted to fund our project. The other wanted to kill it."

Mike felt Valerie's hand close softly around his. It calmed him. "I'm amazed that our project attracted such attention. I guess I should be flattered."

"The ability to create a black hole, in the wrong hands, could be dangerous. Nonetheless, I believed that, given the proper safeguards, it was a research direction that should be pursued. I wanted to meet with three members of the Committee, before the DARPA conference began. We would meet at Grinnell, under the pretense of sightseeing. I hoped to persuade them to keep the project alive.

"Obviously, that meeting never took place. I was ambushed."

Mike nodded slowly.

"How terrible," Valerie said, "to betray you like that."

"It's worse than that. The 'mole,' if you like, is also responsible for Jennifer's death. When Hassan learned about our project, the only people he told were the members of the Committee. He named Jennifer as a source of information. The mole passed her name on to Colton."

"Sealing her fate," Mike said, his voice weak and miserable.

"Yes," Axel said. "I'm sorry, Mike. You must know that you did nothing wrong."

Mike stared at the deck as Valerie's hand squeezed his. He welcomed her touch.

"I wish I could believe that. I wish I knew what to do."

"Save Oleg," Axel said. "Forget about the rest."

Jon Patterson walked along the hallway. In Paul Quinlan's office, Harry downloaded video files from the computer while Paul spluttered about the Bill of Rights.

Jon stopped at the door to Mike Harris' lab. He unlocked the door, opened it, and stepped through crime scene tape into the dark room. He turned on his flashlight and pointed it at the blackened remains of the fume hood, optical table, cryostat, lasers, and capacitors. The air smelled smoky. The flashlight illuminated items left by graduate students: soda cans, burnt notebooks, and a notebook computer. He saw a digital camera, perched on a workbench. Half of it was melted.

He heard footsteps and he swung the flashlight around. He aimed it at the open door.

"Chief!"

The spot of light landed on Harry's sweaty face.

"What do you want, Harry?"

"I've got something to show you."

THURSDAY, JUNE 5

44

The jolt of the landing woke Mike. Valerie's hand still rested on his. He looked out the window and saw runway lights streaming past.

"Where are we?" he asked groggily.

"St. Petersburg," Gunnar said, and added for clarification: "Russia."

The aircraft decelerated. A couple hours ago, as instructed by Gunnar, Mike sent an e-mail to Oleg:

> Oleg,
>
> I got your message. I'm in town. Let's meet at noon, at a place where we can get everything "squared away."
>
> -Mike

He hoped Oleg would get the reference. The last time he visited St. Petersburg, for a NATO workshop on laser physics, Mike made a pun about getting "squared away" when they visited the Palace Square. Despite the lameness of the joke, or perhaps because of it, Oleg laughed with abandon. The rest of the week, every chance he got, Oleg would say "time to get squared away" and giggle like a little kid.

The Palace Square would have open space, light, and tourists, making it as safe a place as he could hope for. However, the chances that Oleg would arrive at the appointed hour were slim. Even if he was alive and checking his e-mail regularly, he could be miles away from St. Petersburg by now.

The aircraft stopped. After a few minutes, the door opened and a Russian in military uniform spoke with the pilots. Gunnar stood up and spoke in Russian. The man nodded and bowed slightly.

"You may go," the man said to Valerie. "Please."

She looked at Mike for a second and followed the man out the door and down the ladder. The others followed. The sun shone low in the horizon. The sky was clear.

"3:55 AM local time," Gunnar said, looking at his phone. "We'll get some rest at the safe house."

The Russian led Gunnar, Axel, Mike, and Valerie across the tarmac, which was deserted save for a couple of helicopters and one MiG fighter. They entered the small airport terminal, where they were greeted by a stocky man in a business suit, flanked by two men carrying AK-47s.

The stocky Russian led them outside to the street, where a convoy of four small cars waited. Gunnar and Mike rode in the second car, Valerie and Axel rode in the third. Military personnel rode in the first and fourth cars. The lead car honked twice and the convoy headed out.

In the back seat, Gunnar barked Russian into his phone. Mike looked out the window. They sped past drab, Soviet-era apartment complexes.

Gunnar hung up. "We're headed to the safe house, north of the city," he said. "We'll try meeting Oleg at the Palace Square at noon. If that doesn't work, we'll send him another message."

The lead car accelerated forward. The rear car shot past them and got behind the lead car. The two cars moved into position at an intersection, blocking traffic. After Mike's car and Valerie's car passed the intersection, the other cars swiftly resumed their positions.

"Russian ballet," Gunnar said with a grin.

They encountered a couple more major intersections, and the

cars repeated their maneuvers. After a few minutes, they turned onto a narrow city street.

"It's important for you to get some rest," Gunnar said. "I have pills."

"Forget it," Mike said, looking out the window.

"Suit yourself," Gunnar replied, and swallowed a tablet.

The cars slowed to a halt. The military personnel got out of their cars and took up positions on the sidewalk. Two men blocked traffic.

Mike's door opened and a man gestured for him to get out. He got out of the car and Gunnar did the same. Valerie and Axel joined them, accompanied by Russians with suits and earphones.

They walked into a plain concrete building with narrow windows. A bored-looking woman sat behind a desk.

"Sign in," she said, indicating a clipboard.

After they signed their names, they were escorted to an elevator that took them to the sixth floor. The elevator doors opened and they stepped into a hallway. A young Russian in military uniform greeted them and handed them keys to their rooms.

Gunnar checked his watch. "4:30 AM," he said. "Get some rest. We'll meet in the hallway at ten." He went into his room and shut the door. Axel went to his room too.

Valerie approached Mike, keeping an eye on the military guy. "I never got to finish that massage the other day," she said, putting her hands around his waist.

"Gunnar said we should rest."

Valerie slipped her hand into his and led him to his door. He fumbled with his key and managed to unlock the door. They walked into the room. The Russian guard didn't seem to care.

Mike shut the door. The room was drab, with a musty odor. Valerie sat down on the small bed, which squeaked in response. She pulled Mike to her. Their lips met and they kissed softly.

"Nice place you got here," she said.

She nudged him onto the bed. He lay face down while she straddled him and massaged his shoulders.

"You're tight."

"Tough day at the office," he said. "Ouch!"

"Sorry."

"No," he said, turning his head to look at her. "I actually liked that."

"I see," she said, kneading his tense muscles. "You're one of *those.*"

Mike hummed in pleasure as he gradually relaxed. His thoughts drifted. Valerie's fingers worked their way down his spine. He thought of the plane ride, when her hand rested on his. He enjoyed the moment.

In a dark room filled with computer screens, Jalen's eyes focused on a set of green numbers.

"Wow," he said, and whistled.

He called Gunnar.

"This Damien Voth guy puts Warren Buffet to shame," he said, watching the green numbers increase. "His portfolio is shooting up. We're talking 200%, and it was already big."

"How big?" Gunnar asked.

Jalen did some mental calculations. "He was up to fifty million a week ago. Now, he's at one sixty."

"It's sitting in an account, right?"

"A bunch of accounts, in places you might expect: Caymans, Switzerland… I guess he knows how to pick 'em."

"Keep an eye on that."

"Roger, boss."

The small jet approached the lush emerald island, framed by a calm blue ocean and cloudless sky. The jet landed on an airstrip near the harbor and taxied to the terminal. A door opened and Jing stepped out, accompanied by two men in Brooks Brothers suits.

A man in khaki shorts and tropical shirt walked up to Jing. His facial muscles were taut. "I am Dr. Sauer," he said, tension in his voice. "I'm coordinating this event."

"Honored," she said.

"If you'll follow me, we will take you to the visitor's quarters."

He escorted her to an automated electric car. She got in and it took off toward the winding road that led up to the region between the twin volcanoes. It would then descend to the west side of the island and arrive at the visitor's center. She would get a nice introduction to the scenic landscape.

A middle-aged woman in a lab coat stood next to Dr. Sauer. Her long gray hair was tied in a bun. "Who's she?" the woman asked.

"A waste of my time," he replied. "Are the Biochips working?"

"Like a charm," she said, her wide grin and crow's feet giving her a gleeful but somewhat maniacal look.

"Any more mishaps?"

"Acutes?" she said, using the medical term for lab animals that expire. "It's a normal part of research. Don't worry your little head."

"I'm not worried about your team," Sauer said, gazing up at the twin volcanic peaks. The car made its way up the road, entering the lush jungle at the base of the mountains. "It's *my* team that needs a kick in the ass."

45

Mike opened his eyes, disoriented. Valerie was gone.

He heard a knock at the door. "Mike!" It was Gunnar's voice.

Mike shuffled to the door and opened it.

"It's time," Gunnar said. "Shower up and we'll move out."

Mike looked at the alarm clock by the bed. It was 10:04 AM. He rubbed his eyes and stepped into the shower. As the water dripped down his body, he realized what happened. Like a fool, he fell asleep while Valerie was giving him a back rub.

There was another knock as he dried himself off.

"Let's roll!" Gunnar shouted.

"Just one minute!" Mike shouted back. "Asshole," he added. He pulled on his clothes, quickly combed his hair, and opened the door. Gunnar and Axel were waiting.

"Follow me," Gunnar said, and took off toward the elevator.

Valerie came from behind. Mike started to apologize.

"No worries," she said, patting him on the shoulder. "It was kind of cute."

They entered the elevator, accompanied by the Russian guard.

The elevator doors opened. The stocky Russian was waiting

for them. He introduced himself as Sergey and led everyone to a convoy of four small cars. Like last time, they got into the second and third cars, and the convoy sped down the avenue. They turned onto a narrow street, the lead car honking at pedestrians. After a series of turns, they parked at a lot outside a government building.

They got out, followed by the Russians with earphones.

"Oleg might get scared off by these guys," Mike said to Gunnar as they walked toward the Palace Square.

Gunnar nodded and spoke to Sergey, who gave the men a hand signal. The men backed off but maintained a watch over them.

"Palace Square this way," Sergey said to Valerie. "Have you been?"

"Nope," Valerie said. "First time in Russia, actually."

"First time! You must visit Hermitage."

They entered the Palace Square, an area of cobblestones surrounded by grand buildings in baroque and neoclassical styles. Russians and tourists walked leisurely in the sun. Young Russian soldiers were in the crowd but paid them no mind. Pigeons were everywhere.

Gunnar looked at his watch. "It's eleven-thirty. Oleg should be here in half an hour. Mike and Valerie, stroll around the square. Try to look casual. We'll watch from a distance. I'll call you every ten minutes."

Valerie and Mike walked toward the Alexander Column, a monument that towered over a hundred feet high. The Winter Palace, home of the Hermitage art museum, was nearby, with a long line of tourists waiting to get in. The low angle of the sun illuminated the green building, brightening its stately white columns and gold trim.

Mike looked over his shoulder. Gunnar had disappeared.

"So now we wait," he mumbled.

"Is Oleg expecting you to be alone?" Valerie asked. "Maybe I should leave."

"You want to?"

"No." She took his hand in hers. "What does he look like, anyway?"

"Oleg? Long hair, glasses. Kind of a coffee-shop intellectual, with a Russian twist."

"I wonder about intellectuals," she said wistfully, "if maybe they're a dying breed. We're becoming a world of 'C' students."

"But we give them 'A's."

"Exactly," she said, looking up at him through thick glasses. "Standards are slipping, dumbing down, every day. What if the smartest people in the world, the geniuses, people like you and Oleg…"

"Or you."

She laughed but did not disagree. "What if those types ran things? Wouldn't we be better off if professors were in charge? Things couldn't be worse, could they?"

"You never sat through a faculty meeting."

A flock of pigeons flew into the air suddenly, startling them. Valerie put her arms around him.

"Kiss me," she said.

He did. Despite being watched, he felt himself respond to her touch. After a long kiss, he ran his fingers through her hair as they gazed into each other's eyes.

The phone rang. It was Gunnar.

"Keep a lookout," Gunnar said. "Don't get distracted."

Mike hung up and put the phone back in his pocket.

"Busted," Valerie said.

They walked around the square in silence, scanning the crowd. Valerie pointed out a few long-haired people, but none of them was Oleg. Even if he were in the square, however, Oleg might very well be in disguise.

"He's not going to show," Mike said when it turned noon.

Gunnar continued calling every ten minutes. After a half hour, Mike began to feel dispirited.

"He might want you to be alone," Valerie said. "I don't want to ruin your plan."

Mike picked up the phone and told Gunnar that he would wait in the square, alone, for an hour. Valerie gave him a kiss goodbye and joined Gunnar outside the square.

The minutes crawled by as Mike waited. After an hour, still no Oleg. He waited for another hour, watching the crowd, hoping to spot the Russian scientist. Finally, Gunnar told him to return. He met the others and they got into the cars, which sped back to the safe house.

Jon glanced at his watch and frowned. It was past midnight and he was in Paul Quinlan's office. Since becoming Chief, he usually managed to avoid late nights. With triplets at home, he knew the value of sleep. Nonetheless, he couldn't pull himself away from what Harry was showing him.

"The format is weird," Harry said, tapping at the keyboard. "Paul Quinlan wrote a program to record long stretches of video. The data are in a compressed format, but nothing standard. I think he made it up. The algorithm is based on prime numbers."

"Prime numbers," Jon repeated, rubbing his eyes. "He mentioned them to me. He's kind of obsessed with them."

"Who can blame him? They're cool. The Chinese thought they were a symbol of masculinity. They're tough, you know, can't be divided."

Harry brought up a window on the computer screen. It looked like an amateurish, out-of-focus photograph.

"That's the passageway outside the lab. Paul recorded video twenty-four seven. When a person appears, the resolution improves."

Harry pressed the "play" button on the window. The scene remained static until a person entered the frame. Then, the picture turned into a multicolored mess.

"What happened?"

"I don't have the key, that's what happened. The key is a password that allows the program to display the high-resolution image. If I had the key, the picture would be crisp and clear."

The picture returned to the fuzzy, low-resolution state.

"We need to get the key from Paul," Jon said.

"Yeah… There's one problem with that idea."

"And that is?"

"I've looked at the source code. The algorithm has a self-destruct built in. If we use a bogus password, then it'll wipe out the information."

"Can't we back up the data?"

"Negatory, Chief. The high-res stuff in the video file is encrypted, and the keys are scattered throughout the hard drive and cloud servers. The file by itself, without the keys, is useless."

"Couldn't you just copy all that information somehow?"

"I could start," Harry said, "but with the wrong passphrase, Paul's computer will send out the self-destruct commands. The servers will respond by erasing the data. *Poof.*" He made the sound of an explosion.

Jon wrinkled his forehead. "Then there's only one option. Get the password from Professor Quinlan."

Harry exhaled and pushed his tinted glasses, which were perched on the end of his nose, closer to his bloodshot eyes. "Just get the right one. If he gives you the wrong one…"

"I'll get the right password. You just worry about analyzing the data."

Back in his room at the safe house, Mike collapsed onto the bed. He thought about Valerie and her soft hands massaging his back. He worried about Seth and Oleg.

A knock interrupted his thoughts. He opened the door. It was Gunnar.

"We got a message."

They walked to Gunnar's room, where a laptop sat on the bed. Mike read the message on the screen:

> Mike,
>
> I saw you today. Who's girl? She has 'naughty librarian' good looking ;-)
>
> Tell others (men with guns) please stay behind. I meet you tomorrow same time. Bring girl, no one else. I see anyone else, I disappear.
>
> -Oleg

"What do we do?" Mike asked.

"We do what he says. We'll keep watch from a distance. You and Valerie talk to him. See what he wants. Convince him to come in from the cold."

Mike nodded and returned to his room. His head ached as he tried to sort through what he should do. Oleg would be safer with Mike and the Praetorians, right? Or was he just leading Oleg into some kind of trap? Clearly, the Praetorians had their own motives. Once again, he didn't know whom he could trust.

After an hour of such thoughts, Valerie knocked on the door. He let her in, grateful for the company.

"You look tired," she said.

"That's because I am. Another backrub might put me under."

"Then I'll skip that."

She took off her glasses and set them on the nightstand. She stared at him, her green eyes intense, illuminated by the afternoon sun filtered through plain white drapes. Valerie brought him to her and their lips met. They kissed frantically, as if they had no time. They unbuttoned their shirts and threw them aside, knocking over a lamp. Her soft breasts pressed against his chest as they collapsed onto the bed. She stroked his hair and kissed him hard, moaning in pleasure. It had been too long. Her free hand unbuttoned his pants. He returned the favor and their remaining clothes scattered onto the floor.

The SUV pulled up to the front of the rustic lodge. Agent Sanchez stepped out, flanked by two agents with "FBI" windbreakers. They marched inside and flashed their credentials at the young employee at the front desk.

"We need to speak to the organizer of the DARPA conference," she said.

"They're on the second floor," the employee said in a shaky voice. "Go right on up."

On the second floor, a group of four sat around a table in a small conference room. Screens displayed the faces of two other people. The adjacent rooms were empty. Speakers in the corners provided acoustic canceling. A man in civilian clothes stood watch in the hallway.

"How can we be sure Mike Harris has not gone rogue?"

A gray-haired man with a somber countenance sat at the head of the table. He considered the question, asked by one of the people on the screens. The room's dim lighting accentuated the worry lines on his leathery face.

"My source is Axel Hansen," he said, gazing intently, one by one, at the members seated at the table.

"Axel's alive?" a woman asked.

"Yes."

"What happened?"

"He was betrayed," he said, a hint of anger in his voice, "by one of us. By one of the Committee."

"Impossible," blurted one.

"I wish you were right, Dr…" He stopped and listened to his earphone. "We'll have to adjourn," he said abruptly.

The screens flickered off. The gray-haired man stood up and walked to the door.

"Your data look promising," he said loudly to the other three as he opened the door. "I suggest that you submit a proposal to the Department of Energy." Face to face with Agent Sanchez, he feigned surprise. "May I help you?"

She showed her badge. "I'm with the Federal Bureau of Investigation. I need to ask you some questions."

"Of course," he said, stepping into the hallway. He grinned genially. "We're scientists. We have no secrets here."

FRIDAY, JUNE 6

46

Jing stepped out of the small pool, water dripping down her lithe body as she wrapped a towel around her waist. She watched the brilliant sunrise and felt the warm morning breeze. She walked back to her room and put on her contact lenses. The spacious room was tasteful and high-tech, with flat screens and soft music piped in through unseen speakers. She removed the towel from her waist and began to dry her hair.

There was a gentle knock at the door.

"Are you decent?" It was Henry Colton.

"You decide," she said, opening the door.

He smiled and admired the woman before him. The swimsuit, compliments of the visitor's center, fit nicely.

"I've missed you," he said, embracing her. "Things have been crazy around here."

"Who are the other visitors?"

"No one as important as you," he said, kissing her hand. "Investors, a couple politicians, scientists…"

He walked toward the deck, where the calm water of the pool reflected the golden-pink sunrise. The water seemed to merge with the ocean beyond. She followed him as he stepped outside.

"I'd like you to stay," he said, staring out at the ocean. "We could build something here, you and I. The world out there"–he waved dismissively in a random direction–"is finished. Here, you can be part of the future."

She arched an eyebrow. "How's that?"

He grinned cryptically. "The details, you mean. This evening, much shall be revealed." He kissed her hand a second time. "Until then, enjoy the beach."

"I will," she said.

He stepped onto a winding path that led along the beach and back to the meeting complex, a gleaming glass structure shaded by palm trees. Behind it towered one of the dormant volcanoes, covered with a carpet of lush vegetation.

"Did you get that?" Jing said quietly.

In the lower right part of her field of vision, her contact lens displayed the reply:

Roger. Keep up the good work. –Jalen

Mike awoke in an empty bed. The scent of Valerie's perfume brought back memories. In the middle of the night, she had disentangled herself gently from his embrace. "I'd better get back," she said, kissing him. "It's past my curfew."

Despite the early hour, the sun was too bright to allow him to fall back asleep. As he languidly took a shower, a thought struck him: his head did not hurt. It was clear. He could think. No migraines, no throbbing pain, nothing. He felt–*fine.* He allowed himself to smile.

He got dressed slowly, reliving his afternoon and evening with Valerie. After their first, frenzied burst of passion, they lay in bed, caressing, saying little, savoring the silence. Their caresses continued and they made love a second time. Afterward, Valerie buried her head in his chest. He felt tears and he held her close.

Mike smiled as he put on his shirt. He didn't know whether they would find Oleg today, or whether they could stop Henry Colton from whatever he was planning. Right now, he didn't care. He was, for lack of a better word, happy.

* * *

Later that morning, Axel came by his room. He had news about Seth. After a brief scare, he was in stable condition. Top medical people were watching over him. Mike sighed in relief. The news, plus Axel's calming presence, set his mind at ease. Things were finally turning his way.

Six men emerged from the dark, cold water and walked onto the beach. They climbed up the cliff swiftly. When they reached the top, they crawled on grass, avoiding the spots illuminated by lights. A building stood before them. A sign identified it:

Kenwood Coast Federal Correctional Facility and Wellness Unit

Inside, Damien Voth sat in his new wheelchair. His vest made a mechanical breathing sound, not as clunky or as loud as the old iron lung.

Doctor Petersen stepped into the room. The lights were off. "You called, Dr. Voth?" he said softly. His face was a picture of kindness, from his soft eyes and long eyelashes to his freckled skin and genuine smile.

"Yes, boy." Voth peered out the window. "You have always been kind to me."

"Is that why you…"

The window pane fell away and shattered on the ground outside. Two men jumped in, clad in wet, dark clothing, aiming laser-sighted rifles at the doctor.

"What's happening?" Petersen yelled.

A security guard entered the room. One of the men fired a silenced rifle and the guard crumpled to the floor. The man calmly aimed his rifle at the doctor again. The second man wheeled Voth toward the large window frame.

"You were always kind," Voth said to Doctor Petersen. "You will be spared pain."

Men carried the wheelchair to the cliff. Behind them, inside the building, there were muffled gunshots. The men attached cables to the chair and rolled it to the edge. On the cliff face, a pair of climbers guided it down while the men above held on to the cables. After a minute, the chair reached the bottom, where the gaunt scientist from Livermore awaited.

"This way, Dr. Voth," he said.

Men pushed his wheelchair along the beach until they reached a gangway that led to a fifty-foot black fiberglass boat. They guided the chair along the gangway, carefully but quickly. Once aboard, the boat's crew retracted the gangway and started the engine.

"The skipper sends his regards," the scientist said. "We'll rendezvous with his ship in due course."

The men wheeled Voth into the cabin as the boat headed for the sea.

Jing arrived at the reception dressed in the sheer black dress Henry had provided for her. A glittering diamond necklace adorned her neck. She caught his eye as she sat down at her assigned seat near the stage. Outside the glass building, the sun was setting over the Pacific Ocean. The waters were calm.

She surveyed the audience in the spacious hall, matching faces to the names Jalen had sent her. There were thirty people here tonight, all of them prominent and dressed elegantly. She recognized Senator Conrad Schmidt of California, chatting amiably with a congresswoman from the other party. Several investment bankers and the CEO of a military contractor sat at another table. At the back of the room, there was a group of scientists, including a biologist who wrote popular books on evolution and atheism, and a Nobel laureate who studied the chemistry of high-explosive materials.

The lights dimmed and people took their seats. Henry tapped the microphone a few times. James stood on the stage behind Henry, his expression stern as always.

"Ladies and gentlemen," Henry said, beaming at the assembled guests, "thank you so much for visiting my island on such short notice. Each one of you has been invited here for a specific reason." His eyes scanned the audience and seemed to linger on Jing.

"While you all bring different talents to this place, we're all here for a common purpose. You all know, as I do, that the world out there"–he pointed out the windows–"has run its course."

A display of the earth appeared behind him. A collection of terms appeared around the planet:

Disease Poverty Financial instability

Climate change Crime

Religious violence Tribal conflict Lawlessness

"You're all familiar with these ills that plague the world. The question is: how do we eradicate them? To understand the answer, we need only look at the barriers to creating a perfect society."

The earth faded to black, replaced by a new collection of terms:

Corruption Ignorance Superstition

Democracy Incompetence Greed

"The spread of democratic rule across the globe has given uneducated, superstitious, religious hoards *unprecedented* control over government operations. Leaders pander to the lowest common denominator. Educational institutions indoctrinate students in propaganda instead of scholarship. Consumers demand 'organic' food, as if Mother Nature–who gave us poisons and parasites–will cure all problems. In such an anti-scientific, anti-intellectual environment, where the ignorant masses are entitled to mob rule, progress toward enlightenment and reason is impossible.

"Ladies and gentlemen, you came here from all corners of the globe, from different professions and backgrounds. After our meeting, some of you will remain on the island. Others will return to your positions in the outside world, where you'll work behind the scenes. All of us will be founders of a new society."

The audience got to their feet and applauded enthusiastically.

Even James cracked a smile and looked admiringly at Henry. As the guests sat down, servants brought wine, water, and glasses to the tables.

"For this revolution to succeed," Henry said, "we require two technological breakthroughs."

The first was the Biochip. As he described its operation, an image appeared of a person implanted with a Biochip, electrical leads running into the brain. The Biochip provided heightened cognitive abilities. In addition, the chip's well-timed stimuli would prevent citizens of the new society from descending into ignorance, apathy, and superstition.

The second technological breakthrough was energy production. Using proprietary technology, Colton Enterprises had developed a clean, unlimited source of energy. While it sounded unbelievable, there was no downside to this new energy source. It would produce plentiful energy with no pollution. The guests would see a demonstration soon.

"I can tell you're impressed," Henry said, smiling broadly, "but there's something I want to say before I conclude. All great civilizations are born from blood, and ours is no exception. A revolution without violence is neither possible nor desirable. As our meeting progresses, I will reveal more details.

"There's a reason why I mention this unpleasant subject tonight. If, for any reason, you do not wish to be part of this revolution, then I shall thank you for your company and put you on a jet tomorrow morning. I will trust you to keep what you have learned thus far to yourself."

He paused. From the attentive, enthusiastic looks of the guests, it did not appear that anyone was considering that option.

"With that caveat, let me propose a toast." He raised his glass and the guests did the same. "A toast," he said, "to our Brave New World, with such people in it."

47

We'll keep our distance," Gunnar said as the convoy headed toward the Palace Square, "but a drone will keep watch. We'll drop you and Valerie off seven blocks from the square. If you need help, press the red button on the phone."

He handed the phone to Mike, who sat in the back. Valerie rode in another car. Mike started to ask a question but Gunnar held up a hand. Gunnar listened to his earphone and his complexion reddened.

"He escaped," he said, his voice atypically soft.

"Who?"

"Damien Voth," Gunnar said, listening to the earphone again. "Dr. Petersen was shot, execution style. Voth disappeared. He's gone."

The car stopped.

"This doesn't change the mission, Mike. It just means things are happening faster than we expected. Do whatever Oleg asks. Lead us to the crystal."

Mike nodded and joined Valerie on the sidewalk.

"Are you okay?" she asked as they walked toward the square.

"Voth escaped."

"You're kidding!"

Mike suddenly felt paranoid. "I have a bad feeling about this."

Somehow, through his computer, Voth found a way to organize an escape. And to think that Mike had felt *sympathy* for the man. Gunnar was right. *A brilliant sociopath.*

Valerie took his hand in hers. "Stay focused," she said.

They walked, hand in hand, along the sidewalk. Mike glanced back. The cars that brought them here were gone. He hoped they were keeping a close watch. They turned down a narrow street and passed an old church. After five minutes of walking in silence, they could see the Neva River. They took a right and headed toward the Palace Square.

"He'd better show," Mike said.

They walked into the square and looked around. Like the day before, the people were a mix of Russians and tourists. A group of Japanese, all dressed in blue, took pictures of the Alexander Column. A young couple strolled. A panhandler muttered. There was no sign of Oleg. Mike glanced at his watch.

"Ten 'til," he said. "We've got some time."

They walked around the square, looking for Oleg. He wished he and Valerie could spend time here–or anywhere for that matter–without worrying about bad guys or silicon crystals.

They turned and were face-to-face with the panhandler, a grizzled man whose jaw jutted out belligerently. He held out an envelope.

"Ten ruble," he said.

Mike looked at the envelope. On it was written

To: Mike Harris

Mike handed the man ten rubles. "Who gave you this?"

"Man in glasses," he slurred, the smell of vodka emanating from his mouth. "He know you." The man took the money and handed over the envelope. He staggered off quickly.

Mike opened the envelope. There was a note, written in Oleg's scrawl:

Mike, meet me in Winter Palace. I will find you. Bring girl.
–O

The envelope contained two tickets. They turned toward the imposing green-and-white building. The Winter Palace was once home to Russia's czars but now housed thousands of Hermitage museum collections. It was vast. How would Oleg find them?

They walked across the square and into the Winter Palace. The interior was stunning, high ceilings and columns crafted in a baroque style. After waiting in line to show their tickets, they went toward the Hermitage Arsenal collection, a display of armor and weapons from the middle ages to the early 1900s. Their footsteps echoed in the cavernous space.

"This reminds me of something that Seth mentioned," Valerie said as she looked at a suit of armor. "He said the black hole could be used as a weapon."

Mike rubbed his chin and looked around for Oleg. "I suppose it could be," he said, "since anything that crosses the event horizon would be toast."

"The event horizon?"

"It defines the boundary of the black hole. If any object crosses it, the gravitational force is such that the object cannot escape."

"What if you had a super-strong rocket or something?"

"Can't be done," he said. "The force is so powerful, nothing, not even light, can escape."

He could not think of how to weaponize a black hole. However, the mere fact that it could suck matter into nothingness meant that it could destroy things more permanently than any weapon on earth.

"Even a nuclear explosion doesn't destroy the individual atoms of a city," he said. "A black hole, in contrast, would remove matter from existence entirely."

"Wow," she said, looking at him through her thick glasses.

He stared at her for a moment, thinking of their night together. His hand touched her hair and stroked it gently. He wanted to take off her glasses, bring her to a quiet place, and pick up where they had left off.

He heard a cough next to him and jumped. A long-haired Russian in wraparound shades and a trench coat stood next to them.

It was Oleg.

"Go to west exit," Oleg said, his lips barely moving. "Get in white car, license DXT 82."

With that, he swept away, leaving them standing in the exhibit hall.

"What do we do?" Valerie asked.

"We do what Oleg wants," Mike said. "Let's go." He looked around. "We came from over there, which was the square. The river is that way…"

"Follow me," Valerie said, walking confidently in a direction that led to the Oriental collections.

"Hold on," Mike said uncertainly, "I think we should be going *that* way."

She pointed at a sign. Below the Cyrillic, it read in English:

WEST EXIT

"Ah," he said. "There's a sign. Well."

They passed Byzantine collections displayed in glass cases, the arches of the Winter Palace accentuating the splendor of the ancient artwork. They weaved through a group of tourists and headed toward the Russian exhibits.

"Move quickly," she said, taking his hand as they dodged a slow-moving group of senior citizens. "We're being followed. Don't look back."

Instinctively, he did just that, and caught a glimpse of a beefy Russian in a suit and shades. The man tried to look casual as he picked up the pace.

They followed another sign, which told them to take a right. As soon as they rounded the corner, they ran. Holding hands, they darted down a staircase and sprinted outside.

"Where's Oleg?" Mike said, looking around in a panic.

They stood in a parking lot with hundreds of cars.

"White car," Valerie said, scanning the lot, "license DXT 82."

A horn honked. It was a white car, under a covered parking area.

"That's it," Valerie said, reading the license plate.

They ran to it. Oleg sat in the back seat and motioned them

in. The engine was running. Mike opened the driver door.

"You drive, Mike," Oleg said, glancing around nervously. "Lady friend ride shotgun."

"All right," Mike said hesitantly. As he got in, he saw the beefy Russian emerge from the Winter Palace.

"Go!" Oleg shouted.

Mike stepped on the pedal and they lurched forward. They got onto a street. Oleg instructed Mike to take a series of turns. They drove to Dvortsovyy Street and onto a bridge that crossed the Neva River. Then they stayed on a road adjacent to the Neva and headed north. The old city of St. Petersburg gave way to housing complexes.

After five minutes, Oleg took off his shades.

"Keep on this road," he said. "We drive for a while. My name's Oleg," he said to Valerie.

"I'm Valerie," she said, turning back to shake his hand.

She yelped.

He was pointing a gun at her.

48

The FBI Cessna landed at the airport near Colton University at sunrise. Agent Sanchez stepped out of the plane and met Chief Patterson on the tarmac.

"We've got some information," he told her.

As they drove to campus, he explained that they had video data that might identify the person who sabotaged Mike Harris' laboratory.

"Do you know who that person is?"

"No," he replied. "But if I had to guess, based on what we have right now–I'd say it was Hassan Zare."

They arrived on campus and walked into Harry's cramped office, stepping over piles of paper and candy wrappers. Harry hunched over a keyboard, tinted glasses perched on the edge of his sweaty nose.

"Harry," Jon said.

Harry bolted upright, sending his glasses clattering onto the desk. He got to his feet and stared at Sanchez with bleary red eyes.

"Ma'am," he said.

"Chief Patterson tells me you have some information about the lab accident."

"No accident," Harry said. He turned around and tapped on the keyboard. "We obtained video footage from a nutty physics professor–excuse my redundancy–named Paul Quinlan. He wanted to catch people stealing his office supplies, so he set up cameras in the hallway. One of those cameras caught someone entering Mike Harris' lab, just before the fire."

The video recording of the hallway appeared on the screen. A person entered the frame and the screen became distorted, like an old television with poor reception.

"I've partially decoded the data," Harry said, "but to get high resolution, we need the passphrase."

The unidentified person walked into the frame and entered the lab. A few seconds later the person came back out and walked down the hallway and out of sight. The distortion of the image made it impossible to tell whether the person was tall, short, black, white, male, or female.

"Hassan Zare made a surprise visit to the lab," Jon said. "After his initial visit, it appears that he stepped back into the lab, planted some sort of device, and left."

Sanchez nodded. "I just came back from the DARPA conference at Glacier Park," she said. "They were hiding something."

"Hassan was part of that group," Jon said. "It all kind of makes sense. Except that he was killed."

"That makes the most sense of all," Sanchez responded. "Once he served his purpose, he was eliminated."

The three stood in the musty office in silence, mulling things over.

"To prove our theory, we need the passphrase," Sanchez said.

"Yes we do," Jon said, "and I know how to get it."

"Keep both hands on wheel, Mike."

Mike's heart pounded. He had moved his hand toward the phone in his pocket. The phone had a red button that Gunnar said he could push in an emergency. Oleg had caught him.

He placed his hand back on the steering wheel. They drove in the fast lane through moderately thick traffic. "What is this about, Oleg?"

"We go to Ioffe Institute," he said, keeping his gun aimed at Valerie as he peered nervously out the back windows. "Take this exit."

"I'm too late."

"Now!"

Mike swerved into the right lane, prompting honks from irate drivers. He hit the brakes to avoid colliding with a small truck. He managed to get behind the truck, without bumping its rear, and onto the exit.

Oleg looked out the rear window. "Coast is clear," he said. "Go on side streets for while, then back onto main road."

They wound their way through narrow streets lined with grim, Soviet-style concrete apartment complexes. After a while, they followed a blue sign that pointed toward the main road.

"Put away the gun, Oleg."

Oleg continued to hold his gun for a few seconds. Then, he holstered it in his trench coat.

"Keep hands where I can see them," he said.

Valerie put her hands on the dash and Mike kept his hands on the wheel.

"I trust no one," he said. "Some bad guys–organized crime?–they come by lab. They would have shot me. Turn here."

Mike turned the car and merged with traffic onto the main road. They resumed their drive toward the Ioffe Institute.

"Who are you with?" Oleg asked nervously.

"I'm not sure who they are, exactly," Mike said. "They call themselves the Praetorians. They saved my life a couple of times, so I'm inclined to trust them."

"Trust no one," Oleg said, seeming to imitate a character from a movie. "These guys who come by lab, I spotted them and hid in storage room. They tore up the place. I figured out what they were looking for."

"The silicon. But where is it now?"

"It's safe," he said. "You will get it for me."

"Okay, but I think we should hand it over to the Praetorians."

"*Nyet!*" Oleg shouted, his eyes wide. "You will give it to *me.* Then, I disappear."

"They'll find you," Valerie said.

"Who is this–'they'?"

"Henry Colton."

Oleg furrowed his brow, looking incredulous. "American billionaire?"

"Yes. Long story short, Oleg: Henry wants the ability to create a black hole."

Oleg sat back and threw up his hands. "What in hell are you talking about?"

"The true aim of the experiment was to create a black hole. I didn't realize it myself. According to Seth's calculations, when we focused high-intensity lasers on the silicon crystal, it would form excitons that condensed into a space-time singularity–in other words, *a black hole.* But we needed an exact isotopic enrichment, one that only you could provide."

Oleg shook his head a few times, sending his long hair flailing. He swept the hair out of his eyes. "A black hole? That's what you guys were trying?"

"I didn't know, Oleg. Seth and Axel knew, along with some other people." He decided not to mention JASON and the Committee, to avoid overloading Oleg with unbelievable data. "Someone leaked information. Colton's people killed my ex-fiancée, colleague, and a grad student. Then they got Hassan Zare."

"Hassan's dead?" Oleg exclaimed.

"Yes. Check the internet if you don't believe me. Seth is in intensive care. And now they're after you."

"Holy crap," he said, sinking in his seat.

"Oleg," Valerie said in a soothing tone, "I didn't trust the Praetorians at first, but I think we need to now. At some point, we have to trust someone, because we can't survive on our own."

Oleg shook his head and groaned, evidently weighing his vow to "trust no one" against the realization that, against a billionaire's army, he was vulnerable. Mike recognized the look on Oleg's face. He knew the feeling of confusion and mistrust all too well.

"Take exit in five miles," Oleg said. "Crystal is at Ioffe Institute. You will get it and hand it to me."

49

Paul Quinlan's beady eyes looked fearful as Sanchez showed him her badge. A morning person, he arrived at the office at 6:45 AM to find the federal agent waiting for him. They sat down. He blanched as she read him a list of statutes that he had supposedly violated, including unlawful surveillance, harassment, and misuse of government property. His computer was paid for with department funds that were matching for a federal grant. Hence, his paranoid video project fell squarely within her jurisdiction.

Jon Patterson knocked and entered the office. Paul looked pale and sick with worry.

"I can handle this," he said to Sanchez.

Sanchez stood up. "This is a federal matter."

"It's *my* campus," he said, jabbing a finger at her.

She stared at him a moment and left, slamming the door.

"Thank you, Chief," said Paul, his eyes welling up with tears. "Oh, thank you. Can you imagine what the Founders would say if they saw this abuse of federal power?"

Jon shook his head sympathetically and handed Paul a mug. "Coffee?"

Paul nodded and took the mug. He sipped slowly. Gradually,

his fear gave way to righteous indignation. "Who do they think they are? The Bill of Rights is supposed to prevent unlawful search and seizure."

"I hear you," Jon said. "Problem is, you might have violated a *state* law too."

"They're just cameras!" he spluttered. "I wasn't the one stealing office supplies!"

"I know, Professor, but the law's pretty clear on this. You can't record video of students at a state institution without their consent. It's a privacy issue."

Paul nearly choked on his coffee and set down the mug. "Privacy, students' rights," he spat. "So-called 'disabled' students get time and a half for their tests. Fifty percent more time! Why? Because some doctor signed a note saying their self-esteem is too precious for a regular exam!"

Jon nodded silently and looked around the paper-strewn office.

"I'll tell you what their 'disability' is," Paul squeaked. "They're dumb as rocks!"

"Be that as it may," Jon said, "we need to think about how to get the feds off your back."

Paul nodded and sipped his coffee.

"We need to examine the video," Jon said, "to make sure there was nothing–improper."

"What are you implying?"

"You know–cameras in the girl's restroom, that kind of…"

"For heaven's sake!" Paul screamed. "What do you take me for?"

"I know," Jon said, holding up a hand. "It's silly, I know. But unless we can see the entire video stream, the feds are going to keep bothering us."

"Fine," Paul said. A hint of a smile crossed his face. "I'll give you the passphrase."

"The *real* passphrase."

Paul looked at Jon with an expression of transparent guilt.

"I know about your self-destruct command. The code that erases the video. We know about it. If you give us that one, the FBI will come down on you like a ton of bricks."

The look of fear returned to Paul's face. His hand shaking, he set the coffee mug on a pile of old papers.

"Let me help you, Professor," Jon said.

They took the exit and approached the Ioffe Institute. Mike recognized the grounds from the NATO conference on laser physics last year. He parked the car.

"Now what?"

Oleg's eyes darted back and forth from behind long strands of hair. "Bad guys will recognize me. Mike, you go inside, up to my office. I wait here with girl."

Mike considered whether to mention that he was a fugitive and the bad guys were out to get him too. Sensing a new level of nervousness from Oleg, he decided against it.

"Okay. Remind me where your office is."

"Room 328. Third floor, that building. I tell guard that I'm expecting you," he said, retrieving a phone.

"And where is the crystal?"

Oleg smiled. "Personal computer under desk. Open it up. You will see it on one of the circuit boards."

Despite the stress of the moment, Mike returned the smile. "Clever," he said. "Who would think to look for silicon inside a computer?" He opened the car door.

"Wait," Oleg said, serious again.

"Yes?"

"Give me your phone."

Mike tried to conceal his disappointment as he handed him the phone. He had planned to call Gunnar. "How will we communicate?"

"Call this phone number when you reach my office. Use desk phone."

Mike looked at Valerie. She appeared relaxed, considering she was a hostage.

He walked toward a plain yellow building, past a guard who read a paperback and barely glanced up. He entered the building and took the stairs up to the third floor. He emerged into a hallway with research posters lining the walls. The place was quiet, almost deserted. He found room 328 and opened the unlocked door.

Oleg's office was messy, but, by the standard of physicists, not unusually so. Mike took some papers off the computer tower under the desk and looked for a way to open it. He found a pair of knobs and, with some effort, turned them. The door of the computer swung open and clattered onto the floor. He peered inside, but it was too dark to see anything. He shut the power off and set the computer on the desk, by the window.

He heard a noise behind him and froze.

He turned around. It was a middle aged man. He looked like a scientist but Mike didn't recognize him. The man asked Mike a question in Russian.

"Sorry," said Mike. "I'm American. I'm visiting Oleg."

"Ah," the man said. "Is Oleg here today?"

"Um, no," Mike said, "I'm getting some files for him. He's in Moscow."

The man wrinkled his brow. "Moscow? He didn't say…"

"Last minute thing. Funding. Short notice. I have his number, though. Would you like me to call him?"

"*Nyet*," the man said with a wave. "It can wait." He shuffled nonchalantly out of the office.

Mike watched him leave and then closed the door. He returned to the computer. The insides looked typical, if slightly outdated. Then he noticed it. Between two cards, there was a Teflon cube. He retrieved it gingerly and put it in his pocket.

He picked up the desk phone and dialed.

Oleg answered: "Mike, you got crystal?"

"Got it."

"I saw bad guy enter building. Get out of there. Use back exit."

"Dammit Oleg, you should have let me take my phone." Mike watched the door nervously.

"Go out, take left, go past elevator and down stairs. Go to basement level. We meet you in loading dock."

Mike slammed down the phone and opened the door. The hallway looked deserted. He felt sweat drip down his forehead as his heart pounded. A Russian walked by him but seemed oblivious. He walked past the elevators and almost took the door to the restroom. On edge, he opened the door to the stairs and broke into a run. He went down three flights and ended up in the gloomy basement, where dusty old equipment lined a wide corridor. He pushed open a creaky set of double doors and spotted Oleg's car. Oleg motioned frantically for him to get in. Valerie sat in the driver seat and Oleg was in the back.

Mike got into the passenger seat. Valerie yelped as they saw the beefy Russian, the one from the Hermitage, run out of the building. She pressed on the accelerator and they drove away from the Ioffe Institute.

"How did he find us?" Mike asked.

"Maybe he know I come back for crystal," Oleg shrugged. "By the way, hand it over."

Mike handed Oleg the Teflon cube. In the light of the sun, they could see the outline of the shiny black silicon cube inside. Oleg put it in his trench coat.

"Are you ready to trust us now?" Mike said.

Oleg did not respond.

Valerie drove adeptly, weaving through cars until they got on the main road. She merged with traffic, thick with afternoon commuters, and slowed to thirty miles per hour. "Where do you want me to go?"

Oleg turned around and looked out the rear window. "Ah, crap. We have company."

Mike turned around too, and Valerie looked at the rearview mirror. A black sedan was in the breakdown lane, approaching at high speed. Valerie drove into the left lane and honked at a stationary truck in front of them. The truck didn't budge.

The black sedan pulled up next to them. Its rear passenger window lowered to reveal the beefy Russian, who aimed a weapon. Valerie screamed and drove the car over the median, into oncoming traffic. Tires squealed as drivers hit their brakes. She flipped a U-turn and drove with the lighter traffic, toward the city. A car clipped the rear bumper and Oleg swore loudly in his native tongue.

"How are they tracking us?" Valerie shouted.

"I don't know," Oleg said. "We should change car."

"Give me my phone."

Oleg regarded him suspiciously.

"We're about to get killed, Oleg, give me the damned phone."

Reluctantly, he handed it over. "What are you going to do?"

"Call 911."

"Nine what?"

"The Praetorians," Mike said. "You need to trust us, Oleg." He pressed the red button.

Oleg looked around, trying to spot the black sedan. Valerie drove fast, weaving through traffic. After a time, the road met with the Neva River, and she turned onto a bridge. They went toward the old part of St. Petersburg.

"Not good," Oleg said, "we go that way, we get stuck in traffic again."

Oleg was right. The bridge led them into a gridlock of tourists and commuters. The car braked to a halt.

"Dammit," Mike said, opening the car door. "Let's go."

"What are you doing?" Valerie exclaimed.

"There must be a trace on the car. C'mon."

Valerie threw up her hands and abandoned the car. Irate drivers behind them honked their horns. The three ran toward the Hermitage.

"We'll wait in the Winter Palace," Mike said breathlessly, "it's a public place."

"Okay," Oleg said, gasping for breath as he ran, clearly unused to vigorous exercise. "I guess these Praetorians can…" He went silent and fell to the ground, twitching spasmodically.

"Oleg!" Mike shouted, panicked. Arcs of electricity enveloped Oleg's body. Mike and Valerie ran for cover. A man in a dark suit approached them. He held a weapon shaped like a smooth black cylinder. A bio launcher.

Valerie's leg swept through the air and snapped the bio launcher out of the man's grip. The weapon fell to the ground. Her right hand jabbed his face, which jerked backward. He stared at her, stunned and perplexed. Mike grabbed the bio launcher and aimed. Valerie jabbed her foot into the man's knee, sending him crashing to the ground. She stepped away as Mike fired the weapon. The projectile hit the man squarely in the chest, sending him into an electrified seizure.

They rushed to help Oleg. He looked up at them and spoke weakly. "Take crystal," he said, reaching into his coat. "Quickly. They're coming. They don't care about me, only crystal."

Valerie took the Teflon container. A projectile streaked past and hit a lamp post. Tourists scattered, screaming. Mike and Valerie ran toward the Hermitage. How could this be happening? Everywhere they went, their enemies found them.

"This way!" Valerie shouted, and they ducked into a service entrance. They walked through a dark corridor and into a room with mops, brooms, and other cleaning supplies. She seemed elated from adrenalin. She pressed her lips to his. Despite the stress of the moment, he responded to her kiss.

"We did it," she said. Her green eyes were intense. She took the bio launcher from Mike, who gladly relinquished it.

Mike looked down the passageway. "I don't know about this, Val," he said nervously. "Keep a watch. They could be anywhere."

50

Paul Quinlan had the tired look of a defeated man. He sat glumly in his office, watching as Harry accessed his computer. Gabrielle and Jon stood beside Harry as he typed. The screen read:

> These data are the property of Professor Paul Quinlan. If you are not Professor Quinlan, then LEAVE NOW!
>
> Enter Passphrase:

"Okay, Paul," Jon said.

Paul sighed and scribbled on a piece of paper. He handed it to Harry, who chuckled briefly as he inputted the passphrase:

> EVEN PARANOIDS HAVE REAL ENEMIES

The computer paused for a few seconds. Then, a new screen appeared, with a menu listing a series of dates. Harry clicked on "May 30" and a series of thumbnail images appeared. He selected one and it filled the screen with a low-resolution image of the empty hallway. After a few seconds, a pair of students appeared. The resolution sharpened, and they could see that they were a boy and girl, both walking slowly and looking at handheld devices. As they ambled out of view, the image returned to its low-res state.

Harry chuckled again. The program, written by Paul, was definitely old school. He fast-forwarded to the time before the lab fire. They waited for the person to enter the frame. After ten seconds, the person appeared.

"I need to see the face," Sanchez said.

The person entered the lab and closed the door. A few seconds later, the door opened.

Jon stood up, staring at the image on the screen.

"Freeze that," he said.

He ran out of the office and sprinted down the hall. Brushing aside crime scene tape, he opened the door to Mike Harris' lab. It still had the smell of smoke. The organic liquids had mostly evaporated, but a sticky residue, like tar, remained on the floor. The lasers, capacitors, and cryostat had been removed. The optical table remained, covered with debris. He bent over a collection of items, bagged and tagged, arranged on the floor. He picked one item up and inspected it intently.

The camera.

Mike peered down the hallway.

"I think I see someone," he said, ducking back into the cleaning room.

Valerie was looking at her phone. She put it in her pocket. With her other hand, she held the bio launcher.

She gazed at him somberly.

"Mike," she said, "I'm sorry."

He saw a blinding flash of light. With sudden clarity, he knew why Valerie had appeared at his lab on May 30, the day of the fire, and why she re-appeared in Glacier Park. He knew how Colton's people had tracked them all this time.

Valerie walked down the hallway, bio launcher in hand. She met the beefy Russian man, an organized crime figure known as Yuri.

"The Praetorians are coming," she said. "We need to move."

"You have crystal?" Yuri asked.

"Yes."

"What about Oleg?"

"Leave him. He doesn't matter to us."

They stepped outside and got into a black limousine. Two rough-looking bodyguards got in too. The limo sped away.

"What about professor?"

Valerie looked out the tinted window, away from Yuri. Her eyes were moist.

"Mike Harris is dead," she said steadily. "I killed him."

Jon Patterson burst into the office. He held the bagged camera in his hand.

On the monitor, there was a clear, high-resolution image of Valerie's face. Jon knew what happened in the moments after that still shot. Valerie went to Mike's office for a minute. Then, she "remembered" that she left her camera in the lab. She walked into the hallway. Moments later, the lasers fired, killing Stefan Schroeder. She screamed. She acted surprised.

Early on, one question nagged at Jon: how did they aim the lasers?

Now he knew. During her visit, Valerie placed the camera on a bench, where it had a clear view of the lab. Miles away, thanks to the malicious software upgrade, some computer jockey on Colton's payroll took control of the lasers. The camera gave him the vision he needed to kill Stefan.

SATURDAY, JUNE 7

51

Dr. Sauer inspected the sample holder in the stainless steel cryostat. Behind him, technicians watched nervously. They stood, dressed in cleanroom bunny suits, in the hangar-sized laboratory with amber lighting. Suspended from the high ceiling by fine wire was a massive array of lasers, all pointing at the cryostat.

"It looks acceptable," Sauer growled, the stress of the past weeks evident in his voice. "What is the isotope ratio?"

A shiny silicon sample was attached to the sample holder. "It's natural silicon," a technician said. "All our tests show that the laser alignment is perfect."

Sauer stared at the sample. Sure, everything was ready to go *in theory*, but they would not know for sure until they swapped out the natural silicon for isotopically enriched silicon.

"When can we expect the sample?" the technician asked.

"That's a stupid question!" Sauer hissed.

"No," said a voice behind him.

Sauer turned around. Henry Colton stood there, clad in a cleanroom suit like the rest of them.

"It's not a stupid question," Henry said. "It's central. The lasers are aligned and ready to fire. The second stage has been ready for weeks. Everything is in place. The only thing we're waiting for is the crystal."

"We'll have it," Sauer said, "I promise."

"Without that crystal," Henry said, gesturing toward the gleaming equipment behind Sauer, "all this is useless. We have thirty guests on this island. They deserve to see a demonstration."

Sauer nodded, his face red from frustration. He had hoped to have everything ready a week ago. Now, the deadline was looming and they still didn't have what they needed. The technicians sensed Sauer's anger and stepped back, knowing they would bear the brunt of it as soon as Henry was gone.

"We will have the crystal," Sauer said. "I promise."

Henry nodded curtly and left.

After taking off the cleanroom suit, Henry proceeded to the visitor's center, dressed casually in shorts, shirt, and sandals. His guests were enjoying a breakfast buffet by the ocean. Little birds flew around the area and pecked at crumbs on the floor. Henry worked the tables, making small talk with his guests. As he casually inspected the buffet, a British scientist approached him. His name was Dennis Ashford and he specialized in evolutionary theory and genetics.

"Mr. Colton," he said.

"Please, call me Henry. Has our hospitality been sufficient?"

"Marvelous, simply marvelous. I cannot tell you how much I appreciate the honor of being invited to your lovely island."

Henry bowed. "The honor is mine."

"Despite the many attractive features of your proposed society, however, I feel that I cannot participate as a founder. You see, while…"

Henry put a finger to his lips. "Not a problem, my friend, not a problem. No reason need be given." He nodded to someone behind Dennis. "I thank you for your company."

Dennis exhaled, obviously relieved by Henry's gracious reaction. He breathed in the warm ocean breeze. "No, sir, thank *you.* I had a lovely time."

James Tyrell came up beside Dennis, startling him.

"Dr. Ashford," James said, "I'll show you to the plane."

Henry shook Dennis' hand. James and Dennis walked down a path that led to a small airstrip behind the visitor's center. Henry groaned and rubbed the back of his neck. The stress was getting to him. Another hand joined in. He smiled at the touch.

"You're tense," Jing said.

He turned to face her. "I'm putting out brush fires."

"No time for a swim?" she pouted.

He shook his head and held her hand gently. "Hold that thought. I have a meeting in ten minutes."

Ten minutes later, Henry entered a soundproof room in the basement of the visitor's center. The door closed behind him and a screen lit up. Damien Voth's face filled it. Most people, Henry knew, would be repulsed by the image. They didn't appreciate the brilliant mind that labored behind the burned and disfigured face.

"Damien," he said, "I'm relieved you're safe."

Voth nodded. "Do you have the crystal?"

"We will," he said, thinking of his earlier exchange with Dr. Sauer. "Valerie Norton has it in her possession. She's on her way to the island as we speak."

"And Mike Harris?"

"Dead."

"Good," Voth said, his gravelly voice descending an octave. "Very good."

"Axel Hansen still lives."

Voth's face broke into a dark grimace. He spoke between clenched, yellowed teeth: "Capture him. I want him alive. I want to see his eyes when he perishes."

"It will be done," Henry said plaintively, approaching the screen, "but we have more pressing matters at the moment."

"*Wrong*," Voth hissed. "Do not underestimate that man."

Henry walked up to the screen. He knew that Damien was right. Damien was always right.

"We'll take care of it," Henry said, his eyes beseeching Damien for approval.

The looming image of Damien's face, dwarfing Henry, relaxed. "You understand my concern. Our plan has worked thus far."

"Yes," he said, touching the screen.

Henry nodded. He knew that, as intelligent as he himself was, Damien Voth towered over him. In his new society, where intellect counted for everything, Voth would reign supreme, lurking enigmatically in the shadows behind the throne.

"Remember who you are," Damien said.

"I do," Henry said.

Damien had told him, years ago, when Henry was still in the haze of an empty life as a partying billionaire. Damien told him who he was. Damien showed him the way, guiding him, teaching him about the new society. Even after the government confined him to a federal prison, Henry and Damien still communicated secretly over the internet. Henry manipulated the stock market to ensure that Damien's investments grew, while avoiding a direct money trail. Now, Damien had a small fortune, enough to command a mercenary navy until he made it to the island.

Two Indonesian men carried Dennis Ashford's bags to the waiting jet, a small white Lear. Dennis stepped out of the car and walked onto the tarmac. James shook his hand.

"Thanks for visiting," James said. He smiled but his eyes were cold.

"Sure," Dennis said, heading for the plane.

He hesitated. Was he making the right decision? After Henry's talk, Dennis tossed and turned all night, unable to sleep. Something about the new society bothered him. Like everyone else on the island, he embraced the idea of a society based on intellect and reason rather than populism and superstition. Being a founder of such a society, on the ground floor of a brave new enterprise, was a unique opportunity. But Henry's words about a civilization born from blood haunted him. Dennis worried about participating in a violent revolution, even as he saw the need for such means. He just couldn't be a part of it. Perhaps that made him weak. All he knew for sure was that he wanted to head back to Cambridge and resume his academic life.

He walked to the plane and ascended the steps. He sat in the back, where bourbon (his favorite) awaited.

"Buckle up, Professor," the pilot said.

Dennis did so, and the cockpit door closed. He took a drink. As his nerves calmed, he became convinced that he was making the right decision. He would wish Henry Colton well, but from a distance.

The jet taxied down the runway and stopped for a moment. Then, it resumed its motion, accelerated smoothly, and lifted into the air. He marveled at the beauty of the clear blue water as the jet flew away from the island.

He downed the rest of the bourbon and settled back in his seat. It was peaceful, being alone in the back of an airplane. One good thing about travel was that it insulated him from interruptions by students and faculty. On a plane, he could think.

Certainly, being chosen as a founder was an honor. He had met Henry Colton at several conferences and, like everyone else on the island, knew that the man was visionary. Dennis' research on evolutionary theory, with its emphasis on logic over spiritualism, appealed to Henry, and they formed an intellectual bond. When he received the invitation, he jumped at the chance.

Now, he realized he could not be part of the new society, at least not directly. He didn't have it in him to fight battles or remake civilization. His role in life was to think and write. Anything else would be a distraction.

After the plane reached cruising altitude, he decided another drink was in order. He unbuckled his seatbelt and knocked on the cockpit door. There was no response. He wondered if perhaps he was being improper. After a minute, he knocked again, but there was still no reply.

He felt a rush of panic. Why did they have a cockpit door in such a small plane? Did they think him a terrorist? He knocked again, harder.

"Pardon me!" he shouted. "Could I get some service here?"

No response.

He pounded the door and it swung open. He gasped.

The cockpit was empty.

He lurched forward and grabbed the joystick, but it was stuck. The plane was on autopilot. Suddenly, the nose swung down. The jet cut through a layer of clouds, its angle of attack steepening. Dennis shouted as the clear blue ocean rushed toward him.

52

Oleg opened his eyes. He looked around the dark room groggily. His hands were tied and he sat in an uncomfortable wooden chair.

Cold water splashed his face and he groaned. His head throbbed painfully. He wished he could pass out. Several figures moved around the room. They spoke Russian but he could not concentrate enough to discern what they were saying.

"What is your name?" a man shouted.

"Oleg Sinitsky," he slurred. "Please, I know nothing."

A fist crunched into his jaw, sending a new surge of pain into his head. He felt nauseous, ready to vomit.

"Why were you with Professor Harris?"

"Please, he's collaborator. We work on science experiments."

The fist prepared for another assault, but another hand restrained it. "The woman Valerie said to leave him alone."

"We don't work for her."

The men–there were three, maybe four–started arguing loudly. One of them dialed and talked on a phone. The voice on the other end yelled.

"I spoke to James," he said, putting the phone away. "He says to kill this rat."

The other men stood in silence. With each passing second, Oleg's feeling of dread increased.

The barrel of a gun pressed against his temple. He pressed his eyes closed and held his breath. Sweat and blood dripped from his face.

He heard the sound of a silenced gunshot.

The gun disengaged from his head and clattered onto the ground. He heard more gunshots. He looked up and saw a thin, pale Russian man with tattoos and a wicked face. The man reached for an AK-47, but from behind him a knife swiftly slit his throat. The man collapsed. Oleg blinked, disbelieving, not sure what had happened. Someone approached him. It was an American. He recognized him.

It was Axel Hansen.

"Breathe," Axel said as another man untied Oleg's hands.

Oleg took a breath and looked around the dank room. Four bodies lay on the floor. They looked like Russian mafia.

"What are you doing here?" he asked Axel.

Axel smiled kindly. "Taking in the local culture. This is Gunnar Stone."

Gunnar walked up to Oleg and inspected his injuries. "We'll get you to medical," he said. "Nothing to worry about."

"Nothing to worry?" Oleg exclaimed, standing up shakily. "These guys come into lab, break everything, shoot lightning bolts at me, put gun to my head. Nothing to worry? No worry? Who in hell *are* you?"

"Where's the silicon?"

"And what is DARPA program manager doing cutting throats with knife?" Oleg demanded, pointing a trembling finger at Axel. "What is going on?"

"We're trying to save your life," Gunnar said, his commanding voice filling the cramped space. "Follow me."

They walked out of the room, down a short hallway, and outside. It was past midnight, although the sun partly illuminated the purplish sky. Axel's eyes scanned the street. A car pulled up and they got in.

* * *

Henry sipped a glass of BenRiach and gazed at the ocean. Years ago, he could not have merely sipped. The liquid would have poured down his throat. Back then, he had no self-control. Now, he enjoyed pleasures in moderation, allowing his mind to chart the course ahead. His mental discipline allowed him to persevere through numerous setbacks. Now, he thought with satisfaction, he had removed the final obstacles.

The door slid open. He turned around to see Valerie Norton. She wore a sheer emerald top that matched her eyes. Her thick glasses were gone.

"Mr. Colton."

"Please, Valerie," he said, "you've been working for me for three years. I think it's time you called me by my first name."

"Okay… Henry."

"You have the crystal?"

She held a Teflon container and opened it. Inside was the shiny black cube of silicon.

He stared at it, mesmerized. There was no way his eyes could discern whether the isotopic composition was correct. Still, he felt that it must be the one.

She snapped the box shut.

"And Professor Harris?" he asked.

She expected this question, and she looked at him with dry eyes. "Mike Harris is dead."

Henry gave her an appraising look. "I imagine it was not easy."

"No, it was not. It was necessary."

Henry nodded and turned to gaze at the ocean. "We're not monsters," he said. "Every great civilization had a violent beginning, and the defense of such civilizations required regular payments in blood. We must be strong, especially in the days ahead."

She stood next to him and watched the ocean pensively. Although she tried to hide it, he could see that her calculated betrayal had taken its toll.

"Bring the silicon to Dr. Sauer," Henry said.

* * *

Valerie drove a Colton electric car up a winding path that led to the high, arid land between the twin volcanoes. She turned onto a two-lane road that led to the Saddle. The complex of buildings and workers was a beehive of activity. She pulled up to building G36 and got out of the car, holding the Teflon box.

Dr. Sauer, waiting by the entrance, unconsciously glanced at his watch. He tried to smile. "Is that it?"

"Yes," she said, handing it to him.

They walked into the locker room and donned bunny suits. Dr. Sauer swiped his badge through a reader and they entered the huge cleanroom.

Kevin Lipman, the project manager, stood by the array of lasers. "Is that it?" he said hopefully.

"It better be," Sauer growled.

"It is," Valerie said. "Load it."

Lipman took the box and opened it with shaky hands. He beheld the shiny cube like it was the Holy Grail.

A technician picked up the cube with Teflon tweezers and placed it into a copper sample holder. He tightened nylon set screws to hold the silicon in place. Then, he fastened the holder to the end of a long rod.

"Careful," Lipman said.

Another technician took the rod assembly and climbed a ladder. She slid the sample holder and rod into the stainless steel cryostat and clamped it in place. Vacuum pumps chugged on. After they produced a vacuum in the sample space, a technician opened a valve and liquid helium flowed into the cryostat. A display showed the temperature decreasing from 298 Kelvin.

"Are the lasers aligned?" Sauer said.

"Of course they're aligned," Lipman snapped. "Don't touch."

The next fifteen minutes crawled by in silence as the temperature fell to two degrees above absolute zero.

Several technicians stood at a control panel and looked at Lipman expectantly. Lipman, Sauer, and Norton donned safety goggles and Lipman nodded. A technician flipped a switch and red DANGER signs lit up.

"Clear the area," a female voice intoned over a loudspeaker. "Laser test in progress. Clear the area."

Power generators ramped up to their operating voltage. Lipman nodded again and the technician pressed a large green button. Dozens of intense laser beams converged on the cryostat, filling the room with light.

The silicon cube flashed a brilliant red. Valerie recalled Mike's explanation. The lasers produced excitons within the crystal. From Einstein's theories of relativity, the intensity of the energy created a gravitational field.

The red turned to blue and then white. The goggles, like welders' masks, went dark. All she could see was a dim white dot, growing brighter.

"Seventy petajoules per cc," the female voice intoned. "Eighty. Ninety."

A plume of helium erupted from a relief valve on the cryostat, shooting white smoke up toward the ceiling.

"Don't worry," Lipman said. "That's normal."

The white light flashed, sending luminous beams out the cryostat windows. Abruptly, the light flickered out.

"Ramp up the field!" Lipman said.

The lasers shut off. A technician turned on the electromagnet power supply, sending amperes of current through superconducting coils in the cryostat.

They took off the goggles. As Valerie's eyes adjusted, she approached the cryostat.

"Oh," Lipman breathed, "oh baby oh my oh my."

They looked inside. The shiny black cube was gone.

Lipman aimed a flashlight through a window. From the opposite side, Valerie could see it: a tiny dark spot, maybe a half-millimeter in diameter, suspended inside the cryostat.

"Why doesn't it fall?" she asked.

"It's confined by a magnetic trap, kind of a small version of the ones that trap plasmas in fusion reactors."

Sauer pushed aside a pair of technicians and stared at the dark spot with wide, greedy eyes. "How soon can you transfer it?"

"As soon as you all get out of the way," Lipman said.

They moved away from the cryostat. Workers slid a stainless steel drum underneath the cryostat and clamped it to the cryostat's bottom. They evacuated the drum with vacuum pumps and turned on a power supply, which hummed loudly.

"Now we're going to transfer the black hole to the magnetic containment bottle," Lipman said to Valerie. "Just before the singularity is formed, some electrons escape, leaving behind a positive electric charge. We use that to our advantage. The magnetic trap is like a prison that keeps charged objects–in this case, the black hole–trapped inside."

Valerie nodded. "What if it escaped the trap?"

The workers monitored the position of the tiny black hole, which began to move slowly downward, toward the containment bottle.

"Tragically, it would disappear," he said. "It's too small and unstable to survive on its own. If it comes into contact with matter, the sudden influx of mass would produce energy that would nonlinearly perturb the event horizon. Not enough to blow up this room, but enough to make the little guy go *bang*."

The dark spot moved downward. It entered a vertical hose, which bulged inward slightly in response to the gravitational constriction. After a minute, the containment bottle shook as its electromagnets went to full power. Lipman nodded and a technician closed a valve, separating the bottle from the hose. The technician disconnected the hose, and other workers wheeled the bottle away.

Lipman wiped his brow. "We did it."

They were too tired to celebrate, but the workers allowed themselves a few smiles and pats on the back. Sauer ran up to Lipman, his eyes wild.

"We must make more," he said excitedly.

"All in good time. We need to study its stability…"

"No! Colton was clear on this point. We must begin production *immediately*!"

Lipman pursed his lips, suppressing his emotions. "We may lose it."

"It's worth the risk. One black hole is worthless. We need more. Do it."

Sauer turned and stalked out of the room.

"This is a first," Lipman said to Valerie, "a real scientific first.

We need to study this thing, understand it."

"I know how you feel," she said, "but Colton has been right about so many things. We need to trust him."

Lipman watched the magnetic containment bottle as the workers pushed it out of the cleanroom. He sighed. *Worthless*, Sauer had said. This was worth a Nobel Prize! Still, he knew what he had signed up for. The brief moment of satisfaction was over. Now the real work would begin.

53

Oleg replayed the scene in his mind, over and over. He felt feverish and shook uncontrollably as he thought of what could have happened, had Axel and Gunnar not arrived. He barely reacted when Gunnar told him of Valerie's deception.

They sped along a road outside St. Petersburg. It was early morning and there was little traffic. The sun was low over the horizon. Gunnar sat in the passenger seat and Axel sat next to Oleg.

They drove for ten minutes. No one spoke. Oleg wanted to go somewhere safe and pour himself a shot of vodka. They arrived at the small airport and were greeted by Russian soldiers with automatic weapons.

Gunnar and Axel led Oleg into a hangar. In the center of the hangar, bright lights illuminated a motionless man on a gurney. Medical personnel surrounded him.

Oleg inhaled sharply. It was Mike Harris. The medical people were standing there, not doing anything. He knew what that meant: nothing could be done.

He ran toward Mike, surprised at the strength of his emotions. He blinked back tears and touched Mike's cold hand. A small arc of electricity shocked him and he recoiled.

"Step back," one of the doctors said.

Oleg knew what had happened. He could see it on Mike's pallid, frozen face, which still seemed to register a hint of surprise. Valerie Norton had killed him. Oleg could picture it clearly in his mind. At close range, she killed him with the bio launcher.

The caravan of electric buses drove north from the visitor's center, along a road that followed the western shore. While the sky over the ocean was clear, clouds formed over the green hills, bringing a sprinkling of afternoon rain. The buses turned onto a road that led toward the northwest part of the island.

Inside the air-conditioned vehicles, the guests talked animatedly, excited by the shared adventure. After a half hour, they arrived at an industrial building in a clearing, surrounded by rolling hills covered with tropical flora. Solar panels and massive light concentrators circled the building.

The guests gathered around Henry Colton, who wore a wide-brimmed hat. Jing moved close to him.

"I'm sorry to tear you away from the beach," he said to a wave of adoring chuckles, "but I want to show you an important component of our new society. Energy production is one of the great challenges of our time. As you can see, we're using state-of-the-art solar technologies, with multi-junction photovoltaic cells and high-reflectivity light concentrators. On the volcanoes, we have geothermal power plants. As useful as these technologies are, though, they will not replace carbon-based fuels. Let's be honest: chemical reactions that produce carbon dioxide give you bang for the buck. To compete with them, we need something else.

"Inside this building, you will see a prototype method of producing energy that is revolutionary. I know a lot of people use that word, *revolutionary*. I mean it. Follow me."

They walked into the building and were greeted by Dr. Sauer. He smiled tensely. Only an hour ago, technicians transported the black hole, housed in its containment bottle, from the Saddle to this building. Amazingly, the transport went off without a hitch. After a series of seemingly unending setbacks, things were finally falling into place.

Still, Sauer could not relax. He tried to keep his voice from shaking.

"As Mr. Colton said, this is a prototype. And as such, it may not work," he said, laughing nervously, "but of course we will do our best. Excuse me."

He nodded to Colton and walked down a passageway, hissing at technicians as he went.

Colton led the group into a spotless, spacious room the size of a basketball court. In the center was a polished copper sphere with dozens of pipes running in and out, like a boiler on a steam ship. The walls of the sphere had several thick, round glass windows, but the inside was dark. Steel supports propped up the sphere so workers could walk underneath it.

Double doors on the far end of the room opened. Sauer and his gang of technicians wheeled in the containment bottle and led it to the sphere.

"Ladies and gentlemen," Colton said, savoring the moment, "this is only a minor demonstration of what is possible with our new technology. Inside that bottle is the first gravitational singularity made by humans."

One of the guests, a physicist, stepped forward. "You made a–a *black hole*?"

"We did," Colton said, and the audience gasped. "And in doing so, we solved the energy problem. Think about it. Matter that falls into a black hole does what?"

"It disappears," someone said.

"Yes," the physicist said, "but only after releasing electromagnetic radiation." He stepped forward, gazing at the copper sphere, growing excited. "When charged particles accelerate toward the singularity, they emit radiation. You could harness that radiation…"

"We *will* harness that radiation," Colton said. "The copper sphere you see before you is only a prototype, a simple boiler with an alloy manifold to transform the photon energy into heat. The point of the demonstration is this: we can use junk–literally, garbage–to produce power."

"You've solved two problems," Jing said admiringly, "waste

disposal and energy."

Sauer ran up to them. "It's ready," he said breathlessly.

"Very well. Stand behind the yellow line, folks. Jing, I'd like you to do the honors."

She looked at him quizzically. A technician handed her a pail of garbage. The group laughed.

"Pour it right in there," Colton said, indicating a metal cylinder.

She poured the garbage in, and it was quickly whisked away under the floor. The group waited in anticipation. Dr. Sauer looked as though he might burst.

Everyone was quiet for a moment. Then a flash ignited in the boiler, sending white shafts of light through the glass windows. The group "oohed" in delight. Behind the windows, water circulated and boiled violently. Incandescent lights in the chamber suddenly brightened, powered by the black hole's energy. One of the lights burst.

Dr. Sauer, grinning maniacally, signaled for the technicians to retrieve the black hole. Adjusting the magnetic field, they extracted it from the boiler and confined it in its bottle. Gradually, the boiling water cooled and the lights began to dim.

They all stared in stunned silence. The physicist's hands clapped together; slowly at first, then faster. One by one, the group joined in, and the applause reached a crescendo. Colton basked in the standing ovation. He held Jing's hand and took a bow.

54

How could she have done it? Oleg thought. Valerie had seemed like a nice enough girl. She appeared to have a real fondness for Mike, regardless of her motives.

Her business card was on a table:

Valerie Norton, Ph.D.
Author, Philosopher, Lover of Science

It was no ordinary business card. It was a tracking device, used to locate Mike and Seth in Glacier Park. The Praetorians had discovered it in Mike's wallet and deactivated it with a large magnetic field.

Oleg gazed somberly at the motionless body. He heard a doctor call "clear" and everyone stepped back. The doctor pressed paddles to Mike's chest. Mike's body convulsed, reacting to the electric shock. An EKG displayed a flat line.

After fifteen seconds, the doctor switched the polarity and repeated the shock. Mike's body convulsed again, more violently than before. He seemed to choke. The EKG showed a spike and started beeping.

* * *

An hour later, Mike sat upright on the gurney. Color had returned to his face but his eyes seemed dead. A monitor showed his vital signs, which were normal. A thermometer was in his mouth.

"You were hit with a bio launcher," Axel explained. "The electrical surge sent your body into a state of suspended animation."

Mike nodded slightly.

"Mike," Oleg whispered, "was it her? Valerie?"

Mike's blank eyes showed a hint of pain. A nurse removed the thermometer from his mouth and noted the reading.

"I'm sorry," Oleg said.

Gunnar walked into the hangar, holding a printout.

"Colton has a black hole," he announced.

Oleg cursed in Russian. Mike didn't react.

"So," Axel said, "we proceed with the invasion plans."

"Like hell. We nuke the island," Gunnar said, slamming the printout onto a table. "Three warheads, here, here, and here. The biological research complex in the north, the physical sciences labs on the Saddle, and the weapons testing range in the south."

"Nuke island?" Oleg said. "Isn't that overkill?"

"Colton is preparing a demonstration that will alter the balance of power on the planet. He has a black hole. *A black hole!* Do you realize what damage it could do?"

"We know that better than you, my friend," Axel said calmly, "but we do *not* know where the black hole, or holes, are. A nuclear blast could drive one into the earth's mantle, with disastrous consequences."

"Or blast it into space, where it will be harmless," Gunnar said, his face turning redder. "That's a chance we'll have to take. If Colton's demonstration succeeds, no nation will dare touch him. His victory will be complete."

Axel shook his head. "The *USS Washington* is in the region. It can be in range in six hours. It has certain capabilities–"

"Not enough time. The demonstration must not succeed."

Mike murmured something.

"Excuse me?" Gunnar said.

"Jing," Mike said. "What about Jing?"

"Everyone on the island will die. The lucky ones will be incinerated by the blasts."

Mike, Oleg, and Axel looked at Gunnar.

"Jing is expendable. As am I, and everyone in this hangar."

"Have you consulted the Committee?" Axel said.

"The Committee is compromised," Gunnar said. "You know that as well as I. We'll take our case to the White House."

During the day, scientists worked to multiply the black holes, like bacteria in a Petri dish. They used magnetic fields to pinch one black hole into two. Then they fed each embryo enough matter to grow to a stable size, and repeated the process.

After dinner, the guests headed to the reception hall where Colton gave his presentation the previous evening. The excitement of the black hole demonstration was still fresh.

James scanned the crowd and spotted Senator Conrad Schmidt. He escorted him to a room behind the stage, where Colton sat.

"Senator," Colton said amiably, standing up to shake his hand. "A situation has come up that perhaps you might help me with."

"Anything," Schmidt said.

James left the room and closed the door behind him.

"This concerns the Committee."

Schmidt nodded. A ranking member of the Senate Armed Services Committee, he knew about JASON and its Committee.

"My source tells me," Colton continued, "that the Committee persuaded the Chief of Naval Operations to send a guided-missile submarine our way."

"Really?" the senator said, taken aback.

"Our demonstration is scheduled for tomorrow. It must go as planned. I cannot be disrupted by a naval attack."

"Of course," the senator agreed, puffing up. "Why, the notion that the United States military would attack its greatest citizen…"

"Conrad," he said, "I'm a citizen of *this* country, the new society we are trying to forge."

"What can I do?"

"Call your contacts at the White House. Tell them you're on the island."

Schmidt nodded. "Understood," he said, and left.

James poked his head in. "You're on," he said.

Colton walked out onto the stage. The lively conversations in the room fell silent. His eyes met Jing's.

"My honored guests," he said, "today you had a glimpse of technological breakthroughs that our new society has produced. Tomorrow, you will witness another example of power, one that is essential to establish our geopolitical position."

The screen behind him displayed a hydrogen bomb exploding into a brilliant mushroom cloud.

"Historically, energy technologies, from fire to fusion, have always found military applications. The black hole is no exception."

The image of the nuclear blast was replaced with a graphic depicting a space-time singularity. It looked like fluorescent water swirling down a funnel.

"The black hole, once created, has a voracious appetite for matter. Any particle that crosses the event horizon–the boundary of the black hole–is doomed. No physical force can retrieve it. For all purposes, that particle is gone from our universe."

On the screen, the black hole dropped into the downtown of a fictitious city. Glass and steel flew off buildings and swirled around the hole. It looked like a tornado blasting through the streets. The gravitational force sucked up cars, streetlamps, and people. An unlucky flock of birds got swept into the vortex, prompting laughter from the audience.

The physicist stood up. "What's to keep it from sucking up the entire planet?"

"I thought you'd ask that," Colton said. "Dr. Sauer?"

Sauer, sitting in the front row, stepped onto the stage. "The black holes created in our laboratory are small, with a diameter of a millimeter or less. Smaller than those found in nature, they are susceptible to space-time fluctuations. After consuming a critical amount of mass-energy–roughly a million metric tons–the fluctuations take over and the black hole implodes upon itself. It, for lack of a better term, vanishes."

The physicist nodded slowly, evidently performing calculations in his head, and sat down. The screen went black and Colton returned to center stage.

"As I mentioned the other night," he said, "our revolution necessarily involves the use of deadly force. We have identified a target for our demonstration."

The screen showed a map of Indonesia and zoomed in on the city of Surabaya. A picture of Santoso, the leader whom James had met, appeared next to the map.

"We will strike the residence of Santoso, a leader in Indonesia. He and his family will be killed, along with twenty to thirty people in the neighborhood."

The audience was silent.

"As a demonstration, it pales in comparison to, say, Nagasaki. But the message will be delivered. While the public will believe it to be the work of the Anti-Globalization Alliance, world leaders will know the truth. They won't touch us."

He surveyed the audience, looking for signs of weakness. He saw none.

"I repeat my offer of the previous evening. We are not a prison. I want volunteers, not slaves. If anyone wishes to leave, for any reason, please let me know."

They returned his gaze. To a person, they were unflinching.

"Very well," he said. "Get some rest. Tomorrow morning, we'll meet in the media room, eight o'clock."

55

The clock on Harry's computer said 12:20 AM. By his standards, it was early evening. The problem was that he had been up for however-many hours without sleep, and his eyes were beginning to glaze over. Harry had not showered for a couple of days and air quality suffered as a result.

He had decoded the program that enabled Colton to take control of the lasers in Mike's lab. Buried in the code, he uncovered an IP address that belonged to the computer that had sent the illicit signals. It was a proxy server, only one link in a chain. The bad guy sent a signal to one computer, which sent it to another, and so on. By searching the net and enlisting the help of some trustworthy hackers, he narrowed down the identity of the original computer network.

The network belonged to Colton Enterprises. He decided to ping the network, using the protocols that resided within the malicious program. It was like fishing. If he got a nibble, he would gently pry information from the nibbling computer and go from there. It would not be easy. In fact, it probably would not work. But he held out hope. With patience and luck, he might worm his way into the Colton network, right into the computer of the guy who killed Charles and Stefan.

* * *

Gunnar slammed down his phone. "Damned politicians," he growled.

"Let me guess," Axel said. "The White House said 'no.'"

"Correct."

"Then we must consult the Committee."

"Need I remind you," Gunnar said, "that the last time you tried to meet with members of the Committee, you were ambushed?"

"There is a mole. That's true. But the Committee has influence. More, perhaps, than you."

Gunnar grumbled, avoiding Axel's cool blue eyes.

"The Committee can get us a ride on the *Washington*."

"The mole will leak our plans."

"Yes," Axel said, "I already thought of that."

"I see," Gunnar said, reluctantly coming around to Axel's point of view. "When can we meet them?"

"Presently."

Mike closed his eyes. He wanted to tune out their conversation. He wanted to go to a mountain shack and forget about everything. The image of Valerie kept reappearing. He remembered her last words. "*Mike*," she said, "*I'm sorry*." Her expression was sincere. After that, a blinding light. Then he was lying on a gurney in a hangar. None of it made sense.

Axel and Gunnar stepped out of the hangar. They walked to the back of a small temporary building, a government-issue trailer with a thicket of satellite dishes on the roof. It was guarded by Russians with AK-47s. Gunnar showed ID and the guards waved them inside.

The room was dark and empty.

"Praetorian code papa-314-echo-271828," Gunnar said.

Monitors flickered to life. They all displayed the same instruction:

GUNNAR STONE–APPROACH BIOMETRIC STATION

Gunnar walked up to a podium and placed his right palm on a smooth black pad. He leaned forward and peered into an optical instrument.

FINGERPRINTS–PASSED
RETINAL SCAN–PASSED

Axel said his code and repeated the procedure. Five of the monitors displayed faces. A meeting was in progress.

"…the uncertainty of the stability calculations suggests that a nonlinear runaway is possible, given the…"

The Committee Chair, a portly man with wispy hair and bags under his eyes, interjected: "We've been joined by Axel Hansen and Gunnar Stone."

Images of the Committee members stared back at them. The Committee Chair was in the center. On the left were Heather Platt, a Los Alamos physicist, and Norman Davidson, the CEO of a defense contractor. On the right sat Victor Jones, a gaunt scientist from Livermore with dark glasses, and Charles Dantsker, a theoretical physicist from MIT.

"Committee members," Axel said, "we have information that Colton will launch an attack within twenty-four hours."

"How do you know this?" Charles asked.

"We cannot discuss our sources and methods," Gunnar said, "except to say that we have overhead surveillance. We request that the Committee approve invasion plans. Navy SEALs will approach the west, repeat, *west* side of the island, where the visitor's center is located. That will allow us to evacuate civilians as quickly as possible. Colton employees will be apprehended or killed. Trained personnel will search and destroy the black holes."

The Committee pondered this. Axel and Gunnar studied their expressions.

The Committee Chair scanned a sheaf of papers in front of him. "You're talking about a military assault on a corporation that has not been formally charged with anything illegal."

"That," Gunnar said, "is why we have a Committee."

The Chair nodded gravely. "Comments?" he said.

"How soon could we begin?" Norman said.

"We can have SEALs on the beach in three hours," Gunnar said confidently.

"Do you have an estimate on collateral damage?" Heather asked.

"There are several thousand employees on the island. Half are what one might call innocent civilians: construction workers, cooks, maids, janitors, and the like. Of those, I estimate thirty to forty deaths and a hundred or so serious injuries. There are thirty visitors on the island. Followers of Colton, they will be killed unless they make a visible and clear effort to surrender. Security personnel and key employees will likewise be terminated on the spot."

The Chair waited a moment to see if anyone else had questions. Hearing none, he said, "We'll discuss your proposal."

"I would remind the Committee that we do not have the luxury of time," Gunnar said.

"We understand that," the Chair said.

The monitors went blank. Axel and Gunnar stepped out of the trailer and squinted in the noontime sun. The guards closed and bolted the doors.

"The mole is Victor Jones," Axel said, referring to the one person who had not spoken during the meeting.

"Yes," Gunnar said. "We should have known."

They walked back to the hangar and told Mike they were leaving right away.

"Where are we going?" he asked.

"A military base in Australia," Axel said. "Jalen set up a control center there."

Mike closed his eyes. He didn't want to hop across three continents in as many days. They didn't need him anymore. Why couldn't they just drop him off somewhere?

As if reading his mind, Axel said, "Relax, Mike. As far as you're concerned, this is over. Leave it to us."

He wished he could, but he felt the weight of responsibility. *He* leaked the project to Jennifer, who then leaked it to Hassan. He misjudged both of them. It was so easy to put them in boxes marked "evil," but the pigeonholing didn't fit. Jennifer was trying to move on with her life after *he* bailed on the wedding. Hassan, whatever his flaws, was on the right side of the scientific debate. He had argued that the black hole project was too dangerous to proceed. In retrospect, he was obviously correct. After Hassan presented his case before the Committee, the mole passed on the names of those who knew about the project. With cold efficiency, Colton's troops eliminated them, one by one.

This raised a question: what about the other members of the Committee? They knew about the black hole project. Were they also in danger?

Mike opened his eyes as he realized something. The Committee was different. Unlike ordinary civilians, they kept secrets. Colton *wanted* the Committee to know. The Committee would inform the President that Colton possessed a weapon more powerful than a nuclear bomb. The President would have no choice but to leave Colton alone. The public, blissfully unaware of this stalemate, would be protected.

A stalemate would not be so bad if Colton merely wanted to be left alone. But Mike knew that Colton, and Voth, would not be content to reside on an idyllic island. Like mad rulers throughout history, they would strike out at neighboring lands. World leaders would be afraid to challenge them. Piece by piece, Colton and Voth would assemble an empire.

SUNDAY, JUNE 8

56

Mike, Oleg, Axel, and Gunnar boarded the jet. Mike sat, strapped in his seat, with a vacant stare. He dimly recalled that, on the flight to Russia, he sat next to Valerie. He remembered the touch of her hand.

The jet took off and banked away from St. Petersburg.

Hours passed. A nurse checked on Mike periodically. As the jet made its southward journey, Axel and Gunnar continued talking, making it hard for Mike to fall asleep. Even in perfect silence, though, he probably could not find the comfort of slumber. Disturbing thoughts and images kept intruding.

Intellectually, he knew Valerie had betrayed him. The facts were clear on that point. He just didn't *feel* anything. Whether it was the medication, the aftereffects of electric shock, or exhaustion, a thick numbness pervaded his mind. The doctors brought him back to life, but he wasn't alive.

After an hour, the nurse gave him a sedative. He felt the numbness grow.

Axel and Gunnar knew, from Jing's reports, that Colton had targeted Santoso's residence in Surabaya. The question before them was whether to alert the Indonesian government. Doing so could compromise Jing, who was their best source of information on the island. Doing nothing could result in innocent deaths.

Gunnar insisted that the point was to stop Colton from launching the attack. Everything else was a sideshow. Axel wanted to formulate contingency plans that would reduce casualties if there *was* an attack.

Gunnar's phone rang. His face reddened as he listened to the person on the other end. He cursed every few seconds.

"Who got to you?" he demanded. After a minute, he said, "I'm sorry too. More than you can possibly know."

He hung up the phone.

"They've called off the invasion," he said.

Axel nodded slowly. "Senator Schmidt."

"Yes. He lobbied them hard. Can't use the military to attack my constituent, blah, blah. The White House referred the matter to the Justice Department."

"We knew this might happen."

"The Justice Department," Gunnar said contemptuously. "I expect they'll issue subpoenas by the end of the year."

They sat quietly, knowing what lay ahead. Barring a miracle, Colton would launch a black hole toward Santoso's residence in Surabaya. The building would implode, killing Santoso, his family, and his neighbors. To world leaders, the message would be clear: this is what will happen to those who confront Henry Colton.

From Jing's report, Colton planned to launch the attack in the morning. On the island, it was 1:30 AM. Time was running short.

James Tyrell and Henry Colton conferred in a small meeting room in the visitor's center. Victor Jones, the Livermore scientist, had told them of the plan to assault the island. Senator Schmidt used his contacts in the White House to prevent the invasion. The machinery worked as planned. Still, they had to be careful. James redeployed several hundred security personnel from the east side of the island to the west, in case the invasion occurred. Dozens of them stood watch around the visitor's complex, their faces obscured by night vision goggles.

"The weapons division is nearly ready," James said. "We can launch as early as five."

"Let's not rush things," Colton said.

"We may need to. The Committee endorsed an invasion…"

"Which was turned down by the White House."

"Officially, yes. But the Committee can act on its own, giving politicians plausible deniability. We must operate on the assumption that they will launch an invasion of some kind."

Colton sipped a glass of whiskey as he pondered James' argument. He knew James had a warrior instinct that he lacked. James had built up the island security force by scouring the prisons and ghettos of Indonesia, searching for innately gifted people in miserable, violent environments. He convinced them that they were special and had a new mission in life. They would be soldiers in the greatest army of the millennium. James put them through exhausting training, sleep deprivation, and torture. Those who survived were implanted with Biochips to enhance their sensory acuity and loyalty.

James knew what he was doing. Colton trusted his judgment.

"Suppose they do invade," Colton said, "what then?"

"We fight. I trust the motivation and ability of my soldiers. Still, I'm a realist. If the invasion force is sufficiently large, then we will be overwhelmed."

Colton nodded. He could not fault James' logic. They could not risk a full-scale invasion. The sooner they launched the weapon, the sooner they would have their deterrent.

"I'm lucky to have you, James. Launch at the earliest opportunity."

The jet continued its southward course, where it would pass over Indonesia before landing near Darwin, Australia. Mike's sedative was strong enough to keep him asleep while Gunnar and Axel debated the merits of alerting Santoso, the leader targeted by Colton.

They pulled up Santoso's file. While he was not above receiving "tributes," he possessed a rare combination of candor and political acumen, and had made strides in cleaning up the local government. Colton Enterprises employed many people from Surabaya, so they had probably had contact with the man. Colton must have decided that an independent-minded leader would make a convenient target for their demonstration.

After an hour of discussion, they decided on a compromise. They would alert Santoso only if an attack was imminent. His neighbors would, regrettably, become collateral damage. On the other hand, Santoso and his family might be saved without alerting Colton to the presence of their spy.

Gunnar picked up his phone. "Jalen," he said, "establish a connection to Santoso's phones."

From Australia, Jalen routed a signal to Santoso's personal cell phone and house phone. He verified that both were ready to receive calls.

The lights of Surabaya were visible on the horizon. The jet's radar systems scanned the dark skies. They knew the black hole had to be carried on a missile of some kind. The warhead would probably be ballistic and would approach from the east. Besides that, they had few specifics.

Jing's contact lenses transmitted a grainy image from the media room. Jing and the guests sat in the theater-like chamber, which had a huge screen in the center and smaller screens all around. The center screen showed preparations underway in the southern part of the island, the off-limits area designated for weapons testing. Employees worked busily around an underground missile silo, illuminated by bright white lights.

The roof of the silo opened rapidly. Even from the grainy image, Axel and Gunnar could tell that the guests were excited by the scene.

The jet engines increased their thrust and Mike awoke. Slowly, he pieced together what was going on. Colton was about to strike.

A message from Jing flashed on the monitor:

LAUNCH IN 10 SECONDS

Axel picked up a phone and dialed.

Santoso lay in bed with his wife. His four-year-old son lay between them.

The phone rang. Santoso fumbled for the receiver, while his wife and son slumbered peacefully. He listened intently. He grabbed his son and said, "Wake up!"

They had practiced this drill many times. His wife went to the kids' rooms while Santoso carried his sleepy four-year-old down the main hall toward the exit. He walked out into the front yard and set his son down on the lawn, which was now illuminated by floodlights. A moment later, his wife emerged with three kids in pajamas. She handed Santoso a small flashlight. Santoso ran to the family minivan and searched it quickly, looking for booby traps.

"It's okay," he said.

The family quietly piled into the minivan. The four-year-old remained asleep during the entire ordeal.

They did not notice that, across the street, a man watched them as they drove away. The man dialed his phone.

On the island, Troy whistled a hair-metal tune as he typed on his computer. He had been up all night, ensuring that the network interfaces were working properly. He wore his lucky vintage 1980s Ratt T-shirt. Now, it was show time. His computer monitor displayed the home page of the Anti-Globalization Alliance. The page showed a list of "global entities that oppress workers and destroy the environment." The empty warehouse in Surabaya, destroyed by arson, was on the list. It had a line through it. Troy added an entry:

LEHMAN TEXTILES FACTORY, SURABAYA, INDONESIA

On another monitor, he watched the missile launch from the

silo, a bright white light saturating the screen. This was so *cool.*

Voices from the control room came through the speakers: "We have liftoff. Trajectory adjustment alpha. Confirmed. Two point two degrees. Confirmed. Wind steady, two knots."

The missile rose in the morning sky and arced toward the west. The bright, fiery exhaust dimmed until it was a dull crimson, and the warhead detached from the rocket. The warhead was now ballistic.

Troy changed the font to strikethrough:

~~LEHMAN TEXTILES FACTORY, SURABAYA, INDONESIA~~

"The boost phase is complete," Jalen reported.

Gunnar nodded. Inside the jet, he watched a monitor that displayed a red dot on a map of Colton's island. Satellites had detected the rocket launch. Now, the jet's radar systems searched for the rapidly moving warhead.

The monitor emitted a beeping sound and a blue square appeared on the screen. The map zoomed out to show the island and Indonesia. The blue square, representing the warhead, followed a trajectory toward Surabaya.

"We're picking up chatter between Indonesia and the island," Jalen said. "I'm putting it through decryption."

"Is Santoso evacuated?" Gunnar asked.

Axel nodded yes.

The blue square approached Surabaya and the monitor zoomed in on the area. According to the map, it headed directly toward Santoso's home.

After a moment, Axel said, "It's deviating."

"What do you mean?"

Jalen's voice came over the speaker. "The warhead's not going to impact Santoso's house. It's going to miss."

Mike felt a sensation of impending doom. "How densely populated is the area?"

"Very," Gunnar snapped.

"Can you intercept the warhead?"

"Impossible."

Axel pointed out the port side window. "There it is."

The warhead streaked across the sky, glowing red from the heat of reentry. They watched the warhead approach a cluster of lights a half mile from the harbor.

"It's headed toward a poor part of the city," Jalen said, "basically a slum, lots of people..."

The warhead disappeared into the lights. For a moment, it was silent and they began to hope that it was a dud. Then they saw a bright flash. A glowing crimson shock wave propagated outward.

"Brace for impact," Gunnar said.

They held on to their seats. Oleg muttered a prayer. The shock wave hit them with a loud, sharp report, causing the jet to roll away from the blast. The pilots corrected and pulled upward.

"I've decrypted a message from Indonesia to Colton's island," Jalen said. "Transmitting now."

Ignoring Jalen's voice, they all watched the monitor that showed the point of impact. A factory building collapsed in toward a dark sphere. The black hole. Bricks and glass swirled around the singularity. The surrounding buildings got sucked in as the radius of destruction widened. Mike noticed a pair of human figures running away from the blast. They became caught in the vortex, tidal forces ripping them apart like rag dolls. More people emerged from homes and tried to run away, but they too were sucked in. The widening circle obliterated rickety homes and apartments.

The black hole flickered sporadically as chunks of matter entered it. Suddenly it emitted a blinding white flash and went dark. Objects flying in the air fell to the ground. An infrared image showed a stark circle of devastation, with debris and bodies in swirled patterns around the epicenter.

Gunnar stared silently at the darkness. "Casualties?" he asked softly.

"Rough estimate, based on population density, one to two thousand," Jalen reported.

They sat, stunned, as the jet accelerated away from Indonesia. *Thousands dead.* Mike felt empty inside and despised himself for it. He was shocked by the terroristic violence but could not seem to empathize with the innocent people whose lives had been extinguished. He thought of the grieving families but could not muster an emotional response. It was too much to take in.

"Gunnar," said Jalen's voice, "I think you need to read the decrypted message."

They all looked up at the monitor:

> CONFIRMED: SANTOSO WAS WARNED. THERE IS A MOLE ON THE ISLAND. REPEAT, THERE IS A MOLE ON THE ISLAND.

57

They had watched with satisfaction but suppressed the urge to celebrate. The demonstration was an unqualified success. It showed technological prowess and ruthlessness, both of which were required to establish the new society. The highest echelons of government were now put on notice. Everything had gone according to plan. Colton's somber demeanor, however, prevented the guests from breaking out the champagne.

The news came in:

Our lead story this morning: terrorist attack in Surabaya, Indonesia. The Lehman textiles factory and surrounding area were destroyed by a massive explosion. The factory had been criticized by labor and human-rights organizations for unsafe working conditions and anti-union activities. Now, it appears that terrorists decided to send a message by destroying the factory. The cause of the blast is not known, but officials speculate that multiple explosives were detonated simultaneously. Some witnesses report seeing a missile or airplane, but those reports have not been confirmed.

Law-enforcement officials point to the Anti-Globalization Alliance, or AGA, as the terrorist group responsible for this devastating attack. The Lehman textiles factory was listed on the AGA web site as a target. This follows a fire that destroyed an empty warehouse in Surabaya several days ago; the warehouse was also listed on the AGA site. The attack this morning inflicted far more collateral damage. Officials are estimating upwards of two thousand people may have been killed, with many more injured.

Police in Oakland, California, report that Kevin Larson, head of the AGA, was found dead in his home, killed by a self-inflicted gunshot wound.

James whispered into Henry's ear and they left the room. They walked down the hallway to a small conference room and closed the door.

"You're absolutely sure?" Henry asked.

James nodded. "You announced to the guests that Santoso was the target. They were the only ones in possession of that misinformation. One of them passed it on."

Henry sighed. James was explaining something that Henry already knew but didn't want to accept. Once again, James' suspicious nature had served him well.

"I'm confident we can identify the spy within twenty-four hours."

"Do whatever it takes," Henry said, brushing back his hair. "We cannot allow our revolution to be compromised."

James left and Henry paced around the room. The betrayal, by one of his handpicked founders, weighed heavily on his mind. It overshadowed the successes of the past few days. He had to focus, soldier on, and allow James to purify the newborn society. As the Biochip technology evolved, loyalty would become a diminishing concern. Thoughts of spying or sabotage would not be allowed to propagate through the brain. Disloyalty simply would not occur to the people of the island. After many human trials, the life sciences lab was on the verge of revolutionary cybernetic technology that would deliver the promise of a population free of corruption, superstition, and sloth. Until the Biochip could be fully implemented, though, he would need to rely on James and his coarser methods.

The jet landed on a runway by the Timor Sea, across the bay from Darwin, Australia. It was sunrise and there was a balmy breeze. Jalen waited for them on the tarmac.

"What's the status of the *USS Washington*?" Gunnar asked.

"In range," Jalen replied.

"We need to formulate an invasion plan," Axel said, "as soon as possible."

"Stick to science," Gunnar growled, "and let me take care of tactics."

The airfield had a small tower and some military helicopters and planes, along with a fuel tanker, personnel carriers, and civilian vehicles. They walked toward a desolate area ringed with barbed wire. He wondered about the connection between the Praetorians and other groups worldwide. There seemed to be a network that included some military or quasi-military organizations but excluded law-enforcement agencies like the FBI. He was curious but knew it was pointless to ask.

"Jing's in danger," Jalen said.

"And she's expendable!" Gunnar shouted, his face red. "We do *not* have a contingency plan for extracting compromised assets."

Gunnar led them past armed sentries, who waved them through the gate. They entered a plain brown building. Mike followed slowly, as if in a trance. Inside, several computer screens showed maps of the island.

"We have evidence," Jalen said, "that Colton is building up an arsenal of black holes."

"Not surprising," Gunnar said.

"An arsenal…" Mike mumbled.

Gunnar turned impatiently toward the disheveled professor. "You have something to add?"

"The one we saw," he said tentatively. "The black hole. It was small and unstable."

"Yes," Axel said, understanding.

"But a larger one… Beyond the Schwarzschild radius…"

He hardly wanted to acknowledge it, but Mike could not refute the physical facts. By combining the smaller black holes, it was theoretically possible to create a big, stable one. Once that happened…

"It would consume matter," he said, almost in a whisper. "Suck in matter and grow larger. Eventually–a few days, I don't know, I'm not an astrophysicist–the earth would distort into an accretion disk."

Matter from the earth would swirl around the black hole, slow at the outer edges but terrifyingly fast near the event horizon. Rapidly moving particles would emit gamma rays, which would shoot out in two streams of intense energy, perpendicular to the swirling disk. When particles crossed the event horizon, they would disappear. Forever.

"Like water spiraling down a drain," Axel said somberly. "The planet as we know it would cease to exist."

Gunnar pondered this. People talked glibly about nuclear war destroying the planet, but it really wasn't true. Even at the height of the Cold War, the most horrific nuclear exchange between the superpowers would not have come close to destroying all human life, much less other species. Colton's doomsday device was something different altogether. It was the ultimate deterrent.

"All the advances of humanity, the good with the bad, *gone*," Axel continued. "There won't be any weapons after this. Colton has made the last weapon."

"The Secretary of Defense ruled out a military invasion," Gunnar said. "Senator Schmidt saw to that."

"But this is world-ending event," Oleg protested. "Surely American president would do something if you told him about black hole."

Gunnar shook his head. "Two problems with that idea. First, Senator Schmidt and others will argue against an attack, on the grounds that it's too risky. Faced with the prospect of annihilation, the White House will choose negotiation over direct confrontation. Second, even if they *did* authorize an invasion, the senator would leak that information to Colton, putting him on alert. We would walk into a trap."

"Then what do we do?" Oleg said plaintively. "Ask Colton please be nice?"

Gunnar walked around the room, looking at the computer monitors. He turned to the others with a resolute expression.

"We must stop Colton. All other considerations are secondary."

He pointed to a map of the island. It showed the visitor's

center and energy labs on the west side, and the biological research complex on the east. Twin volcanic peaks separated the two sides. South of the biological complex was a small harbor.

"Colton believes that if an invasion occurs, it will come from the west. That was a calculated deception. In reality, we will send a small team to the *east* shore. Their mission will be to determine the location of the black holes."

"What then?" said Oleg.

"Once we find the black holes, the *USS Washington* will take care of them."

"But your Defense Secretary prohibited attack!"

"What attack?" Gunnar asked slyly. "I said nothing about an attack. The *Washington* is conducting weapons tests in international waters. Sometimes, accidents happen. One of their guided missiles might veer off course…"

58

Harry read the message on his computer monitor:

~~LEHMAN TEXTILES FACTORY, SURABAYA, INDONESIA~~

He had intercepted the transmission from the island to the AGA website by casting a wide net around the Colton computer network. Fortunately, the AGA website used an outdated encryption protocol, allowing him to read the uploaded text. There was no doubt about who was behind the attack in Surabaya. It had to be Colton.

Despite his excitement, or perhaps because of it, Harry felt lightheaded. A sugar-caffeine crash was hitting him hard and he knew he could pass out any minute. He fired off a message to Agent Sanchez. He tilted his head back and closed his eyes.

Henry felt sick in the pit of his stomach as he waited in the soundproof room. He wondered how he would explain the presence of a spy on his island. He had assured Damien Voth that his people were completely trustworthy.

Voth's image appeared on the screen.

"Have you captured Axel Hansen?" he asked, without preamble.

"No... But something else has come up. It's my fault entirely." His throat constricted and he looked away from the screen, ashamed. "We have a spy. Damien, I trusted all of these people, but one of them is a spy."

"I see," Voth said.

"James tells me I'm too trusting. It's true. Please forgive..."

"There is nothing to forgive."

Henry approached the screen, tears in his eyes.

"Every revolution has its traitors," Voth said. "You will take care of it."

"Yes," Henry said, a wave of gratitude rushing over him. Voth had every right to be furious with him, but instead showed him kindness. It was more than he deserved. "I will stop at nothing. I'll find the traitor."

"My boy, don't be too–hard on yourself. Remember who you are."

"I do."

"You are the product of two geniuses–the genius of science and the genius of power. Never has such a person–walked the earth."

Henry wiped his eyes and smiled.

"Thank you, Damien. Your words are kind. I won't let you down."

Not far from the soundproof room, Jing walked along a wandering path that led up the hill behind the visitor's center. Brightly colored tropical birds squawked in the trees overhead. After a half hour, she reached an observation platform, where a pair of guards watched the ocean through high-powered binoculars. She showed one her guest pass. He nodded and continued scanning the horizon.

She turned her gaze toward the physical sciences lab, perched on the Saddle. Her contact lenses zoomed in. She saw workers loading a canister onto a truck, which sped away toward the north and out of view. A second truck moved into the loading dock. Workers hurriedly wheeled a canister down a ramp and into the trailer. The second truck took a different path, a narrow road that led from the arid land into the eastern jungle.

She headed back to the visitor's center. She stepped to the side of the path to let a Colton electric car go by.

The car stopped. James and Valerie stepped out.

"That's her," Valerie said.

James raised a weapon. "Don't move."

Jing slowly put her hands in the air.

"Always a pleasure, James. What do you think you're doing?"

The guards saw what was happening and rushed over, guns at the ready.

"Take her into custody," he said.

One of the guards roughly put her hands in cuffs. She glared at James angrily.

"I want to talk to Henry, *now*."

"Get in the car."

She sat in the back seat of the electric car, which sped down the path toward the visitor's center. The two guards sat to her left and right while James drove. Valerie rode shotgun. Jing knew that her contact lenses transmitted the scene back to Gunnar and the others. They could see and hear everything.

"You're making a mistake," she said.

They followed a road to the visitor's center loading dock and stopped abruptly. A guard led Jing out of the car. They took her through the entrance and up a flight of stairs. More security personnel joined them and they went into a spare, dark room.

"Sit down," James said.

Jing sat in the only chair in the room. One of the guards attached her cuffed wrists to the back of the chair.

"This is ridiculous," Jing spat. "I demand to see Henry."

James produced a stainless steel rod about the length of an orchestra conductor's wand. He pressed a button and wormlike appendages shot out, wriggling, as if searching for prey.

"What the hell is that?"

"Pain," James said. "Pure, unadulterated pain. Even a trained agent like you cannot withstand it. Don't try. Just tell me who you work for."

The guards kept their eyes on Jing. Valerie looked away.

James pressed the rod against Jing's arm. The tentacles spread out and attached themselves to the skin. Blue sparks shot from the tentacles and enveloped her body. She arched her back convulsively and screamed. The pain was beyond intense, an infinity of needles penetrating her core. After a moment, James retrieved the rod. Jing hyperventilated and her eyes rolled toward the ceiling.

"That's just a sample," he said. "We can go further, but I'm sure you realize there would be no point to that."

"I know who the mole is," she whispered, "but I want Henry here."

James moved the rod toward her arm.

"Listen!" she shouted. "If you torture me, I'll tell you what you want to hear. I'll say whatever will make the pain stop. It won't mean a thing."

He jabbed the rod into her collarbone. Her eyes bulged as the tentacles wrapped around her neck, sending agonizing jolts of electricity through her body. She screamed until she was hoarse. Tears streamed down her cheeks. Following her training, she forced her mind to regress into childhood. She rode a bike along the sidewalk in her old neighborhood. A car backed out of a driveway and she swerved to miss it. She lost her balance and crashed, skinning her knees. The image shifted and she was scampering up a climbing wall. At the top, she rang a bell and started belaying down. Her mother held the rope, worry lines on her face but trying to look encouraging.

Her memories catapulted forward in time. She saw an image of her mother and father. They sat on the sofa and looked away, disappointed. She had told them about getting a job with a financial firm instead of going to graduate school. She couldn't tell them that the financial firm was a CIA cover. If she told them the truth, the neighborhood would know within hours. So she fed them the story about her new profession as an international hedge fund manager. Thus began her life of lies.

She recalled Gunnar Stone, recruiting her to join the Praetorians. She tried to concentrate on his image and push the pain away. But he vanished, obliterated by searing torture. She tried to focus her mind but it was impossible. She knew she would crack. No one could withstand this.

After what seemed an eternity, James pulled back the rod and set it aside.

"Okay," Jing said, gasping for air, "I'll tell you."

Valerie stood in a corner, obviously disturbed by the scene. Jing tried to catch her breath.

After a few seconds, she nodded in Valerie's direction.

"*She's* the mole."

James laughed mirthlessly. "Nice try," he said, turning to reach for the rod.

"Listen to me!" Jing shouted desperately. "Ask Valerie if she killed Mike Harris."

She saw James' confident façade crack slightly. "We already know the answer to that."

"Ask her."

James looked at Valerie.

"She's playing games," Valerie protested. "It's obvious. She's trying to deflect attention away from herself."

"Humor me," James said.

"Of course I killed Mike Harris!" she exclaimed. "I gave him a lethal dose from the bio launcher."

"Did you confirm the kill?"

"Yes," she said, flustered. "I'm not the one under interrogation here."

Jing stared at James intently. "I can prove that Mike Harris is alive."

James regarded her for a moment. He didn't trust Jing, but if her assertion was correct, then it would mean Valerie was compromised.

"I'm listening," he said.

"I'm a reporter. I have contacts."

"She's with *them*," Valerie said, pointing an accusing finger. "The Praetorians. I *saw* her!"

"Fine," Jing said. As the pain receded, she felt herself regain her composure. "Hook us up to lie detectors. See who passes."

"Lie detectors can be defeated by trained spies."

"That's enough," James said impatiently. "Jing, where's your proof?"

She hesitated. "I'm a journalist. Like most of my sources, Mike Harris contacted me directly. I can have him on the phone within the hour."

In Darwin, Gunnar and the others listened to the conversation intently.

"She sold me out," Mike said.

"She improvised," Gunnar corrected. "I would've done the same. It preserves her cover."

He handed Mike a phone.

"What am I supposed to do?" Mike asked.

"When it rings, answer it."

Mike massaged his temples, trying to get his bearings. The revelation that Mike was alive would uncover Valerie's lie and expose her to Henry Colton's wrath. She would be punished for sparing Mike's life. He may become responsible for yet another casualty.

The phone rang. On the screen, they saw the image of James holding a phone.

Mike answered in a weak voice. "Mike Harris."

James handed the phone to Jing. "Mike," she said, "this is Jing Shen from the *London Financial Times*. Is this a good time to talk?"

"I guess..."

"I wonder if you could briefly recap your experiences of the last few days. Just to make sure I have my facts straight."

He monotonously recited his story: the lab disaster, escaping to Glacier Park, Hassan's death, his chance encounter with Valerie... He provided enough details to establish his identity, while omitting the parts about the Praetorians.

"Thanks Mike," said Jing, trying to sound casual, "that's all I need for now. I'll be in touch."

James inspected the display on the phone. "The voice checks out. It's him."

Valerie shook her head slowly.

"I'm not surprised that you couldn't go through with it," said James. "I always thought you were too soft for this line of work. What surprises me is that you thought you could get away with deceiving us."

Mike and the others watched the screen as security personnel handcuffed Valerie and led her away.

James' face loomed large as he leaned in close to Jing, staring malevolently. "We're not finished," he said.

59

In Darwin, a door opened, letting in bright sunlight. A pair of large Australian guards walked in.

"No offense, Oleg," Gunnar said, "but we're going to have to move you to a secure location."

Oleg looked at Gunnar with a perturbed but resigned expression. "Oh, don't trust Russian," he said. "Fine with me. Just get me to bed."

The guards led him away. Mike barely noticed as the doors slammed shut. He kept thinking about Valerie. By delivering the silicon to Harris, she facilitated the destruction of innocent lives. She couldn't claim ignorance. She knew the black holes would be weaponized. And yet, there was one line she could not cross. She was ordered to kill Mike but, for whatever reason, did not.

The screen went dark.

"What happened?" Gunner demanded.

Jalen peered at his computer screen. "Jing shut off the transmission."

Gunnar understood. Jing was following protocol, minimizing communications to avoid incriminating herself further. At the first opportunity, she would swallow the contact lenses, which would quickly dissolve in her stomach and disappear.

Axel stood up. He had been thinking, silently, and appeared to have reached a conclusion.

"We have an opportunity," he said.

"Our only asset, Jing, is in confinement," Gunnar grumbled.

"And so is Valerie. She knows where the black holes are. She can lead us to them."

"She betrayed and nearly killed Mike Harris!"

Mike listened impassively. He knew he should be furious at Valerie, but he still felt nothing.

"Nearly," said Axel. He turned to Mike. "Valerie is no psychopath. She doesn't want to destroy the planet."

"I agree," Jalen said. "That's consistent with her psychological profile."

"What do you propose?" Gunnar said.

"We invade the east side of the island, as planned, but at two points." Axel pointed to a screen that showed a map of the island. "A diversionary force will attack the harbor. In the ensuing confusion, a smaller group will infiltrate the northeast region, near the biological labs. From there, one can hike to the detention facility on the north shore, which is inaccessible from the sea. That is where we'll find Valerie."

"What if you're wrong?"

"Then we'll change our plans accordingly."

Gunnar rubbed his chin. If anyone other than Axel had suggested the plan, he would have rejected it out of hand.

"Who will be in this smaller team?"

"It will consist of a landing party of six to eight, and me."

Gunnar's eyes widened. "Are you insane?" he boomed.

"The landing party will get me to the shore. After that, I go alone."

Mike cleared his throat and stood up. "I'm going with Axel," he said, surprised by his own words. Yet he knew, deep in his gut, that he had to do it.

Gunnar stepped back and regarded Mike and Axel. "You physicists are nuts. *Nuts!* Axel going alone is reckless enough, but Mike, you're a rank amateur. We can't rescue you when you do something stupid."

"Nor do I expect it." He felt a sense of detached confidence, like he was beyond feeling pain. "You want to flip Valerie. Turn her to your side. Use her. I'm your best chance."

"Don't flatter yourself," Gunnar scoffed.

"He has a point," Jalen said. "Mike's presence would disrupt her psychological equilibrium, which is already off balance after being detained. This disruption would increase the chance of obtaining the needed information."

"Spare me the psychobabble," Gunnar said, turning red. "I cannot have a civilian on this mission."

"I'm expendable," Mike said calmly. "If I can't keep up with Axel, then he can leave me behind."

"Let me be clear," Gunnar said. "If you cannot locate the black holes, I will use every trick, pull every string, and move every mountain, to convince the White House to *nuke the island*, to obliterate it once and for all. I will not save you or any other member of my team."

"Of course," Axel said with a smile, knowing they had won. "We would expect nothing else."

Axel gestured for Mike to come with him. They left before Gunnar could change his mind.

Gunnar stared at the map of the island. He needed to come up with a plan B. His bluster about nuking the island was just that. Modern politicians couldn't afford that kind of courage, he knew. In a world of human rights organizations and international law, leaders who defended their nations or even the entire world could expect arrest warrants in return. Today, Harry Truman would be locked up at The Hague. There was no way the president would agree to a nuclear strike.

In his darkest moods, Gunnar wondered whether the world was even worth saving. People were capable of admirable bravery and sacrifice when faced with an external threat. But as soon as the perceived threat recedes, citizens invariably turn on the soldiers who defended them. He felt resigned to that fate. Gunnar knew that, if the planet survived, he would someday be called to account for his actions, hauled before a tribunal like a war criminal. Compared to that, annihilation didn't seem so bad.

After the doors closed, Jalen said, "Gunnar?"

"Yes," he replied absently.

"There's something we need to discuss. It's about Colton's psychological profile."

Henry marched toward James, his hair even more disheveled than usual. James was outside the room where Jing was locked up. Two guards stood by the door.

"What have you done?" he demanded.

"I obtained information from Jing," James replied calmly. "Valerie Norton did not kill Mike Harris as ordered. She's being transported to the detention facility."

"But Jing…"

"We have to ask ourselves some questions about Jing. First, how did she know that Mike Harris is alive?"

"She's a reporter," Henry said, pulling at his hair. "She knows everything, it seems. James, tell me you didn't hurt her."

Henry could tell from James' stony face what happened. He knew about the methods that James used. Hell, he sanctioned them. James had a suspicious nature, which was an asset, but his distrust of Jing bordered on obsessive. It went beyond just protecting Henry. He seemed oddly jealous of Jing's relationship with Henry, chaste as it was. James took Henry's charge too far. To claim that Jing was a spy was ludicrous. He had courted her, practically *begged* her to come to the island.

"I know you mean well," Henry said, looking away, "but I'm going to have to relieve you of your command. *Temporarily*, James, just temporarily, until I get this sorted out."

"Of course," James said stoically. "I serve at your pleasure. But there is a second question to consider. How did Valerie identify Jing?"

"Valerie has no credibility," Henry said, waving dismissively. "You said as much yourself."

Before James could respond, Henry motioned to the guards.

"Escort James to the detention facility," he said brusquely, walking to the door while avoiding James' gaze. He waved his palm in front of a black panel. The door clicked and opened. He walked into the bare room.

His heart leapt at the sight of Jing, her arms handcuffed behind the chair. Her face was pale.

He closed the door behind him.

"Jing, I'm so sorry," he said, tears in his eyes. "I didn't know."

"Henry," Jing said in a hoarse voice, "promise me…"

"Never again," Henry said firmly, stroking her long black hair. "It won't happen again. It never should have happened. I've sent James away."

She smiled weakly. "If you don't trust me…"

"I do trust you, Jing." He dropped to his knees. "James was just trying to protect me, like always. But we found the mole. It was Valerie. I should have known. She doesn't have the killer instinct. She obviously lost heart and alerted the authorities..."

"Kiss me."

Henry was taken by surprise but recovered gamely and leaned forward. Jing did the same, straining against her handcuffs. Their lips met and they kissed softly.

"Just one problem," Henry said, his heart racing. "I don't have keys to the handcuffs."

"Is that a problem?" she said, and they both laughed, followed by a longer, more passionate kiss.

Gunnar tried to make sense out of what Jalen had told him.

Damien Voth's insight into human manipulation equaled his scientific brilliance. He interjected himself into Henry Colton's life just as Colton hit bottom. He knew Colton had been adopted by an elderly couple who died when Colton was in college. Colton's personal life was a mess. He had no family or true friends. Behind the veneer of a successful businessman was a sad, empty life. The more Colton tried to conceal his inner torment, the more intense the pain became.

Voth stepped in and assumed the role of father, role model, and mentor. He gave Colton a singular purpose in life, to create a great new civilization. In redeeming himself, Colton developed a powerful psychic bond with Voth, to whom he felt he owed everything.

Voth could have left it at that. He would have had profound

influence over Colton.

But that wasn't enough, for Voth had schemes within schemes that required unquestioning obedience. He needed total control.

Gunnar imagined how the conversation must have gone.

Henry, Voth would have said, using his most kindly, avuncular voice. *I must tell you about who you are.*

Jalen's team pieced the story together from altered records scattered across the internet. Obscure documents, of interest to no one, comprised the framework of an elaborate deception.

The deception was based on fact. At the Swiss Federal Institute of Technology, Albert Einstein had a love affair with another physics graduate student, Mileva Marić. They had a daughter, Lieserl, born out of wedlock in 1902, and gave her up for adoption or to an orphanage. What exactly happened to the baby girl was never made public, but it tormented Mileva for the rest of her life.

You are destined for more than mere commerce.

Next came the lies: Lieserl grew up in Eastern Europe and had two children who died of influenza. Later, Lieserl herself died after giving birth to a son, Piotr. In the chaos of World War II, family members shuttled young Piotr from place to place. He suffered from malnutrition and never received a proper education. Despite these disadvantages, he became a successful technician at a state weapons factory in Poland. Toughened by adversity, when he reached adulthood, his health was excellent.

Piotr fell in love with a visiting American college exchange student named Kayra, a fertile young woman who got pregnant after their first coupling. Kayra came from an immigrant family that traced its ancestry back to Ataturk, the leader who forcibly transformed backward, religious people into a modern, secular power.

You are the product of two family lines, a union of science and power.

Kayra worried about how her family would react to the news. In an echo of Einstein, Kayra and Piotr decided to give the baby up for adoption.

That baby was Henry Colton.

Henry would surely have checked the claim and found the

altered documents that supported it. Once satisfied, though, he would not have investigated deeply and skeptically, as Jalen's team had done. That was because he *wanted* to believe.

"Information is power," Gunnar mused. "What if we confronted Henry with evidence of Damien's deception? We could drive a wedge between them."

"That would be dangerous," Jalen said, "in the extreme. He's integrated this story into his psyche. He would rally every defensive mechanism in an attempt to reject the evidence. If pressed, he could have a psychotic episode."

Gunnar nodded. Humans were resourceful when it came to blocking out information that contradicted their world view. Some people still denied the Holocaust or believed that the United States was behind the September 11 terrorist attacks.

The deep connection with Voth was especially worrisome because Gunnar knew how the sick bastard's mind worked. If it were just Colton, he could imagine a *détente* between his society and the rest of the world. With Voth in the picture, he knew there would be no Cold War standoff. One day, he would release the black holes. He would destroy the world.

60

Troy cracked his knuckles and congratulated himself on a job well done. As cool as laser-beaming that German guy was, obliterating a couple thousand people with a black hole was truly epic. He stood up from his workstation, which was located in the "mission control" building in the weapons testing complex. From here, the team monitored the transport and deployment of black holes. The physical sciences lab was churning them out routinely now, confining them in magnetic bottles and loading them onto trucks. The trucks took circuitous routes across the island but they all ended up here. Troy got the impression that they were merging the black holes to create a Big Daddy black hole that could be put on a missile. Mental images of the destruction wrought by such a weapon gave him a pleasing tingle.

The spacious building had vaulted ceilings and a constant air-conditioned breeze. He strolled along a catwalk and looked down at banks of computers. They were used, in part, to calculate the optimum radii for weaponized black holes. The physics of the calculations did not interest him. Instead, his talent and passion lay in harnessing the results of those calculations to wreak maximal devastation.

The weapons testing complex was in the southern part of the

island. In contrast to the lush vegetation and beaches of the east and west shores, the volcanic landscape here was bleak. That suited Troy just fine. He would much rather hack on a computer than lie on a beach or go on a nature hike.

Troy walked to the vending machine and got a cold can of soda. He took his time walking back to his workstation. The network was running slowly and his current job was taking a while. He sat down and was about to have a video chat with a system administrator when he heard a voice above him.

"What's wrong with the network?"

He looked up and saw Greg, a member of the weapons deployment team, on a catwalk about ten meters up. "I was just about to ask," Troy said.

Troy got the system administrator on the screen and asked him what was up. He replied that the entire network was slow and they were running a virus scan. This was fairly typical. Although security was good, viruses did occasionally slip in from the internet. They were always eliminated quickly and never did any real damage.

On the opposite end of the island, guards led James into the detention facility, located a half mile from a black sandy beach. Large waves crashed onto the shore. The guards were obviously uneasy about escorting their former boss.

Sensing their emotions, James said, "Don't forget that Henry Colton is our leader. Take your orders from him and his designated representatives."

They led him into the windowless gray building, signed him in, and took him to a sterile cell with a desk, bed, and toilet.

"How long will you be in here?" asked one of the guards.

"That's not your concern," James replied. "If Colton asks you to fall on your sword, do so willingly."

The guards nodded and left James in the cell.

James knew that his stoic serenity flowed, in part, from the Biochip. It enhanced his loyalty to the point where he didn't feel the slightest resentment over being detained. Instead, he perceived things analytically. Like a master chess player, Jing had outmaneuvered him. She won this round. James' goal was to protect Henry Colton, regardless of the costs to himself. Everything he did, everything he *was*, served that end.

Valerie was also locked in the detention facility. After Henry calmed down, James would request permission to interrogate Valerie about the Praetorians. Henry would surely see no downside to this proposal. The task would keep James away from Jing and might yield useful information.

Mike had never gone scuba diving and it showed. He breathed heavily, practically gasping for air, and couldn't achieve neutral buoyancy. He flipped upside down and had uncontrolled ascents. The instructors were patient and praised him whenever he didn't completely screw up.

He got out of the swimming pool, exhausted. The instructors removed his tank and weight belt.

"I can't do this," he said between breaths.

"You're doin' fine, mate," one of the Australians said. "You'll be with experienced divers the entire time. Just don't worry or panic. If you think you're breathin' too slow, you're just right. If you think you're breathin' just right, you're too fast."

"I should have taken lessons in Maui."

Axel, calm as ever, emerged from the water. "Remember to go slow, never overreact," he said. "Don't inflate your vest too much or you'll rise to the surface. Just use a little air at a time. Use your lungs to make small adjustments in buoyancy, but never hold your breath. If you get scared, just stay still and someone will help."

They took off their dry suits. Underneath, they were wearing green fatigues. Mike felt totally out of place. Like most academics, he had zero military experience, not even the Boy Scouts. Axel, in contrast, looked the part. Mike could easily imagine a young, blue-eyed Axel on some top-secret NATO special operations mission. He regretted his woeful lack of skills and realized, with a sinking feeling, that he was in over his head. Even if he and Axel made it to land, somehow they had to evade the enemy, find Valerie, and get information from her. They had no exit plan.

They walked outside with the six divers who would accompany them to the island. Mike didn't know where the divers came from but suspected they were military or ex-military. From their accents, the team seemed to be half American and half Australian. They all tried to put Mike at ease. If they resented having to babysit an amateur, they didn't show it.

As the sun set, a large helicopter landed quietly. The divers quickly loaded gear onto the helicopter and got in. Axel and Mike followed. Mike's legs felt wobbly. He considered stopping and telling Axel that he couldn't go through with it. Axel would understand.

After a moment's hesitation, he inhaled and climbed into the helicopter. The door shut and they took off. This was it, he thought. There was no turning back now. He was committed.

The helicopter flew north, keeping close to the water. After a half hour, it was dark. Mike reviewed the plan, such as it was, over and over in his mind. He tried not to dwell on the multitude of ways that things could go wrong. After another half hour, the helicopter hovered and they donned their scuba gear. Two of the divers helped Mike put on his tank, BC vest, and weight belt. They attached a small propeller thruster to the tank. Then they all filed into the rear of the helicopter and got into the landing craft. The aft hatch opened, letting in water. The craft backed out of the helicopter and onto the sea. The helicopter ascended and flew away.

It wasn't too cold but Mike shivered uncontrollably. The landing craft accelerated and quietly skimmed over the surface of the water. Saltwater sprayed into his face. It was dark and he felt totally disoriented. The trip seemed to take forever. Just as he was about to get seasick, the craft stopped.

"It won't be a long swim," one of the divers said. "Don't hesitate to use the thruster. And let us know if there's any trouble." They reviewed the hand signals.

Two divers got into the water. Two others helped Mike to the edge of the boat. He jumped in awkwardly, inflated his BC vest, and gave the "okay" sign. Axel and the other divers jumped in. They deflated their vests and descended into the inky black sea.

Mike's mask flickered and the sea came to life as the night vision turned on. They swam through a school of fish and descended to a depth of ten meters. Mike tried to control his breathing but he couldn't shake the feeling that he was suffocating. Axel flashed the "okay" sign and Mike returned it limply. He started to ascend and one of the divers tugged him back down. After a while, he felt he could control his buoyancy somewhat. The divers checked on him continually and gave him gentle nudges as needed.

Getting closer to the island, they swam through a coral reef that was teeming with fish, eels, urchins, sea anemones, and a lone manta ray. They passed through a coral arch and the sea floor gradually sloped up toward the shore. After a few minutes, he could stand, albeit unsteadily. With the night vision, he saw the tropical island against a backdrop of bright stars. Two divers helped him remove his scuba gear. The other divers scanned the shore, weapons at the ready.

They walked to the shore. The two divers unzipped a waterproof bag and handed boots to Mike and Axel. They gave Axel a small handgun, which he put into his belt holster, and a backpack.

"Thanks for your help," Mike said.

"What help?" the diver said, as he and his partner retreated toward the sea. "We were never here." They disappeared into the water, leaving Axel and Mike alone on the shore.

They put on night-vision glasses and headed for the jungle. Mike felt dangerously exposed. He knew that his dark green fatigues provided little camouflage against motion sensors or infrared cameras.

Mike turned to his left and saw a burst of white light, followed by a sharp report. Then, a flurry of tracers and machine gun fire.

"That's the diversion," Axel said. "Follow me."

They ran into the cover of dense vegetation. A shrill alarm sounded in the distance. Mike stumbled over the undergrowth, trying to keep up with Axel. They reached a narrow, rocky gorge, carpeted with moss, vines, and various tropical plants. At the bottom of the gorge was a shallow stream. They splashed through the stream and made their way uphill.

Henry had just drifted off to sleep when he was awakened by one of his lieutenants. He blinked drowsy red eyes as he walked along the passageway in sweatpants and T-shirt, absorbing the news. The Praetorians had assaulted the harbor on the east side of the island. A contingent of security personnel that had been stationed on the west shore were now rushing across to help secure the area.

They walked into the windowless situation room in the visitor's center, the same one where he and his guests had watched the black hole missile demonstration. Monitors showed oil fires at the harbor. An orange explosion ripped apart a Colton boat.

"They attacked from small boats, using RPGs and 50-cal machine guns," the lieutenant reported. "We counterattacked and prevented them from landing. We're now establishing a perimeter around the harbor and are sweeping the area."

They had been tricked, Henry realized, into thinking the assault would come from the west. Since Senator Schmidt had prevented an all-out military invasion, the Praetorians resorted to a desperate attack with small boats. While the damage they inflicted looked impressive, in fact Colton's operations would not be disrupted significantly.

They had to regroup and prepare for a possible follow-up attack. He had enough confidence in James' lieutenants to put them in charge of that task. Still, he questioned the wisdom of sending James to the detention center. What James had done to Jing was inexcusable, but no one had James Tyrell's tactical abilities and unwavering loyalty.

Longer term, Senator Schmidt would initiate a congressional investigation to expose the out-of-control tactics of the Praetorians. The world would be shocked by the methods of this rogue group and would demand their dismantling and prosecution. Politicians, citing plausible deniability, would readily appease the public.

The more he thought about it, the more he believed that the

Praetorians had made a fatal mistake. This error, coupled with finding the mole, Valerie, strengthened his hand. Two events that seemed like setbacks had been turned into victories. Tired though he was, he felt his old confidence return.

Axel and Mike continued slogging through the stream until they came to the end of the gorge. A waterfall spilled down a sheer cliff, surrounding them with a cloud of fine mist. Axel checked the map displayed by his night-vision glasses. He took off his backpack.

"We'll have to go up the cliff," he said

"Of course we will," Mike said wearily. "And then we'll try hang gliding."

Axel got a gun from the backpack and aimed it at a tree near the cliff's edge. He squeezed the trigger and a hook shot out, connected to a fine black rope. The hook missed and fell into the water. He reeled it in and tried again. This time, the grappling hook attached to the base of the tree. He tugged firmly.

"The rope is made of a lightweight carbon nanotube composite," Axel said. "It won't break. The tree I cannot guarantee. Hold on."

Mike held on to Axel's backpack straps and the rope yanked them up. The acceleration frightened Mike and he tightened his grip. Axel grabbed a thick tree branch and heaved them onto the edge of the cliff. Axel put the gun in the backpack while Mike got his bearings.

"You're doing fine, Mike," he said kindly. "We'll follow the stream for a mile and then head north."

They headed up the stream, like before. The stream narrowed and they walked along the right bank. Axel said a device in his backpack emitted a broadband signal that partially cloaked them from detection. It was experimental technology and therefore unreliable, but Axel didn't think it would hurt.

Mike was about to take a step but Axel's hand halted him. He gasped as he saw a snake, about a meter long, slithering across the path. Another snake stared at him from a tree.

Axel motioned for Mike to follow him away from the stream.

They walked quietly. Mike glanced behind him and saw the two snakes, joined by two more, following them. He bumped into Axel, who had stopped. Axel slowly retrieved a knife from his ankle holster. The ground glistened with slithering snakes while more snakes descended from the trees.

"This isn't right," Mike whispered.

A snake, coiled around a branch, slowly approached Mike's face. It had a bulge on the top of its scaly head and its eyes scanned him robotically. Other snakes began to coil around his legs. He shook them off frantically. With a swift motion, Axel sliced off a snake's head. Red light flickered from its brain, making its eyes glow.

"They found us," Axel said.

Mike felt a painful bite and fell to his knees. His glasses fell off and he was nearly blind. He felt a dull, groggy sensation overtake him. As he lost consciousness, he saw that Axel too had collapsed.

MONDAY, JUNE 9

61

They awoke in a dark, musty concrete room. They lay on the cold floor and their hands were cuffed. A thick stainless steel door opened and two Indonesian men with guns walked in.

"Get up."

Axel and Mike stood and the men escorted them out of the room and down a narrow, dimly lit passageway. They entered a circular chamber with hundreds of specimens in jars of formaldehyde–fish, eels, snakes, pig embryos–arranged around the perimeter. The early morning sun filtered in through a skylight at the apex of a domed ceiling. In the center of the underground laboratory, a middle-aged woman in a lab coat worked at a bench. Her long gray hair was tied in a bun.

She placed a test tube in a rack and walked over to them, grinning. Crow's feet around her intense eyes gave her the look of an amiable but eccentric aunt.

"I see you met my pets," she said loudly. "Welcome to my lab. You can call me Jan."

She extended her hand and noticed that Mike and Axel wore handcuffs.

"For Pete's sake, take the cuffs off," she scolded. "They're scientists."

The guards reluctantly complied, eyeing their prisoners warily.

"I wouldn't go outside," Jan said apologetically but with an undercurrent of intimidation. "My robosnakes are pretty stirred up. They're liable to use their lethal venom next time. Just relax and make yourselves at home. C'mon, let me get you something to drink."

She led them to a small break room with vending machines, a coffee maker, two tables, and a computer monitor. The monitor displayed a slide show of scientists at work against scenic backdrops or in labs with shiny equipment. They sat down and she handed them bottled water. Mike drank thirstily.

"Henry Colton's put together quite an operation here," she said, stirring a mug of hot tea. "I tried academia, and I tell you what, this is a lot more fun. You know how it is, Mike. You spend evenings and weekends writing proposals that have a one-in-five chance of being funded on a good day, less if you actually have an original idea. The rest of the time you sit on pointless committees, babysit grad students, and try to teach privileged kids who don't want to learn. When you actually start to do experiments, you're hindered by safety regulations, animal testing restrictions, human subjects boards, administrative red tape… All of that nonsense leaves, oh, about ten minutes a day to think about science.

"Contrast that wretched waste of time with what I do on this island. I have unlimited resources–and when I say unlimited, guys, I mean, *unlimited.* No one has ever told me 'no.' There are no nettlesome restrictions, no human or animal subject boards, and no students. No time burned on grant proposals, committees, or conferences. I live and breathe science every day."

"At what cost?" Axel said, piercing her with his blue eyes.

"With respect, Dr. Hansen, you're part of the problem. Government agencies don't fund discoveries any more. They give money *after* the discovery. Even your DARPA has become conservative–it killed Mike's project, for Pete's sake. Colton knew it was a winner and brought it to fruition."

"Killing how many people in the process?"

Jan chuckled, genuinely amused, and took a sip of tea. "Oh

Axel, you know that NIH-funded scientists go through lab animals like toilet paper. How many rats are equivalent to one human? Ten? A thousand? Let's suppose a new medical procedure saves a million human lives. Suppose further that a thousand humans were sacrificed to develop that procedure. Why, that means you 'only' saved nine hundred ninety nine thousand people. Goodness gracious, what an outrage. Better to have saved none at all."

"You're playing God," Mike protested.

"I'm an atheist, dear, so that doesn't mean a whole lot. But I think you're alluding to disease prevention, surgery, genetic modification, and the like, and how they might interfere with nature, or 'God's plan.' Back in the day, villagers protested against hot air balloons. People are primitive and superstitious about technology, even when the benefits are staring them in the face. Their view of risk is all topsy turvy. They're complacent about real dangers but get their panties in a twist over stuff that's harmless. But hey, gentlemen, enough philosophy. We're adults, and scientists to boot, so I'm sure we can agree to disagree. I'd just as soon show off my lab while you're here."

They walked down a hallway and through a set of stainless steel doors, into a lab with rats in cages, lobsters in aquariums, and snakes in terrariums. One rat was by itself in a large cage with a maze. A computer chip stuck out the top of its head. An overhead monitor displayed the world from the rat's perspective.

"Here," Jan said, handing Mike a joystick. "Go to town."

Mike tentatively pushed the joystick forward. The rat twitched and straightened its body. Then it scurried in a straight line until it encountered a wall. Mike pulled back on the joystick and the rat turned around 180 degrees and began to walk. He let go of the joystick and the rat stopped.

"Kinda fun, you have to admit. The snakes you guys ran into have computer chips attached to their brains too. Basically the same idea, except those critters can kill you. We're also testing lobsters for shore surveillance. They would've come in handy when you all decided to pay us a visit," she said with a wink.

As they walked to the next lab, she explained that the computer chip sent laser pulses and electrical impulses to measure and control the brain. Through a complex feedback mechanism, a computer program effectively commandeered the motor functions, while optical signals were reconstructed and displayed on the monitor.

"Now, these animals don't really have free will as we understand it. I suppose we could debate whether free will exists at all, but that would take all day and then some, so let's say it does, at least in some humans. The challenge is how to suppress those parts of free will that elevate your own ego over the good of the team. That brings us to our integrated brain scanner, or IBS."

She picked up a helmet and handed it to Mike. It was lightweight and looked like a bike helmet. An array of laser diodes and detectors covered the inner surface. He put the helmet on and a false-color image of his brain appeared on the screen. Mike remembered reading about this type of noninvasive brain scanning. Lasers or LEDs would send infrared light into the brain. The light passed through the neural tissue and was received by detectors. If a certain part of the brain was active, it would absorb light differently than if it was dormant. By compiling the data from all the sources and detectors, the computer constructed a map of brain activity.

"This helmet is already obsolete," she said, "but the basic idea hasn't changed. We get a pretty good idea of what's going on in there, without having to dig in with scalpels. Once we build up the subject's baseline, we attach wires and optical fibers. Follow me, guys. This'll knock your socks off."

They walked into a dim concrete chamber with two chairs on one side and stainless steel double doors on the other.

"Have a seat, gentlemen."

Mike sat down.

"I'd prefer to stand," Axel said.

"Suit yourself," she said and waved her palm across a sensor. The steel doors opened, revealing thick glass. Behind the glass sat an Indonesian man, his eyes unfocused and glazed. His wrists were bound to a steel chair. Wires and glowing fibers streamed from the back of his neck to a computer. Two technicians were checking the connections.

"They can't see us," she said conspiratorially, "kinda like a lineup."

One technician released the man's wrists. "Raise your left hand," the other technician said, and the man complied. "Lower your hand. Touch your nose…" He went through two dozen simple commands. The man's eyes betrayed nothing as he robotically carried out the tasks.

"Hey guys," Jan called into a microphone, "we have some visitors. Let's do an acute."

The technicians nodded. One of them retrieved a gun from a locker and placed it in front of the man.

Axel approached the glass. His jaw dropped. "You can't be that barbaric," he said.

"Pick up the gun," the technician said.

The man complied.

Axel pounded on the glass. "Stop it! You've made your point!"

"Point the gun at your right temple."

The man picked up the gun, his hand shaking slightly, and pressed it against his head.

Axel turned toward Jan. "Tell them to stop."

Jan looked at him, amused.

"Squeeze the trigger," the technician said.

Immediately there was a muffled explosion and blood spattered on the wall behind the man. He crumpled into the chair. The technicians quickly wrapped towels around the head and carried the body out. A moment later, a pair of custodians entered the room and began cleaning.

Jan's eyelids fluttered and she took a deep breath. "Remarkable," she whispered, enraptured. "No hesitation. None at all."

"You're a monster," Axel seethed. He lunged toward her and grabbed her by the throat. She gasped, her face turning red.

An arc of electricity struck Axel and he fell back, paralyzed. Armed men piled into the room. Mike put his hands in the air. Jan steadied herself and put a hand to her throat.

The commander looked at Jan. "What are they doing here?"

"Just enjoying the show," she said, catching her breath. She pointed to Axel, who lay on the ground. "The humanitarian there tried to kill me."

The security force pushed Mike roughly out of the room while one of the men used a fireman carry to transport the paralyzed Axel. They hustled through a corridor lined with large glass cylinders, two meters high and a meter wide. The smell of formaldehyde permeated the place. Mike felt sick and dizzy. He could pass out at any moment. His knees went wobbly and he fell against one of the cylinders. He came face to face with a cadaver. Its bulging eyeballs stared right at him. He yelled hoarsely as they pushed him down the hallway. Each of the hundreds of cylinders, he saw with horror, contained a human body.

62

Gunnar gazed at the computer screens. He had lost contact with Jing, Mike, and Axel. The room was quiet.

"Ever been on a submarine before?" he said casually.

Jalen stiffened.

Gunnar sensed Jalen's fear. He expected it.

"If we get the coordinates of the black hole, you'll feed them into the sub's fire control system. The guided missile will detonate underneath the black hole and blast it into space."

"Why…"

"You need to be on the sub. The Pentagon ordered the CO not to attack the island. He cannot refuse that order, nor can any member of the crew. He *can*, however, allow a nonmilitary person on board. It's done all the time."

"But *inside*?" he asked, his voice a dry whisper.

"As part of the weapons test, the sub's computer firewalls will be disabled. That will allow you to hack into the fire control system and re-direct the missile. But you have to be physically in the boat to make that happen." He looked at Jalen sympathetically. "I realize what I'm asking you to do. If there were anyone else… but there isn't. It has to be you."

Jalen nodded morosely as he turned away from Gunnar.

* * *

At sunrise, Jing dressed in shorts and a T-shirt and casually jogged up the hill behind the visitor's center. Her new visitor's pass dangled from her neck. With James locked up, she had a narrow window of opportunity to investigate.

She jogged along a winding path and found a small parking lot with several Colton electric cars. The cars were for visitors to use and had no keys. She climbed into one and said, "Mission control building, weapons complex."

"I'm sorry," the car replied, "this car is not authorized to go to the weapons complex. If you would like a list of authorized destinations, please say 'list.'"

She activated the manual override and drove along the path, which led up to a gentle hill south of the Saddle. After a half hour of driving, she could see a parched, volcanic landscape below. Several gray buildings were clustered in a rocky plain. An electrified fence surrounded a broad region around the buildings.

Jing watched a truck approach the area. It entered the loading dock of a short, squat building.

Somehow she had to gain access to the complex. She logged on to the car's computer and searched the internal web site. She came across a description that caught her attention:

> Colton Enterprises Weapons Division. Through cutting edge innovation and teamwork, we supply the free world with the very highest level of defensive capabilities. Our Pacific Island Research Center facility is a pioneer in force-multiplying technologies. By combining the world's fastest supercomputers with an integrated testing range, Colton is a leader in…

Supercomputers. One of the buildings must house the computers, Jing thought. Her mind went back to her visit to Colton's compound in Montana. It seemed like ages ago. One of the computer guys had awkwardly returned her camera after downloading the pictures. He had also gazed at her body with the terahertz scanner. She teased him about it. "*You can't tolerate Peeping Toms*," she said. She remembered how he blushed and scurried away.

The computer technician's name was Troy Orton. She knew that Colton transferred him to the island, along with James and other key personnel.

She browsed the personnel directory and found his contact information. She dialed his number.

"Troy," he answered.

"This is Jing Shen, Henry Colton's guest."

"Who?"

"Jing Shen. We met in Montana."

Pause. "Yeah, I remember."

"Colton suggested that I visit your building and see your hardware."

She visualized his pale face blushing crimson, caught between lustful fantasizing and dorky awkwardness.

"Do you have a gate pass?"

"I have a visitor's pass," she said.

"I'll have to ask my supervisor…"

"Okay. There shouldn't be a problem. I'll be at the north gate."

She hung up and drove until she reached a guard tower. Two guards approached and asked what business she had. She said she was meeting Troy Orton and flashed her visitor's pass.

Troy arrived in a Colton car fifteen minutes later. He got out and talked to the guards. From inside her car, Jing read the group's body language. Troy explained sheepishly that this was a Colton visitor with special privileges who wanted to tour the complex. The guards, realizing that this was above their pay grade, relaxed and gave Troy a document to sign.

"You can leave the car here," Troy called to Jing.

They got into Troy's car and drove along a dusty road. "I'm not sure what you want to see," he said. "The interesting stuff is classified."

"I'm here all week," she said. "I'd rather see your stuff here than lie on a beach."

"You gotta point there," he said, turning into a parking lot.

They walked into the tall glass building that housed most of the island's supercomputers. After signing in, they strolled along a hallway with windows on either side. They looked down at the floor below, where thousands of computers, working in parallel, were housed in black towers.

"It's impressive," Troy said, "but the POS on my desk is being lame."

"Really?" she said, looking into his eyes. "Have you tried…"

"Defrag, virus scan, spybot scan, repartition, yadda yadda. I know all the tricks."

"You tried Zipline?"

He cocked an eyebrow.

"It's a multiple threading algorithm developed at MIT. You should try it."

He looked at her, skeptical but intrigued. "Follow me," he said.

They walked to his cubicle. He cleared papers off a chair and they sat down. Troy did a search for "Zipline computer program," resulting in a link to the zipline.com site along with favorable user reviews. He clicked on the site.

> **Zipline!** Your system never moved so fast. Zipline goes beyond virus and spyware scans and provides an integrated, multi-threading approach to system optimization. Click here for your *free* copy.

"Can't hurt," Troy said.

He downloaded the program. His computer scanned it for viruses and gave the all-clear. Troy groaned at the slow progress.

"We can simulate a binary black hole in-spiral," he said, "but we can't get a decent operating system."

"Is it frustrating?" Jing asked, leaning close, "working here?"

Troy's cynicism vanished and he gazed at her with an oddly earnest expression. "This is the best job ever," he said. "More than a job, really. The rest of the world is clueless. They have no idea. Colton is a genius. A freaking genius. One sentence from him is like a book or entire series from some philosopher. Except that the philosopher is old and useless and probably buggers young boys. Colton knows that the outside world is corrupt and weak. We're helping it implode. It's a job that's awesome, necessary, and, to be perfectly blunt, fun."

The program finished loading. A window appeared that asked

to reboot the computer.

Onboard a helicopter flying over the Pacific, Jalen shouted into his headset.

"We've made contact with Jing!"

He showed Gunnar the screen on his phone. Zipline, Jalen's proudest creation, fed him data. An image appeared. They could see Jing talking to Troy.

"That's from a webcam," Jalen said, elated. "Way to go, girl."

63

Jalen's euphoria faded as they approached the drop site. A crewmember spotted the *USS Washington* and they moved into position. He fastened a harness on Jalen, who looked down apprehensively at the choppy seas and the waiting submarine. The sub looked like an enormous gray whale.

"You can do this," Gunnar said.

Jalen said a prayer as they lowered him. He dangled helplessly from the helicopter as two men on the deck of the sub waited. One of them snagged the cable with a grounding hook as the other steadied him on the deck. They released his harness and opened the hatch.

Jalen took a deep breath and entered the sub. The men shut the hatch and Jalen immediately felt the steel walls close in. After a moment, he felt faint. He forced himself to breathe.

"Seasick?" one of the men asked.

He shook his head and shakily climbed down the ladder. A petty officer met them and led Jalen down the passageway, past massive cylinders that held six missiles each. He explained the boat was converted from an SSBN boomer, which carried nuclear missiles, to an SSGN that launched guided missiles. Other petty officers in blue coveralls moved along the passageway, busy with numerous tasks.

"You picked a good day to visit," he said. "We're launching a new kind of missile. Watch your head."

They ducked into a small stateroom and an officer greeted them. Jalen perspired and started to hyperventilate. The tiny compartment seemed to press against his brain, squeezing his field of vision into a narrow, dark tunnel.

"Take a seat," the officer said. "Can I get you something to drink?"

"Water," Jalen said weakly.

The officer glanced at the petty officer, who took off toward the galley. In a moment, he returned with a cup of water, which Jalen sipped tentatively.

"I'm Lieutenant Kresge. Call me Bryan."

Jalen nodded. Sweat dripped down his brow. He closed his eyes and memories rushed up like a monster from the sea. He was a ten year old boy in a Detroit suburb, hard hit by foreclosures. Bad families moved in, with bad kids. A pair of thugs found him one night as he walked home from the school computer lab. They tackled him and bound his hands together with duct tape. They threw him into a steel cage formerly occupied by a pit bull, locked the door, and ran off, howling with laughter. Jalen spent the night in the cage, shivering. The cops found him the next morning. They never caught the thugs. More injurious to his psyche, the police and other adults didn't seem to care. No one acknowledged the terror he had suffered. His parents, who usually doted on Jalen, were stunned and could not say the right things.

He tried to steady his breathing as he wiped his brow.

"You okay, man?"

"Tell me about the missiles," Jalen said.

"Sure," Bryan said, closing the hatch. This only heightened Jalen's claustrophobia. "The skipper said you have Top Secret clearance and a need to know. You sure you're alright?"

"The missiles. Why are they special?"

"They've got some new explosive developed at Los Alamos," he said. "Polymeric nitrogen. More bang than a conventional high explosive like RDX, with none of the radioactive fallout from a nuke."

Jalen had already been briefed on this but he wanted to keep his mind off the fact that the sub was descending. Scientists at Los Alamos, guided by theoretical calculations performed at Livermore, synthesized the material by compressing nitrogen to pressures exceeding those at the center of the earth. Under such extreme conditions, nitrogen molecules transformed into long chains. These polymers stored a huge amount of energy. When ignited, they made a major boom.

"So you're an engineer?"

"Yeah," Jalen said. "I'll be monitoring the missile trajectory."

"With what?"

Jalen held up his phone.

Mike and Axel sat in the back of a windowless van, handcuffed and guarded by silent, armed men. They arrived at the detention center. The guards led them into the gray building and signed them in. The place was quiet and nearly empty. The guards locked them in a sterile cell with a desk, two beds, and a toilet.

"So this is it," Mike said glumly.

Axel's eyes scanned the cell. "The walls are hardened steel. We won't break out by ourselves. Maybe someone will help us."

Mike thought that sounded pathetic but he kept quiet. After a few minutes of silence, he said, "Tell me about the Praetorians."

"We're a network," Axel said, "loosely connected, international, integrated with–yet separate from–the governments of the world."

"Sounds dangerous."

"It is," Axel said. "The Committee, a group of citizens with the highest ability and integrity, was created to keep this extralegal organization under control. The system worked. Then, a scientist loyal to Damien Voth, Victor Jones, infiltrated the Committee."

"How did that happen?"

Axel closed his eyes. "I've been asking myself that ever since they ambushed me at Glacier. Victor Jones is a brilliant scientist. When one encounters such intelligence, one tends to miss things which, in retrospect, were obvious red flags."

Mike did not have experience with such high-level deception, but he did recall an instance when a professor voted to fail a Ph.D. student, merely to spite another professor. The transgression shocked him because he had always assumed scientists were fundamentally fair and objective. His experiences with Hassan further heightened his cynicism. He understood how postmodernists could embrace the idea that there was no objective scientific truth. They went too far, of course–there *is* an objective reality–but he wondered how many *scientists* were truly objective. When presented with the right incentives, maybe scientists could be corrupted like anyone else.

They talked about the Praetorians for a few minutes. Typical of a university professor, Mike was curious about their sources of funding.

"Does the government fund the Praetorians?" Axel asked rhetorically. "No. Does the government fund organizations, which decide to give money to the Praetorians? Ah, now there's a question. Ask Gunnar when we get back. You can also ask him what happens to the bad guys' assets."

The steel doors swung open and guards entered. They pushed Mike and Axel out of the cell and led them down a hallway, to a door labeled INTERROGATION.

Jalen watched the data that flowed from Troy's computer. As he focused on the numbers, he felt release from the oppression of claustrophobia. Jalen loved Zipline because it actually did a great job of cleaning up computers and making them run faster. What users didn't know was that the program gave the Praetorians control over their private data. In this case, he had access to Colton's network, including a real-time webcam view of the area around Troy's computer.

After a few minutes, Jalen noticed that the network was being slowed by a second intruder. He used Zipline's capabilities to track the worm. In the stream of data, an IP address jumped out at him. Somehow, it looked familiar. He did a quick search. The address was from an academic institution in the northwest

United States. Colton University.

Harry had penetrated the network.

64

As predicted, Henry calmed down enough to see the logic in James Tyrell's proposal. James would interrogate the intruders, Mike and Axel, and later the mole, Valerie.

Now, James hovered like a predatory animal over the two physicists, who sat bound to steel chairs. Five guards stood uneasily around them. Their charge was unusual: they had to let James do his job but keep him confined to the detention center.

James walked over to Mike. "When did you first meet Valerie Norton?"

"A few days ago," he said, sweat dripping down his back. "She visited my lab. Then we ran into her at Glacier Park."

James scanned him with his eyes and nodded. "Correct. You are telling the truth. When did you first meet Jing Shen?"

"Who?"

James showed him a picture.

"She's a reporter," he lied, feebly. "Maybe a few weeks ago."

"Under what pretense?"

"What do you mean?"

"Why did she contact you?"

"I don't know. She was interested in physics, I guess."

"I'm not talking about Valerie. Why did Jing contact you?"

Sweat glistened on his brow. James' gaze penetrated into his brain. He felt himself sinking into a trap. The more lies he told, the worse it would get.

"Mike, you're not even trying. We know all about you, the Praetorians, and Jing Shen."

"Then you know more than I do."

"Jing is a member of this group, the Praetorians, isn't she?"

"I'm the one you should ask," Axel said.

James smirked, amused. "Excuse me?"

"I have much more knowledge about this business than my colleague. He's a bystander. If you have questions about Jing Shen, then ask me."

James regarded Axel superciliously. "Dr. Hansen, I'm surprised that a man of your intellect can be so willfully dense. Of course you have information. I know that and you know that. But I also know that you're a tough old bird, practically impervious to physical methods of persuasion."

He walked back to Mike. "Axel, one of you is going to tell me what I need to know, or I will torture your colleague to death."

Axel flinched slightly but held his gaze with icy blue eyes. "You want some sort of confirmation that Jing is a spy. Mike knows nothing. If you torture him, he'll tell you whatever you want to hear. Anything he says will be useless. I will only tell you one thing: *Jing is not a spy*. You can torture me. You can torture Mike. It won't matter. I will not say anything different."

James nodded to a guard who held a remote control. A piercing current of electricity surged through Mike's arms, sending him into spasms of pain. Axel stared straight at James, giving no indication that he noticed Mike's agony. After a few seconds, it stopped. Mike gasped for breath, tears running down his face.

"You're wasting time," Axel said.

"Tell me what I need to know."

Axel said nothing. James gave Mike a second dose. This time, Mike looked like he might faint. Axel maintained his silent stare.

"Fine," James snapped. "I overestimated your humanity." He pointed at Axel angrily, his finger shaking. "Give it to him. Maximum power."

Axel's body convulsed, his eyes bulged, he bared his teeth, as a loud buzzing sound emitted from electrical transformers. Sweat poured from his brow and arms.

"Stop!" Mike yelled.

The torture continued ten, twenty seconds, each moment sending Axel into further depths of unimaginable horror.

"We need him alive," a guard said. "Colton's orders."

"Keep going," James replied.

Axel gasped and his eyes rolled to the back of his head. His face turned deep crimson.

"He's past the lethal dose."

"Keep going."

Axel's body stiffened like a plank. Finally, James signaled for the torture to stop. Axel abruptly slumped into the chair. A guard felt his wrist.

James leaned over him.

"Now let's try this again. Is Jing a spy?"

Axel's eyes closed and his breathing stopped.

"I'm not getting a pulse," the guard said.

James stepped back. For the first time, he looked unsure of himself. The guards eyed him warily.

The lead guard took charge. "Take James back to his cell," he said angrily. "Administer CPR."

Two guards escorted James out. James did not resist. His gaze lingered on Axel's body. The doors closed. One of the remaining guards released Axel from the chair. Axel's body collapsed limply to the floor. The guard set up a defibrillator, applying pads to Axel's chest. The device beeped three times and the body twitched.

Mike had a sinking feeling. Just a minute ago, he felt resentment that Axel would allow him to be tortured. Now, he watched helplessly as his friend's body lay on a cold steel floor.

"We need him alive," the lead guard said, panic in his voice.

The guard with the defibrillator peered at Axel's face, searching for signs of breathing. He saw a swift motion in the corner of his eye. He looked back at his holster and saw that his gun was missing. The last thing he heard was a *boom*.

Axel sat up and fired two shots at the lead guard. He swung ninety degrees to the left and fired at the third guard. He took out the security camera.

Mike inhaled sharply. The three guards lay dead on the floor.

Axel grabbed the remote control from a dead guard. After a minute, he figured out how to release Mike from the steel chair.

"We don't have much time," Axel said.

The guard at the check-in desk, a man named Johan, tapped the monitor labeled INTERROGATION ROOM. It showed static.

Johan went to his computer and started the lockdown protocol. The gates around the perimeter would close. No one would be allowed in or out. All inmates and guards would need to be accounted for. That task shouldn't be difficult because only a handful of inmates were housed at the detention center.

He looked at the array of monitors and began checking off the inmates. Three men and one woman, all custodial staff, were incarcerated for a drunken brawl the previous night. James was in his cell, pacing like a caged lion. Valerie was in her cell, reading a thick book. Mike and Axel were supposed to be in the interrogation room.

Johan spoke into the radio. "I'm not getting a feed from interrogation, over."

"Hansen's in a coma. Send medical, over."

"Shit!"

He immediately dispatched the paramedic on duty, an English woman named Hannah. Two guards accompanied her to the interrogation room. Johan looked at the image of James in his cell. What happened?

The guards opened the steel doors of the interrogation room. Hannah approached Axel, who was lying face down on the floor.

A shot boomed and a guard fell. Axel spun around and shot the second guard.

Mike held a submachine gun, his hands shaking. He stared at the man he had just killed.

Axel put his gun to Hannah's temple.

"Come with us," he said, his eyes and voice cold.

They marched her to the reception desk. Johan hit an emergency button and sirens wailed. Mike pointed his gun and Johan put his arms in the air. Mike took the guard's gun.

"Unlock Valerie's cell," Axel ordered, "or you and the doctor will die."

Johan did a quick calculation. The lockdown procedure was underway, so no prisoners could escape. Even if they managed to vault the electrified fence, they had nowhere to go. Reinforcements would arrive in five minutes. Everyone would be rounded up soon enough.

"Fine," Johan said. He accessed his computer. "Okay, it's unlocked."

Mike fumbled with a pair of handcuffs and locked Johan to the desk.

Mike, Axel, and the paramedic headed to Valerie's cell. Axel kept his gun trained on Hannah while Mike opened the door.

Valerie looked up, her expression a mix of shock, fear, and guilt.

"Mike," she said. "What are you…"

"Come with us," he said. "The doc will stay in the cell."

They closed the steel door and locked it. Mike and Axel escorted Valerie to the reception desk.

"I don't know how you got here," Valerie said, "but you can't escape. We're on an island, you know."

They reached the reception desk, where Johan was handcuffed. The sirens continued blaring.

"We're not planning to escape," Mike said. "We just need some information."

"Where are the black holes?" Axel asked.

"I can't tell you that," she said.

Mike's face flushed as he fought the urge to strike her. "You have blood on your hands already, Val, but it's going to get a lot worse. They're combining black holes as we speak. The singularity is growing. That's Colton's insurance policy. He can end the world."

"Is that so different than nuclear weapons and mutual assured destruction? We need a deterrent while our new society grows. Otherwise, how can we defend ourselves?" She stepped closer to Mike, her green eyes beseeching him. "I know you're angry at me, but please, at least consider the potential of this new civilization. Think of it: a society ruled by the brightest citizens, guided by reason and free from superstition. Colton is a great man. He won't destroy the world, Mike, but he needs the threat, at least temporarily."

"We can't take that risk," Axel said. "Colton is unduly influenced by Damien Voth, who is, I assure you, mad."

"How can you defend them? They put you in prison!" Mike yelled.

"Which I deserved," Valerie said, "because I willfully disobeyed orders."

Axel looked down the passageway. "We don't have much time." He accessed Zipline on the computer and typed in a few characters.

They could hear guards approaching.

"Tell us how to open the front doors," Mike said, pointing his gun at Johan.

"The doors won't open. We're in lockdown."

Two guards arrived and took up positions. Axel pointed his gun at Valerie and held her close.

"Back off!" he shouted.

The guards took a half-step back but kept their weapons up. One spoke into a headset. Reinforcements were on the way.

65

In the sub, Jalen received the message from Axel, sent via Zipline. Decoded, it told him to terminate the detention facility lockdown. He forwarded the message to Gunnar.

This would not be easy. The lockdown status was supposed to be maintained until reinforcements arrived. However, false alarms did occur. There was surely a way to turn off the alarms and allow the front door to be unlocked. Jalen searched through the emergency fire protocols. In case of a fire, personnel would require means of egress from the facility.

He worked furiously, tapping away at his phone, knowing that the focus and urgency of the mission held off claustrophobia. He navigated through lists of subdirectories until he found the one he wanted.

"I said, back off!" Axel said and fired his weapon, narrowly missing a guard. Valerie screamed. The guards stepped back and spoke urgently into their headsets. More guards arrived and took up positions along the passageway.

"Tell us where the black holes are," Mike pleaded, "and we'll surrender now."

Valerie stared back at him, her face silent and defiant but tinged with regret.

"Put down your weapons!" a guard shouted.

"Go for the door," Axel said. "Take the girl. I'll cover you."

Mike grabbed Valerie and ran toward the front door. A guard raised his weapon to fire. Axel squeezed off a round and the guard fell back. The guards unleashed a fusillade of machine-gun fire. Axel ducked behind the desk. Mike and Valerie reached the steel door and crouched down.

Axel crawled to the edge of the desk and peered over the top. The guards charged. He fired at them, dropping one. He ran to join Mike and Valerie by the door.

Abruptly, the sirens stopped. They heard a click as the front door unlocked. Mike pushed the door open and they ran out. Axel covered them, methodically shooting at their pursuers. A bullet grazed his thigh but he kept running.

At least ten guards followed them outside. A bullet whizzed by Mike's ear. They couldn't survive this, he knew. They were outgunned.

Valerie fell to the ground.

"C'mon!" Mike yelled. "Get up!"

She didn't respond.

The men approached, relentless.

A flash of light ignited above them. Suddenly, the guards were consumed in a fireball. A shock wave knocked Mike and Axel to the ground.

They saw the helicopter hovering above them, blocking the sun.

Mike got up and went to Valerie. Her face was pale and she lay in a pool of blood.

"I'm sorry, Mike," she whispered, "for everything."

The helicopter landed, kicking up sand.

"The black holes," she said weakly. "Building 10-250. South."

Her eyelids closed and she exhaled for the last time.

Gunnar motioned from inside the helicopter. "Get in!" he shouted.

* * *

Reinforcements arrived at the detention center and set up a perimeter. At the reception desk, they unlocked Johan from the desk. One of the surveillance monitors showed James in his cell, gesturing emphatically.

Johan turned on a microphone. "What is it, James?"

"Ask Colton to release me. I can contain this."

Johan sent a text message to Colton. While he waited for a reply, he considered the situation. Colton had already authorized James to leave his cell in order to interrogate Mike and Axel.

"James, I'm unlocking your door," Johan said. "Report to reception."

"Thank you."

James arrived promptly. "How did they unlock the front door?"

"No idea," Johan said. "We were under lockdown. Axel typed something into the computer."

James peered at the computer monitor and looked the main security program settings. Everything seemed normal. He brought up the web browser and listed the history. The visited sites were internal, plus some news and weather sites. One unfamiliar name was Zipline.com. James clicked on it and glanced at the page.

"This is how they communicated with the Praetorians," he said confidently. "Tell IT to scan for devices that accessed Zipline."

James picked up a phone and dialed Colton's number.

"This is James, sir," he said. "I have information and a request."

The helicopter flew along the west shore at a safe distance, heading toward the weapons complex at the southern tip of the island. Mike sat back, his mind in a fog, as Axel and Gunnar talked animatedly. His relief at escaping with his life was overshadowed by guilt over Valerie's death. Whatever her faults, Valerie had spared his life. He could not return the favor.

Gunnar and Axel discussed what to do next. Axel argued that he should go in, alone. He and Jing would determine the exact location of the black holes. The *USS Washington* would strike with cruise missiles packed with polymeric nitrogen explosives.

"They're on high alert," Gunnar shouted over the sound of rotor blades. "It's a suicide mission. Let Jing handle it."

"You can help me from Darwin," Axel said. "Jalen has access to the Colton network."

"Suicide, I say!"

"I'm expendable, remember?"

Gunnar shook his head in exasperation and spoke to the pilot. The helicopter headed south, away from the island. It then doubled back and headed toward a desolate stretch of volcanic rock on the southern tip. Most of the security personnel had been deployed to the east shore and the detention facility, leaving this area undefended. The weapons complex, however, was encircled by an electric fence and guarded heavily. How Axel hoped to get inside was anyone's guess.

"You're a damned fool," Gunnar said. "Good luck."

Axel nodded.

The helicopter hovered over a patch of black rocks and Axel jumped out. In fatigues, wearing a nanocomposite bulletproof vest with a 9mm pistol, knife, grenades, and ammo, he looked like some kind of Special Forces instructor. He ran to an area of dry bushes and volcanic steam vents as the helicopter turned away.

"They escaped," Henry said, running a hand through his disheveled hair.

"Axel is alive," Damien said, his face looming on the monitor.

"Yes."

"Defenses are useless at this point. Deterrent is your only option."

"The black holes, you mean."

Damien gazed at him intently. "You must go to building 10-250 yourself. Prepare to initiate the omega sequence."

"Surely that won't be necessary!"

"Of course not," Damien snarled. "Your adversaries are

weak. They will retreat. But you must be there, to provide–a plausible threat."

The screen went dark. Henry ran into the hallway, his heart pounding. Things were falling apart. He could sense it. He never should have incarcerated James, his most talented security person. That was a foolish mistake.

James had called him minutes ago with information about Zipline, the web site that Axel used to communicate with the Praetorians. He also requested to be put back in charge of security, which Henry granted without hesitation.

One of James' lieutenants accompanied Henry to his car, an emerald green sedan. They sped away from the visitor's center and headed south, toward the weapons complex and building 10-250.

James peered out the window of the helicopter as it flew past the waterfalls and lush vegetation of the island's east coast. A voice crackled through his headset.

"We have the report from IT."

"Go ahead," he said.

"Zipline was accessed from a terminal in the supercomputer building. The terminal is assigned to Troy Orton."

"Good work," he said. "Detain him."

The Praetorian helicopter landed at the Darwin base. Gunnar and Mike got out and headed toward the plain brown building that served as their headquarters. Once inside, Mike collapsed in a chair and buried his head in his hands. He could not shake the image of Valerie.

"Moscow," Gunnar said.

"Excuse me?" Mike said, looking up.

"A while back, when I had a different job, I met a woman in Moscow. Valentina. Not her real name, of course. I'll spare you the details, but suffice it to say she snagged me, hook, line and sinker. I gave her info that I shouldn't have. Later she entered the United States and I led an operation to arrest her. The CIA traded her for some of our assets. Not a bad outcome, overall."

"Your point?"

"As she was led off to prison, she told me something. She said that she hadn't faked her feelings for me, that our time in Moscow had been real. I know how trite that sounds, especially coming from a professional liar, but I believed it. I *still* believe it. And not a day goes by that I don't think of her."

Several monitors turned on, illuminating the dark room. One of them showed the view from Troy's webcam. He was explaining something to Jing, who listened attentively.

A voice came over the audio: "Gunnar, this is Jalen. We have a problem."

"Go ahead."

"They're on to Zipline. Jing needs to get out of there."

"Send a coded message to Troy's computer."

"I did. I don't think it got through."

At that moment, the webcam screen went blank.

"They set up a new firewall," Jalen said. "Zipline's quarantined. I can't get in."

Taking her eyes off Troy for an instant, Jing glanced at the computer screen. The Zipline site was down, replaced with an error message. Troy talked at length about the difference between 1980s hair metal and "classic" bands like Black Sabbath and AC/DC.

"Excuse me," she said, softly patting his shoulder. "Could you point me to the ladies' room?"

"Down that way, I think," he said. "I usually don't go there," he said with a loud chuckle.

"Be right back."

Jing noticed movement and sensed danger. She picked up her pace, heading to the restroom like someone who had drunk too much coffee. She ducked inside and went into a stall.

In Darwin, Gunnar stared at blank screens. Jalen told him he suspected that Harry, the computer hack from Montana, had managed to infiltrate the system.

"Call him," Mike said.

"Too risky," Gunnar snapped. "We can't bring him in."

"We're about to get obliterated by a black hole," Mike said in an emotionless monotone, as though he couldn't care less. "What do we have to lose?"

Gunnar paused.

"Good point," he said, and picked up a phone.

In his office, Harry's eyes popped open at the ring tone. He leaned back in his squeaky chair and fished for his phone. After the third ring, he found it and mumbled hello.

Gunnar tersely explained the situation. Then Mike got on the line and confirmed that what Gunnar was saying was true.

"Right," Harry said, reaching for his glasses. "I need to know the network address of Troy's computer."

A minute later, Jalen joined the conversation and told Harry the address.

Harry's stubby fingers tapped at the keyboard. After a few false starts, he gained access. The webcam image appeared again. Troy was at his computer, a bored look on his face.

"Troy's about to be apprehended," said Gunnar. "He'll blow Jing's cover. We need him out of there!"

"Not sure what you're talking about," Harry mumbled. "Is Troy the one who killed Stefan?"

"Yes," Gunnar said. "He controlled the lasers remotely."

"I see," Harry said, shaking the cobwebs and starting to focus. "Tell me what message to send."

Gunnar recited a message and Harry typed it:

We need you upstairs, level 14. Come up NOW. –Greg

Troy glanced at the message quizzically. He left his desk and climbed a series of ladders that led to a catwalk thirty meters up. Apparently the computers on level 14 were acting up again. He would probably need to code a patch or two.

As he reached the catwalk, he saw a dozen guards below, walking around like there was a drill or something. Employees were showing their badges.

"Greg?" he called. "What's up?"

He walked along the catwalk toward a storage space that housed new alpha-3 computers. They were kept here until the upper floors were completed. Bundles of cables ran along the ceiling and underneath the metal grate flooring.

Troy dialed Greg's number. After the automated greeting he left a message to call him back.

He stepped back onto the catwalk, phone in hand.

"Hands up!" one of the guards called.

A light shone in Troy's face and he dropped the phone. It bounced off the catwalk, fell thirty meters to the floor below, and shattered. His arms quavered as he reached for the sky.

66

Axel crouched behind an obsidian rock formation and watched a lone patrol vehicle make its way along a dusty road south of the weapons complex. It was a Colton electric car, not heavily armored, used primarily for routine surveillance. The car was about fifty meters away.

He pulled the pin out of a grenade and threw it toward the car. It landed between the car and Axel, exploding with a loud bang. The car halted abruptly. A guard got out and took cover behind it while the driver called for backup.

Axel crept on the sand, behind the obsidian wall, peeking over the top every few seconds. He reached the end of the wall and aimed his pistol at the guard, but the man was out of range. He holstered his pistol and walked toward the car.

"Stop right there!" the man said.

"I'm Axel Hansen," he said, raising his hands slowly. "Tell Henry Colton I would like to speak with him."

"On your knees!"

Axel complied. The man kept his weapon trained on Axel as the driver called security headquarters.

"We're supposed to take him alive," the driver said.

The man cursed and walked cautiously toward Axel.

"Lie down. Face on the ground, hands where I can see them. Okay, now put your hands in front of you like you're Superman. There you go."

The driver got out and covered Axel while the man unhooked two grenades from Axel's belt.

"You were planning quite a party," the man said as he carried the grenades back to the car. He popped open the hatch and placed them in back.

"What else you got?" the driver said.

"Knife on my left ankle," he replied. "Echo five."

"Echo what?"

The man noticed blue LEDs light up on the grenades. A loud blast erupted from the back of the car, blowing him back twenty feet. The driver's mouth dropped as he turned to watch the explosion. Axel whipped out his 9mm and took the driver out with a single shot to the head.

The car's hatch was torn off and the rear passenger windows were shattered. Black smoke billowed out. Axel jumped into the car. His eyes watered from the smoke and he coughed. He pressed the "on" button and, surprisingly, the car started right away. He accelerated forward.

Jing emerged from the restroom to find security personnel focused on Troy, who stood unsteadily on the catwalk. They barked for her to get away and she did so. As she walked toward the exit, she pieced together why they were arresting Troy. They had tracked Zipline to his terminal. It would not take them long to figure out that Jing had shown him the site. She needed to get out of the building.

A guard stopped her at the exit and swiped her badge. She stepped outside and looked around. She had no way to contact the Praetorians.

She turned and recognized Colton's emerald green sedan, coming down the road toward her. She waved excitedly.

The car stopped and the passenger window lowered. Henry stuck out his head. He looked pleased but confused. "Jing, what are you…"

"I was touring the supercomputer center," she said. "Where are you off to?"

"Building 10-250."

"Can I come?"

"Well, I don't know… Your visitor badge doesn't have sufficient clearance." He looked into her eyes and his boyish smile returned. "What am I saying? I run this place! C'mon!"

She got into the sedan. It was really more like an electric limousine. She reclined and Henry poured her a glass of whiskey.

After they clinked their glasses, Henry said, "Don't be alarmed, my dear, but 10-250 contains a black hole that could destroy our planet."

"Oh really," she said.

"It's merely a deterrent," he said, patting her thigh gently. "I would no sooner use it than the American president would launch a nuclear first strike. Still, the 'omega sequence,' as we call it, is a credible threat to head off interference from the outside world."

"When you say, destroy our planet…"

"I'm not speaking metaphorically. I am, quite literally, the first human to possess the ability to destroy Earth."

"I guess I'd better be nice then."

"Dear," he said softly, "I'm not a monster. After our civilization is established, we can discard the black holes. But we are in a fragile state right now. Even as I speak, invaders and spies crawl on my island, seeking to destroy humanity's one chance to establish a society based on rationality and science." He topped off his glass. "We'll get through it, though. I've seen crises before and I'll see them again."

The car passed through the gate and sped down a dusty road. Black volcanic rock dotted the dry landscape. They could see the ocean in the distance. After a few minutes, the car stopped in front of a plain, windowless building. Building 10-250.

They got out and walked into the building, accompanied by Henry's armed lieutenant. From the outside, the structure looked like a one-story building. On the inside, though, an open foyer extended down five floors. They went into an elevator. The lieutenant pressed the button for floor B-30, thirty floors underground.

James' helicopter landed outside the supercomputer building. He got out, flanked by two guards, and walked inside. Troy was being held in a conference room near the entrance. Shivering nervously, he told them about Jing and Zipline. James could see that he was holding nothing back.

James tried to reach Henry Colton on the phone but was directed to voice mail. He dialed the operator.

"Mr. Colton is in building 10-250," the operator said.

"10-250?" James exclaimed. "Why?"

"I don't know, but I can transfer you to the front desk."

The receptionist at the front desk told James that Henry had taken the elevator and was currently incommunicado.

"Who was with him?"

She listed the names of two technicians, the lieutenant, and one visitor, Jing Shen.

"Dammit!" James yelled. He pointed to a guard. "You! Get us to 10-250!"

Jing, Henry, and the others stepped out of the elevator into an enormous, cavernous room. The massive scale reminded Jing of St. Peter's Basilica in the Vatican. Two spherical stainless steel containers were suspended from the ceiling. They looked like smooth metallic hot air balloons floating in the air. Pipes of various diameters fed into the spheres. Two large pipes led from the spheres down to a hemisphere on the floor. The hemisphere was surrounded by a bright orange rail and warning signs.

"This is my masterpiece," Henry said. "Each of those spheres up there contains a black hole. In the omega sequence, magnetic fields guide the black holes to the hemisphere, where they merge, forming a black hole that's large enough to exist in a stable form. The gravitational force from this singularity would be enough to tear down the building and swallow the entire island. Consuming matter, its mass would grow rapidly. The earth's gravity would pull the black hole toward the planet's center. As the black hole descended through the earth, it would consume more and more matter, eventually transforming the globe into a spiraling accretion disk. Humanity would come to an abrupt and final end."

They walked along a wall, their footsteps echoing in the vast chamber.

"It is the ultimate deterrent."

They reached the control room and stepped inside. Through tall glass windows, they could see the two spheres and one hemisphere, arranged symmetrically like an upside-down isosceles triangle. The technicians sat at computer desks and went to work.

"We're now going to initiate phase one of the omega sequence."

"What?" Jing exclaimed.

"Don't worry," Henry said soothingly. "Watch."

A panel on the wall slid down to reveal a computer screen and black pad. Henry put his palm on the pad. The screen came to life:

Omega sequence step 1, fingerprint / blood scan OK.
Please stare at the green dot.
Retinal scan OK. Please say current passphrase.

Henry cleared his throat and said, "Victor two."

Omega sequence step 1, complete.

"I'm the only one who can complete the sequence," Henry said with a touch of pride.

Jing approached him and touched his chest softly. "Henry, turn it off. It scares me."

"That's up to the Praetorians," he said, snapping his fingers.

A technician nodded.

"Gunnar Stone!" Henry shouted. "I believe you can hear me!"

A large screen switched from plain blue to a scene of Gunnar and Mike at the Darwin headquarters. Gunnar approached the camera.

"I'm here. We got your message. What do you want to discuss?"

"The terms of your surrender."

"What do you mean?"

Henry pointed upward. "I want your death squad off my property."

"I don't know what you're talking about."

"Call off the attack," Henry said emphatically, "or I'll destroy the planet."

Gunnar stared back at him, unblinking. "I don't think you're that crazy," he said, "but I have no reason to attack you. So, fine, I surrender."

"Henry," Mike said, approaching the camera. "I'm Mike Harris."

Henry took a step back and brushed back his hair. "I know. We've already met."

"You hurt people important to me," he said in a stony monotone. "I suppose I should be angry. Fact is, I don't feel a thing right now. I don't care whether I live or die. But I can tell you one thing, and it's not bravado, it's just the analytic truth. You're in a bunker, below ground, like some holed-up rat trying to survive one more day. Best thing you can do is get rid of this weapon. You're not a monster, Henry. The fact that *I* can say that means something. You killed my ex-fiancée, my student, my colleague… But despite that, and the hell you've put me through, I believe you're not the kind of genocidal freak who would exterminate an entire civilization. So don't waste our time. Come back to reality. Do the right thing."

Henry took another step back. He looked dazed. Jing gazed at him intently.

"Eliminate the black holes," Gunnar said, "and we'll leave you alone. I'll have a presidential pardon e-mailed to you within the hour."

Henry looked at Jing, who nodded encouragingly.

"It's your only way out," Gunnar said.

Henry held on to a rail unsteadily and stared at Gunnar's image on the screen.

"Begin omega sequence step two," he said, his voice wavering.

Red lights flashed throughout the building and a beeping alarm sounded.

Omega sequence step 2, voice command received.
Please insert key into interlock alpha.

Henry pressed his palm against a black panel and a door swung open. Inside was a steel key. He grabbed the key and inserted it into a keyhole on the control panel. Pressing a button below the keyhole, he turned the key clockwise, lighting up several red LEDs.

Omega sequence step 2, proceeding…

"Henry, what are you doing?" Jing asked.

"That idea you had, about destroying the black holes," he said, staring at Gunnar accusingly, "the plan where you blow 'em up with a missile strike? Think again."

They watched as the tubes leading to the hemisphere deformed, pulled inward by the gravitational force of the black holes as they slowly descended.

"By themselves, the two black holes are unstable and relatively harmless. But if they combine, they exceed critical mass, and it's *over.* Curtains. The only thing keeping them apart is a magnetic barrier produced by the hemisphere. If you destroy this building, the magnetic field will shut off and the black holes will merge. Mutual assured destruction."

Gunnar raised his hands in a conciliatory gesture. "Okay, Henry, you're in control. Tell us what you would like to do."

"I want you to *leave us alone!*" he shouted.

From the distortion in the pipes, the black holes appeared to reach the edge of the hemisphere and stop. The room was silent. Jing tried to remain calm, pushing aside thoughts of the extreme danger they were in.

"We can do that," Gunnar said.

"I expect so," Henry said. "Now get your people *off my island.*"

67

The car arrived at 10-250. Before it came to a complete stop, James bounded out, followed by his two guards. He tried calling Henry again but there was no response.

"Tell IT to compile the evidence against Jing and send it to me," he said as they walked briskly toward the entrance. "Henry will want to see proof."

The guard nodded and dialed on a phone. He stopped abruptly and collapsed.

James whirled around. He saw the guard lying on the ground. A bullet wound had snapped the man's backbone. James' mind, enhanced by the Biochip, performed rapid calculations. He saw a man in fatigues aiming a weapon at him. It was Axel Hansen. His vision zoomed in. He saw Axel's finger squeeze the trigger. James could project the trajectory of the bullet, perceived as a bright yellow streak of light that intersected his chest. Immediately, he twisted his body to the side. In slow motion, he heard the click of the trigger and the muffled explosion of the gun. The bullet whizzed past his chest as he continued his twisting motion. In his peripheral vision, James saw the second guard take aim, but the guard hesitated. Axel took him out.

James rolled onto the ground and retrieved his pistol. He

caught a glimpse of Axel running behind the building. James gave chase, swiveling his head, searching for other Praetorians. James approached the building and peered around the corner. He saw footsteps in the dusty ground, leading to the back.

He knew Axel could be leading him into an ambush. James stopped and listened. He heard insects in the distance, the buzz of an electrical transformer, and the gentle breeze. Other than that, silence.

James followed the footsteps, pistol in hand, his eyes continually scanning the area. He stayed close to the building. The ground was covered with tall yellow grass and the footsteps ended. He cautiously approached the corner and peered around it. The rear of the building housed electrical equipment and a loading dock, but there was no sign of Axel. The area was fairly desolate and there were not many places to hide.

He tensed as he heard a running sound. *Sprinting.* He glanced around and suddenly realized that it was coming from the other side of the building. Axel was sprinting toward the entrance.

James turned back the way he had come and ran. He rounded the corner and reached the entrance. Sweating, he burst in. Two guards lay on the ground. The receptionist, panicked, pointed toward the elevator.

It was Axel. As the elevator door opened, he fired at James, but James had already anticipated the action and evaded the bullet. Suddenly a loud explosion shook the room and the elevator plummeted. He heard it crash below, thirty floors down, followed by a bright flash. He aimed his weapon at Axel and fired. The bullet struck Axel's chest.

Axel fell backward and disappeared into the elevator shaft.

The beeping alarm in B-30 was now augmented by calm voice that repeated "fire warning–do not use elevator" continually.

Jing touched Henry's arm gingerly. "This is scaring me," she said, looking into his eyes. "Could you at least dial it back to omega one?"

A door thirty meters away burst open and James ran in, his face drenched in sweat.

"Detain that woman!" he shouted.

Henry's lieutenant approached Jing but Henry held up a restraining hand.

James stepped into the control area and pointed at Jing. "We have evidence that she contacted the Praetorians, using a program called Zipline. Access the IT file, you'll see."

After a pause, Jing stood tall and returned James' gaze. "No need," she said, "James is correct."

"What?" Henry said, astonished.

"You've changed, Henry. Look at what you've done. We're one step away from the end of human civilization!"

Henry staggered backward, stunned. His gaze drifted to the two tubes that led to the hemisphere. The twin black holes, held apart by magnetic fields, waited.

"I contacted the Praetorians. I'm sorry. I was frightened. I can explain everything, but *please* send back the black holes."

"Jing," he whispered. "I…"

"I'll take her to the detention center," James said.

"No," Henry said, trying to clear his head. "Let me think." He sat down and brushed back his hair with a trembling hand.

Axel crept along a narrow passageway. His face was scarred but he was intact.

Minutes earlier, he had tossed a grenade into the elevator shaft, causing the elevator to crash onto floor B-30. James shot at him and the bullet hit the bulletproof vest. Axel fell down the shaft and grabbed hold of a ladder rung. From his vest, he retrieved the carbon nanotube rope and rappelled down nine levels until he found a service entrance. He then ran down the stairs to floor B-31, which lay underneath the hemisphere and control area.

He glanced at his phone, which displayed his GPS coordinates.

"Are you reading me?" Axel said.

"Yeah," replied Jalen through the crackle of static. "The signal is crud but I got your position."

"I'll need to send you the coordinates directly underneath the hemisphere," Axel said.

They knew that a missile strike under the hemisphere would blow both black holes away from each other. The missile would wreak horrible damage, destroying the building and everyone in it, but the black holes would fizzle out due to their instability. The world would be spared.

Axel opened a hatch but it led to a dead end. He tried another and it opened into a curved hallway. It seemed to go in a circle. Bulky electromagnets stood every few meters. Large electrical cords ran from the electromagnets to join bundles of cables overhead. The smell of grease and ozone permeated the musty air.

He found a locker painted bright blue and opened it. Inside were boots and a large metal suit.

"We're getting a message from Dr. Voth," a technician said.

"Yes," Henry replied, standing up, "put him on. He'll know what to do."

Damien's face appeared on a monitor opposite the one that displayed Mike and Gunnar. He grinned slightly but his eyes were black and cold. Henry gazed at him expectantly.

"Initiate omega sequence three," he intoned in a gravelly voice.

The room fell silent. Jing watched the unfolding scene with a sense of dread. Henry's lieutenant stood next to her.

"Omega three?" Henry said. "But Damien, the black holes are just a deterrent."

"You've been betrayed, not only–by this Asian whore, but by–your own parents. This new society–it was your only hope. The hope is gone. Mike is right, you–are a rat in a cellar."

Henry turned pale. He looked at the screen, his face pleading and pathetic. "Why are you saying these things?"

"They're coming, Axel and the rest. You have failed."

"But you always told me who I am…"

"I lied!" he spat. "Your mother was a disease-ridden addict. A petri dish of human scum. She left you in a ghetto hospital where–your adoptive parents took pity on a–weak runt!"

Henry collapsed and buried his head in his hands, shaking uncontrollably.

"You are *nothing* without–the new society. The world means nothing! End it!"

A man possessed, Henry ran across the room and slammed his palm against the black panel.

James rushed toward his boss. He could see the dangerous control Damien was exerting. He yanked Henry's hand away from the panel.

"Shut off the transmission!" James shouted, pointing at the malevolent face of Damien Voth.

"No!" Henry said, running up to the technician.

James pointed his gun at Henry.

"I'm sorry, but I have to protect you from yourself."

James felt a sudden, splitting headache as his primal loyalty battled the knowledge that Henry was leading them to disaster. His reflexes slowed. The Biochip seemed to turn on him. He struggled to keep the gun pointed straight. His hands shook.

He heard a *boom* and a bullet ripped through his torso. Henry's lieutenant prepared to shoot him again. James swung his gun around and shot the man before collapsing to the floor. The lieutenant fell.

"Henry," James whispered as blood rushed from his body. "Henry…"

On the screen, a message:

Omega sequence step 3. Awaiting voice command...

Jing swiftly retrieved the dead lieutenant's weapon and fired at Damien's face. The screen shattered. Henry rushed at her. She fired, hitting his chest, knocking him back. Blood spattered onto the black panel. He stared at her with a wild, angry look.

"Einstein alpha!" Henry yelled as he slid down to the floor, a streak of blood on the wall. He gasped and his eyes rolled back. "To hell with you," he croaked. "To hell with Earth." After a brief gurgling sound, silence.

Voice confirmed. Omega sequence step 3 underway.

* * *

Underneath the hemisphere, Axel donned the titanium alloy suit, looking like a cross between a medieval knight and Iron Man. The suit would protect him from flying debris that would soon be sucked into the black hole. If he crossed the event horizon, however, no suit–or anything else for that matter–could save him.

The hemisphere, he discovered, was actually a complete sphere, but only half was visible from the room above. Axel walked toward the sphere, making loud clanging sounds as boots struck the metal floor. The thick glass visor fogged up.

He called Jalen.

"I'm almost there," Axel said. "I'll send you…"

He winced as the earsplitting sound of metal grinding against metal pierced the chamber. The sphere began to implode.

Axel ran toward the sphere and lodged himself underneath. He pressed the SEND button. Just then, a man-sized chunk of the sphere disappeared into inky blackness. The rest of the sphere began to disintegrate. Axel was pulled inexorably toward the black hole. He looked into it and saw total, complete darkness. Then, a blinding flash.

Jing ran. Behind her, the tubes leading to the sphere collapsed with a groan, and the sphere itself cracked. Like an imploding light bulb, the sphere emitted a bright light and broke into hundreds of fragments.

The black hole remained stationary, held in place by hundreds of superconducting electromagnets on the floor below. They would not last long. Metal fragments spiraled around the singularity and vanished. Gravitational forces ripped the orange rail from the floor, sending bolts flying. The rail orbited the black hole once before disappearing with a flash. The walls began to buckle.

She sprinted up the stairs, knowing it was futile, that soon the black hole would consume everything. She lost the sensation of time as she ran up thirty flights. Sweating and gasping for breath, she ran out of the building. She kept running.

As she passed an obsidian rock formation, a missile streaked across the sky. Like a Peregrine falcon, it performed a nose dive, blasting its way into building 10-250, drilling down to floor B-31. Jing crouched behind the rock wall as a mushroom cloud billowed forth, sending debris into the sky. She held her hands to her ears as the shock wave hit. The force hit her like a truck, throwing her across the dusty plain.

In Darwin, Mike and Gunnar watched the satellite imagery. Dust and debris from the explosion settled over the volcanic landscape. A moment later, an image came in from an Air Force space telescope. In false color, it showed the black hole streaking away from Earth.

"Jing, come in, over," Gunnar said into his phone.

Mike tried to comprehend what had happened. He knew he should feel jubilant, for humanity's sake, but he just felt tired and numb.

"Jing, this is Gunnar, over."

Building 10-250 was obliterated, replaced by a deep crater.

"Please reply, Jing."

The radio crackled. "This is Jing. Get me out of here."

Gunnar's face broke into a smile. "Roger that," he said, wiping tears from his eyes. He typed a text message.

Mike's attention turned to the image of the crater. The cruise missile had detonated directly underneath the black hole. Most of the explosive force was absorbed by the black hole, propelling it away from Earth. The rest of the shock wave's energy was directed upward. This turned out to be fortunate for Jing, who managed to take cover and survive the blast.

Mike turned to Gunnar. "Axel?"

Gunnar's smile faded. He shook his head.

EPILOGUE

32 killed in tragic accident–Henry Colton among the dead

Legendary CEO Henry Colton died in an explosion at the Colton Pacific Research Center today, which left an estimated 32 employees dead and scores injured. The blast is believed to have been caused by a malfunction at an experimental energy-efficient power plant. Navy personnel have secured the area and are searching for survivors. According to a statement put out by the company, "We mourn the loss of our leader, colleague, and friend. The world is a better place for having had Henry Colton in it. Rest assured that Colton Enterprises will investigate the cause of this tragic accident and ensure that nothing like it ever happens again."

Mike put down the newspaper and walked into the Johns Hopkins hospital room, where Seth was chatting up a pretty young nurse. He didn't seem surprised to see Mike.

"I'm fine," Seth said, anticipating the question. "They've got me on painkillers but I'll be out in a couple days."

That morning, Mike had attended a secret ceremony at the Pentagon, where the deputy director for special operations awarded him a certificate and a check for $70,000. Mike signed a nondisclosure agreement. A series of government officials paid respects to Axel Hansen and his distinguished service to the nation. They mourned the loss of a true patriot and friend.

Mike and Seth talked for hours. Seth was back to his usual self, mostly, but tired easily and nodded off a few times. They recounted their experiences the past few days while avoiding the most painful parts. Seth must have known about Valerie because he didn't ask about her.

"I guess I should head back," Mike said, yawning.

"Sure," Seth said. "But before you go, you should know something."

The Committee sat in a soundproof room.

"It was close," Norman Davidson said, "*too* close, but we should still congratulate ourselves on a job well done. This is exactly why we have a Committee."

"Hold your celebration," the Chair said. "We have a problem, you know. Damien Voth ripped a *hole* in the space-time continuum."

"People don't need to know that," Charles Dantsker said. "The black hole can only be observed by government telescopes. We can edit out the evidence." The old days of astronomers peering through telescopes were long gone. Nowadays, scientists got time on major facilities like Hubble, and images were sent to their personal computers. It would be straightforward to digitally scrub any trace of the singularity.

"Was this Voth's plan all along?" Heather Platt asked.

The Chair sat back and stared into space. "I'm not a psychologist," he said, "so I don't know what goes in Voth's mind. But I keep thinking about his idea for contacting alien civilizations. It involved the warping of space and time to get around interstellar distances. We all dismissed it as crazy."

"Quantum gravity teleportation," Norman said.

"Yes. Exactly. It required creating a singularity, as I recall."

They sat in silence.

"What are you suggesting?" Charles said.

"Nothing," the Chair replied wearily, dark rings under his eyes. "Nothing at all."

* * *

Mike impulsively decided to buy a car and drive west rather than fly. He was in no hurry to return to Colton University. He stayed at hotels located in generic mall/restaurant/hotel complexes along the interstate highway system. The familiarity of these developments was somehow reassuring. Still, he slept fitfully. During the day, he sometimes had to park at a rest stop and doze for a few minutes. As he approached the Dakotas, the wide open spaces and silence calmed his turbulent mind.

He had long periods to ponder what had happened. The missile strike succeeded in blasting the black hole away from Earth and into space. Seth speculated that it could someday return, like Halley's Comet. The odds that it would collide with Earth were slim but nonzero. Government scientists would monitor its position while suppressing evidence of its existence. If necessary, they could divert its path with a nuclear explosion. How long they could keep it a secret was anyone's guess.

Meanwhile, Damien Voth hid, somewhere, surrounded by people loyal to him.

Mike wondered how he could piece his life back together. He considered whether he could return to research. He now knew it was possible to create a black hole in the lab. The problem was that the Praetorians would never allow it.

Could he have a relationship? Could he learn to trust again? It seemed impossible.

His mind lingered on what Seth had told him. Seth had a fanciful side and shouldn't be taken literally, especially in his medicated state. Still, Mike could not shake it. Seth's words haunted him.

"You should know something, Mike."

"Yes? What?"

Seth had stared at him intently, without a trace of doubt.

"Axel is alive."

ABOUT THE AUTHOR

Matthew McCluskey is a physics professor at Washington State University. He received his B.Sc. from MIT and Ph.D. from Berkeley, and was a postdoctoral researcher at the famed Xerox Palo Alto Research Center (PARC). A world leader in semiconductors, high-pressure science, and optics, he has authored or co-authored over 100 publications, including a major graduate textbook. *The Last Weapon* is his first novel.

www.ingramcontent.com/pod-product-compliance
Lightning Source LLC
LaVergne TN
LVHW020518100826
845148LV00010B/1273

* 9 7 8 0 6 1 5 8 2 3 2 2 5 *